"Keely," Brock called as he moved up the flight of steps to where she stood. "Keely, will you marry me?"

"Why?" she challenged, hoping he didn't hear the pounding of her heart.

"Don't you ever do anything on impulse?" His dark eyes locked with hers. "Because it feels right?"

"Does this . . . does this feel right?" she murmured, suddenly dizzy with confusion.

"This does." Brock pulled her roughly against him, taking her breath away as he forced his mouth down on hers. Instead of resisting, Keely parted her lips to savor his sweet, searching kiss. She shivered as he planted the seeds of desire.

When he let her go, she spoke before she thought. "Yes, I'll marry you." She swallowed hard, frightened by her own words . . . and by the realization that she *did* want this man more than she'd ever imagined she could want anyone . . .

ZEBRA'S GOT THE ROMANCE
TO SET YOUR HEART AFIRE!

RAGING DESIRE (2242, $3.75)
by Colleen Faulkner

A wealthy gentleman and officer in General Washington's army, Devon Marsh wasn't meant for the likes of Cassie O'Flynn, an immigrant bond servant. But from the moment their lips first met, Cassie knew she could love no other . . . even if it meant marching into the flames of war to make him hers!

TEXAS TWILIGHT (2241, $3.75)
by Vivian Vaughan

When handsome Trace Garrett stepped onto the porch of the Santa Clara ranch, he wove a rapturous spell around Clara Ehler's heart. Though Clara planned to sell the spread and move back East, Trace was determined to keep her on the wild Western frontier where she belonged — to share with him the glory and the splendor of the passion-filled TEXAS TWILIGHT.

RENEGADE HEART (2244, $3.75)
by Marjorie Price

Strong-willed Hannah Hatch resented her imprisonment by Captain Jake Farnsworth, even after the daring Yankee had rescued her from bloodthirsty marauders. And though Jake's rock-hard physique made Hannah tremble with desire, the spirited beauty was nevertheless resolved to exploit her femininity to the fullest and gain her independence from the virile bluecoat.

LOVING CHALLENGE (2243, $3.75)
by Carol King

When the notorious Captain Dominic Warbrooke burst into Laurette Harker's eighteenth birthday ball, the accomplished beauty challenged the arrogant scoundrel to a duel. But when the captain named her innocence as his stakes, Laurette was terrified she'd not only lose the fight, but her heart as well!

Available wherever paperbacks are sold, or order direct from the Publisher. Send cover price plus 50¢ per copy for mailing and handling to Zebra Books, Dept. 2611, 475 Park Avenue South, New York, N.Y. 10016. Residents of New York, New Jersey and Pennsylvania must include sales tax. DO NOT SEND CASH.

TRAITOR'S CARESS

COLLEEN FAULKNER

ZEBRA BOOKS
KENSINGTON PUBLISHING CORP.

ZEBRA BOOKS

are published by

Kensington Publishing Corp.
475 Park Avenue South
New York, NY 10016

First printing: March, 1989
Printed in the United States of America

*For my great-grandfather,
William H. Faulkner,
who taught me the importance of
storytelling in our lives*

Chapter One

July 26, 1777

The howling wind ripped at the canvas of the schooner's sails, and Keely Bartholomew lowered her head against the driving rain. Holding fast to a hempen line she lowered her lashes to shield her hazel eyes from the bitter onslaught and took a deep breath.

The icy Atlantic beat at the hull of the *Tempest*, filling the air with one deafening boom after another. Keely licked the salt spray from her lips, refusing to let the northwesterly best her as it tore at her rain-drenched skirts, threatening to knock her off her feet.

"I'll not go below," she murmured stubbornly, shuddering at the thought of the cramped cabin she'd been locked in since the night before. "Not to escape the devil himself!" Her voice was lost in the drone of the wind and the wail of the bo'sun's pipe.

This was sheer folly, this journey of her aunt's!

What God-loving English woman would travel to the American Colonies in the midst of a rebellion? Word was that it was full-scale war, but the Crown still denied it, assuring loyal subjects that it was a few degenerate colonials who had raised arms against their King. Keely leaned into the wind, resting her forehead against the taut line she clenched so tightly. She was caught between wanting to see Uncle Lloyd again and wanting to remain safe at home in London. She couldn't understand why Aunt Gwen was returning to her husband's side after all this time. They hadn't seen each other since his last visit to England fifteen years ago!

The icy downpour beat at Keely's face, reviving her. She had never liked dark enclosed places, not even as a child. The dismal ship's cabin that she shared with her aunt had been more than she could bear. If Keely hadn't escaped its smothering confines, she'd surely have gone mad; even in a storm the deck was a haven.

Without warning, a pair of massive hands encircled Keely's waist. She cried out, whipping around to face her assailant. "Unhand me!" she shouted above the whistling wind. Her eyes widened as she stared at the huge man dressed in oil cloth, with a wide-brimmed hat pulled down over his face.

"Like hell!" The stranger tightened his grip, his fingers digging into her sides. "Didn't I order you below decks before you were washed overboard?"

"Some mealymouth boy-child was here mumbling something about a woman's safety, but I sent him packing." Her words were nearly lost in the squall.

"I sent the sailmaster to get you below!" the stranger roared.

"Who are you to be telling me where I can and cannot go? Do you know who I am?" Keely gripped the line as a gust of wind whipped her bonnet from her head and sent it whirling into the

8

spray. Her auburn hair tore from the pins to plaster her cheeks and fall dripping down her back.

The man raised the front brim of his hat with the back of his hand to reveal bronze skin, high cheekbones, and raven eyes. "*I,* mistress, am the captain of this vessel."

Keely stared through the blinding rain, her hands trembling. Something about this man was deeply frightening. "I'll have you know my aunt hired this boat!"

"I am the captain and your safety is my responsibility." He raised a dark eyebrow, lifting a hand to wipe the rain from his full mouth. "Either you go of your own accord or . . ."

"Or what?" she dared, tightening her grip on the hemp.

Without a word the stranger grasped Keely by the waist and threw her over his shoulder. She screamed and pounded her fists against his broad back, shouting for help, but he ignored her, taking the slick steps that led below decks with ease.

"Hush your mouth, wench. I've no time for a female's hysterics."

"Hysterics!" Keely sputtered, hanging upside down. "You want to see hysterics you just . . ."

With a great flourish the copper-skinned man swung her down and dumped her unceremoniously to the deck. "You were saying?"

Keely tried to get to her feet, but her rain-drenched skirts tangled about her legs, making it impossible. Her rich red hair clung to her face and she spit a lock from her mouth. A rosy circle burned on each cheek and her gray-green eyes snapped in rage. Her mouth dropped open but no words escaped her lips as he swept off his hat.

A lantern's light shed streaks across the stranger's face revealing the most magnificent man she had ever seen. Michaelangelo's David was shameful in

9

comparison with this bronze devil. Well over six feet tall, he had brawny shoulders that filled the narrow passageway. His face was sculpted from the finest clay, red in hue and molded by a master. His eyes were as black as the depths of hell and down his back hung one long ebony braid.

"God . . ." Keely whispered, her eyes wide with panic.

"Pardon?" A mocking grin spread across his arrogant face.

"Who are you?" she breathed, trying to regain her composure. The passageway was so narrow that she could feel his hot breath on her cheek.

"I told you." He put out one huge callused palm and she grasped it. "I am the captain of this vessel." His voice was a deep tenor, strong, with a lace of bemused humor.

"No." She shook her head, rising with his aid. *"Who* are you? Some Saracen brigand?"

"You ask of my heritage?" His pitch black eyes rested on hers. "I am half Englishman"—he paused, tightening his grip on her trembling hand—"half red savage, my lady."

Keely's mouth dropped open and she ripped her hand from his grasp. "An Indian?"

"Indians, my dear child, live in India. My father was a Lenni Lenape warrior."

A mixture of embarrassment and fright made her reach for the knob of the cabin door, but before her fingers made contact with it, it turned of its own accord and the door swung open. Relief flooded Keely's face as she spotted a familiar form in the doorway. "Aunt Gwen!" she cried.

"Brock . . ." The plump, middle-aged woman gazed past Keely at the stranger and held out her arms.

Keely stood frozen in confusion.

"It's been too long." Ignoring his wet oilskin,

10

Aunt Gwen threw her arms around the captain.

"Good to see you again. I've missed you." He returned the embrace, kissing her forehead.

Keely stared from one to the other in utter confusion. What was happening? Why was Aunt Gwen hugging this lunatic? "Aunt Gwen?"

Her aunt turned and smiled. "Keely, you must think us mad. Brock, this is Keely, Marley's girl. Keely—my son, Brock Forrester Bartholomew."

"Your son?" She stumbled back in disbelief. "You have no son!"

"I beg to differ with you, little cousin." Brock chuckled deep in his throat. "I may be an embarrassment to certain members of the family, but I do indeed exist.

"An embarrassment to some perhaps, but never to me, my dear." Gwenevere gazed at him proudly before turning back to Keely. "I'm sorry you had to find out about Brock in this manner."

Dazed, Keely turned to meet her aunt's gaze. Why did she feel betrayed by this revelation?

"I know I should have told you long ago, but I wanted to protect you."

"Protect me? Protect me from what?" The ship was yawing harder now and Keely had to lean against the bulkhead for support.

"From my past."

Keely looked from her aunt to the red-skinned captain and then back to her aunt again. "I don't understand. How can he be your son?"

"I think you do understand." Gwen squeezed Brock's hand, smiling up at him. "It was not for want of love for him that I never told you, Keely."

"Mother, I've got to get up on deck; Milady *Tempest* calls." He motioned topside, then leaned to brush his lips against his mother's cheek. "We can talk later, after this has passed." He glanced back at Keely. "You and my little English cousin

11

obviously have some things to discuss."

Just then a wave hit the ship broadside, sending Keely sprawling. Brock caught her beneath the arms, pulling her against his chest to right her. For an instant Keely found herself pressed against him, inhaling the strange masculine scent that enveloped him. She'd never been this close to a man before, never felt his hard muscles pressed against the soft curves of her breasts. Breathless, Keely pulled away, refusing to look up at the dark face she knew would be grinning. Without a word she passed him and ducked beneath her aunt's arm, disappearing into the small cabin and slamming the door behind her.

Brock raised a dark eyebrow. "You should have warned me, Mother. A bit of a witch, this cousin of mine."

Gwenevere laughed, her voice echoing in the narrow passageway. "Just young, Brock. You'll like her, I promise."

"That's precisely what I'm afraid of." He smiled at his mother, pleased to see she was as ageless as he remembered her. Her rich chestnut hair was without gray, her skin as smooth as a maiden's. She was dressed immaculately in a rich brocade, beribboned and befitting a woman of her rank. She was Lloyd Bartholomew's wife, but she was also the Duchess of Morrow, the last living heir to the Morrow estates.

"Keely's just not herself—the message you sent concerning Lloyd—our hasty departure." Her warm brown eyes studied her handsome son. "Tell me, how is the old goat?"

Brock lifted his hat and pulled it down over his head. "I was wondering when you would ask. Actually, I'm surprised you came at all."

"Brock!"

"Mother, you've always known this was a bone

12

of contention between us. He's your husband, you owed him more."

"I owe him nothing except perhaps thanks for looking after you. He got what he wanted from me years ago. There've never been any hard feelings between us." She reached up to straighten his wide-brimmed hat. "Now go on with you and keep this tub afloat. We'll have plenty of time to talk later."

Bowing slightly, with a click of his heels, Brock turned and climbed the ladder, disappearing above decks.

With a sigh, Gwenevere stepped inside the captain's cabin she shared with Keely and closed the paneled door quietly behind her.

"Why didn't you tell me?" Keely demanded. She was stripped to her chemise and drying her hair with a cotton towel.

"I didn't know how. When you first came to live with me, I thought you too young to understand such things." Gwenevere shrugged, seating herself on a wooden chair before a chart table. The captain's cabin was small, no more than ten by eight feet, but with the bunk and table built into the bulkhead, there was room to move about. "Then as you got older, I just didn't tell you. Oh, I had a thousand reasons why it would be better for you not to know." She raised her eyes to meet her niece's. "None of them very good."

Keely got to her knees, taking her aunt's hand. "You should have told me. I'd have thought no less of you."

"Here I am trying to bring you up to be a respectable woman. How could I tell you of such an indiscretion?" She pushed aside a lock of the auburn hair that clung to Keely's face. "Fetch me a brush and I'll comb it out for you."

Keely did as she was told, returning to her aunt and seating herself on the floor. "How did it hap-

13

pen? Were you . . . were you raped?"

Gwen laughed, running the brush through her niece's hair. "Goodness no, child! The truth of the matter is that I fell in love with a savage! His name was Adam, but he was full-blooded Lenni Lenape." The sound of the Algonquian words on her tongue felt good. It had been many years since she had dared to speak them. "He worked for my father, lived in a cabin only a few miles from our plantation on the Chesapeake. That was before my father inherited the title from his cousin and went back to England to live."

"You loved him?" Keely breathed, wide-eyed.

"I loved him." Gwenevere laughed again, only this time it was a sad laugh, a laugh of regret, of bittersweet sorrow. "We had this foolish idea we'd run away and be married. We'd move west to where his family lived. I was going to be his squaw!" It had been a long time since she'd allowed these memories to wash over her. Too long.

"So what happened?"

"We were children. Young, foolish. My father found out, beat me nearly to death, and then locked me in my bedchamber for two weeks." Gwen's voice caught in her throat. "Adam came down with smallpox and died in his cabin alone before I could reach him."

Tears welled in Keely's eyes. "Oh, Auntie, I'm so sorry."

"I was already carrying Adam's child. The rest you know. I was married off to Lloyd before my delicate condition became noticeable."

"Uncle Lloyd knew?"

"He knew, bless his sweet soul, and he didn't care. He needed my dowry to finance his shipping business. But he was a good man, Keely. He accepted Brock and would have taken him for his own if I'd permitted it. But I was young and still

14

in love with my Adam. I wanted no part of the old goat nor his life in the Colonies." She sighed, her capable hands braiding Keely's wet hair. "After three years of putting Lloyd through hell, I packed my things, with his consent, and Brock and I sailed for Papa's estates. He and my brother were dead by then, and being the only heir, it was all mine."

"But why did I never hear of any of this?" Keely turned, leaning on her aunt's billowing skirts.

"My dear, up until now, you've led a rather protected life. By the time your father had died and Lloyd had sent you to me in England, Brock was long gone. He had resigned his commission in the Royal Navy and set sail for the Colonies. In fact, I believe he left England within weeks of your departure from the Colonies. I simply instructed my friends not to discuss my indiscretion and they didn't."

"Is it indiscreet to love someone?"

"If only it were that simple." Gwen caressed her niece's cheek. "Now get into your sleeping gown before you come down with the ague."

Late that night, long after the tiny cabin was filled with the sound of Aunt Gwen's soft snoring, Keely lay awake staring into the darkness. She still couldn't believe her aunt had a son. A son! All these years and she had never revealed her dark secret. Keely's thoughts turned to the red-skinned captain who was suddenly and inescapably her cousin.

Punching the goose-down pillow, she rolled over, smoothing the covers that made her bed on the floor. She couldn't get him from her mind. "Brock," she whispered in the darkness. His name rolled off her tongue like some forbidden word. He

15

frightened her and she didn't know why. Was it because he was half red man . . . half savage? Or was it the way he looked at her with those disquieting ebony eyes? Keely squeezed her eyes shut, but still she saw his face haughty, laughing. She didn't like him; he was too arrogant, all too sure of himself. Who did he think he was, lifting her off her feet and toting her like a sack of flour?

Keely groaned, sitting up. The storm had passed now and the ship rolled easily, making its way toward the Colonies. With that thought, a shiver passed down Keely's spine and she got to her feet, dragging a woolen comforter behind her. Moving quietly to the chart table, she sat down, pulling the comforter close to ward off the dampness that seeped through the bulkheads of the ship. Their accommodations were small, but Auntie had explained this was the only suitable cabin on board. The crew slept in a berthing area in the fo'c'sle. This was the captain's cabin . . . Brock's.

Keely leaned back in the wooden chair, listening to the sound of the waves and the distant voice of a man. She still found it difficult to believe she was on a ship bound for the Colonies. An illegal privateering vessel no less! Where was Aunt Gwen's head? She was an English noblewoman. She had no business aboard this vessel, no business traveling to the American Colonies.

Toying with the end of her braid, Keely stared at her aunt's sleeping form. The middle-aged woman lay on her side in the bunk, her arm thrown over one of her King Charles' spaniels. She was all Keely had. Of course, there was Uncle Lloyd, her father's brother, but it was Aunt Gwen who had raised her since she was ten. Keely's memories were sketchy of her own life before she came to England. Her mother had died shortly after she was born, so it was her father who had cared for her.

16

Keely slipped her hand beneath her cotton sleeping gown and caught the cold metal of the amulet she wore around her neck. She smiled in the darkness, fingering it. It was only a copper tuppence, worn smooth by the years, but it was given to her by her father when she was four, and it was her most prized possession. "Take this and keep it always, daughter," her father had told her, smiling. "And someday it will grow; someday you will have wealth beyond belief." At the time, his words had meant little. What did a young girl care about wealth? But it had been a present, given out of love, and Keely had not gone a day without it since he had given it to her. With a hole punched in it, she wore it around her neck on a delicate gold chain.

Keely's mind swept over the years that had passed since her father had given her that coin. Father and Uncle Lloyd's shipping business had prospered, then Father had died and she had been sent to England to be brought up as a proper lady. Keely laughed aloud at the irony. She had been sent home to England so she could be raised decently, only to return to the wilderness of the uncivilized Colonies. What good would her lessons do her now? Did it matter that she could read and translate Latin? Did it matter that she could plan a banquet for three hundred guests? She hoped she would not be exiled there for long; London was her home now.

Sighing aloud, she crossed her arms over her chest. Keely was sorry that Uncle Lloyd was dying. Though it had been a long time since she'd last seen him, memories of his laughter and his love for her were still fresh in her mind. It would be good to see him again . . . if only it was under different circumstances. Still, she wished it wasn't necessary to travel all the way to the Colonies to be with him. And she wished Aunt Gwen hadn't had her bastard son come fetch them.

Brock . . . Her thoughts settled on the heathen captain again, and for an instant she recalled the feel of his hard chest pressed against her cheek. Leaping up from the chair, Keely climbed back into her bed on the floor and pulled the covers over her head. She had never met anyone in her life that frightened her — or excited her — as much as that red devil did.

Chapter Two

August 25, 1777
Dover, Delaware

"Keely, I truly wish you'd curb your tongue in Brock's presence." Aunt Gwen arranged the abundant skirts of her brocaded silk dress on the carriage seat. "One would think you were some fishmonger's brat!"

"Me? Curb my tongue? What of him? You know he baits me." Keely sat across from her aunt in a small horse-drawn phaeton sent by Uncle Lloyd. "He's been doing it for weeks."

Brock had brought the *Tempest* up the Saint Jones River to Lloyd's private dock at midmorning and sent word to the Bartholomew household that they had arrived. As soon as Brock completed his immediate duties aboard ship, he would be escorting his mother and cousin to Lloyd's home in Dover.

"I know this trip has been difficult for you, and I'm sorry for that, but there really is no other way. If Lloyd is dying, there are things to be settled."

"Things to settle?" Keely sighed, fiddling with the reticule she held on her lap. "What kind of things? There are solicitors to settle wills, your son said so

19

himself." She pushed open the tiny window of the phaeton, letting the light breeze ruffle the curls that peaked from her green silk calash. Outside, rough-looking men on the docks scurried like ants on a hill, moving crates and shouting orders.

"Nothing for you to concern yourself with, dear. Your Uncle Lloyd and I will take care of it all." She stroked the chin of the spaniel sprawled on the seat beside her. Brock had suggested the dogs be brought later, but Gwen insisted they'd been cooped up long enough. "The inheritance you will receive from your uncle, combined with your father's assets," she continued, "will make you a woman of considerable wealth. We just want to be sure you'll not be taken advantage of."

Keely turned sharply to face her aunt. "You mean you'll be marrying me off?" Her hazel eyes flashed with indignation.

Gwenevere opened her mouth to speak, but the door of the phaeton opened and Brock stuck his dark head inside. "I'm coming, Mother. Just one more thing." He shut the door.

"Well?" Keely asked. "Is that your intention?"

"Dear, we've discussed this before. You knew the time was coming. A lady of nineteen should be wed by now. You should have accepted Lord Larten's proposal last year."

Keely gave a snort. "Easy for you to say. You wouldn't have been locked up with the perfumed dandy for the rest of your life." She looked away. "I know that I have to marry, but I'd like some say in it. A proper Englishman, educated, so at least I have something to say to him." Her eyes narrowed. "I'm warning you, Auntie, I'll have no colonial clod for a husband, not as long as I draw breath!"

Gwenevere's mouth twitched. "I've been far too lax with you, child. You know better than to speak like that to me."

"I'm sorry," Keely's voice dropped. "You're right, I do know better. It just seems so unfair that a husband must be chosen for me, or for any woman for that matter. I should think you'd trust me to choose for myself."

"And who would you choose, tell me that, child. I have given you more than adequate time; we discussed this a good three summers past."

"I don't know," she answered thoughtfully.

Gwenevere reached out to take her niece's hand. "Don't worry. You have a good life ahead of you." She unfolded the young girl's hand, flashing a smile. "It's in your palm."

Keely tried not to smile. "Palmistry is a lot of nonsense and you know it. Last year you were reading my fortune in a crystal ball." The phaeton door latch clicked and she looked up to see Brock climbing into the carriage.

"My apologies, ladies." He glanced down at his mother's seat and realized the futility of finding room beside her. An assortment of wicker baskets, yapping spaniels, and worn leather valises filled every inch of space and spilled over into her ample lap. He looked to Keely. "Am I to stand, little cousin, or are you going to move over? I can run behind the carriage if you prefer."

Bright spots of color tinted Keely's cheeks as, flustered, she slid over. Brock made her so uncomfortable that during the journey across the Atlantic she had avoided him as much as possible, trying desperately to keep out of his way.

Brock dropped into the seat beside her as he knocked with a fist on the roof of the vehicle.

The carriage leaped forward and Keely pushed back on the leather bench, trying to keep her arm from brushing against her cousin. The man was unnerving with his heathen black eyes and cynical laughter. But for some reason the bronze hue of his

21

skin, the slope of his nose, the height of his cheek-bones intrigued her, even haunted her. Though by day she hid beneath the decks from him, by night she found herself thinking of him. He angered her with his overbearing manliness, yet her eyes strayed to his at the evening meal.

"All's well, I take it?" Gwenevere asked her son.

"Well enough. I'll have to return this evening. I've business to attend to, but I've time to sup with you ladies and see Lloyd before I go."

Keely kept her eyes on the window, watching the passing scenery as they followed the road that ran along the river. As much as she hated to admit it, the Delawawre Colony, the place where she'd been born, was beautiful. The dirt road was lined with ancient oak and maple trees that had grown tangled, forming a thick canopy of lush green. In the distance she could see fields of crops running down toward the river and the dots of scattered men working the land.

It had been nine years since Keely had left the place where she'd been born, though she now considered England her homeland. Until she was ten, she'd been raised in Dover by her doting father, his brother Lloyd, and a bevy of servants. She never missed the mother who had died of milk fever when she was only a week old. The Bartholomew brothers had grown wealthy through their shipping concerns despite the crown's growing demands on the American colonists. Then her father died and Uncle Lloyd had not thought it proper for a young maid to be raised in an old bachelor's household. Instead, he sent her to his estranged wife Gwenevere in England.

The sound of angry masculine voices and heated discussion outside the carriage startled Keely from her revelry as the vehicle came to an abrupt halt. "What is it? What's going on?" she demanded, standing to stare out the window.

A group of angry men surrounded the carriage, shouting and shaking their fists. "Come out, you traitorous puddleraker!" someone shouted.

"Come out and face your maker," another demanded, jerking open the door of the phaeton.

"Stay where you are," Brock ordered the women tersely.

Two men reached into the carriage and yanked Brock out by his arms. "We have to do something," Keely shouted.

"Sit!" Aunt Gwen hissed, holding tightly to one of her spaniels.

But Keely was already up off the seat, pushing her way out the door. Ignoring her aunt's command, she leaped out of the carriage.

"Stop it!" Keely shouted at the men who were laughing and shoving Brock from one man to the next. "Let him go or I'll have the *watch* after you."

A sudden hush fell over the men. All eyes turned to the defiant young woman standing ankle deep in a puddle of water. Only Brock's muffled chuckles broke the stillness.

Keely suddenly realized that something was wrong.

A stocky man in a scarlet coat burst into laughter, knocking Brock on the shoulder. "Got a lady fightin' your battles, have you, Bartholomew?" He swept off his befeathered cocked hat, bowing gracefully. "Mistress, my apologies. George Whitman at your service. We didn't realize the good captain here was traveling with company. We simply recognized the carriage and meant to welcome him home."

The other men followed suit, sweeping off their hats as well and murmuring words of apology. Only Brock kept his hat on his head, watching her, his mouth twitching to the barest of a smile.

At a loss for words, Keely dipped a brief curtsy, ignoring the water that ran up over her polished black slippers. "Gentlemen. Master Bartholomew." She shot Brock a venomous look. "I have an ill uncle to attend to." Turning gracefully, she swung back up into the carriage and closed the door behind her.

George Whitman broke into laughter, stuffing his hat back on his head. "Christ, Brock, we're sorry. We didn't mean to offend. But who's the fierce little blue hen with her feathers ruffled?"

Brock raised his hand. "None taken, I'm glad to see you, all of you. And that, gentlemen, is my dear little English cousin, Mistress Keely Bartholomew, Lloyd's niece. My mother's returned to Dover as well."

"Gwenevere! By the King's arse, I didn't realize she was still living. Is she as beautiful as she was when she left?" Joshua Kane beat his three-cornered hat against his knee.

"She is," Brock answered. "And now, gentlemen, that you've had your fun and stopped traffic" — he glanced up at the wagons and carriages lined up to pass — "I should be on my way."

Micah Lawrence offered his hand. He was a well-featured man with a head of yellow-gold hair tied in a club. "Good to see you, Brock. Missed you." He glanced at the carriage. "If you wouldn't mind, I'd like to come calling." He smiled. "Just to catch you up on the news, of course."

Brock laughed, starting for the carriage. "You're always welcome, you know that, Micah, but you'd better get in line fast. I imagine my mother and Lloyd will have her on the auction block by the end of the week." He flashed a grin. "That *baggage* is a wealthy woman, you know, or shortly will be if Lloyd's surgeon knows his business."

Micah's eyes twinkled mischievously. "A beauty and an heiress, hmm. You certain you don't intend to keep her for yourself?"

24

Brock threw up his hands in self-defense. "Not for all Howe's ships in the Chesapeake."

Micah grew serious. "So you heard, did you? There's fear he'll take Philadelphia and we're wide open to it. We've heard talk of the Continental Congress moving to higher ground."

Brock shook his dark head. "I'll be by the King's Head tonight, Micah, you can tell me the details then." He tipped his three-cornered hat. "Gentlemen." Then with a nod, he swung open the carriage door and leaped up. "Onward," he ordered the driver, then closed the door behind him.

Brock looked from his mother to Keely on the seat beside him and then back to his mother again. "My apologies, madam. They're friends. They didn't realize you were with me." He shrugged. "Their idea of a joke." He glanced back at Keely, who sat stiffly, peering out the window. "I hope the mud didn't ruin your slippers, but you should have stayed when I told you to."

Keely pointedly ignored him, continuing to stare out the window. Her new leather heels were beyond repair, yet she refused to give him the satisfaction of admitting it.

Gwenevere made a clicking sound with her tongue. "Men . . . always boys," she said with amusement. "You gave us quite a start."

"A start!" Keely whipped around, unable to remain silent another instant. "Not very funny if you ask me. It's my understanding that these wandering bands of so-called patriots are burning houses and tarring and feathering anyone who doesn't side with your disloyalty to the Crown." She folded her hands on her lap. "And you, sir, call these vagrants friends?"

"Vagrants?" Brock scoffed. "Who are you to judge? Those vagrants, as you call them, are the members of the Committee of Inspection and Observation. They are men of considerable wealth, education, and power. George Whitman is a judge and an assemblyman, Manessah Lewes, a portentous solicitor."

"Portentous or not, I fail to see the humor." Keely looked away, unable to stand under her cousin's scrutiny.

"There, there, Keely. No harm done, you've been too sheltered, and it's no one's fault but my own." Gwenevere scratched one of her spaniels behind the ear and the dog whined, thrusting its head beneath its mistress's hand again. "That, Keely, is the sort of thing men do. They *are* loud and boisterous; they *do* play inane pranks on one another." She shrugged, glancing out the window, the subject obviously closed.

Keely crossed her arms over her chest, looking away as a lump rose in her throat. She felt like a fool. Why would she do such a stupid thing? What did she care if someone carried the heathen off?

Brock sighed irritably, leaning back on the well-oiled carriage seat. His little cousin suddenly looked younger than her years. The sunlight came through the tiny window, setting on fire a red curl that peaked from beneath her bonnet. Brock had to suppress the urge to reach out and tug the curl. He pushed his hands down on the seat, promising to find himself a willing fair-haired woman as soon as possible.

The remainder of the bumpy journey to Dover was made in silence, and when the carriage finally came to a halt only a street from the town's center green, Brock leaped out of the phaeton, offering a hand to his mother to help her down. Hesitantly, Keely accepted her cousin's hand just long enough for her to step from the carriage and then she released it.

The house that loomed above them was a two-

and-a-half-story, L-shaped, red brick structure with a center door and nine windows across the front, upstairs and down. The shutters, the simple woodwork trim, and the front stoop had been freshly painted, in the last day or two, Keely surmised; she could still smell the fumes of fresh whitewash. The house was simple, yet elegant, just as she had remembered it.

A long-forgotten glimmering from the past flashed through Keely's mind. She remembered the stoop, standing on it, waiting for her father to return home. He had thrown his arms out to her and she had leaped into them, laughing. He was a kind-looking man with a frosted beard and a coat that always smelled of tobacco. How many times had he caught her off that stoop, she wondered.

"My pups, Brock," Gwenevere said, startling Keely from her remonition. "They can't be left in the carriage."

Brock shook his head. "You and those damned dogs. What I'd have given to throw them to the fish a hundred miles offshore."

"You'd better thank the heavens you didn't or I'd have had your head on a chopping block, son or not," Gwenevere retorted.

"I'll see to them. I'll have Blackie take them around to the kitchen and feed them." He tugged at the braid running down his back. He'd forgotten how difficult his mother could be.

"Feed them? Don't you dare let one of those servants of Lloyd's feed them! My babies would be dead in a week. They have a special diet, you must realize that." Gwenevere's dark eyes grew large. "Are you to care for them or I?" she asked, planting her feet firmly on the brick walk.

Brock started for the front door. "I'll do it, Mother, now come. Lloyd will be waiting." Brock stepped onto the front stoop just as the door swung open.

A young girl in a starched mobcap threw a hand up to her mouth. "God's teeth, Master Brock, don't be steppin' in the wet paint."

Brock lifted a booted foot and cursed beneath his breath at the sight of white paint covering the soles of his fine leather shoes. "Why the hell didn't you warn me before I stepped in it, Lucy?"

"I'm sorry, I'm sorry, Master Brock! Blackie tole me to watch fer you, but you see, there was this mouse hidin' behind the table in the front room, you know the table with the little legs that looks like—"

"Enough, enough, Lucy." Brock dropped his hands to his hips in exasperation. "We'll just go around the back."

"It's wet there, too, sir," the girl answered sheepishly.

"And the side door from the garden?"

"Wet, too." She clutched her small hands.

"And how in the hell did he expect us to get in if he painted all of the stoops?"

"Well, that's what I asked him, I said, Blackie, if you paints them steps then how is—"

"Lucy! Go tell Master Bartholomew that we've arrived. I'll take care of this."

"Yes, sir." She bobbed a curtsy and then disappeared.

"Mother." Brock put out his arms, trying to make the best of a bad situation. "Come on, I'll lift you in."

Gwenevere chuckled. "I can see nothing has changed in this household, not even in thirty-five years."

Keely watched as Brock lifted his mother. Buried in a heap of brocade skirts and bustling crinolins, he deposited her inside the front door. "Put on a stone or so, haven't you, Mother?"

Gwenevere spun around. "So what if I have?" she

28

asked with mock severity. "It's an old woman's pre-rogative to indulge in a sweet meat or two."

"Old woman!" He laughed, stalling for time, knowing it would be Keely he had to pick up next. "Joshua Kane was just asking about you. Sounds smitten to me."

"Oh, pshaw!" Gwenevere waved a lace handker-chief. "But next time you see Joshua, send him my greetings, tell him to come by and visit. I haven't seen him in near on four years. He visited me on the Morrow estates on several occasions, you know." Her eyes sparkled mischievously. "Well, fetch Keely, son, and let's get on with it."

Brock turned and came across the stoop. "Keely?"

She stood on the brick front walk, her arms crossed over her chest, her reticule dangling from her arm on a velvet string. "I can walk on my own, sir."

"Don't be difficult. I can't let you walk through the paint, now come on." Brock wondered vaguely why he was arguing with the chit. What did he care if she stepped in the paint?

"Keely, stop being a goose and come along. I swear, girl, you've not been yourself since we left England."

Biting her lower lip, Keely took a step forward. She was caught between not wanting Brock to lift her and not wanting to make a scene.

Brock swung Keely into his arms, hesitating as he gazed into bewitching hazel eyes framed with thick dark lashes. "How is it that I find myself toting you again," he asked softly. She smelled of lavender and freshly scrubbed skin. He groaned inwardly. What's wrong with me, he wondered, spinning around. I've been at sea too long when I start finding virgins appealing.

Keely held her arms wrapped tightly around Brock's neck, trying not to lean against his chest.

29

The man was huge! He smelled of the salt air, of tobacco, and of the forest. As he lowered her to her feet, their eyes met for a second and then she turned from his striking face.

Chapter Three

Keely stood outside the closed door of Uncle Lloyd's office, waiting for Aunt Gwenevere to call her. A flood of happy memories washed over her as she ran her hand over the dusty wood of the hallway's paneled wall. Little had changed in the nine years that had passed since she left Dover for England. On the floor, the same blue and gold Persian rug ran the length of the hallway; the same hand-painted, vined wallpaper ran from the ceiling to the chair rail. The house smelled of cinnamon and clove, and the rumble of servants' voices could be heard in the distance. The home she had grown up in was filled with familiar sights and sounds that had once made her comfortably content and now reassured her. She smiled at the sight of cobwebs hanging from a wall sconce. Though the servants had obviously been lax in their household duties since Lloyd had taken ill, there was nothing wrong with the house that a mop, a broom, and a little elbow grease couldn't solve.

The door to Lloyd's office swung open and Keely looked up. "Aunt Gwen?"

"Go ahead in, child, he's waiting."

Keely reached out to take her aunt's hand. "Aren't you going in with me?"

"Don't be silly, he'll not bite. He wants to see you alone." She squeezed her niece's hand reassuringly. "Now go on while I see to supper." She released Keely's hand and started down the long hallway.

Taking a deep breath, Keely smoothed the knot of auburn hair at the nape of her neck and then knocked lightly on Lloyd's door.

"Come in," a masculine voice beckoned.

Stepping into the room, Keely saw her uncle seated in a chair at a massive oak desk. Across the room was an identical desk, the one that had once belonged to her father.

"Come in, kitten," Lloyd Bartholomew said, turning in his chair.

Keely smiled. Her Uncle Lloyd looked no different than she had remembered him. He was a tall, slender man with silver-white hair and a clean-shaven face. He didn't look as if he was dying to Keely. "Uncle Lloyd."

He put out his hands to her. "Come, come, give your old uncle a hug." His brilliant blue eyes glistened with moisture. "I was afraid I wouldn't live to see your sweet face again."

Bending over Lloyd, Keely wrapped her arms around his neck, lowering her head to his shoulder. "I've missed you," she whispered.

"Is that all of the hug I get after nine years? Give me a squeeze, kitten, I'll not shatter. You've grown up to become such a beautiful woman."

Laughing, Keely squeezed him tight, inhaling his familiar scent. He smelled of tobacco and whiskey and hair powder, just as her father had. Withdrawing, she straightened up, studying his wrinkled face. "Uncle Lloyd, I can't believe it. You don't look a day older than when you put me on the boat for England."

He chuckled, indicating a straight-backed chair. "Excuse me if I don't stand, but my surgeon has

32

forbid me; I'm not even to be out of bed." He winked. "Now sit and let me look at your lovely face."

Keely sat down, looking at the bookshelves that lined the interiors of two closets. Lloyd's office was distinctly masculine, with dark paneled walls and ominous rows of dusty leather-bound books. A fireplace took up one wall while another had two windows heavily draped in faded crimson velvet. "You haven't changed a thing," she murmured. "Not even Papa's desk."

Lloyd glanced at the twin oak desk that had been his brother's. "Matilda suggested I move it out of here often enough, but I just didn't have the heart."

"Matilda?"

"You don't know her. She came here after you'd gone. I hired her to run the house—" he waved a wrinkled hand—"do my sewing and the like."

She nodded, sliding back in the chair. "I'm glad you didn't move it." She ran her hand over the smooth-grained desktop, smiling sadly.

"So tell me, how was your journey? Not too arduous, I hope."

She shook her head. "I can't tell you I'm anxious to make the trip home again, but it wasn't as bad as I thought it would be."

Lloyd took a long-stemmed clay pipe from his desk and reached for his tobacco tin. "And what of Brock?"

Startled, Keely looked up. "What of him?"

"Do you like him?"

"Like him?" She blinked.

Lloyd chuckled. "Fine specimen of a man if you ask me. Bright, a head for business, and a full set of teeth. Not a rotten one in his mouth. Good stock, I suppose." He tamped at the bowl of his pipe and reached for a tinder box tucked in his faded gray-twill waistcoat. "What more could a female ask for?"

Keely shifted uncomfortably on the chair. What was her uncle getting at? What did he care what she thought of Aunt Gwen's illegitimate son? "Sir?"

"Oh, nothing." He sucked on the stem of his pipe, exhaling slowly.

An uncomfortable silence filled the room as Lloyd concentrated on his pipe, seeming to forget Keely for the moment. Finally, he looked up. "Well, kitten, I know you must be tired. Go on to your room and rest. I'll see you at supper."

Keely rose. "I am tired."

"Then go on. I'll have Matilda or one of the others show you to your room. If there's one thing I've got here, it's servants. Coming right out of my ears they are."

Keely laughed. "Then why do you keep them all?"

He shrugged. "Some folk collect prized chickens; I seem to collect misplaced help. I inherited Matilda when Mistress Samkins passed on. Lucy came off the stocks in Annapolis and Blackie—I caught him trying to steal horses at Sunday services."

Keely smiled, her hazel eyes twinkling with pride. "And what of Ruth? Is she still with you?"

"She is."

"And does she still make the best gingerbread in the three lower counties?"

Lloyd grinned, his pipe still clenched in his teeth. "She does. I sent her to the Solomons' with a tincture for Daniel, but she'll be back shortly."

Keely brushed her lips against the old man's wizened cheek. "I'm glad I came, Uncle Lloyd."

"So am I, kitten, so am I."

Keely lay awake in her childhood four-poster bed, staring at the forest-green drapes that floated dreamily on the hot August night air. The tall case clock

34

on the landing down the hall chimed midnight, and she rolled restlessly onto her side. Her stomach churned, growling, and she ran a palm over it irritably.

Brock had reigned over the evening meal like some foreign prince, making it impossible for her to eat. He had monopolized the conversations, entertaining Uncle Lloyd and Aunt Gwen with his sharp wit and intelligence until Keely thought she would scream. He had made no attempt to draw her into their discourse, politely ignoring her except to ask that she pass the bread pudding. While Brock rattled on of his adventures at sea, Keely had pushed her roasted chicken and boiled peas around the plate with her fork until Matilda had come and cleared away the dishes.

Keely couldn't for the life of her figure out what it was about Brock that Uncle Lloyd and Aunt Gwen found so fascinating and she found so infuriating. Whenever she was in the same room with him, she found herself tongue-tied or saying foolish things. How was it that she could carry on an intelligent conversation with the Prince of Wales, yet she sounded like a ninny in her cousin's presence. At least now that they had arrived in the Colonies, he wouldn't be so near. She realized that he would still visit with his mother on occasion, but at least now he would go home to his own house to sleep.

Keely's stomach growled again and she sat up, slipping her feet into a pair of silk mules that rested on the floor near her bed. Midnight or not, she knew she'd not sleep until she had something to eat. Shrugging on a robe of filmy cotton, she opened her bedchamber door quietly and listened.

The only sound she heard was the whining of one of Aunt Gwen's spaniels. The entire household seemed to be asleep; not a single candle burned. The tall case clock ticked ominously as Keely made her

35

way down the steps. There was no need to light a candle—she knew her way by heart, even in the pitch blackness. Many times since she had left the Colonies she had dreamed of this house she'd grown up in; in her mind she had wandered its long hallways and explored its elegant boxwood gardens. England was her home and had been for quite some time, but still this house in Dover had haunted her.

Reaching the bottom landing, she followed the back hallway into the winter kitchen, out the door, and down a breezeway to the summer kitchen. Lighting a candle, she rummaged in the pantry, coming up with a peach, a slice of fresh-baked bread, and a sliver of yellow-white cheese. Spotting a row of dusty ale bottles, she snatched one up on impulse. Placing her bounty on a wooden tray, she slipped back into the main house and went into the parlor to enjoy her feast.

By the light of the three-quarter moon shining through the open window, Keely enjoyed the simple meal. The sound of peepers chirping in the woods filled the night air and she sighed, leaning back to draw her feet up beneath her. She was content with her life in England, but she had to admit there was something about his land that stirred her. There was something about the clean, fresh smell of the air, the vast openness, the vivification of the colonists that made her heart swell, her skin tingle.

Spotting an ancient chess set on a small table between two high-backed chairs, Keely rose to study the pieces. Lifting a delicately carved queen, she rolled it between her fingers, remembering the hours she had spent on winter evenings watching her father and Lloyd play the game. Setting the piece down lightly, she pushed a pawn forward. "Pawn to king four," she murmured.

"Knight to king's bishop three," came a deep, masculine voice from behind.

36

Startled, Keely turned to see Brock lean forward to move the black knight to the indicated position. "What are you doing here?" She clutched her robe at the waist, lifting the collar to conceal her bare neck.

"Doing?" He smiled roguishly, making her cheeks color. "I live here, my dear."

Keely's face fell. "Live here?"

"Well, where did you think I live, in a wigwam outside of town?"

He had changed his clothes since the evening meal and now wore a working man's garb. His high black leather boots led to fawn-colored breeches stretched taut over massive thighs, joining smoothly with the pristine white of his shirt and stock. His thick, blue-black hair was tied with a leather thong to hang like a mane down his back. He was the most handsomely intimidating man Keely had ever seen in her life.

Flustered, she took a step back. "Well, I . . . no, of course not, I just thought somewhere . . ." She shrugged taking another step back. ". . . I just thought you had a home . . ." She let her voice trail off into uncomfortable silence.

Brock laughed. "I do. My home is here. After I returned from my father's people on the Ohio, Lloyd took me in. He set me up in the shipping business; he's been very good to me."

"I should say so, *considering!*" Keely blurted.

Brock's eyes narrowed. "So young you are, my English cousin. So little you know about the world. My being an honest man meant far more to Lloyd than being a bastard, even his wife's bastard." He turned to the window, not wanting her to see the tears welling in his eyes.

Keely trembled. She had hurt him and she was sorry. She ran her fingers softly across his shoulder and he turned back toward her. Her eyes locked on Brock's dark, brooding features.

"I'm sorry," she whispered. "That was uncalled

for. But I am not as young as you think."

Brock took her chin between his thumb and fingers, making her tremble. His touch was hot against her skin, the scent of his male flesh rising to taunt her senses.

"Nor am I as naive."

"No, maybe not." Forgetting himself for the moment, Brock leaned into her. Her face was delicately oval in shape, her skin a creamy satin. He could see her soft, shapely lips trembling, daring him to kiss them. He was so close that he could feel her sweet breath on his face.

Keely lowered her lashes instinctively, her breath catching in her throat.

Brock withdrew abruptly. "No, you're no child, but you play childish games I've long outgrown."

Keely's eyes flew open. His face was a mere inch from hers, his dark eyes laughing. She pulled back, her cheeks growing flushed with embarrassment.

"Your move," he said, taking a step back.

"My . . . my move?" Her heart was beating wildly, her hands trembling. What did he mean? What did he expect her to say, to do?

"The chess set, mistress." He pointed at the table. "I take it you play . . ."

"Oh, Lloyd!" Gwenevere giggled girlishly, curling up at his side beneath the light cotton spread on his massive oak bed.

"We never got along so well when we were together, did we?" He lifted a wrinkled hand to brush a stray lock of hair off her cheek. The light of the candle on the stand next to the bed cast an aura of golden light over Gwenevere's face, making him smile at the memory of her once youthful features. Even now, in his eyes, with the creases of age and the plump curves, she was still one of the most

38

beautiful women he had ever known.

She caught his hand, pressing a kiss to his palm. "Too young and foolish, I suppose. I should have made an attempt to stay here with you and be happy."

"You're right, you should have, but I should have insisted you stay." He sat up slowly, propping himself on a plump goose-feather bolster. "I should have thought less of the damnable business and more of my wife."

Gwenevere shook her head, lifting the counterpane to cover her bare breasts. "Should have, could have, the soup has stewed, Lloyd. 'Twas in the stars." She smiled, leaning forward to kiss his lips. "Admit it, you and I were never meant to be. Our fate was sealed before we breathed our first breath."

"So why did you come to me? To make an old man happy on his death bed?"

She laughed, sitting up beside him. "Or to kill him. I'm certain your surgeon's instructions didn't include futtering." Her rich brown eyes grew serious. "Actually, I don't know why I came — guilt?" She looked away, staring at the ancient crimson bedcurtains. "I hope not. I like to think of it as good friends saying good-bye." She turned to study his aged face.

"Then a man could receive no finer a farewell." Lloyd took her hand in his. "And now on to the business at hand. You must know why I called you."

"I do, but are you certain you're dying? You seem healthy enough to me." She smiled coyly.

Lloyd chuckled. "You could always make a man feel like a king, Gwen. But yes, I'm certain. I've had two heart attacks in the past year. My surgeon says I can't possibly survive the next." He smiled sadly. "My time's run out."

She nodded. "Then what's to be done? Why do you need me?"

"I wanted your consent, in person. I have a proposal to make, but I wanted your word on it first."

She looked at him, puzzled. "A proposal?"

"I have a niece not of legal age who will inherit a great deal of money when I die; you have a son with a large shipping business and no means to run it when I'm gone . . ." He paused, letting the information sink in. "My proposition is a legal union between the two parties."

Gwenevere gasped. "Marriage? You want my son to marry Keely?"

He shrugged. "And why not? They're of no blood kin. Do you not think it fitting?"

"Well, no, it's just that it didn't occur to me that you would think Brock of high enough station to marry her."

"Bastard or no, I've never met a finer man, Gwen. I'd trust him with my life, so why not the life of my only living heir?"

Gwenevere sat back in the pillows, her hands clasped. "You're right." She nodded thoughtfully. "The perfect solution. Keely's inheritance is safe . . ."

"If I were to die without appointing a guardian, one would be appointed. No telling how mismanaged her funds would be. And Brock would no longer have the money to continue financing his ventures."

"If they married, no matter who wins or loses this bloody war, the Crown or you traitors," she said good-naturedly, "the union would retain the money."

Lloyd nodded, pleased with himself. "The only question is, will Keely and Brock agree the solution is so simple?"

She turned, slipping her hand beneath the coverlet. "Certainly not. They've been at each other since the minute she set foot on board his ship, but I can speak with him if you're willing to take on Keely."

Lloyd chuckled, leaning to blow out the candle. "All right, I'll speak with her. But as usual with you, Gwen, I believe I've gotten the short end of the stick."

Gwenevere's laughter filled the darkened bedchamber as Lloyd's hand crept up her ample thigh.

Chapter Four

"You're late," Keely announced as Brock came through the front door.

"And since when are you my keeper, little cousin?" He whipped off his cocked hat, tossing it onto a side table. He couldn't help noticing that the exquisite piece had been polished until the patina of the cherry wood shone. "Been busy, have you, tidying up? Practicing for that bridegroom, whoever he might be?" His well-shaped mouth twitched into a smile.

Keely's hand ached to slap Brock's mocking face. This morning in the parlor he had challenged her to an ongoing game of chess and then proceeded to chat while they made their first moves. He told her that her uncle and aunt intended to marry her off and soon. He had made her feel like some prized sheep being sent to the auction block.

"Indeed, I have been cleaning. The two of you live here like swine." She pointed to his booted feet. "Wipe them. I just had the carpets swept."

Brock chuckled, wiping his boots on the rag rug in the entranceway. "So where is tea being served?"

"Uncle Lloyd wants us in his office, but you're certainly not going like that." She gestured with a hand. "You look like some field hand." Wrinkling

42

her nose, she added, "and you smell like one, too."

"Perhaps that's because I have been working, something you wouldn't know anything about."

"Unloading illegal goods, I suppose?"

"Check, but not checkmate." He smiled. "All right. For you I shall change into my most presentable costume."

"Not for me, I assure you, sir, but for your mother and her husband." Keely's triumphant eyes met his. " 'Tis common courtesy."

He studied her oval face. "And is it common courtesy to look so beautiful for your long-lost colonial cousin?"

She blushed scarlet, turning away. "I'll tell them you've arrived."

Lucy poured Keely a cup of sassafras tea and set the pot on the table, offering a plate of tiny iced cakes.

"That will be enough, Lucy," Lloyd said kindly. "You're dismissed."

"Yes, sir." She lowered the plate to the table, dipping a brief curtsy, then left the room, closing the paneled door behind her.

Brock sipped his tea, leaning back in the winged chair to stretch out his long legs before him. "Well, Lloyd, let's not keep us in suspense any longer. What have you summoned us all here for?" His voice was light and teasing, yet was underlaid with a deep respect for the elder man.

"You've no patience, boy; I've told you that again and again." Lloyd shook his head, sampling a cake. "Of course I had none at your age either."

Gwenevere shifted uneasily in her chair beside Lloyd's. She was dressed outrageously this afternoon in something she referred to as a caftan. Keely thought she looked utterly ridiculous in the flowing silken shirts with her head wrapped high in a sheet of silk, but there was no point in commenting—her aunt was well content in her odd ways.

Gwen glanced up at Keely and then fixed her attention on her china teacup. It was a delicate porcelain thing, shaped without handles and hand-painted, one of a set given as a wedding gift to her and Lloyd many years ago. "Do go ahead, Lloyd."

"Very well." The silver-haired man cleared his throat, setting his teacup down on the table. He lifted his gaze to meet Keely's. "I first ask that the two of you, you and Brock"—he nodded to Keely—"keep silent until I've finished."

Keely's hand trembled ominously. What was he going to say that would concern both her and Brock? Why was Auntie looking so guilty?

"Gwenevere and I have thought long and hard on your future, child." He looked to Brock. "And on yours as well."

Brock stiffened, the lazy smile falling from his face.

"With my death imminent, I want to be certain that you, Keely, are protected and well provided for as you should be. Your father and I built a great fortune, most of which will soon be yours." Lloyd took a deep breath. "But I am also concerned for Brock's welfare." His eyes turned to his wife's child seated across from him. "You have been a son to me, Brock, and a better son a man could never ask for, of my loins or not. But I worry for you and this cause we support. Your future seems so unstable."

Keely swallowed hard as she leaned to deposit her teacup on the table. There was a loud buzzing in her head as she tried not to draw any conclusions from her uncle's rambling. Her eyes grew wide with knowing, however, as Lloyd continued.

"And so, Gwenevere and I have come to a solution to my worries. We have thought of a way to secure

44

both of your lives, no matter which way this dirty warring business falls." He reached with his withered hand to take Gwen's plump one. "It is our wish, Keely and Brock, that you marry and marry soon, so that I may die in peace."

Keely bolted out of her seat, speechless.

"Marry her?" Brock let his teacup hit the table with a clatter. "You jest?"

Keely turned to him with a mixture of shock and indignation. "Have no fear, I assure you I have no desire to wed *you!*"

"Now, now . . ." Lloyd raised his hands. "Sit down, kitten. I asked that you not speak until I'm finished, now hear me out."

Keely exhaled sharply, dropping into her seat. Her eyes still rested on the heathen seated beside her. Had her uncle gone mad? Marry Brock? An uncivilized, colonial half-breed? Not if he was the last man on God's green earth!

"It's the only logical thing to do. If you marry, Keely, you will be safe from some court-appointed guardian who might rob you of your due, or marry you himself. And you, Brock." He turned his attention to his wife's son. "You will have the money necessary to continue financing your ventures. If you do not accept this arrangement, once I am gone, your funds will be cut off and you'll lose the *Tempest.* You realize your mother would never see fit to support our *traitor* cause."

Seeing the light of reasoning in Brock's dark eyes, Lloyd paused. "And this way," he said soothingly, "the inheritance will be safe whether we win this blasted war or not, for you will have an Englishwoman for a wife." He smiled, quite pleased with himself as he leaned back in the chair. "Besides, the two of you are quite fond of each other as I understand; a greater match neither of you could make." He retrieved his teacup. "Now, you may speak."

45

Keely slid forward in the chair, her hands clasped tightly in her lap to keep them from shaking. "No. Absolutely, certainly not. I'll not marry him. I told you, Aunt Gwen, I'll not marry some colonial clod! Why, why, he's not even Christian," she choked.

Brock got to his feet. "Clod? And how would you know my religious convictions, cousin?" he asked hotly. He looked to Lloyd, lowering his voice a notch. "She's not much more than a child, surely you don't . . ." His voice trailed off into silence. From the look on Lloyd's face he could see that they were indeed quite serious. He shook his head, looking away. " 'Tis absurd."

"I'll tell you what's absurd," Keely said, leaping to her feet. She scrutinized Brock's scowling face, holding him captive with her livid hazel eyes. "It's absurd that you would think I would even consider marrying you!" She planted her hands on her hips. "You're rude and unmannerly, ungentlemanly and . . . and someone's going to hang your arrogant neck from a rope for this treason you commit."

"Now, now, Keely," Gwenevere murmured, shaking a hand. "Calm down!"

"Calm down! Would you be calm, Aunt Gwen?" Her voice weakened against her will. "*You* of all people I should think would understand!" Turning away, she fled the room, slamming the door behind her.

Brock stood at the window, his arms crossed over his broad chest, listening to the sound of Keely's footsteps as they died away. The room was silent for several moments before he spoke. "Clever, you two. I have to admit that."

Gwenevere got up from her chair and went to stand beside her son. "We don't mean to be clever, just sensible. Are you really that violently opposed or is your dander just ruffled?"

"*Mother,* I have no dander. But yes, I am opposed. I have no room in my life for her, not just for Keely but for any woman." He turned his dark gaze on Gwenevere. "She's right, you know. I might very well find myself swinging from the hangman's noose. Do you think that fair to her?"

"She's of good stock. She would bear you sons you could be proud of." Gwenevere rested her hand on her son's arm.

"She's naught but a child," he flared. "I'm a good fifteen years her elder."

"Tell me you don't like her," Gwen reasoned. "Tell me I don't see that sparkle in your eyes when she passes you in the hallway."

"That's lust, Mother. Nothing more."

"So that's as good a place as any to start. You could learn to love, her, couldn't you?"

Brock looked out over the elegant boxwood garden, watching the branches of an apple tree sway with the light August breeze. Yes, he thought to himself . . . it's possible, but I can't let it happen. Not again. "Love's not necessary in a marriage of convenience," he murmured aloud.

Gwenevere chuckled, giving a nod of her turbaned head. "There then, it's done."

"No! It is not done," Brock said sharply. "I'm no fortune hunter. I'll not marry the chit against her will." He ran a bronze hand down the length of his neat black braid. "She's right, you know — you of all people *should* understand, Mother. You would never have married Lloyd if you had been given a choice." He glanced over at the old man. "No offense meant, sir, but you know 'tis true."

Lloyd reached for his pipe. "No offense taken."

Gwenevere sighed with exasperation. "You want Lloyd to go to his grave sick with worry for her?"

Brock shook his head. "Oh, no, Mother, you'll not pin that on me." He turned to Lloyd. "Can't you find another suitor? There are plenty of men right

47

here in Dover who would take her today if they heard what she was worth."

Lloyd sucked on his pipe until the tobacco in its bowl glowed red. "But I want her to be happy."

"And what makes you think she'd be happy with me, for Christ's sake?"

"You're a good man."

Brock ran his palm over his face. He couldn't help imagining what it would be like to lie beside her in a great bed, to touch her silky flesh, to kiss her soft lips. "It just doesn't seem right to take advantage of the girl like this."

"She has to marry someone and soon," Gwenevere said, going to the table to pour Lloyd another cup of tea. "And you have to admit this would solve your financial concerns."

"Yes, yes, I know," Brock commented irritably. "But even if I agree, she said she'd not marry me. She thinks me uncivilized."

"Oh, that's just the young, foolish girl in her talking. She cares for you, Brock." Gwen stirred her tea with a small silver spoon. "Tell us you'll marry her. She'll come around."

Brock looked from his mother to Lloyd, both calmly drinking their tea. "I don't like having decisions made for me like this." He looked away. "But I'll think about it," he conceded quietly.

Gwen smiled, patting Lloyd on the knee. "You see that, you old goat, I told you he'd agree to it."

"I have not agreed," Brock insisted. "I just don't have the time to stand here and argue with the two of you. I've got work to do; I'll not be back for the evening meal so don't wait for me." He gave a nod. "Good day to you both."

Gwenevere watched her son disappear through the office door and then turned to Lloyd, a smile plain on her face. "Well, my part's done. Now it's your turn."

Lloyd exhaled, watching the smoke from his pipe filter through the air. "He hasn't agreed."

"No, but he will." She smoothed the skirts of her brilliantly colored caftan. "He's an intelligent boy. He realizes what a superb wife she'd make."

"You mean he realizes what an advantage it would be to have her money."

"I didn't raise him to be an idiot, Lloyd. Finances are an important concern in marriages and he knows it," Gwenevere answered haughtily.

Lloyd chuckled. "Don't put on your duchess airs with me!" He patted her hand. "Now I suppose I have Keely to contend with."

"You do, but since I've done so well here, perhaps I'll speak to her too." Gwenevere pushed up out of the chair, leaning to peck him on the cheek. "My dogs need their exercise. I'll be in the garden if you need me."

"Very well, old girl," Lloyd said, unable to resist patting her on the bottom as she went by. "I'll see you tonight." He winked at her as she went out the door, and her shameless laughter filled the hallway.

The moment Gwenevere was gone, the housekeeper, Matilda, entered Lloyd's office. "Will there be anything else, sir?" She picked up the teacups one by one, placing them on a tray she balanced in her hand. She was a tall, middle-aged woman, with gray hair and translucent skin. Her mouth twitched as she went about her chore.

"And what are you in such a pucker about?" Lloyd asked good-naturedly. "Leave my cup be, I'm not finished."

"It's her, sir." Matilda's pale blue eyes met his.

"Gwen? What on earth's she done to you?"

"It's not me, sir, it's you." Matilda lowered her head, scooping up the teapot. "I know it's not my place to say so, but it's sin. She's gone all of these years and then comes back like some vulture when

49

you're dyin'."

"Now, now, Matilda, that's a little severe, isn't it?"

"She should have been here with you. It's not Christian living apart from your husband." Her eyes grew wide. " 'Tis the devil's work, she is, with her funny clothes and strange ideas!"

Lloyd laughed aloud and then winced, gripping his left arm.

Matilda dropped the tray on the table and got to her knees in front of him. "Are you hurtin', sir? Should I get the surgeon?"

"Hurting? No, no." Lloyd took a deep breath, straightening up. "I feel better than I've felt in years. It's Gwen. I'd forgotten just how much fun she could be. I'm just a little tired, that's all."

Matilda made a clucking sound between her teeth, daring to take Lloyd's withered hand. "Shame on her, exciting you like this. You know what the surgeon said. Tryin' to kill you, she is. The devil's work if I ever saw it. She'll burn in hell for it, you can be certain of that."

"That will be enough of that talk, Matilda. I'm too lax with you and your mincing ways. I'll not have you speak of Gwen with that tone. She's still my wife."

Blushing under the heat of Lloyd's reprimand, Matilda got to her feet. "Excuse me, sir. I apologize. It's only for your welfare that I'm concerned." She lowered her gaze to the floor.

"I know. Now go on with you. I've some papers to draw up and then I'll be needing my solicitor. Can you send a message to him?"

"Right away." She swept the tray off the table. "Are you certain, though, sir, that I shouldn't get the surgeon? I hate to see you suffer like this."

"Suffer? I feel absolutely grand, just grand. Just do as I ask, Matilda. I'll be the one to decide when I need my surgeon."

"Yes, sir."

Keely paced the floor of her bedchamber. "I can't believe it," she murmured aloud. "They actually thought I'd consider taking him as a husband." She scoffed at the absurdity. And to think that colonial had the audacity to say *he* wouldn't take *her!* Keely balled her hands at her sides, seething.

She was hurt that Aunt Gwen and Uncle Lloyd would have rallied against her like this. Imagine, she being married to Brock! The truth was, she couldn't imagine being married to anyone. It seemed so unfair that she be forced to wed a man she hadn't chosen herself, a man who hadn't chosen her. But then Aunt Gwen was right, what young woman was allowed to chose a mate out of love? Especially a woman with an inheritance of the size that she could expect.

But if Uncle Lloyd and Aunt Gwen were going to chose a husband for her, why not an Englishman? She had told them she was homesick; she had told them she wanted to return to England as soon as possible. She wondered now if she should have accepted Lord Larten's proposal. He would have at least been a husband she could have ignored. How could she ever ignore a man like Brock; he made her jump every time he spoke. A woman couldn't marry a man she was afraid of—and she was afraid of her cousin.

A knock came at the door, startling Keely. "Yes, come in," she managed.

Lucy stepped inside the door. "Your aunt is askin' for you in the garden, mistress."

Keely sighed, fingering the worn amulet she wore around her neck. "Very well, tell her I'll be there directly."

"Yes'm." Lucy's eyes twinkled mischievously. "Word is in the kitchen that you'll be marryin'

51

Master Brock. Quite a man, that one is . . ."

"Well, the word is wrong!" Keely snapped. "The whole bunch of you had better quit gossiping and get to work or you'll all be out on your ears!"

Lucy dropped the grin from her face, bobbing her head. "Yes, mistress." But as she ducked out the door, she was chuckling to herself. There wasn't a serving girl in the county that wouldn't give a year's wages for a tumble with that man!

Keely found her aunt in the garden, seated on a bench in the sun. Her spaniels ran in circles, chasing each other through a patch of knee-high Queen Anne's lace.

"Oh, there you are." Gwenevere patted the small stone bench. "Sit down, I want to talk with you, Keely."

"I'd rather stand."

Gwenevere studied her young niece, her nut-brown eyes sparkling with pride. Keely was certainly a beauty with her blue-green eyes and rich red hair, but more importantly she was a woman of character. Seeing her standing there on the brick walk, her arms folded stiffly over her chest, convinced Gwenevere that Keely and Brock were the perfect match. "Very well, stand then."

One of the spaniels, Rupert, nipped at Keely's heels and she brushed him aside. "You should have told me. It was humiliating for me to stand there in front of him and have him say he wouldn't have me. He's right, you know, I am nothing more than a piece of livestock being auctioned at the Sussex fair."

"Perhaps I was wrong in not speaking to you first. But you were the one who popped up first insisting you wouldn't have him." Gwenevere picked up a ripe peach from the bench and began to peel it with a small paring knife. "You injured his pride, and pride is important to men. You'll soon learn that."

Keely watched a bumblebee alight on a hollyhock blossom. "And what of *my* pride? He called me a child." She couldn't admit to her aunt that her son frightened her, or that he made her heart pound when he spoke.

"And in many ways you still are. Only a child would not consider every facet of this proposal."

"I know I have to marry but isn't there someone else, someone—"

"Someone who will bore you to death? Someone who will gamble away your father's money or beat you into submission?"

Keely's cheeks colored. "No," she said quietly. "Just someone who lives in London. Someone who will let me continue my life as it was with my friends, people of my own class. I expected to marry an educated gentleman, a man with some couth."

"We all grow up, Keely. Brock is a good man who could make you very happy."

"I could never be happy here in the colonies. Besides, he's arrogant."

Gwen nodded, nibbling on a slice of peach. "He probably is, but what man isn't?" She paused for a moment. "Lloyd is in a hurry to have this done, be it Brock or someone else. Your uncle won't force you, but there will be a wedding shortly and you may not like his next choice any better."

"So what you're saying is that I really have no choice." Keely's eyes grew moist and she brushed at them.

Gwen lowered her lashes. "No. Not much. The only other suitable man would be Lord Calvin in Essex."

"Lord Calvin!" Keely uttered in amazement. "The man is sixty-two years old!"

"He's a cousin by marriage to your Uncle Lloyd, a wealthy man in his own right."

"He's deaf! I can't marry him!"

53

Gwenevere shrugged. "Then you'll marry my son."

Keely covered her mouth with her palm, muffling her words. "I can't believe you're doing this to me . . ."

"It's not to hurt you, dear. You have to believe me when I tell you that I honestly think you will be happy here with Brock. He's half in love with you already. Your love for him will come in time."

"Love?" Keely laughed bitterly. "Me? I think not."

"Then you're a fool." Gwenevere returned her attention to her peach.

For several minutes Keely was silent. She listened to the buzz of the bees in the garden and the sound of laughter in the summer kitchen. The sun was hot on her face. She turned into the cool breeze, away from her aunt. Tears dried on her face. "He said he wouldn't marry me."

Gwenevere looked up. "He'll reconsider."

"Because of my money?" Keely asked numbly. She couldn't believe they were forcing her to marry that heathen savage!

"Yes, partly, but also because he likes you. The two of you have so much in common. You said yourself he plays chess as well as you do."

"Better," she admitted with defeat. "He ignores me mostly and when he does speak he calls me little English cousin." She sat down on the bench beside her aunt dejectedly. "He's a traitor to the Crown."

Gwenevere nodded. "That is my greatest concern. If the union is to take place, you must keep yourself out of this conflict. No matter what happens, you must remain neutral."

"What if they hang him? He could drown at sea. What then?"

Gwenevere shrugged good-naturedly. "Then as a widowed woman you may return to London to live with me."

"I want to go home with you now. I don't want to

live here." Nervously, she jingled the household keys she wore attached to a narrow cloth belt around her waist. "If I must marry, couldn't you find me a younger English husband?" she pleaded desperately.

"This was your home first. Have you no recollections of this house?"

Keely frowned, looking off into the distance. "Oh, some. I remember Papa, I remember a cat who had a litter of kittens in the garden. I remember the parties at Christmastide."

Gwenevere looked up. "They say that if you're colonial born, it runs in your blood. They say you can be happy nowhere else. It's true enough with Lloyd and Brock."

"Well, it's not true with me. I don't belong here, not with him. I miss my friends and I miss my home in England."

"When you're older, Keely, you'll realize you've made the right choice." Gwenevere took Keely's hand. "Tell your uncle you'll agree to the match."

Keely sighed. "Maybe I'll get lucky and they'll hang him. . ."

Chapter Five

Keely stood at a window that looked out over the gardens, laughing at Gwenevere and Blackie's mock tennis game. Gwenevere cursed, stomping her feet as she waited for Blackie to toss her another ball. She was dressed outrageously this morning in Turkish pantaloons and a wide-brimmed straw bonnet.

One of Aunt Gwen's passions was tennis. She said she refused to let her game go to hell while she was in these godforsaken Colonies, so each morning she went out into the garden, a servant in tow, and had balls tossed to her so that she might practice her swing. It was a comical sight, with Aunt Gwen racing back and forth in her silk pantaloons over a bed of mint and Blackie running to retrieve the leather balls.

Spotting Keely in the window, Aunt Gwenevere waved her racket, then swung hard. The leather ball hit the catgut with a resounding crack and Keely ducked as the ball came flying in the open window and hit the plastered wall. It bounced aimlessly down the hall as Lloyd stuck his head out of his office.

"Is she at it again?" he asked, feigning irritation.

Keely bit back a chuckle. "She tells me her game is improving, but I'm not so sure."

"Well, come in here, kitten, before you're beheaded. I want to talk to you anyway."

Keely stiffened. "If it's about Brock, I don't want to hear it. You know what I think of your proposal."

"Well, you're going to hear it, so get your tail in here," Lloyd chided.

Keely's eyes grew wide with surprise and Lloyd softed. "Amuse an old dying man and hear me out. I give you my word this will be the last I'll say on the subject."

Keely came slowly down the hall. She didn't want to talk about Brock with Uncle Lloyd or anyone else, but she couldn't deny her uncle's request. He was too dear to her; he reminded her too much of her own father.

Closing Lloyd's door, she leaned against the polished wood, her hands tucked behind her back. "Well, speak if you must. Everyone in this entire household thinks we should marry—everyone but Brock and I. There are no secrets in this house," she scolded. "First it was Lucy telling me what a catch he is and then last night Ruth asked me what I wanted served at the wedding party."

Lloyd sat down in a chair near the small fireplace. "We just want what's best for you. We want you to be happy."

"If you think marrying that man will make me happy, you're wrong."

Lloyd leaned back in the chair, folding his hands neatly in his lap. "I didn't think you to be a woman of prejudices. Perhaps my wife did not bring you up to be the young lady I had hoped."

Keely lowered her head, shaking it. "It's not just that, it's everything." She looked up. "I'm a loyal

English subject, Uncle, and England is where I belong. I want to go home."

"Why are you so opposed to this union?"

"He doesn't even like me! We could never get along. He's a traitor," she spit.

"If it's wooing you want, rose petals and silly poems scribbled on sheets of perfumed paper, you'll not get them from Brock."

"I'm not that naive," Keely flared. "But I want to marry a man I can respect. I've no respect for someone who has betrayed his King!"

"Does that mean you have no respect for me?" Keely looked up. "No, of course not."

Lloyd forced his face to harden. "Then out of respect for me and your aunt you will marry Brock."

"That's it? My unwillingness means nothing?"

"Keely, Keely, dear, don't be so serious! You've been reading too many of your aunt's romantic novels." He felt for his pipe in his waistcoat. "Oh, granted, there are men who will play those games, men in England with nothing better to do with their time, but you'll not get that here. What you'll get here in these United States is honesty, hard work, and undying loyalty. Brock is no powdered, wigged gentleman, but he would come to love you with all of his heart."

"Yours was an arranged marriage. The two of you were never happy."

"We were young and foolish. I take full responsibility for the failure of that marriage. I was too busy with my work to make Gwen feel welcome." His eyes grew misty and he looked away. "I was too occupied with the shipping business to help ease the pain of the loss of the man she had loved."

"But 'tis done now," Keely said softly.

Lloyd turned back to her. "Yes, it's all in the past now, but I'll tell you, if I had it to do over again, I'd never have let her go. I'd have made her stay here. I'd have made her love me."

"But she loves you now, Uncle Lloyd."

He shook his head, glancing on the table. "Have you seen my pipe? No, now I'm an old man. It's not the same love, not the love we could have had. Nothing can change those years of loneliness."

Spotting the pipe on Lloyd's desk, Keely crossed the room to retrieve it. "Here 'tis."

Lloyd took Keely's hand in his. "Please, kitten, say you'll marry him. You'll not regret it in the years to come."

Keely studied her uncle's wrinkled face. "The decision has already been made," she said with defeat. "Why do you need my consent?"

"I want no tears on your wedding day. I want you to accept what we think is best." He squeezed her hand then suddenly released it, wincing with pain.

Keely's face became a mask of concern. "What's the matter, aren't you feeling well?"

"No, no." He waved a hand. "I'm quite fine. I just want this matter to be done with. I want your permission to cry the banns."

A knock at the door interrupted them, and Lloyd nodded for Keely to open it.

"Mistress Keely"—Lucy bobbed her head—"there's a gentleman here to see you."

"Me?" Keely looked to her uncle. "Who would be here to see me?"

Lloyd chuckled, lighting his pipe. "Go and see why don't you."

"It's Master Micah Lawrence from Fortune's Find, mistress." A sassy smile played on Lucy's lips.

"Fortune's Find?"

Lloyd sucked on his pipe. "A large plantation east of here. He's a friend of Brock's."

Keely rolled her eyes, turning back to Lucy. "Very

well, tell Master Lawrence I'll be pleased to receive him in the parlor."

"Yes, ma'am." The serving girl dipped a curtsy and turned to go.

"And Lucy . . ."

"Yes, mistress?"

"Try to keep your hands off my guest, will you?"

Lucy grinned, shaking her head. "Oh, no, I'd not lay a finger on him." She winked at Lloyd. "But you wouldn't mind if I ogled him a bit, would you?"

"Out with you!" Keely ordered.

"Yes, mistress."

Keely shook her head as Lucy went down the hall. "You really are too lax with them, Uncle. That one's going to find trouble with her loose ways."

"She's harmless enough. Now go on and attend to your guest. I want to have these legal papers drawn up immediately." He looked up at her. "Now I want no vapors and no fits. You go to your bridegroom with dignity."

"Do what you must," Keely conceded. "I'll not embarrass you." She stared at her uncle for a moment, her face frozen in unhappiness, and then she let herself out of the office, closing the door behind her.

Smoothing her dimity skirts, Keely's hands went to the knot of hair at the nape of her neck. Patting her unruly auburn tresses, she glided into the parlor. She wouldn't let herself think about Brock right now, because if she did, she knew she'd go mad. "Master Lawrence?"

Micah rose up out of his seat, coming forward to take Keely's hand. "Mistress Bartholomew, please excuse me for coming without being invited"—his lips brushed the back of her hand—"but Brock has spoken so fondly of you that I had to come see you for myself."

Keely smiled, looking up at the handsome stranger as he released her hand. This was the first friendly face she'd encountered since her arrival. "Oh really, that surprises me. My cousin, you say? Please sit down." She indicated with a hand. "I've called for tea—good English tea."

Micah lifted the tails of his finely tailored coat and sat down. "English tea? I'm surprised you could find such an amenity in this household. It's illegal here in Delaware to trade for English goods, you know."

She sat down in a high-back upholstered chair just opposite Micah. "Oh, there wasn't a leaf to be had before we got here, but it was one of the first things my aunt insisted on when we arrived—good English tea. She told Uncle Lloyd that she didn't care what he had to pay for it or who he had to pay, she wanted tea. Brock was furious."

"So my dear friend is drinking English tea now, is he?" Micah grinned. "I should think his acquaintances at the King's Head tavern would like to hear that."

"Oh, no. Brock won't drink it himself. When he has tea with us, he's brought a separate pot of herbal stuff." She studied her guest's well-featured face, taking notice of shining blond hair tied neatly in a queue.

Micah nodded smiling. "He's right, you know . . ."

"About the tea?" She liked this Micah; he was charming. He made her forget her troubles.

"No, about how beautiful you were. His words don't do you justice."

"I think you're a liar, Master Lawrence, though a flattering one. But I can hardly believe my cousin would say anything so pleasant."

"He says you play chess as well as he does and

61

that is a compliment, coming from Brock Bartholomew."

"He said that?" Keely asked with surprise.

"I'm also told he's asked you to marry him," Micah dared.

"That's what he told you, did he?" She lifted a sooty eyebrow.

"No. He didn't. In fact, I haven't seen him in several days."

"Business to the north, I'm told," Keely said tartly.

He nodded. "Actually, it was your maid who spoke of your pending betrothal; Lucy, I think she said the name was."

"Lucy has a loose tongue. He didn't actually ask for my hand," she said, looking away.

"I see," Micah responded kindly. "Marrying you off, are they?"

"Yes, I'm afraid so." She wondered vaguely why she was disclosing all of this to a near-stranger, but she couldn't help herself. Besides, he'd have known soon enough, wouldn't he? It would certainly only be a matter of time before Brock would have everyone in town knowing the story.

"And let me guess. Brock is your guardian's first choice."

Keely's hazel eyes met Micah's with uncertainty. "There's nothing particularly wrong with him, we just don't get along," she said hedgingly. "The truth is that he's just a little too . . . too . . ." She cut herself off for lack of the right word.

"Arrogant, sarcastic, unrefined?"

"He's your friend. I shouldn't have said anything."

"Yes, he is my friend. But who knows a person better than their friend? Brock would be my first choice to be the man at my side in a fight; he's the man I would trust with my life above all others, but no, I wouldn't want to marry him either."

62

Keely smiled, then laughed. "You have a good sense of humor, Master Lawrence. I like that."

"Please, call me Micah."

She nodded. "Micah, then."

He adjusted his pristine white stock at his neck. "It's easy for me to be humorous though, isn't it. I mean it's not me that's in the predicament. A pity, but it happens to all women of your age, doesn't it?"

"So I'm told."

"You could always marry me . . ."

Keely lifted her dark lashes. "Excuse me?"

"I said you could always marry me."

"Is that a proposal?" She couldn't help smiling.

He chuckled. "Yes, I suppose it is, although I certainly didn't come for that purpose."

She clasped her hands, leaning forward. "You're not serious?"

"Oh, but I am. My father has a large plantation not far from Dover. I don't need your money and I'm not nearly as free with my finances for the *cause* as Brock is. I think I'd make a rather good husband. Don't you?"

A blush crept across Keely's cheeks. "I . . . I don't know what to say."

He shrugged. "Say yes then."

"But I don't know you."

"How well do you know Brock? Your uncle can attest to my good character. I can go and ask for your hand right now if you like." He got to his feet.

Flabbergasted, Keely stood up. "You're not serious." She looked into his clear blue eyes. "You are serious, aren't you?"

He caught her hand. "I am indeed. Tell me you'll marry me, Mistress Keely Bartholomew."

"I couldn't accept." She knew she was mad to even contemplate marrying this man, but she couldn't help thinking this would be a way out of this trap.

63

"But . . . I will consider it." Wouldn't it be wonderful to choose a man for herself, she thought slyly. Wouldn't she like to see the look on Brock's face when he discovered he'd lost the chance to have her inheritance?

"I'm honored." He kissed her hand gently. "Now how about that tea you offered?"

"Oh, yes." She stepped back clumsily. "Lucy must have gotten lost. I'll fetch it myself."

An hour later Keely was seeing Micah out the door. "Thank you so much for coming."

"You're most welcome." He accepted his cocked hat from Lucy. "And thank you for seeing me." He glanced at the servant, who had obviously been listening in, and lowered his voice. "You will consider my proposal, won't you."

She laughed, crossing her arms over her chest. "I'm tempted. But I'll have to think about it. My uncle has his mind set."

Micah Lawrence winked and let himself out the front door.

"God a'mercy!" Lucy breathed the moment he was gone. "You've got the two best-lookin' men in Dover after you!"

"Lucy! Were you eavesdropping on my conversation with Master Lawrence?"

"Eavesdroppin'? Certainly not!" Lucy said indignantly. "I was just polishin' the chair railin' in the front hall; I couldn't help but hear a word or two."

"Well, let me warn you." Keely held a fist up to the dirty blonde. "If I hear that one word of my conversation has been repeated by you, I'll have my uncle dismiss you. Do you understand?"

Lucy's smile fell from her face. "God's teeth, mistress. I didn't murder no one! But my mouth is stitched." She ran a finger over her rosy lips. "I swear it!"

Long after everyone had retired for the night, Keely paced her bedchamber restlessly. She knew she was foolish to have led Micah on like that, to have made him think she would consider his proposal. Uncle Lloyd had already started the paperwork necessary to make her and Brock's betrothal official. It had been wrong not to tell Micah, but it had felt so good, if only for a few hours, to pretend she had a choice. Micah was so kind, so unintimidating. He was the kind of man she would have liked to have married. Now she would have to contact Micah and apologize, turning down his offer.

Pushing that unpleasant thought aside, Keely slipped on her nightrobe and padded barefoot down the front steps. She found herself suddenly hungry and wanted something to eat. To her surprise, a lamplight shone through the summer kitchen windows. Cautiously, Keely pushed open the door. Light spilled onto the brick walk and illuminated the summer night air. "Is someone there?" It seemed odd to her that anyone would be up at this hour.

"Evening," came Brock's deeply masculine voice.

Startled, Keely stepped into the kitchen. "I thought you were gone."

"I'm back." He was seated at the worktable in the center of the room, his boots propped up on it. On the table sat a pewter mug, a small wheel of cheese, some bread, and a bowl of peaches.

Keely was tempted just to return to her room. She hadn't seen Brock since the other day in Lloyd's office when their marriage had been proposed and she had no desire for a confrontation now. But slowly she came to the table, as if drawn to him by some unholy spell.

Tonight Brock was dressed in a pair of navy

breeches and a lawn shirt, minus a stock and waistcoat. Keely's gaze came to rest on the triangle of bronze skin that peaked from the V of his shirt. She swallowed hard, mentally chastising herself for being such a ninny. What was wrong with her that a glimpse of bare male skin could make her heartbeat quicken?

She cleared her throat, reaching for a slice of aged cheese. "I trust your business went well . . ."

"Well enough."

"You certainly are the talkative one," she murmured sarcastically.

"I didn't know what they had cooked up, Keely." He tried to keep his gaze from straying to her slender neck, where wisps of auburn hair fell from a neat braid to entice him.

"Then you don't approve?"

"The truth?" He dropped his booted feet to the floor.

She nodded slowly, lost in the depths of his ebony eyes. "The truth," she whispered.

He tapped a stool beside him. "Sit." He waited until she had done so and then he spoke. "At first I was violently opposed. I had no intentions of marrying any time in the near future, though I'd like to have children."

Keely tore her gaze from his and reached for another bit of cheese. "But now?" She didn't know what made her so daring.

He reached out tantalizingly slowly to touch a lock of the dark red hair. "What do you think?"

His low rumbling voice was a caress, like the sound of the wind in the forest on a late afternoon. She moistened her dry lips. "I don't think I'm the woman for you. I think—"

"I think you're frightened of me . . ." He twisted the wisp of hair around his finger, mesmerized by its magical color.

Keely lifted her chin to study his sculptured face. "Why should I be frightened of you?"

"Oh, you know"—reluctantly he freed her hair and reached for the pewter mug—"me being a savage and all." When Keely said nothing, he changed the subject. "I understand Micah Lawrence came to call today."

"He did." She reached for a peach and a small paring knife.

"What did he want?"

He eyes narrowed, smiling secretly. "To propose marriage, I think."

"He what?"

Keely slipped with the knife, cutting her thumb. "Ouch!" she cried out as the knife fell to the floor with a clatter.

Brock rose up out of the chair. "Are you all right?" He took her hand, holding the thumb that oozed blood.

Keely watched Brock bring her thumb to his lips. His mouth was warm and moist on the injured flesh, sending an odd shiver down her spine. "It's all right," she whispered. She knew she should pull away, but her limbs were frozen, and she could do nothing but stare into Brock's dark eyes.

He sucked gently on her thumb, holding her in the countenance of his ebony eyes. "Micah is not the man for you," he said.

Gaining control of herself, Keely snatched her hand angrily from his. "And why not? He's your friend, isn't he?" She was angry at him for being so familiar with her and angry with herself for allowing it.

"Aye, that he is, but he's not right for you."

"Why, because he doesn't need my money as badly as you do, cousin?" she flared.

Brock's face grew taut with checked anger. Why did he care who she married, he wondered. Was the price of his privateering ventures worth the chains of marriage to a woman who came to him against her will? "I can't explain it," he said stiffly.

Keely took a step back. "It seems to me that even Lord Calvin would be better than you!"

Brock said nothing as she spun around and ran out the door and through the breezeway to the house. It wasn't until she was halfway up the front steps that she heard his voice come out of the darkness.

"Keely," he beckoned as he moved silently up the flight of steps.

Against her better judgment, she stopped and turned. "Yes?" she demanded.

Suddenly he was one step below her, bringing them eye to eye. "Keely, will you marry me?"

"What?" Only the moonlight shining through the window on the landing illuminated his bronze face.

His hand brushed the nape of her neck. His breath mingled with hers. "I said marry me," he whispered.

"Why?" she challenged, hoping he didn't hear the pounding of her heart.

"Because . . . because I don't know why . . ."

"Not a very good reason for a girl to marry," she retorted.

"Don't you ever do anything on impulse?" His obsidian eyes locked with hers. "Because it feels right?"

"Does this . . . does this feel right," she murmured, her head suddenly dizzy with confusion. His presence was so overwhelming that she seemed to lose all conscious thought.

"This does." Brock pulled her roughly against him, taking her breath away as he forced his mouth down hard against hers. Instead of resisting, Keely's lips parted to accept his sweet, searching tongue. She shivered as he planted the seeds of desire, combing his fingers through her thick hair as his mouth made its shocking assault.

When Keely withdrew, she spoke before thinking. "Yes, I'll marry you." She swallowed hard, frightened by her own words. "Though I'll probably regret it."

He laughed, releasing her so abruptly that she nearly lost her balance. "That's all right," he assured her as he went up the steps, "I'll probably regret it too."

Chapter Six

Brock ducked into the King's Head tavern and swept off his cocked hat, squinting as his eyes adjusted to the dim light of the smoke-filled room.

"Brock, where the hell have you been?" cried a voice from a table along the far wall.

"Christ, George, don't ask. I'll not be the brunt of your jokes for the next fortnight." He shrugged off his brass-buttoned sea jacket and tossed it onto a bench, along with his hat.

"Been with the tailor being fitted for a wedding coat, I suppose," Micah's mouth twisted and for an instant Brock saw a flicker of red-hot anger before his comrade laughed with amusement.

Brock's gaze met Micah's as Brock slid into a chair at the end of the rectangular wooden table. "You've a big mouth, friend."

"Wedding or a hanging?" George dissolved into raucous laughter. "I never thought I'd live to see the day Brock Bartholomew was caught in the noose."

"I knew it was only a matter of time," chided Joshua Kane.

"Who's the fortunate lady?" Manessah Lewes asked, then signaled for a barmaid.

"Well, Micah," Brock said irritably. "You might as well have finished what you started." Two days ago

Keely had sent a message to Micah declining his proposal, but thanking him graciously. The following day, Brock and Keely's betrothal had been announced.

Micah rose to his feet. "My trusted friend, Brock, has beguiled his cousin, the lovely Mistress Keely Bartholomew, into marrying him."

The men cheered, banging their copper-bound leather jacks on the table. "Hurray!" one called. "Congratulations," cried another.

Brock raised his hands. "Enough gentlemen, we have business to attend to."

"Not so fast," George interrupted. "When does the miraculous event take place? We're to be invited, aren't we?"

"That depends entirely on whether or not you can behave yourselves," Brock responded dryly, turning to the barmaid who stood at his side.

"Afternoon to you, Master Brock." The pox-faced barmaid dipped a curtsy, giggling behind her dirty palm. "Your usual, sir?"

He nodded, flipping her a copper pence. "Where's Jenna?" he asked as the serving girl skittered away.

"Haven't seen her," Joshua answered.

"No one's seen her since she went north?"

Micah lifted a jack of ale. "Not to my knowledge."

"Damn!" Brock muttered. "I knew we shouldn't have sent her."

"Now, now, my sister will be here," Manesseh assured him. "With Lord Howe marching toward Philadelphia, Jenna was the best choice. She's just late."

A week ago, on August 25, Commander Howe of the King's army had landed his warships at Head of Elk in Maryland. Some 18,000 British troops had disembarked, leading to skirmishes with the patriot

71

army at Wilmington and Cooch's Bridge in Delaware. Now, General Washington and the rest of the new nation waited to see what Howe's next move would be.

"She should have been back last night. Is there word from anyone else?" Brock accepted his china cup of herbal tea and dismissed the barmaid with a wave of his hand.

Micah shook his head. "All's quiet."

Just then the tavern door swung open. "Sorry I'm late," came a feminine voice.

Brock swung around. "Jenna, where have you been?"

The young woman laughed, shaking her mane of silver-blond hair. "You worry too much, Brock." She gave him a peck on the cheek as she swung around the table to take a seat beside Micah.

Brock leaned across the table. "So what's the word?"

"Howe's pigs are making a mess of things. Raiding and the like. I guess you heard they burned the courthouse records, ransacked the storehouses, and destroyed the army depot at Head of Elk."

Brock struck his fist against the table. "I *knew* we should have had the militia on that depot. We can't afford to lose supplies like this."

Jenna shrugged, taking a sip of ale from Micah's jack. "We should have expected it. Howe's men have been on those ships nigh seven weeks. Any army's going to pillage after being cooped up that long."

George leaned back against the wall, propping a foot on the back bench. "A commander ought to have better control over his troops."

Jenna reached for a crusty slice of bread. "If it's any consolation to you, gentlemen, I understand one man was hanged and three got the lash for their ill behavior."

"Hmph! Little good that'll do our soldiers this winter," Joshua muttered.

Brock sipped his tea. "What about our army? What are they lacking; what can we get them?"

Jenna laughed, her rich feminine voice echoing in the small public room of the tavern. "What do they always need? Black powder, cornmeal, soap . . . shoes. I understand they're terribly low on salt. My guess is that Washington had better be prepared to defend Philadelphia—Congress had better get their coattails out of there."

"Well"—Brock lowered his voice—"I have it from a good source that there's a fat English brig only a few days offshore . . ."

George leaned in. "Think you can catch her?"

"If there's a man who can do it, it's Brock." Joshua raised his jack in salute.

Brock shook his head, deep in thought. "She's going to be knotty," he said slowly. "There are two more in the fleet, but the scuttlebutt is they're a good day behind her."

"What's she carrying?" Jenna tugged off her mobcap and dropped it onto the table.

He smiled. "Salt and lots of it. Woolens, flour, salt pork, and the like."

Jenna's dark eyes danced mischievously. "When do you set sail?"

Brock glanced behind him to be certain none of the tavern's other customers were nearby. "On the morning tide."

"Good luck to you then." She rose to her feet. "And now, gentlemen, if you don't mind, I've got to get home. The rest of the information can wait. I've got a young son to tend to."

Brock stood up, following her to the door. "I'm going to be married, Jenna."

"Married? You?" She looked up at him with

73

surprise. "I didn't know there was anyone. I'm glad to hear it."

He ran his hand over his head to smooth his dark hair. "Lloyd's niece. I brought her back from England with my mother."

Jenna grinned. "I hope she'll make you happy. You deserve it if anyone does."

"Happiness has nothing to do with it, but the cause can well use her dowry. I can buy another ship." He grinned. "Come for the evening meal tonight. I'd like you to meet her."

"And if I don't approve?"

He chuckled. "Too late. I signed the betrothal papers this morning."

"I suppose this means I've lost my chance. You're not going to fall madly in love with me, kidnap me, and sail off into the sunrise with me in your arms." Her voice was laced with good humor.

He lifted his hands. "You had your chance."

"Yes, Brock, I'd love to come. But would it be all right if I bring Max? I've been gone for days."

"Certainly, bring him along. I just want Keely to meet you. She could use a friend."

Jenna squeezed Brock's hand. "See you tonight."

Keely had been standing on a wooden stool in the center of her bedchamber until her arms ached from holding them out at her sides. The rotund mantuamaker had been making circles around and around, creating tucks and adding pins to the green damask wedding gown for nearly two hours.

"Please, Mistress Schmidt, you've got to hurry. My head hurts, my back is stiff, and I've got to use the *necessary*," Keely moaned irritably.

"Ja, ja. Helga is almost finished," Mistress Schmidt soothed through a mouthful of dressmaker's pins. "Lift deine arm just a bit. Gut! Gut! Ve are almost done." The mantuamaker turned to one of the three maidservants she'd brought with her. "Janey! Das scalloped lace on das bed. Hurry!"

The young woman scurried to do her mistress's bidding, and then stepped back admiring Keely in awe. "Beautiful," she breathed. "Ye've outdone yourself with this'n, mistress."

The bedchamber door swung open and Gwenevere hustled into the room, her spaniels barking and leaping at her skirts.

"Aunt Gwen! Help me!" Keely dropped her arms and a pin stabbed her in the armpit. "Ouch!" tears came to her eyes as she lifted her arms again.

"Enough! Enough!" Gwenevere proclaimed with a sweep of her arms. "Get her out of it, Helga."

"But Mistress Bartholomew, I have not complete meine vork." The mantuamaker's eyes grew large. "I cannot be expected to create a perfect gown if I cannot be allowed to vork!"

"Get her down this minute! Look at the child, she's near to fainting!" Gwenevere went to Keely, helping her down off the stool.

"I've never fainted in my life," Keely whispered in her aunt's ear.

"I know, but it sounds good," Gwenevere returned with a wink. "Now get it off her before I take it off," she said, raising her voice.

"But it vill not be right," moaned the mantuamaker, near in tears. "It vill be ruined!"

"I thought the whole idea was ridiculous anyway. She's being married in the parlor, for God's sake." She looked to Keely. "It was all Lloyd's doing, I want you to know. I wouldn't care if you wore your shift to your wedding if that was what you wanted."

Keely managed a smile. "He thought it would make me happy. He's never been fitted for a gown."

Helga Schmidt circled Keely, the spaniels ducking beneath her skirts as she tried to loosen the gown to remove it. "I can make no promises how it vill come out," she moaned, shaking her head. Stepping over a dog, she gave a squeak as the spaniel dove to catch the toe of her leather slipper in its mouth. "Vhat are these dogs?" she shouted.

Gwenevere laughed, clapping her hands. "Rupert, Annabelle, you poor pups," she crooned, shooing them out the door. "You've hurt their feelings."

Keely held up her hands as the dressmaker pulled the gown over her head. Sighing with relief, she slid down to sit on the wooden stool. "It's like an oven in here!"

One maid fanned Keely's face with a paper fan while another handed her a glass of lemonade.

"Give it another few days, the weather will turn," Gwenevere assured her. "But nothing is certain in this beastly wilderness. In England one always knows the climate will be abominable. Now," she announced to the others in the room. "It's time you all were out. Shoo, all of you!"

The mantuamaker muttered in German as she ordered her maidservants about, gathering scraps of damask and packets of lace.

"Send a message when the gown is ready," Gwenevere commanded imperiously.

"Ja, ja, one last fitting vill do it," the dressmaker answered, still flustered.

"No. I think not. There will be no more fittings. My niece is about to become a bride, she's distraught! I'll not have Keely pierced with your sharpened bayonets again. If I'd had my way we'd have wrapped her in yards of chine silk . . . perhaps an East Indian sari—magenta—with a rope of pearls around her waist. Fashion is not limited to his majesty's realm, you know. Eastern garb is becoming quite the thing among the traveled."

Keely rolled her eyes heavenward.

"Now out with you!" Gwenevere smiled. "And thank you. You'll be well paid."

The mantuamaker made her exit with a great flailing of her arms and muttering beneath her breath. "Magenta. Saris?"

Keely laughed as the entourage of maids burdened with silks and laces followed their mistress out of the bedchamber. "Thank you," she told her aunt as the door was closed with a resounding bang.

"No need for such a fuss. Does Mistress Schmidt think Brock won't take you if the dress isn't to his liking?"

At the mention of Brock's name, Keely scowled. "I've made a mistake, Auntie. I don't want to do this; I don't want to marry your son. Maybe Lord Calvin wouldn't be so bad."

"Too late, the betrothal papers are signed." She took Keely's glass from her. "But just out of curiosity, tell me why you agreed in the first place. You seemed so obstinate in the garden the other day. Whatever Brock said to you that night must have been quite convincing."

Keely's cheeks colored. "It's not what he said, it's what he—" She cut her sentence short, moving to the window.

Gwenevere chuckled deep in her throat. "I thought you needed a good kissing! I was just telling Lloyd the other day that you needed some proper kissing."

Keely swung around. "You didn't!"

He aunt laughed, obviously pleased. "It must have been quite a kiss to make you agree to spend the rest of your life with him."

"I said I changed my mind."

"And I said you can't. Now just marry him and make the best of it, the love will come with time."

77

Keely sighed, realizing the hopelessness of any argument. The savage was to be her husband, whether she liked it or not.

"Now I won't have you sulking. Put on something pretty and come downstairs. Brock's just arrived and he's invited a guest."

"A guest? Who? Micah?"

"Micah, is it?" Gwenevere crossed her arms over her ample bosom. "Let me give you some advice. Stay away from Micah Lawrence."

Keely lifted a brush from her dressing table. "He's Brock's friend."

"Friend, is he? Then what was he doing proposing to you?"

Keely lifted her dark eyelashes indignantly. "He thought he was helping me out of a difficult situation."

"Hmph! Helping you into one if you ask me."

Keely dropped the brush on the table irritably and went to retrieve her gown from the bed. "I didn't know you didn't like Micah. Why not?"

"I don't know. I just don't."

"He's certainly better mannered than Brock . . ." Keely dared.

Gwenevere nodded. "I'm quite sure he is, but one day you'll realize what's important in a man and what's not."

Feeling chastised, Keely turned away, pulling her gown over her head. She was confused. She never argued like this with Aunt Gwen. Wasn't anything ever going to be right again?

Gwenevere came to Keely, resting a hand on her niece's shoulder. "I didn't mean to be sharp with you, child. Who your friends are is certainly none of my business. The truth is that I never cared for the boy's parents. Micah's mother, Eve Lawrence, was a scandalous slut. Quite the jezebel. Everyone knew it.

78

His father was little better—cheated at cards. Naturally I transferred my dislike to their son. You must think me quite an old fool, I know. Every woman has lightskirts now. It's quite the fashion."

"You could hardly say your life has been the model of propriety, Aunt," Keely chastised gently.

"You simply cannot compare my youthful peccadilloes to Eve's transgressions! You are too much an innocent to know the difference between high spirits and common sluttery." Gwenevere kissed Keely's head. "Now finish your toilette and come down."

"Who's the guest?"

"Jenna Williams. Her husband was Brock's first officer until he was killed on board the *Tempest* last year."

"How horrible! She continues to associate with the man that was her husband's undoing?"

Gwenevere laughed, turning Keely around so that she might button up her gown. "You have a lot to learn about these patriot fools. When her husband fell, she lifted the banner for him."

"Whatever do you mean?"

"Meet you downstairs in the parlor. I have to see to the pups' baths. Rupert strayed from the path on his morning walk and muddied his paws." Gwenevere blew a kiss across the room as she went out the door, leaving her niece to stand, staring in perplexity.

A half hour later Keely descended the grand staircase and went in to the parlor. To her dismay, there was no one there but Brock, seated before the chessboard.

"Good evening," he said, looking up. A spark leaped in his dark eyes as he admired Keely's slim form. She was dressed in a simple azure cambric gown.

"Don't you stand when a lady comes into the

79

room?" she asked tartly.

"A lady, yes, but you're to be my wife."

She came to him, her hands planted on her hips. "And I'm no lady?"

"I didn't say that. It's just that I'd be a'bobbin' up and down like a cork on the sea with you coming in and out of the room for the next forty years or so." He turned his attention back to the chessboard.

Keely supposed he was right, but just the same, they weren't married yet. Wasn't she due a little respect?

"A good move that was of yours yesterday," came Brock's deep voice.

She leaned over to study the board. They had an ongoing game between the two of them, each one getting a full twenty-four hours to make a move when Brock was not away. "You think so?"

"I just said so, didn't I?"

"This marriage business, it's never going to work when neither of us can keep a civil tongue!"

"It's too late, you agreed." He took her hand, smiling wickedly. "And you have to admit, I am charming in a crude sort of way."

"As charming as a sewer rat." Her gaze settled on Brock's obsidian eyes. He was dressed handsomely this evening in his fawn-colored breeches and red waistcoat and he knew it.

"A sewer rat, is it? The lady kisses sewer rats?"

Keely twisted her hand, trying to escape his grip. "Why are you doing this? I said I would marry you; you're getting my money. Can't you be nice to me?"

He deepened his voice, getting to his feet as he still gripped her hand. "Nice? I'd die of boredom with niceties. I'd rather have a little fire, a little savagery in my life, wouldn't you?"

"Are you trying to frighten me?" She forced herself to stand stock-still as he lowered his head until

80

his lips nearly touched hers.

"Certainly not," he whispered. "But I did want to warn you." Her scent enveloped him, making his chest tighten. Careful, his inner self warned. Don't get too attached, don't let her beneath your skin. Women are all alike, unworthy of love, too fickle, too cruel.

Keely lifted her dark lashes to stare into Brock's eyes, a smile tugging at the corners of her mouth. "Your mother says you like to play Indian on occasion. Is this what she means?"

"My mother has a big mouth." Brock released her hand slowly, reluctant to break the intimate contact. It had been a long time since he'd felt this kind of burning desire for any woman. An image of Lady Elizabeth Cubitt and her azure eyes flashed through his mind and then was gone as quickly as it had come. *Liz* . . . She'd betrayed him . . . scorned him . . . and he must never allow himself to forget.

Keely chuckled, tucking her hands behind her back. "She says that's why you refuse to cut your hair."

Brock tugged at his long black braid of hair. "You don't like my hair?" he asked, his voice feigning injury.

Slowly, Keely reached to grasp the long mane that trailed down his back. "Would it matter?" His hair was thick and glossy; it felt good in her hand.

"No . . ."

Lucy stuck her head in the door. "Sorry to bother you two"—she giggled—"but Mistress Williams and her son are here."

"Send them in," Brock said. He turned to Keely the minute Lucy was gone. "Now I want you to behave yourself tonight. Just pretend that you like me. Jenna is a good friend."

"And what am I to get in return for this bargain?"

He smiled. "Another kiss?"

Keely turned crimson. "That's not funny." She folded her arms over her chest. "I think an even exchange would be that you will behave like a gentleman and not some sea-sailing redskin."

Brock laughed. "Your price is high. I'd prefer the kiss," he teased, "but all right, little cousin. My behavior will be impeccable. Now let's greet our guests, shall we?"

To Keely's reluctance, she found she liked Jenna Williams immensely. She was well educated, honest in her opinions, and most importantly, she was fun. Jenna wanted all of the gossip from England and wanted to know the latest fashion news. For nearly an hour they chatted while Brock took her four-year-old son, Max, out to the stables for a ride on a horse.

"Brock is good for my Max," Jenna said. "I appreciate his interest in the boy."

"My aunt told me about your husband. I'm so sorry."

Jenna shrugged. "We knew the risks."

"But now your son has no father," Keely leaned forward in her chair. "Aren't you bitter?"

"I'm not a bitter person. It's for my son that my Garrison died. It's for my son that I support independence from the Crown."

Intrigued by her new friend's conviction, Keely's eyes narrowed. "Aunt Gwen says you're a part of Brock's *business*."

"I help out when I can."

"A woman? They have a woman fighting their battles? What do you do?"

Jenna laughed. "Brock said I would like you." She smoothed her fashionable lawn skirts. "I can't tell you what I do."

"Because I'm English?"

"Because Brock told me not to."

"But what of your son? What if you're killed?" Keely asked.

"I take the risks like the rest of us. My mother raised nine children, she can raise one more."

Keely shook her head, rising at the sound of the dinner bell. "How can any cause be more important than your life? I just don't understand."

Jenna stood up, linking her arm through Keely's. "Then I shall have to make you understand, won't I?"

Chapter Seven

"He isn't coming," Keely stated flatly, staring out the window of her bedchamber. Her skin was a dusky pallor, her hazel eyes dull and lifeless.

Gwenevere leaped to her feet. "He's coming. I spoke to him last night before he went to the tavern. He was quite anxious for the day to come. He's just late."

Keely wheeled around, her hands caught up in the skirts of her emerald green wedding gown. "Four hours!"

"Dear, he's obviously run into some trouble." Gwenevere patted her niece's sleeve affectionately.

Not to be mollified, Keely continued to work herself into a rage. "Thirty-five people in the parlor. Thirty-five wedding guests and no groom. He'd better be dead!"

A sharp knock came at the door. "Come in!" Keely demanded.

Lloyd came storming through the door, dressed in a suit of rich burgundy brocade with matching stockings and high-heeled shoes. "Where the hell is he, Gwenevere?" he demanded, moving like a man half his age. He pounded a fist in his palm. "There can be no excuse for this impertinence! I knew this idea of yours would never work!"

"My idea, you old goat! 'Twas you who came to me with the thought in the first place!" Gwenevere's face grew redder with her rising anger. "I don't know where he is, but I'm certain there's an explanation."

"An explanation!" Lloyd drew himself up stiffly. "There can be no explanation to excuse leaving my niece at the altar!"

Gwenevere planted her hands on her well-rounded hips. "You'd better calm down before that fancy coat of yours becomes your death shroud. You're going to get yourself so excited that you're going to fall right out on the floor of Keely's bedchamber. Now wouldn't that be a handsome wedding gift!"

Keely turned from her aunt to her uncle and back to her aunt again as they volleyed their heated remarks until finally she couldn't stand it. "Please!" she protested over the din of their angry voices. "Please stop this. The guests are going to have to be sent home. He's not coming."

Lloyd and Gwenevere grew suddenly silent. "Don't you think we should wait just a little longer?" Gwenevere asked quietly.

Keely stripped off her gloves, throwing them dejectedly on the bed. "What of Micah or Jenna? Hasn't anyone seen Brock?"

"Micah didn't come, business elsewhere. George and Joshua are here, but they say that when they left the King's Head near midnight, Brock was preparing to leave."

"Drinking inebriants, I suppose," Lloyd wheezed, suddenly out of breath.

Concerned at his condition, Gwenevere went to her husband, pulling up a chair for him and pushing him gently into it. "You old goat, you know Brock barely drinks."

"Every man drinks on the eve of his wedding . . . if he's got any sense," Lloyd muttered dryly.

"And he's not on the *Tempest?*" Keely plucked the

green bows from her glossy auburn hair, one at a time.

Lloyd shook his head, cradling it in his pasty-colored hands. "I sent Blackie down to inquire nearly two hours ago. The quartermaster says he was aboard yesterday afternoon accepting good wishes from his crew. From what I can gather, the boy intended on being here."

"Uncle," Keely said gently, kneeling in front of him. "Why don't you go lie down in your chamber for a little while?" She patted his bony knee.

"Guess I am a little winded."

Keely nodded grimly. "Walk with him, Auntie, then you can go down and tell the guests Brock's been detained and that they might as well go home. I don't think I can face them," she said with dry-eyed determination. No need to weep now, she thought. Her throat was so constricted that she could barely breathe. *The colonial bastard, if he's not dead, I'll kill him!*

Slowly Lloyd got to his feet and shuffled out of the room on Gwenevere's arm. Just as they made their exit, Jenna came to the door, knocking softly. "Could I come in?" she asked gently.

Keely nodded. "Please."

Jenna came to Keely, taking her hand to give it a sympathetic squeeze. "I don't know where he is, but I'm sure he would be here if he could."

Keely laughed, choking back a sob as she spun around to face the window. "No. He changed his mind. Ours was to be a no love marriage. He was only wedding me because my uncle wanted him to."

"Brock Bartholomew has never been a man to be forced into anything."

"Well, maybe not forced. He needed my money. Did he tell you I was to inherit a great deal of money besides my handsome dowry?" Keely asked bitterly.

"He did. But it doesn't matter; if he hadn't wanted

86

to marry you, an entire King's ransom would not have been enough to persuade him."

"Then why isn't he here?"

Jenna walked slowly to the window to peer out on the gardens below. "Unavoidable business would be my guess."

"Business!" Keely's harsh voice shattered the silence of the room. "I'm sick of this *business* already! What is his business besides importing illegal goods? He takes on British ships, doesn't he? What else? What else?"

Jenna stood at the window with her hands folded demurely. "I can't tell you."

"Because you don't trust me? He doesn't trust me?"

"You've been under the King's influence for a long time, Keely. You're not to blame him. He just wants to be certain where your allegiance lies."

"Does he think me stupid? I know that when I agreed to marry him, my allegiance went to my husband, no matter what my personal opinions." Her lower lip trembled. " 'Tis the way of the world. Doesn't he think I know that? Though I may not agree with his politics, I'd never endanger his life! How are we to be man and wife when I don't know what it is he does when he leaves this house? Isn't a marriage built of trust?"

"Mine was, but not all. There are women right here in Dover who watch their husbands steal out of the house into the darkness, and yet ask nothing. Some have no wish to know."

"But I want to know!" Keely paused, sighing heavily. "This could never work. I don't belong here. Maybe it's just as well he didn't come."

"Don't say that. When Brock told me of your impending marriage, I saw a light in his eyes I'd not seen in many years." Jenna's dark brown eyes met Keely's. "Maybe he has underestimated you; why not prove it?"

Keely's hazel eyes narrowed. "Was there ever some-one else?" What she wanted to know was if Jenna was in love with Brock, but she couldn't bring herself to say it aloud.

Jenna smiled sadly. "There was long ago. Her name was Lady Elizabeth Cubitt; he served with her brother in His Majesty's Navy. Brock was young and a little innocent. Apparently the lady led him to believe that she was in love with him too, that they would marry. She used him to make the ac-quaintance of another officer and Brock became the butt of their jokes. It seems she had no intentions of marrying a 'colonial half-breed bastard." She looked away. "It was then that he resigned his commission and left England forever."

"And he never saw her again?"

"No, but I don't think he's ever gotten over her betrayal."

"And that's when he went to live with the Indi-ans?" Keely asked.

"Yes, but he doesn't talk about it. He spent two years on the Ohio River with his father's people. Then he returned to Dover, joined with Lloyd, and petitioned for his privateering commission." Jenna faced Keely. "You have to understand, Brock is a man caught between two worlds, Indian and white. He once told me he doesn't think he belongs in either world."

There was silence for several minutes and then Keely moved from the window. "Still, it's no excuse for leaving me here like this," she said, her sympathy fast turning to anger once again. "He had no right. If he wanted out of the agreement, he should have seen the solicitor."

"He wants to marry you. He'll be here, or he'll send a message. I'm sure of it; I know Brock."

Keely spun around, presenting her back to Jenna.

"Could you unhook me? There'll be no need for this gown now."

Brock leaped out of the hired coach. "Wait here a minute," he instructed the driver in a tired voice. "I'll fetch your coin." Fumbling with the key to the lock on the front door, he cursed beneath his breath. Finally hearing the satisfying click of the mechanism, he pushed open the door.

Though it was nearly dawn, the Bartholomew household remained silent as Brock slipped into Lloyd's study and swept up some coins off the end of the mantel. Returning to the hired carriage, he pressed the cold coins into the driver's hand. "My thanks."

"Aye, Cap'n. If ye ever need a driver again, just gimme a holler. Jimmy Jo McCoogen's the name. I'll be in Phili 'til the redcoats run me out."

Brock waved farewell and walked slowly back into the house. Peering into a French mirror that hung on a gold cord in the front hall, he groaned aloud. His face was dark with the makings of a beard, his raven hair dirty and tangled, his eyes sunk back in his head from lack of sleep. The first thing he needed was to bathe and rid himself of his stinking clothes, then sleep. Only after he slept would he be able to deal with the force of the anger he knew would be bestowed upon him.

Moving quietly up the steps, he passed Keely's bedchamber, heading for his own. Just before his hand met with the polished brass of his doorknob, Keely's door flew open.

"There you are, you son of a bitch!" she accused, coming down the hallway after him.

Brock couldn't control the smile that tore at the corners of his mouth. He didn't think a lady like Keely knew how to curse.

"Wipe that simple smile off your face," Keely shouted, shaking a fist.

"Listen, I'm sorry. There's an explanation."

She padded barefoot down the hall, dressed only in a flimsy cotton sleeping gown of the lightest blue. "Explanation! There can be no explanation! They thought you were dead; I was hoping they were right!"

"Keely." He put up his hands in defense. "I'm sorry; it wasn't my fault."

"Not your fault! Then who the hell's fault was it?"

He sighed, trying not to stare at the soft curve of her breasts through the nearly transparent gown. "It's a long story, one that I think can wait until I've bathed." He pulled at the soiled material of his waistcoat as proof of his statement.

"There can be no story good enough to change the fact that two days ago, Brock Forrester Bartholomew, you and I were supposed to be married!"

He ran a bronze palm over his ill-tasting mouth. "You have a right to be angry but—"

The sound of a door swinging open interrupted them as Gwenevere came out of Lloyd's chamber and hurried down the hall. "Brock! Thank God you're safe," she cried out.

Lloyd came out the door just behind her in only a pair of breeches. "Where have you been, boy? We thought the redcoats had got you!" He stood there bare-chested, relief evident on his face.

Brock leaned against the paneled door of his bedchamber. "If you'll just let me bathe and dress, you will have your explanations," he said hotly. "Now, please!"

"Master Brock's home! Master Brock's home!" came Lucy's voice up the front staircase.

Lloyd ducked back into his room as the maid came tearing up the steps. "God's teeth, Master Brock! We thought you were feedin' the

90

fishes in the Delaware. Me and Blackie, we had a bet going, see . . ."

Brock ducked into his room and slammed the door behind himself, turning the key of the lock. Keely wheeled around in a rage and stalked back down the hall toward her bedchamber, passing Gwenevere and Lucy.

"Where's he been?" Lucy asked Gwenevere as Keely slammed her door so hard that one of the ancestral portraits on the wall fell to the floor.

Gwenevere opened the door of her own bedchamber and her two spaniels came bounding out. "We haven't heard yet, Lucy, but it's bound to be a quiz of a story." She knelt to pat the nearest pup. "You better get Ruth on breakfast. Tell her to make it a good one—Master Brock's going to need to fortify himself for what's coming."

"Yes, mistress." Lucy dipped a curtsy and bounded down the steps to tell the other servants what had just transpired.

An hour later, after a hot bath, a shave, and a change of clothes, Brock came down the grand staircase. He'd gone over and over in his mind what he was going to say, yet he couldn't help thinking how ridiculous it all sounded. How could he explain to his betrothed that he missed their wedding because of a practical joke? How could he tell her that he'd gotten drunk at the tavern, passed out, and that Micah had put him on a coach bound for Philadelphia?

In the dining room Brock found Lloyd and Gwenevere and a pot of steaming coffee. "Where's Keely?" he asked, scowling as he poured himself a cup of the rich, dark brew.

Lloyd leaned back in the upholstered chair at the head of the table. "She hasn't come down. Now sit and tell us what this is all about," he said angrily.

Brock gave an exasperated sigh. "No. I owe her an

explanation first. Pardon." Setting his cup on the cherry dining table, he left the room.

Going up the stairs, Brock stopped at the first door on the left and rapped on it. He felt bad that all of this had happened, but still, he had no desire to deal with a raging female. All he wanted to do now was get the marriage over with and get back to work. He'd already received most of the dowry from Lloyd, so the wedding had to take place, and soon.

"Go away," came Keely's voice. "I don't want anything."

"That's good because I've brought nothing," Brock responded. "Nothing but an apology."

"I don't want to talk to you, now go away."

Brock turned the knob and swung open the door to find Keely seated at a small writing desk. "How dare you. Get out of here! Get out!" she shouted.

"Not until you've heard my explanation."

Her hazel eyes narrowed venomously. "I told you. It's too late for excuses. The betrothal will have to be broken."

Brock caught Keely by the elbows and lifted her to her feet. He lowered his face within inches of hers as a sudden stroke of genius came to him. "Keely, listen to me." He shook her gently. "I was kidnapped." Not exactly a lie, he thought to himself.

Keely's mouth fell. "What?" she breathed.

"Keely, I didn't make it to the wedding because I couldn't. I was bound like a common criminal and carried off," he told her in a low whisper as he recalled the horror stories told around the campfires of the Delawares.

The anger in Keely's voice had vanished, replaced by genuine concern. She reached up to stroke his bronze cheek. "Are you all right? Are you hurt? Who did this to you?"

He shook his head, trying not to smile. He suddenly felt so damned guilty. He hadn't realized she was so gullible. "I don't know, but it was sheer luck that I escaped," he murmured in her ear. His arms went around Keely's shoulders and she lifted her hands as if by magic to rest on the broad expanse of his chest.

"I'm so . . . so sorry," she said softly. "I've been so stupid. Jenna told me what you did was dangerous. I just never imagined!"

"Shhh," he hushed, pulling her against his chest. His eyes drifted shut as the scent of her thick, fiery tresses enveloped him, making him shudder inwardly. What was a little lie, he rationalized as he brushed his lips against her ear, if the lie could turn this snarling she-cat into a soft bundle of female fluff.

Keely lifted her head from Brock's chest, her senses spinning. She was so confused. Why was her body betraying her like this? Why did she wish he would kiss her? "Have you told Uncle Lloyd? These men must be found."

"No, no, we mustn't. It wouldn't be safe."

"Brock, you must stop this insanity! Next time it will be your life . . ."

He pressed his fingers to her lips. "It's too late," he murmured. "Too many lives involved, too many at risk. I could never abandon my country now. This is my home. But we mustn't tell anyone about my being kidnapped, not even Lloyd or my mother."

"But you told them you would explain." Tentatively, she lifted a hand to smooth his lawn shirt. This was a different Brock than the man she knew. This man was soft-spoken and sincere. . . .

"Just tell me you'll marry me, Keely. I'll have the minister here to say the words, today." He smoothed her unruly hair, looking deep into the frightened hazel eyes. Child or no, he suddenly realized just how much he desired this girl. English or no, consequences be damned! He was going to have her, and

93

tonight!

"I don't know," she breathed, mesmerized by his haunting dark eyes. "My logic tells me it could never work. We agree on nothing. You're a traitor to the Crown, for God's sake!"

"We agree on this," he whispered, bending to press his mouth hard against hers. Keely succumbed to him without hesitation, accepting his advance with a breath of startling innocence. She tasted of honey, and unfulfilled dreams, stirring him as no woman had ever done before.

"Who says unrest is not good for a marriage?" Brock reasoned huskily. "Say yes, Keely. You'll not regret it. If you must marry, why not me?"

"All right."

He broke into a grin. "You will?"

She laughed nervously, detaching herself from his arms. "You took my money, we signed the papers. But it will have to be today, before I have a chance to change my mind again."

He nodded. "Done."

"No, he won't tell me a thing, Gwen." Lloyd settled himself in a chair in his bedchamber to roll up his stockings. "All he said was that his explanation for missing the wedding was acceptable to Keely and that was all that mattered." He waved a burgundy stocking. "Oh, you know how the boy is!"

Gwenevere heaved a sigh, turning back to the mirror that stood on the floor. She was dressed only in her chemise, dusting her face with Italian face powder. "I got much the same and Keely was worse. I don't know what's gotten into her. She's never been secretive with me before."

"Smitten females!" Lloyd chuckled dryly.

Gwenevere scowled in the mirror. "And what's that supposed to mean?"

"Only that I think we were asking too much of Keely. Of course she's hesitant to marry, what young girl isn't? You spoil her too much, Gwen. You should have just told her she was to marry him and that should have been the end of the discussion. These young people today, I tell you, they have no respect for their elders. In my day . . ."

"You old goat! You were the one that told her she didn't have to marry him." Gwenevere reached for her gown on the bed and pulled it over her head. "You'd have let her marry a two-headed dragon if she'd expressed the desire!"

Lloyd slipped his feet into his shoes and stood up. "Now don't get into a state with me, Gwenevere. Your son is about to be married; you wouldn't want to go downstairs with wrinkles at your mouth." He moved slowly toward the bed to retrieve his waistcoat.

"Now I know why I didn't stay. I never liked you, Lloyd Bartholomew! Never missed you a bit all of these years." She snatched his waistcoat out of his hand and helped him into it.

"No, you may not have missed me but I know what you did miss!" He caught her by the waist, burying his face in the valley between her breasts.

She laughed. "If you think you've been the only one, you're crazier than they say! And don't think you'll be the last either."

"Never missed me, not a bit," he said, his voice muffled.

"Well, maybe occasionally when I was looking for a good fight." She ran her fingers through his snowy hair. "Look at you, you old goat, you've gone so gray you don't need to powder!"

"You're going to miss me, Gwenevere. You're going to miss me when I'm gone," Lloyd warned, releasing her.

Her face grew sober. "I am," she murmured. For a

95

moment there was silence and then she took his hands in hers. "I'm glad I didn't let my pride keep me from coming to you. I've enjoyed this time we've had together. It makes me wonder what we could have had if I hadn't been so stubborn. It makes me regret."

Lloyd reached with one hand to stroke Gwenevere's plump cheek. "What I wouldn't give to be them right now—young, energetic, a whole life in front of them."

"You mean you would have done things differently?" Gwenevere's dark eyes searched her husband's.

"No. I'd probably have made the same mistakes, and you would have too."

She nodded. "You're probably right."

Lloyd smiled tenderly. "Brock says he has no time to take Keely away now. Business to attend to. What would you think of going to visit the Adleys? We could spend the night and come back tomorrow."

"I think it's an excellent idea. Give them a little time to themselves."

"Give us a little time to be by ourselves too, wouldn't it?"

Gwenevere's ribald laugh filled the bedchamber.

"Now," Lloyd said, "give this old goat a kiss and let's go downstairs. We've got a wedding to attend."

Chapter Eight

Keely's laughter mingled with Brock's as they stood at the front door, waving farewell.

"Take care of my pups, Keely, and we'll see you tomorrow!" Gwenevere fluttered a purple handkerchief through the window of the departing carriage.

"They'll be fine," Keely answered. "You and Uncle Lloyd have a good time."

The carriage lurched forward and Brock closed the door, taking Keely's hand. "What's say the first thing we do is put those damned spaniels out on their ears?"

Keely laughed, her clear voice ringing in the front hallway. "What, and let Rupert soil his paws?"

"Worse yet, we could let Annabelle mingle with Lloyd's foxhounds!" Brock offered, his hand still linked in Keely's.

Her nervous laughter died away as her eyes met his. Suddenly she was frightened again. This odd, arrogant man was now her husband, for better or for worse for the rest of her life. What did she have to look forward to? A house of cold stalemates and unfulfilled dreams?

Sensing Keely's sudden apprehension, Brock smiled. "I sent the servants packing, gave everyone the night off. I thought I'd make us something to eat."

"You? I could do it."

"No, no." He led her down the back hall, toward the kitchen. "Let me. You just keep me company while I work."

Releasing Keely's hand as they entered the summer kitchen, Brock shrugged off his coat and waistcoat down to a simple lawn shirt and breeches, rolling up his sleeves. He pulled a high kitchen stool out for her, and before she could get up on it, he lifted her by the waist, setting her gently on the wooden seat. "A kiss is the fee, cousin," he told her playfully, his hands still on her waist.

Tentatively, Keely lifted her hands to rest on his shoulders. "And if the price is too high, cousin?"

"Back on the floor you go."

When Brock made no attempt to collect his compensation, Keely leaned forward, brushing her lips ever so lightly against his. Since she'd never initiated a kiss before, it felt odd, but it sent a tingle of sensation down her spine.

"That was nice." He turned away. "And now for a wedding supper fit for a Lenni Lenape princess maiden."

Keely watched her husband move about the kitchen with confidence, taking notice of the way his back muscles rippled beneath his lawn shirt as he lowered a cast-iron pan from a peg in the rafters. "I didn't know you could cook."

"There's much you don't know about me." Seeing her stiffen, he smiled assuredly. He had vowed to himself that he would be the perfect bridegroom tonight with sweet words and wooing. Once he had the bedding done with and she was carrying his child, then he would let her be. "So you've much to learn." He turned back to a mixing bowl, adding two fresh eggs to the cornmeal mixture. "I'm not much with a leg of lamb but give me a side of venison or a basket of squash and my talents are adequate. I spent time with my father's people when I first returned to the Colonies after the Royal Navy. An old aunt taught me how to cook on an open fire, how to skin a deer, how to clean and dry fish."

Keely folded her hands in the skirts of her emerald damask wedding gown. "Don't do much fish drying, do you?"

He laughed. "No. But at the time it was important to me that I know what kind of life my father led."

Keely looked away thoughtfully. "My father was a wonderful man."

Brock spooned the cornmeal into a square pan, which he pushed into the beehive oven alongside the fireplace. "You remember him?"

"A little. He used to buy me licorice." She slipped her hand beneath the neckline of her gown, retrieving the amulet she wore around her neck. "He gave me this." The instant the words slipped off her tongue, she felt foolish. Only a child treasured such worthless baubles. What would Brock think of such fancies?

"Did he?" To Keely's surprise, he came across the room to lift the delicate chain with his finger.

She shrugged. "It's just a copper tuppence. I should put it away."

A frown creased Brock's handsome brow. " 'Twould be bad luck at this point, don't you think?"

Her hazel eyes met his, the barest smile on her face. "What do you mean?"

"How long have you been wearing it?"

"Ten, fifteen years, I don't know."

"If it were my charm, I'd keep it." He gave her a wink, releasing the amulet. "After all, maybe it brought you me!"

Keely's cheeks colored. Somehow, as nervous and

frightened as she had been after the wedding, Brock had managed to calm her shattered nerves. He had managed to put her at ease, to make her laugh, to make her enjoy his company. She was fast learning that her new husband was a many-faceted person and that thought was encouraging. Perhaps Aunt Gwen and Uncle Lloyd were right—perhaps they could build a happy life together.

The wedding feast Brock prepared for Keely was a strange assortment of foreign dishes, but a hearty and delicious feast nonetheless. He prepared succotash—an Indian mixture of corn and beans—hot buttered corn bread, and a spicy meat dish of venison and herbs. They dined in the garden, on the grass, in the fading autumn light . . . laughing and talking, each exploring the other's personality with quiet diligence.

Keely stared into the dregs of her mulled wine then looked up at Brock, who sipped from a teacup. "Are you an abstainer?" she asked impulsively.

Brock set his teacup down and reached for a slice of rosy apple. "Inebriants seem to get me in trouble." A wave of guilt washed over him as he remembered the last time he had succumbed. "My father's people do not seem to be able to tolerate the white man's brew, so I try to stay away from it as much as possible."

Keely nodded. "Rather admirable for a man, I think."

He lifted a dark eyebrow. "Admirable? You think me admirable, cousin?"

"I hate it when you do that." She drained her glass.

"What? Admirable things? I shall try to refrain myself in the future."

"No!" She laughed, looking away. "Call me cousin." She forced herself to meet his gaze.

"But you are."

"I know, but I am also your wife now," she said softly.

For a moment Brock gazed into the depths of her rich, blue-green eyes. A man could lose himself in those limpid pools, he observed thoughtfully. He had to remind himself that theirs was an arranged marriage. He would be expected to provide for her, to give her children, and to protect her, but never to love her. He didn't want to love her, not the way he had loved Elizabeth. Love like that could tear a man in two.

But as he studied Keely's delicate oval face, he felt his heart stir against his will. For the briefest fleeting moment, he allowed himself to contemplate what it would be like to hear those simple words flow from her mouth — *I love you.*

Breaking from his reveries, Brock took Keely's hand in his. "Come, wife, let's retire." Getting to his feet, he guided her gently upward. "You go upstairs and do what ever it is ladies do before they go to bed and I'll clean this up."

She nodded, with a gulp. Suddenly she realized what was before her. She knew all along that, whatever husband would be chosen for her, she would be expected to allow him to bed her, but Brock? Her breath caught strangely in her throat and she turned from him, hurrying out of the garden and into the house.

Once in her bedchamber, Keely managed to get the wedding gown off on her own, and nervously she slipped out of her underthings and into a sleeping gown of the palest green. Going to sit at her dressing table, she lifted a silver-handled hair brush to her head. In the reflection on the mirror, she caught sight of a china doll sitting on a carved shelf on the far wall. She couldn't help smiling. The doll, Roxy, had been a gift from her father on her fourth birthday.

101

There were so many memories in the house; only after returning had she realized how much she loved it here. Though the town house in London and Auntie's estate house had been opulent, her bedchambers had never been this comforting. The houses in England had never welcomed her home like this house her father had built.

When Brock rapped softly on the door, Keely swallowed against her rising fear. Though there was a part of her that was frightened of the idea of sharing intimate relations with this man who was now her husband, another part of her yearned to see just what this was between a man and a woman that was as ageless as time itself. "Come in," she murmured, turning back to her mirror.

Brock slipped into the room, surprised to find that he was nervous in Keely's presence. Slowly he came across the room and stood behind her, watching her brush out her long, luxurious tresses. "Beautiful," he whispered, reaching out to lift a handful of auburn hair. He inhaled, his eyes drifting shut. "What is it that makes a woman's hair so magical?" he asked.

"Magical?" Keely laid down her brush and came to her feet to stand before her husband. "Is it?"

Brock threaded his fingers through her hair until he reached her scalp and then he leaned in to kiss her tempting mouth. "My father's people say one's hair is sacred, never to be left behind to fall into enemy hands." He laughed softly. "Your lips are so soft, so fragrant." He brushed his thumb against her lips and Keely pursed them, kissing it. "Don't be afraid," he told her quietly, his fingers stroking her collarbone, which peaked from the lace of her gown.

"I . . . I'm not afraid, just nervous." She smiled.

Catching her hand in his, Brock planted soft, fleeting kisses the length of her pale throat, steadily making his way to her mouth. When his lips finally met hers, there was an urgency in her breath as she leaned into him, lifting her hands to his shoulders.

As Brock kissed his virgin bride in her bedchamber, he tried to remember when he'd ever made love to an untried woman. Had there ever been a virgin? Names, blurred faces streaked through his mind. Only Elizabeth, and now Keely. How ironic. It was Elizabeth he had meant to wed and now here in his arms was the most desirable woman he had ever come upon. Instead of being a hindrance, he found her innocence refreshingly arousing. Her body was without knowledge of love and yet she responded unhindered by prudish notions.

Keely moaned softly as Brock's hand met the soft curve of her breast, his thumb brushing against her nipple. He smiled, burying his face in her tresses. "Come," he whispered, his breath hot and damp in her ear.

She lifted her languid eyes. "Come? Come where?"

He bent to slip his arms behind her knees and lifted her until her cheek rested on his chest. "Not here, *kikileuotte.*"

She smiled at the sound of the foreign word on his tongue, knowing it must be some Indian word of endearment. "Where?" She stared up at him in utter trust.

"I had a chamber made up for us in the other wing. I'll not make love to my wife in the room where she grew up." He nodded in the direction of the doll seated on the shelf across the room. "Look, she's watching me," he whispered, feigning uneasiness.

Keely's laughter filled the room, putting them both at ease. Blowing out the candle on her dressing table, Brock carried Keely down the hall and through a closed door to the unoccupied wing. Carrying her into the master bedchamber, he set her gently on the bed.

The room had been swept and dusted, the bedcurtains aired and fresh, sweet-smelling linens put on the bed. The windows were each open a crack to let in the sounds and smells of a September night. Lighting a candle on a side table near the windows, Brock lifted his shirt from his back and came to her, stretching out beside her on the massive bed.

"I hadn't realized you were so tall," Keely teased, studying the length of his body compared to her own.

"My father was a big man, though the Delawares are usually shorter, no more than Lloyd's height." He reached with a finger to toy at the bow on her neckline. "We don't have to do this tonight, you know. We've a lifetime. I'm in no hurry."

Keely rolled back onto the pillow in laughter and he lifted himself on one elbow to study her dancing hazel eyes. "What's so funny?" he asked, her laughter contagious.

"I was just wondering if I had married the right man. I don't know *you*. The man I crossed the ocean with was arrogant, impolite, aggravating, but you, here . . ." She laughed again, letting her voice trail into silence.

"Don't worry, I'm still those things too." His arm went around her waist and he kissed the lace of her neckline. "I'm just on my good behavior; have no fear, it will pass."

She lifted her dark eyelashes to gaze into obsidian eyes. "I want to know, Brock. You are my husband and I am no longer a girl. Show me what it is to love." She took his hand, laying it gently on her breast. "I think I've wanted to know since that first night I met you on the ship."

Brock nuzzled her neck, his lips seeking hers as he molded his body to hers. Her words had brought an aching desire to his limbs that only she could put to rest. When his mouth met hers, she parted her lips, her tongue meeting his halfway in a timeless dance of lovers united. His hand swept the curves of her lithe body, bringing him soft moans of encouragement.

Every nerve in Keely's body called out with wanting as he stroked her gently, exploring her pliant flesh through the thin gown. As if under their own command, her hands lifted to stroke the thick cords of his back. In awe, she moved her fingers over the broad expanse of his bronze skin, feeling the wonder of a man's whipcord muscles and taut flesh.

Keely's innocent exploration sent Brock's unhurried patience spiraling. His heart beat hard beneath his breast; his hands trembled as he stroked her flat stomach. Taking care not to frighten her, he lifted the gown slowly over her head, to reveal a perfect feminine form of pale curves and sleek limbs.

Drunk with sensation, Keely made no protest when Brock lowered his mouth to take her nipple, but she nearly sat up in surprise at the first rise of intense pleasure. She had never realized how glorious this would be! Threading her fingers through the wisps of raven hair that framed Brock's face, she arched her back in encouragement. Aching, searing want flowed from the center of her being to bring every nerve in her limbs alive with wanting as Brock stroked one breast and then the other, his tongue teasing her throbbing nipples until she thought she would go mad with burning frustration.

Brock's fingers fumbled with the tie of his breeches as Keely clung to him. Pressing soft kisses to her cheeks and closed eyelids, he lifted his body over hers, reveling in the feel of flesh against flesh as she moved beneath him. Unable to hold back another instant, he separated her legs with his knee and in one quick motion he entered the core of her womanhood.

Keely arched her back in expectation of pain, but felt none. Her eyes flickered open for a moment, but then closed in relief. The lack of her own pain seemed to go unnoticed as Brock began to move slowly within her. Relieved that he wouldn't accuse her of coming to his wedding bed tainted, Keely relaxed against the pillow, lifting her knees slightly to cradle his body.

Slowly Brock moved, stroking her with the evidence of his desire as he fueled his own flames of long-awaited fulfillment. His head swam with joy at the thought that he had married a woman so receptive to pleasures of the flesh. Though they might not ever agree over matters at the dining table, here in the privacy of their bedchamber, he knew they would always meld until they were one.

Catching on to the rhythm of Brock's movement, Keely lifted herself in reception of each stroke, exploring each sensation as his body rose and fell above her. All too soon he moved rapidly and then groaned, collapsing at her side.

For a long moment he rested beside her, his eyes closed, then finally he lifted his dark lashes to meet her gaze. He laughed, drawing her into his arms. "It seems the groom was a little anxious," he told her, making light of his own performance. "It's always a man's dream to satisfy his wife on their wedding night."

"Satisfy!" Keely's cheeks burned bright. "It was wonderful!"

He laughed again, pulling her against him so that he might kiss the top of her perspiration-beaded forehead. "Ah God, girl, you were made for love," he said hoarsely.

At the sound of breaking glass, Keely sat up in the bed, drawing the covers modestly over her breasts. "What was that? It sounded like it came from downstairs. I thought you said no one was to be here tonight."

Brock turned his head to listen and was rewarded by the sound of crashing furniture. Jumping up out of bed, he reached into the drawer of the table next to the bed and extracted a loaded pistol. "You stay here," he commanded.

Keely grabbed her green nightgown from the floor and pulled it over her head. By the time Brock reached the hallway, she was already behind him.

"I thought I told you to stay put."

Keely kept behind the huge frame of the man who was now her husband. "That's what this new country of yours is to be about, isn't it? Freedom to come and go as one likes?"

Brock scowled, entering the main hallway that led downstairs. "Just stay back, all right?"

She placed her hand on his bare back, nodding in the darkness. As the two came down the steps, Keely was amazed at how quietly Brock could move. Each time she took a step, the stairs creaked beneath her feet, but he moved as if gliding on air, soundlessly. Another crash echoed from the parlor and Brock turned, lifting a finger to his lips. "Stay here. Whoever the intruder is, he's come to the wrong house."

Keely watched Brock turn in the front hallway and then she scurried after him. Pressing his back to the wall, Brock held the pistol in front of him, poised to shoot. Taking a deep breath, he whipped around the corner of the parlor and then dropped the pistol to his side with a groan.

"What is it?" Keely stepped into the parlor and bit back a chuckle, covering her mouth with the palm of her hand. She looked from Aunt Gwenevere's spaniels seated on the horsehair settee to her nude husband, pistol drawn, and back to the dogs again. Unable to control herself, she burst into laughter. "My patriot hero." She giggled, bending over to pick up the bottom half of a broken vase. "Well, if you're

107

going to shoot them, now's the time to do it!"

Feeling like a fool, Brock set the weapon on the spinet near the door and leaned to right the tea table. "How the hell did they get in here? I thought Mother said she locked them in her room."

Keely piled the shards of broken vase on the table, trying not to laugh. "We were supposed to take them out for their evening walk and then they were to have their tea and cakes before retiring." She scooped up wildflowers that were strewn across the Persian carpet. "You probably didn't remember to give Rupert his hot brick for his bed either. You know how easily he catches a cold."

"Goddamned dogs! Promise me, wife, you'll never bring dogs into the house."

"Not even a small lapdog to keep me company when you're at sea defending your liberties?" Keely baited.

"No dogs! I hate dogs!" He pushed Rupert onto the floor and the spaniel fled. "Filthy flea mounds! Get down, whatever your name is!"

"Annabelle."

"What?"

Keely bit down on her lower lip. "Annabelle. You have to call her by her name if you want her to do something."

Brock glanced up at his wife. "This isn't funny. I brought that vase from China!" He grabbed Annabelle by her silk collar and pulled her to the floor, giving her a push out the door.

Keely turned her back on Brock to keep from further aggravating him, still chuckling as she searched for the rim of the broken vase.

Brock turned to study his wife in the dim moonlight that poured through the window. Her sleeping gown was hitched beguiling over one knee to fall gracefully over her round bottom. The thought of her tempting lips pressed to his brought a stirring to his loins, making him smile. Giving an animal-like growl, he swept Keely into his arms, forcing a squeak out of her as she dropped the retrieved bit of vase.

Keely's arms snaked around Brock's neck and she lifted her chin to let him nuzzle her throat. "What of the pups?" she whispered.

Brock carried her out of the parlor and up the grand staircase toward their haven in the far wing. "Let them find their own beds tonight," he murmured against her lips.

Chapter Nine

"Damnation!" Lloyd slammed his fist on the dining table in response to Brock's words. "Defeated?"

"I'm afraid so, sir," Brock took his seat beside Keely at the breakfast table and signaled for Lucy to bring him the plate of sliced ham and dish of baked egg and cheese. "Apparently it was quite a mess," Brock went on. "General Washington assumed that the main point of attack was to be at Polly Buckwater's Lane, when actually that was just a diversion—a Tory command. When the general learned that the main thrust of the army was to come from Scanneltown, out of Osborne's Woods, it was nearly too late for John Sullivan and his men on the Brandywine River." Brock paused to lean back long enough to allow Lucy to pour his herbal tea.

"Go on," Lloyd urged. "What happened?"

"General Washington sent Nathaniel Greene and his Virginians and they held the British off until dusk." Brock smoothed his weary brow. "Our army retreated to Chester and then moved on to Philadelphia to defend her. Howe's hot on their trail. Congress has moved north to higher ground."

Unable to contain herself another instant, Keely laid down her fork. "And you were there?" she demanded. "That's why you left the day after we

110

were wed? You could have been killed!"

Brock scowled, sampling a slice of ham. "I was safe enough," he told Keely, then returned his attention to Lloyd. "Howe and the bulk of the British army are settled in Chester right now but no one knows how long they'll sit."

"Why didn't you tell me that's where you were going? I have ears," Keely broke in. "I knew the King's army was nearby. I'm your wife! I should have known."

Brock sighed heavily, turning to his new wife. "Can this wait? Lloyd and I have business to attend to. Why not go with Mother to visit the Marshes? I think Devon's wife Cassie's going to be there. You'd like her, she's one of the few females in Dover who's got a head on her shoulders."

"Visiting? I think not. You and I have some talking to do." She threw down her napkin. She was mad enough when Brock had left the day after they'd been married, but then to discover that he was off playing men's warring games! It was too much!

Lloyd cleared his throat, getting slowly to his feet. "I think I'm through here. Why not have breakfast with your wife? Get cleaned up and come to my office. We can talk there." He dismissed Lucy with a wave of his hand. "That'll be enough, girl. Go about your business."

"Yes, sir," Lucy answered, taking her time to exit the room.

Keely waited until her uncle and the maidservant were gone and then she turned on Brock. "You said you had to speak with Micah and that you'd be back in two hours. It's been two days, husband!" she said, using the endearment none too fondly.

Brock poured himself another cup of tea, wincing at the sound of her raised voice. His head was pounding at the temples and he was sore from riding horseback all night. "I suppose this means the honeymoon is over," he said dryly.

"I am your wife! I have a right to know!"

"I did not intend to have this conversation now, but if you insist . . ." He put down his teacup, settling a dark glower upon her. "You are my wife, but you are my English wife. I no longer consider myself a British subject; however, you are surely one. Are you following the conversation so far?"

Keely leaped to her feet. "Don't you treat me like some sullen child, Brock Bartholomew. I won't stand for it!"

"Then sit and listen, because I will say this once and only once." He pointed to the chair and she did his bidding. "My business with the cause is just that, my business. But you have married me and now you must abide by my rules. There will be no more English goods brought into this household, and you will not betray me in word or deed. This so-called *business* I'm involved in could get me hanged and I do not want to have to be cautious of every word I speak in my house before my wife."

"This isn't your house—it's Uncle Lloyd's house! It's my house—my father built it."

"Lloyd turned the deed over to me." His hand snaked across the linen tablecloth to catch Keely's before she could escape. "Now give me your word as my wife and a Bartholomew that you will keep your English thoughts to yourself and that you will not reveal to anyone anything what is said within these walls."

Tears stung Keely's eyes. For what did she deserve this distrust? What had she done to make him think she would ever betray him? Her lower lip trembled as she forced herself to speak in a clear, true voice. "I will not! You have no right to say these things to me."

"Swear it!" Brock insisted angrily.

She twisted her hand, snatching it from his. "You have no right to say what I can and cannot speak of! I know none of your dark secrets!" Without another word she got up from the table and left the room.

When Brock entered Lloyd's office and closed the door behind him an hour later, Lloyd was waiting for him. "I had a fire started," the elder man said, nodding toward the small fireplace, "Just to take the chill off the air."

Brock nodded, taking a seat in one of the high-backed chairs. "I apologize for the outburst at breakfast; that should have been taken care of in the privacy of our bedchamber. I meant to wait a few days and then discuss our political differences."

Lloyd sucked on his clay pipe thoughtfully. "Don't you think you were a little harsh on her?"

"I meant to be." Brock's eyes narrowed. "You were listening? That's not like you."

The gray-haired man laughed, waving his pipe. "Hell no, I wasn't listening. I haven't the energy to stand that long these days. Lucy told me."

"Something's got to be done about that wench's loose tongue before she gets herself or us into trouble."

"Lucy's harmless—you have my word on it. Now back to Keely. I don't want her hurt; I don't want to see her spirit trampled. She's seen a lot of changes in her life in these last few months."

Brock's dark eyes met Lloyd's. "I must be hard on her; I have to make her understand the severity of our situation. My contacts are none too pleased to hear that I've married a proclaimed British subject. It's been suggested she be sent home to England."

Lloyd's eyes narrowed. "And will you, when I'm gone?"

"No . . ." Brock sighed. " . . . I don't know. It would make things easier."

"You've never been one to take the easy road, son.

You know it's my wish that she remain here. This is where your sons belong, here on freedom's land."

Brock ran a hand through his raven hair. "All I can tell you, sir, is that I will watch and wait and see what the situation commands. Hopefully she'll learn her place as my wife and accept my political affiliations, or at least tolerate them."

Lloyd chuckled. "You've your hands full then. She'd never betray you, son, but she's got her own thoughts on what's right and what's wrong. She'll not be an easy one to win over. Gwen's brought her up to be awfully hardheaded."

"Well, she's my wife and I wanted things straight between us from the beginning. Once she begins to take over household business, this will all be forgotten. Women aren't interested in politics."

"And what of Jenna?"

"She's different, you know that. Now don't worry, I can handle my wife, sir."

"I'm glad to hear it." Lloyd lifted his booted foot to a footstool, a smile pulling at the corners of his wrinkled mouth. "Now, tell me what's about in Philadelphia and leave nothing out . . ."

For the next few days conversations between Keely and Brock were cool and kept to a minimum. It hurt Keely to think that her husband found her untrustworthy, yet Aunt Gwenevere and Uncle Lloyd both assured her he was just being cautious. Both were certain that they would come to an understanding and that it would just take time. Keely knew she should confront Brock on the matter of her loyalty and explain to him that she knew when she married him that her first loyalty would have to be with her husband, but he was so accusing and angry that he filled her with fear and fury. There was just no talking to him.

When Brock set sail a week after they'd been married, Keely couldn't help feeling glad he was leaving. She didn't like sleeping with her back to him, listening to his light breathing, wondering what he was thinking. Since their wedding night, he had made no attempt to make love to her and that was worrying her. Was that it? Had he done what he considered to be his duty? Would she ever see that tender, warm side of her husband again? Had he really desired her, or could a man feign ardor? By the time Brock set sail for some unknown destination, the man she had spent her wedding night with was barely a shadow in the recesses of her mind.

Two days after Brock had gone, Micah came calling. Keely received him in the garden, where she was reading a leather-bound copy of Homer's *Iliad*. "Micah, how good to see you." She set her book on the bench, rising to offer her hand.

Micah's lips brushed the back of her hand. "By the King's hounds, you just look radiant today, Keely."

"Oh, sit down. Your flattery is wasted on this old married maid."

"Nonsense. Married life must suit you well. You're utterly breathtaking this morning." He sat beside her on the bench.

She straightened the woolen shawl she wore over her brocade morning gown. The September air had turned crisp in a day's time, bringing a refreshing breeze off the ocean to cool the heat of August and ripen perfectly shaped apples on the trees in the garden. "Well enough."

"If only it could have been me, Keely," Micah said wistfully.

She looked at him with open surprise and then frowned. "Oh Micah, please don't say that or I'll have to ask you to leave. Brock is my husband now and of my choosing."

115

"You want me to go?" he asked quietly. His yellow-gold hair peaked from beneath his beribboned cocked hat to shine brilliantly in the morning sun.

"No, I don't. I want to be your friend. I liked you from the moment we first met. It's just that I wanted you to understand. I really had no right to make you think I could honestly consider your offer. It was my uncle's choice that I wed Brock." She looked away, slightly embarrassed.

Jealousy flickered in Micah's eyes. "I'm no proud man. I'll take the spoils."

Keely turned to him, a frown creasing her brow. "The spoils?"

Micah's scowl turned so quickly to a sincere smile that Keely missed the transformation all together. "Your friendship, my dear. If I cannot have your undying devotion, I shall just have to accept your friendship."

"Oh." She smiled. "Good."

"And while we are getting things straight here, I want to apologize about what happened to Brock the night before you were to marry."

"I'm certain you would have helped if you could have."

"Helped?" He erupted into laughter. "I could have prevented the whole thing; it was my idea to put him on that carriage in the first place. Though, I have to admit I was well in my cups when the idea came to me."

Keely tried to mask the shock she knew was evident on her face. "The carriage?"

"The carriage I put Brock on after he passed out — the carriage to Philadelphia. It was just a joke. I didn't realize he'd sleep ten hours." The smile faded from his face. "You didn't know about the carriage?" he said haltingly.

Keely shook her head, turning away. She was

116

mortified at the thought that she'd been so gullible. Brock had told her he'd been kidnapped and she'd believed him! The colonial bastard had lied to her!

"I'm . . . I'm sorry," Micah murmured. "I didn't mean to—"

"It's all right, Keely interrupted, getting hold of herself. "I just had some English tea brought in this morning. Would you like some?"

Micah lifted a brushed golden eyebrow. "Your husband is allowing you to accept English goods?"

"Certainly not, so don't tell him. Tea or no?"

"Yes, indeed I will, thank you. Unlike my other patriot counterparts, I've not lost my taste for it."

"Then come into the parlor." She stood, picking up her book. "I'll have Lucy bring us a pot and some of Ruth's gingerbread."

"Excellent." Micah offered his arm, thoroughly pleased with himself. "My lady."

"Sir."

When the *Tempest* entered the Saint Jones River more than a week later, Keely was on the Bartholomews' private dock, tapping her foot decisively.

Had she not been so furiously angry with Brock, she might have taken more notice of just how breathtakingly beautiful the *Tempest* was as she sailed up the river, her pennants fluttering in the breeze. Long boats towed a British brig behind her, its ensign flying upside down in defeat.

Yesterday Joshua Kane had brought Keely a message sent by Brock. The tiny piece of foolscap had been crumpled, the ink smudged, after being passed from the *Tempest* to another privateering vessel and then to Joshua before it finally came into her hands. The brief note was in Brock's own scrawled handwriting:

Keely,

Mission was a success. I am well. See you on the morrow.

Brock

Instead of bringing her relief by saying that Brock was safe, the note only fueled her anger. Did he think he could just march off whenever he pleased and justify it by sending a silly note? Brock had lied to her about why he had missed the wedding and she wanted an explanation. Who was he to be concerned with her loyalties when he had come into their marriage with an inexcusable lie on his tongue? Keely had said nothing to Aunt Gwen or Uncle Lloyd about what Micah had told her, seeing no need now, but she had counted the hours until her husband returned so that she could confront him.

When the wooden hull of the sleek vessel scraped the dock, sailors in tarred pigtails ran to catch the lines that were tossed overboard. Keely could hear Brock's voice, carried by the sea breeze, as he called out instructions in a deep tenor. When he spotted her on the dock in her sapphire brocade gown and bonnet, he lifted a hand in salute, smiled, then turned away to speak to one of the crewmen.

Shortly, a gangway was lowered from the *Tempest* and a hulking black man disembarked, making his way to Keely's side. "Mistress," he beckoned in a soft, lilting voice, "The captain asks that I escort you aboard." He lifted a dark hand in the direction of the sharp-hulled privateering vessel.

Keely nodded, swaying with the crowd of men gathering to see the English vessel captured by the *Tempest*. "Lead the way, sir."

118

Isiah stepped forward and the crowd of cheering patriots moved back, allowing the lady and her escort to pass. Unassisted, Keely crossed the gangway, setting foot lightly on the deck. Spotting Brock just forward of the foremast, she stalked up to him, her face taut with anger. "Brock . . ."

"Keely." He turned to her smiling. "Good to—"

"Don't you Keely me, you—"

With one swift motion Brock leaned forward, catching Keely's hand and forcing his mouth hard against hers. She struggled to disengage herself but he held his mouth pressed to hers until she was faint. In the back of her mind she heard the roar of men's voices, catcalls, and clapping. When Brock finally released her, she could do nothing but sputter, gasping for breath. With a forceful hand on the small of her back, Brock hurried her across the deck and down the steps below. He didn't let up on the pressure of his hand until they were in his cabin, the door closing out the sound of raucous male laughter.

"How dare you do that in front of all those men!" Keely spit, tugging off her bonnet.

Brock's raven eyes narrowed dangerously. "How dare you launch a tirade in front of *my* men!"

"You lied to me, you son of a bitch!" She raised her hand to strike his face but he caught it in midair.

"I what?"

Realizing her mistake, she lowered her hand, suddenly frightened by his booming voice. "You lied to me! You were never kidnapped," she murmured bitterly.

"That's it, is it?" He released her hand. "Then, I'm sorry." He turned away. "I'll have Micah's head for this."

"Why is he to blame when you're the one who played me false? You tricked me; made me feel sorry for you!" She took a step toward him, shaking a finger. "If I'd known the truth, I'd never have agreed

119

to marry you the second time. I'd have had Uncle Lloyd withdraw the betrothal agreement. I'd have sooner married old Lord Calvert than a liar."

"That's why I did it," Brock said calmly.

"You . . . you . . ." She took a deep breath, suddenly without words.

"It was wrong, but I just thought it would be easier than telling the truth. I wanted you to marry me."

"You mean you had to marry me because you'd already spent part of my dowry on your stupid ship."

"True."

Keely's hazel eyes grew moist with defeat as she turned her back on him. Brock's brutal honesty was almost more than she could bear. On their wedding night she had been so optimistic; she had hoped that his behavior, his tenderness, was a reflection of what would be.

Silence stretched between husband and wife for a moment. Brock studied Keely's slim figure, noting the auburn curls that sneaked from beneath her linen snood to curl beguilingly at the nape of her neck. Seeing her tremble, he had to restrain the urge to take her in his arms and kiss her creased brow. Suddenly her unhappiness seemed important to him. But he held his ground. "I apologized. What else am I to do?"

"That's it? You expect forgiveness because you say you're sorry," she said in disbelief.

"I told you why I lied."

"And it was a rotten excuse," she countered.

He shrugged. "I got what I wanted . . . you."

Keely met Brock's dark eyes with cool contempt. "How could you be so cruel to me? What have I done to you?"

"It's not cruelty, it's truthfulness."

"Well, I'm sick of your damned truthfulness. I

don't want truthfulness! And I don't want you, you stinking traitor! I want to go home!" Taken aback at the words that slipped from her mouth, Keely stood for a minute in shocked silence then ran out of the cabin, slamming the door behind her.

"Keely, come back here," Brock cried out in fury, slamming his fist into the door. How could he have been so stupid as to have married her, money or no? How could he have been so idiotic as to allow himself to care for her? She was right. She should return to England, but the truth was . . . he didn't want her to go.

That night Keely retired early, not wanting to have to see Brock when he finally returned home from the ship. She had heard him shout after her, she had heard the sound of a fist or a foot hit the door behind her, and she hated him. Tears ran unchecked down her cheeks. She was homesick and she wanted to go home. She *would* go home! But Keely knew that she couldn't go running to Aunt Gwen or Uncle Lloyd. She was a married woman now so she would just have to get up her nerve and settle it with her husband herself. If Aunt Gwen and Uncle Lloyd could live their married life apart, so could she and Brock. But even as she lay in her bed making plans to return to England, a small part of her protested. Why?

Their wedding night. That's why. Keely rolled onto her side, drawing the counterpane to her chin. Brock's lovemaking . . . he had been so tender, so sincere. Even now, the thought of Brock's hands touching her brought a moistness between her legs. She was ashamed that she had allowed him to make her feel so deeply. She was ashamed that she had wanted him, that she wanted him even now. With that thought, Keely drifted wearily into a dreamless

121

sleep.

Sometime in the middle of the night Brock shook Keely gently, calling her name.

She was slow to wake, drifting pleasantly on the sound of Brock's soft, beckoning voice. The warmth his skin radiated enveloped Keely as he lifted her, sliding onto the bed to cradle her in his arms. She lifted her dark lashes deliciously slowly to stare up at her husband. Half-asleep, she forgot her anger. The only thing she felt now was his warm breath on her face and the fingertips that brushed her breasts.

The light of the candle at the bedside glowed golden, casting an aura of peacefulness over Brock's bronze face. "Keely," he called softly. "Wake up, *ki-ti-hi*."

"Brock?" She smiled drowsily, lifting her hand to stroke his broad cheek. He's come to me to beg my forgiveness, she thought with heavy-eyed contentment, her eyes drifting shut again.

"Keely, please." Brock smoothed her mussed hair, kissing her temple. "Come on, sleepyhead. You've got to listen to me."

She forced her eyes open. "What is it," she whispered softly.

"It's Lloyd, Keely. You've got to wake up," Brock murmured. "He's dead."

Chapter Ten

Keely blinked, uncomprehending. "What, Brock?" she murmured.

"It's your uncle. He's died in his sleep." His dark eyes shone with compassion. "I thought you would want to see him."

"Uncle Lloyd?" she was fully awake now, still cradled in Brock's arms. He hadn't come to apologize, he'd come to tell her Uncle Lloyd was dead! Keely slipped out of bed to escape the warm embrace of her husband. "Dead?" She moistened her dry lips in confusion.

"I'm afraid so," Brock answered quietly. "I'm sorry."

She turned to him, noticing for the first time that he was fully clothed. "What time is it? When did he die?"

"Apparently he died in his sleep. Mother sent Blackie to get me down at the dock. I was still aboard ship; I had British prisoners to unload." He wondered why he felt the need to explain to Keely why he wasn't home, here in bed with her at two in the morning.

"He died and Aunt Gwen didn't call me?" Keely ran a hand through her thick unruly hair. Untended like this, it was a mass of fire-lit waves, nearly reaching her waist. "I don't understand. If he died in his sleep, how did Auntie know?"

Brock could not resist the briefest smile. This English wife of his was such an innocent. "Because, Keely, they've been sleeping together since you arrived. She was with him when he died."

"Sleeping together?" She laughed, an edge of hysteria in her voice. "They were not!"

Brock got up from the bed to fetch Keely's night robe and hold it up for her to slip her arms into it. "It's all right, you know; they were married."

She shook her head in disbelief, fumbling with the silk frogs that ran the length of her robe. "You're crazy, everyone in this house is crazy, and now you're making me crazy."

He laid his hand gently on her shoulder. "Come on, if you want to see him. I wanted you to have a moment alone with him before I got the whole house up."

Keely nodded dumbly, allowing him to usher her out of their room and down the hall toward her uncle's room.

When Brock reached Lloyd's bedchamber, he turned to her. "Stand here a minute." He slipped into the room then returned to the door. "Come on." He offered his hand and she accepted it without question.

Candles were ablaze on every table in the distinctly masculine bedchamber. The room smelled of hair powder, of tobacco, and of her uncle. Gwenevere sat on the edge of the bed, beside her husband's still body, wiping her eyes with a lace handkerchief.

"Auntie . . ." Keely cried out.

Gwenevere looked up, her eyes swollen and streaked red from spent tears. When she saw Keely, she smiled sadly, rising to take her niece in her arms. "It's all right, honey. He went peacefully," she soothed as tears slipped down Keely's cheek.

Brock left the room, closing the door discreetly behind him.

"He kept saying he was going to die, Auntie, but I didn't believe it." She sniffed. "He seemed so healthy!"

Gwenevere laughed, dabbing Keely's eyes with her own sodden handkerchief. "I know. The old goat was such a good actor, I nearly believed it myself." She kissed her niece's damp cheek. "But you mustn't be sad. Death is a part of life, it just completes the circle."

Keely nodded, accepting the handkerchief Gwenevere offered. "I just wish there'd been more time. There were things I wanted to tell him."

"There always are, sweetheart." Gwenevere released Keely. "Now, say your good-byes. The coroner's been called and we've a lot to do before the funeral." Running her palm against her niece's cheek, she smiled then left the room.

For a moment Keely didn't have the nerve to look at her uncle, but finally, she took a deep breath and turned to face the huge old bed that stood in the middle of the room. The hand-loomed counterpane had been pulled to Lloyd's chin, his hands folded over his chest, his silver-gray hair combed carefully back off his forehead. She smiled, studying his pale, withered face. He didn't appear to be dead; he just looked as if he were asleep.

"Oh, Uncle Lloyd," she murmured to the empty bedchamber. "Why did you have to go so soon? Couldn't you have stayed just a little longer?" She gripped her hands. "You've left me . . . left me here with him. I know you thought he would make a good husband, but I'm not so sure now." She paused. "I'm afraid, Uncle Lloyd."

"Afraid of what?" came Brock's distinctly masculine voice.

Keely spun around in surprise. "Must you sneak up on a person like that?" She shivered, despite the warmth of the room. "I never heard the door open!"

"Then you must learn to listen, to pay more attention to your surroundings. More than once my life has depended on moving without being heard."

"Yes, well, I don't spend my time sneaking about and committing treason!" She took a deep breath. "Listen to me. Here I am standing in a room with my dead uncle and I'm arguing with you!" She brushed passed him. "Please excuse me, but I have to dress."

Lloyd Bartholomew's funeral was a long-drawn-out affair that whittled at Keely's nerves. Following a lengthy service in the chapel at Christ's Church, there were graveside blessings and then the family and what seemed like half the town of Dover returned to the house for food and drink. All through the weary day Keely played the part of the new bride, accepting congratulations and condolences in the same breath.

Brock played the new bridegroom to the hilt, lavishing attention on his bride and seeing to her needs in her time of grief. He brought her a plate at mealtime, ushered her from room to room introducing her to the townspeople, and insisted she withdraw from the crowd when they became too oppressive. So why did Keely find herself growing angrier with him as the day passed?

Excusing himself on the pretense of seeing his wife to bed, Brock strode up the steps beside Keely, his hand resting possessively on her hip.

The moment they turned down the hall, she brushed his hand away. "No one can see us now, you don't have to do that," she said with tired aggravation.

"Do what?"

"Act like you give a damn about me!"

Brock shook his head in incredulity. "Damn, woman, you've got a sharp tongue. What have I done wrong now?"

"Nothing! You've done nothing wrong. Just leave me alone."

Brock stopped in the hallway, watching Keely continue on her way. "I'll give you the benefit of the doubt and take this to be grief, but I'm warning you, I'll not live like this in my own house. If you have a reason to be angry with me, then you had better tell me or keep it to yourself."

She ignored him, disappearing into the far wing of the house, and Brock sighed heavily.

The morning following the funeral, Keely was the last to enter the dining room for breakfast. "Good morning, Auntie." She kissed Gwenevere's cheek, sliding into her seat beside Brock's. Immediately, she sensed something was wrong. "What's the matter?"

"While you, princess, were sleeping, we had a visit from the authorities." Brock looked up from his teacup, his face grim.

Her anger with Brock was lost for the moment. "The authorities? You're in trouble?"

"I could be. But it's Mother they're questioning now. Lloyd's surgeon says Lloyd didn't die of a heart failure. The high sheriff came calling an hour ago."

Keely stared into Brock's dark eyes. "What? I don't understand."

"It's nothing to worry about, Keely," Gwenevere told her from the head of the table. "The whole thing is ridiculous. Imagine, me killing the old goat!"

Brock broke in. "He was poisoned, Keely."

"Poisoned?" Keely grew sick in the pit of her

stomach. "Why would anyone poison Uncle Lloyd? He was dying anyway."

"According to the sheriff, a woman who did not live with her husband might hurry an old dying man on his way so that her son might inherit a fortune."

Keely's face grew pale. "They think Aunt Gwen did it?"

Gwenevere reached for a slice of freshly baked bread. "You would think John Clark would have better things to do these days than falsely accuse people of killing their husbands."

"Well, it's obviously all a mistake," Keely announced shakily.

"It's no mistake. He was definitely poisoned. The coroner, Joe Stidhan, was here just before the sheriff. He came to apologize for having to go to him, but he was Lloyd's friend. It would have been unethical for him not to have reported his suspicions."

"Well, someone did it then," Keely murmured aloud. She gazed up at her husband. *Could it have been Brock?* The thought was preposterous. . . .

"Someone, indeed." Brock lifted the china teapot and poured his wife a steaming cup. "Their next suspect, of course, is me."

Keely gulped. "You?"

"Everyone knew we were business partners, Lloyd and I. What if I got greedy? First I married his heir and then the old man seemed to get better instead of worse. What if I couldn't wait? What if I'd already agreed to the purchase of another vessel? What if it was being built in a shipyard on the Chesapeake right now?"

"Oh Brock, you didn't?" Keely breathed. A murderer certainly wouldn't provide his own motive, Keely reasoned. But what if he was such a clever murderer that he did, just to throw everyone off his path?

"Lloyd was just going to give me the money, but

how am I to prove it? There was no written agreement. I'm due to make a large payment at the end of the week." He picked up a muffin and lathed it thick with butter.

Keely lifted her teacup to her mouth, her hand trembling. "So what are they going to do—the authorities?"

"For now, nothing. Just questions." Brock looked up. "Don't worry about it. They can't prove a thing. There has to be evidence for an arrest and there's no evidence. Besides I have a lead . . ."

Keely glanced over at her aunt. She seemed calm enough; of course, she would never suspect her son of such a crime. "Are . . . are they certain he was poisoned? I mean it *could* have just been his heart, *couldn't* it have? Are you certain the coroner was telling the truth?"

"It's Joe, for God's sake. He and Lloyd used to play cards."

"Oh." Keely's face fell. She had heard the man's name in letters sent from Lloyd when she was still in England. Joseph Stidham's honor was impeccable.

"Brock's right, Keely," Gwenevere said. "No need to get yourself overly excited about this."

"No need!" Keely bolted upright out of her chair. "Aunt Gwen! Uncle Lloyd was murdered!"

"Brock has several suspicions. Let him take care of it."

"I . . . I think I should talk to the sheriff myself," Keely reasoned nervously.

"No!" Brock commanded. "You'll stay out of this! I don't want you talking to anyone."

Keely turned on her husband. "Why?" What was he trying to hide from her, from the authorities?

"Because I said so. There are too many delicate matters that were discussed behind Lloyd's office doors. There are too many people that could have wanted him dead."

"Uncle Lloyd! That's absurd, Brock Bartholomew, and you know it. He was an old man."

He pushed away from the table. "Don't speak of what you don't know. It could be dangerous."

Threats? Keely wondered. Is he *threatening* me?

"Now stay home and keep out of this," Brock went on. "I'll handle it, and I'll let you know as soon as I know something. Now I've got to go."

"Go? Go where?" Keely was confused and a little frightened. Wouldn't she know if her husband was a murderer? But what did a murderer look like? What did he say? Was he different from any other man on the street who wanted something for himself or some cause he believed in?

"The ship. To add to this, one of the British prisoners I brought in escaped, and that brig we captured is taking on water."

"That's what happens when you fire cannon balls through her . . ." The moment the words were out of Keely's mouth, she was sorry.

Brock shot her a deathly black scowl. "Just be sure your comments remain in this house, wife. I don't want you talking to anyone until this matter of Lloyd's death is settled. Do you understand me?" he demanded harshly.

Keely nodded her head. She had no intentions of obeying him, but she didn't want to make him any angrier than he already was. After all, once you killed one innocent person, what difference would another make? Wouldn't Brock's life be easier without his English wife in the way?

Brock looked to his mother, who was still seated. "I've got a lot to do on the ship today so I'll be late, Mother. Don't hold supper for me. If you find out anything concerning what you and I discussed, send Blackie with a message. He can be trusted."

Gwenevere waved a hand, dismissing her son. "Go on and don't worry about this. We'll get to the bottom of it."

"I hope to God you're right." He swept his hat off the sideboard and left the room.

The moment Brock was gone, Keely ran to her aunt's side. "What did you discuss? What was he talking about? What doesn't he want me to know?"

Gwenevere heaved an exasperated sigh. "Keely, there are things that have gone on in this house that he doesn't want you to know about. I'm not saying that I agree with him or what's happened, but that's the way it is. The truth is that I trust his judgment and you're going to have to as well."

Trust him, Keely thought. Trust him so thoroughly that you wouldn't know if he killed your own husband for monetary gains? Vowing to keep her thoughts to herself and not alarm her aunt, she nodded in submission. "Maybe you're right." She went back to her seat and sat down, picking up her napkin.

"I am. Brock is a good man. He'll find Lloyd's killer."

I hope it's not him, Keely prayed fervently. But if it is . . . I'll see him hang for it.

After Gwenevere had retired for a nap, Keely slipped on her cloak and went down the back staircase and through the servant's quarters out into the late afternoon sunshine. Going directly to the barn, she waved to one of the stable hands. "I'll be needing a carriage, now."

"Now, Mistress Keely, without an escort?"

"What's your name?" Keely asked the young mulatto boy. He was not more than fourteen and dressed comfortably in homespun breeches and a coat.

"Samuel, ma'am." He twisted his hands behind his back, staring at the clean straw that covered the

131

floor of the barn.

"Well, Samuel, as you know, I'm the mistress of this house now, so that means I can request a carriage when I want one."

"Yes, ma'am. But Master Brock, I don't think he'd be wantin' me to let you go alone."

Trying not to seem overly anxious, Keely went on patiently. "Did Master Brock instruct you not to let me leave?"

"No, ma'am. But Master Brock, he always says he wants us to have a little sense of our own. He says we've got to make our own decisions about what's right and what ain't right." He wrinkled his nose. "And this ain't right, not with Master Lloyd just being dead at the hand of some murderer."

Only in this house would servants be giving orders, Keely thought irritably. "Samuel, just do as I say, please. Master Brock will never know I was gone. He's going to be at the docks until late, but if he does find out, you can tell him I told you it was an order."

"Yes, ma'am." Samuel nodded his head, but stood his ground.

"Samuel!" Keely raised her voice. "Get the carriage!"

"Yes, ma'am!" The boy scurried off and in a few moments time he brought around a two-seated open carriage drawn by a handsome chestnut mare. "This is Sally Mae, ma'am. She's old, but she's a good'n."

Keely rolled her eyes heavenward. How was a person to go on a secret mission to investigate a murder in an open carriage driven by an ancient horse? "Thank you, Samuel," she murmured, getting into the carriage. "Now give me the reins and let me be on my way."

The boy begrudgingly handed the leather reins to his mistress. "Don't you want to tell me where you're goin', just in case someone asks?"

"No, Samuel, I do not." Keely clicked to the horse, giving her free rein, and the carriage creaked forward.

Though it had been nearly ten years since Keely had been about Dover, she found herself easily recalling which roads led where. Without too much trouble she located the sheriff at his home. Though John Clark was pleasant enough, he refused to discuss Lloyd's case with Keely, except to say that he was unready to make an arrest yet. Within ten minutes of speaking to the gentleman, Keely realized her attempt to get information was futile, and so she left.

Seated in her carriage on the edge of town, Keely watched the lamplighter as he moved up the street. The September sun was just setting in the western horizon, casting an arc of bright orange over the frame houses that lined the paved street.

Though her visit with the sheriff was less than revealing, Keely was undaunted. If the investigator in charge would tell her nothing, she would go straight to the most frightening suspect — her husband. Her first idea was to go to the *Tempest,* but then realizing how foolish that would be while he was aboard, she devised a new plan.

What of the King's Head, that patriot tavern he was always having those meetings in? What if she just had dinner there, giving the illusion to be on an assignation? Many ladies certainly did so these days. Who would bother her? She could sit quietly in a booth and eavesdrop on conversations. Everyone who frequented the tavern knew Brock — someone was bound to speak of him, considering his latest victory at sea.

"Excuse me, excuse me, sir," Keely called the lamplighter just passing by.

"Me?" The bowlegged little man looked up with surprise. "You callin' me?"

133

"Yes. Might you tell me how I could find the King's Head tavern?"

The man's eyes narrowed suspiciously. "King's Head, is it? And what would you be wantin' there?"

"I'm to—" she cleared her throat—"I'm to meet a gentleman there in an hour and I'm not certain where it is."

The old lamplighter broke into a grin. "I knew you was one of us, the minute I set eyes on you!" He slapped the patched knee of his breeches. "Meetin' some young patriot feller, are you?"

Keely smiled prettily. "I assure you, sir, it's nothing of the sort. Now could you point me in the right direction?"

He nodded, chuckling. "Yup, yup, I can tell you. Just follow this here street through The Green and make a left turn past the apothecary on the far edge. Can't miss it." He looked up at her, his face changing to one of concern. "But shame on that man of yours expecting you to come alone, and it being near dark!"

"I'll be quite all right. Thank you." Keely signaled the old mare to move forward and the lamplighter swept off his beat-up three-cornered hat as she passed him.

Locating the tavern with little trouble, Keely jumped out of the carriage just as the sun set. In the dim light of dusk she tied the old mare securely to a hitching post behind the wood-structured establishment and reached for her drawstring reticule on the carriage seat. Adjusting the hood of her woolen cloak, she started around toward the entrance of the King's Head.

Bright light and men's laughter spilled from the back door as a kitchen girl in a mob cap threw a pan of soapy water out onto the ground. Sidestepping the puddle, Keely hurried along the side wall of the two-story building, ignoring the sound of footsteps

134

behind her.

"Hey there, little lady," came a drunken voice. "Why you in such a hurry?" There was laughter and the sound of added footsteps.

Walking faster, Keely mentally counted the separate voices. There were at least five or six men to her guess. Stifling the fear that threatened to overwhelm her, she gripped her reticule, taking care not to lose her footing in the damp grass. Up ahead she could see light from a lantern she guessed hung at the front door.

"Come on, missy," came the gang leader's brash voice. "Don't ya know to speak when you're spoken to? We ain't gonna hurt you, just want to talk, that's all."

Again there was raucous laughter. The instant the man came after her, Keely was running. Twice he caught the sleeve of her dress and she wrenched free before he tripped her with his foot. Hitting the ground, Keely instinctively rolled over to face her attacker. Above her loomed a burly sailor in a short military jacket and red breeches.

"Need a hand?" The sailor stood with his foot on the hem of her cloak. In the dim light Keely could see broken teeth in his leering smile.

Refusing his dirty hand, she scrambled out of her cloak and onto her feet, leaving her reticule and the cloak on the ground. "Take it," she offered, backing up slowly. Behind the sailor were six more hard-faced men, forming a semicircle behind their leader. "There's . . . there's money and not that white paper patriot stuff, real money."

The man laughed. "Money's not what we're lookin' for, love." With one clean jerking movement, he caught the bodice of her gown and ripped off the front panel.

Screaming, Keely whirled, ducking the sailor's fist, and raced around the corner of the building. Hollering as loud as she could, she threw open the door of the King's Head tavern, nearly colliding with the huge form of a man.

"Keely?"

She stopped short in the doorway. "Brock?" Her hand flew to her mouth just as the sound of the sailor's voice came from behind.

'Hang on to her, will you, mate? Paid good money for her and suddenly she's unwilling."

Brock's iron grip settled on Keely's shoulder and he pushed her behind him, into the tavern. "She's mine now," he answered gruffly. "Be on your way."

"Oh, no," the leader argued, slipping a knife from his belt. "Ain't that easy, mate, 'cause me and my friends, we got a good look and we aim to see more, so hand her over before someone gets hurt."

Taking a step back into the tavern, Brock glanced over his shoulder at the men who stood behind him. "Rig for a squall," he shouted.

Chapter Eleven

A group of gentlemen and several sailors leaped to their feet at the same time that Keely felt someone tug on her arm. "Jenna!"

"Get back before you're hit, Keely," she warned.

"Fight?" Keely glanced from her husband to the group of sailors moving slowly in through the tavern door. "They're going to fight?"

Jenna laughed, propelling Keely to the rear of the public room as the first punches flew. "Down on the floor," she ordered, dropping on all fours.

Craning her neck to see Brock's fist connect with her attacker's jaw, Keely ducked just in time to miss being struck by an airborne chair.

"Get down!" Jenna shouted, pulling Keely beneath a table.

Crawling on the floor, Keely positioned herself beneath a battered trestle table, where she had a good view of the pandemonium above. Men stumbled back under the impact of smashing fists as shrill shouts of encouragement came from two barmaids standing on a table near the rear of the smoke-filled room.

"Crack 'em!" a coarse feminine voice shouted. "Give 'em hell, Georgie!"

Keely cringed as Brock took a punch to his midsection, her hand flying to her mouth to stifle a scream.

"Keep quiet," Jenna ordered. "You'll distract him!"

"But he's going to get hurt!"

Jenna gripped Keely's arm. "I can guarantee you this isn't the first fight Brock Bartholomew's been in, nor will it be the last, now shut up!"

Caught between horror and fascination, Keely watched her first brawl. Fists flew and men shouted as glass bottles shattered and bodies hit the floor with a resounding bang. One sailor lay motionless, slumped over a table, while the other men still threw punches, falling over chairs and slamming each other against the tavern's rough-hewn walls.

Joshua Kane stumbled forward, hitting the table Keely and Jenna had taken refuge under, his arms locked around a bearded sailor. On impulse, Keely grabbed a pewter tankard from the floor and struck the sailor hard on the foot. The man yelped in pain, releasing Joshua long enough for the patriot to sink his fist into the sailor's stomach and watch him fall. One by one the sailors went down, or retreated out the door until only the leader remained. Brock circled him slowly.

Keely caught the glimmer of a steel blade as the burly sailor slipped a knife from his stocking and her breath caught in her throat. The only thing that kept Keely beneath the table was Jenna's bulldog grip on her arm.

Brock moved in silence, his breath even, his obsidian eyes boring into his attacker.

"Come on, you red-skinned bastard!" the sailor sneered. "Take me, if you can . . ."

Without warning, Brock leaped forward, catching the sailor in the side of the head with his fist. The man lashed out, slicing Brock's forearm with the tip of the knife, staining the sleeve of Brock's muslin shirt crimson.

Brock never flinched, sidestepping the sailor's next onslaught to knock him soundly on the back of the neck. The gang leader went down on one knee to the cheers of the barmaids. In one fluid movement Brock kicked the knife from the sailor's wrist and shoved him facedown on the floor.

"Do you go in peace or do I slit your throat?" Brock bellowed.

"Broke my wrist," the gang leader moaned. "Stinkin' Indian, you broke my goddamned wrist!"

Brock yanked the man up by the collar of his coat and dragged him to the door of the tavern. "I don't want to see your face in Dover again! You understand me?"

Swearing beneath his breath, the leader staggered off into the darkness.

Brock turned to spot the remaining sailor, sprawled senseless across a table. Heaving him on his shoulder, Brock carried him across the public room and dumped him onto the walkway just outside the door. "Take this with you," he shouted after the fleeing sailors.

The moment Brock shut the door, Keely scrambled out from under the table. "Brock! Are you all right?" Cheeks flushed with excitement, she hurled herself against her husband.

"What are you doing here?" Brock demanded. "Look at you! You could have been killed!"

Keely glanced down at her gown in shame, realizing for the first time that the front panel of her brocade gown was missing, revealing the soft curves of her breasts beneath her wispy-thin ivory shift. Instinctively her hands went up to cover her breasts. Not knowing what to say, she remained silent.

Brock snatched his coat up off the floor and

held it up for her to slip her arms into. "Put this on. Christ, Keely, what are you doing in this place? Is something wrong at home? If you needed me, you should have sent Blackie."

Keely's lower lip began to tremble. Brock had put his life in danger to save her from that bunch of ruffians! Shame brightened her cheeks as she blinked back salty tears. Were her suspicions concerning Uncle Lloyd's death unfounded? Would a man like Brock commit that kind of murder?

"Well?" Brock demanded impatiently. "What did you need of me so badly that you'd risk your virtue to reach me?"

The sound of men's laughter in the public room seeped into her thoughts and she glanced up at Brock. "I don't think you want to know . . ."

"What?" he bellowed.

She dashed at her eyes with the back of her dirty hand. "I said I'd rather not tell you here . . . rather not tell you at all."

Jenna came up behind Keely, her dark eyes dancing mischievously. "You ought to be proud of this little English wife of yours, Brock. She saved Joshua from a good licking. I'll warrant you there's a sailor limping home with a broken foot tonight." She laughed. "I take it the meeting is over?"

Brock heaved a sigh of exasperation. "We had more to discuss, but I suppose I've got to take her home now else she'll be stopping at every taproom on the road."

"Don't let this brute keep you shut away in the house. Come have tea with my mother and me tomorrow, will you, Keely?"

"I'll try," she answered quietly.

Brock moved away to locate his hat and Jenna leaned to whisper in Keely's ear. "I'm sure you had good reason to come; don't let him bully you. He has no patience for people who can't stand up for themselves." She smiled. "I'm counting on you for tomorrow."

"Shall we go?" Brock asked Keely with mock politeness. Together they walked to the door as he waved a hand over his head, bidding the men in his group farewell. "I'll get back to you, tomorrow on that issue, Manessah," he called.

"No hurry, Brock," Jenna's brother answered jovially. "I can see you've your hands full right now."

There was laughter as Brock ushered Keely out of the tavern and closed the door behind them.

"Well, did you bring a carriage or did you walk?" Brock asked angrily. He gripped her elbow none-too-gently.

"Of course I brought the carriage. It's in the back."

"Good place on a dark night on this side of town," he responded sarcastically.

"I'm sorry," Keely muttered as they came to the place where the sailor had tackled her.

"What?" Brock swept her cloak off the ground and continued walking. The reticule was gone.

She raised her voice. "I said I'm sorry."

"And what good would sorries have been after the bunch of them had raped you?"

Reaching the carriage, Keely climbed up onto the seat, refusing Brock's assistance. "I didn't think . . ."

"Do you ever think?" he demanded, taking a seat beside her. "Now tell me, little cousin, what the hell did you want?"

She gripped the lapels of his coat she wore, inhaling the heavenly masculine scent that clung to it. "I wasn't actually looking for you."

He clicked to the old mare and she moved forward. "What?"

Keely kept her eyes focused in the darkness on the mare's ears which twitched as she walked. "I

141

went to investigate."

"You're making no sense, wife. Now out with it." Brock demanded hotly.

Struggling against tears that threatened to flow, words spilled from Keely's mouth in rapid fire. "I was investigating Uncle Lloyd's murder. I went to the sheriff and then I came to the tavern to see what I could find out about you." She turned to him, her gaze settling on his angry face. "I thought . . . I thought maybe you killed my uncle."

He gripped the reins so tightly that the leather bit into the flesh of his hands. "You what!"

Keely cringed.

"Why in the—" Brock cut himself off, looking away as he shook his head. "How could you be so—"

For several minutes Brock was silent. The sound of the horse's feet hitting the hard dirt echoed in Keely's ear, mixing with the soft even rhythm of her husband's breathing.

When Brock finally spoke again, his anger was checked, but the rage lurking beneath the surface gave his voice a razor edge. "What the hell made you think I would do such a thing?"

She shrugged. "Who else would do it? I thought you needed the money."

"I already *had* the money."

"Maybe you wanted him out of the way." Keely swallowed hard. "Then you could get rid of me."

"Why would I want to get rid of you? I need you," Brock responded unemotionally.

Keely's heart skipped a beat. "You what?" she asked with surprise.

"I need you. The war is going so poorly that Lloyd may have been right. I may need you and your English loyalties."

For an instant Keely felt a strange sense of regret, though she didn't know why. What else could he

142

have meant? "Well, I don't need you," she managed through clenched teeth.

"According to you uncle, you did, now stop avoiding the subject. You had no right to accuse me of murder, wife."

The manner in which he said the word *wife* made Keely tremble. "I said nothing to anyone."

"I'm no murderer of innocent men and certainly not Lloyd's murderer. I loved that man as much as I could have loved my own father." He turned to her, the anger in his voice subsiding slightly. "But I'm glad you acted on your suspicions, however silly they might have been."

She looked up at him beside her on the carriage seat. "I don't understand."

"It was stupid. Your conclusions were without basis, but"—he held up a finger—"you acted on your conjecture. You didn't just sit like a useless female and worry yourself into a spell."

"But I was wrong."

Brock chuckled dryly, taking her hand in his. "You were wrong, quite wrong, my dear." He lifted her hand to brush his lips against the back of it.

Keely tried to ignore the shiver of pleasure Brock's touch created. "But if you didn't do it, who did?"

He laid her hand on his thigh, patting it gingerly. "While you were off *investigating,* I was checking into a few things myself."

"And?" Keely asked, removing her hand from his leg.

"Wait until we get home. I'll show you."

Half an hour later Brock helped Keely down from the carriage and escorted her in their home through the back kitchen door. "Go on upstairs and change your dress. No sense in giving Lucy anything more to gossip about. Then meet me in Lloyd's office; I'll get Mother."

When Keely came downstairs a few minutes later, the office door was open. Inside she found Brock pacing the floor and Aunt Gwen and the housekeeper, Matilda, seated in two high-back chairs.

Brock glanced up at Keely, flashing her a hint of a smile before he turned to the servant. "Matilda, tell me what you know of Lloyd Bartholomew's death."

The white-haired woman looked up. "What, the sheriff don't know who did it yet?"

"No arrests have been made. Right now we're just talking to everyone who knew him. I know you two talked, what do you think?" he asked solemnly.

Matilda's eyes darted to Gwenevere. "There's evil in this house, I can tell you that, Master Brock. Evil just come of late, but been here before."

Gwenevere's eyes met Matilda's but she kept silent as Brock had instructed her.

Brock crossed his arms over his chest. He still wore the shirt with a torn and bloodstained sleeve. "Evil? What kind of evil? Tell me, Matilda."

The old woman worried at her bony hands. "Devil spawned, what other kind is there?" She licked her dry lips. "I warned Lloyd, I told him there was evil about, but he was in so much pain that he didn't understand."

"Lloyd was in pain?" Brock probed.

She nodded vigorously. "Didn't you see him always rubbing at his chest? And then when *she* came it got worse, only he couldn't see it because he was under her spell."

"Whose spell?"

Matilda rocked her frail body in the chair. "You know—*her*." She lifted her chin, motioning toward Gwenevere.

"His wife?" Brock asked. "His wife was the evil?"

"Hmph! Wife! She tweren't no wife . . . not the kind of wife he deserved, not what he needed." She

144

rocked faster. "I offered. I'd of made a good wife to him, I'd have never traipsed off across the oceans. Me and Lloyd we knew each other as children. Then she came and he married her and then she went."

"Matilda," Brock said softly. "What's that got to do with Lloyd's death?"

The old maidservant looked up at him. "Don't you see? You were caught right betwixt it! First she brought back the girl and told Lloyd to marry the two of you off. I heard them whispering in his bedchamber, head him laughin' under her spell. And then when it was legal, she kilt him so that her son might have it all!"

Brock studied the old maidservant's translucent blue eyes. "Gwenevere? You think Gwenevere did it?"

Distressed, Keely looked up at Brock. He shook his head ever so slightly, lifting his finger to signal for her to hold her tongue.

"And how did she do it, Matilda? Can you tell me that?"

" 'Twas simple enough. Laudanum." Matilda's eyes grew round and glazed as she began to rock back and forth again. "A little slipped into that sleeping tincture Blackie took him. He'd been drinkin' the stuff for years, a bitter awful potion . . . to make him sleep, he said. " 'Twas enough for that old heart of his to give in. He's gone now, bless his soul, gone to a better place far from the evils and pains of this wretched world."

Brock laid a hand gently on Matilda's thin, ragged shoulder. "Why did you do it, Matilda? He was always good to you."

Crystalline tears ran down her wrinkled cheeks. "I sent him on without me, sent him far from her evil hand. He's in peace now." She looked up at Brock. "Don't you think he's in peace?"

145

Brock nodded slowly. "He is, Matilda, now go on upstairs and pack your things. Someone will be here for you shortly."

The old maidservant got up slowly, making a semicircle around Gwenevere's chair. She hummed quietly to herself as she walked out the door and down the back hallway.

"She killed Uncle Lloyd?" Keely cried in disbelief. "Matilda did it?"

Brock ran a bronze hand across his forehead. "Her mind was always weak, but I never thought she'd ever do any harm. I blame myself for allowing her to stay."

Gwenevere shook her head. "You were right, Brock. Saints in hell! She was in love with the old goat! She killed for unrequited love!"

"No, Mother, I think she did it because she thought she was helping him. In her own twisted way she was saving him from the pain of life"—his eyes met his mother's—"and from you."

"Save him from me!" She laughed. "Poor soul. Why'd he ever bring her here in the first place?"

Brock perched himself on the arm of a chair. "You know how Lloyd was. He was always taking servants from other people when they didn't work out. When Annie Samkins died a few years back, John dismissed Matilda. He said she made him nervous and now that his wife was gone, he didn't need her. Apparently Lloyd knew her from his childhood, felt sorry for her, and took her in."

"If he'd only known . . ." Gwenevere muttered.

"If he'd known, he'd have hired her anyway," Keely said thoughtfully.

Brock's eyes met his wife's and he nodded, holding her in his gaze. "You're right, Lloyd would have." He smiled sadly. "It was the kind of man he was."

"Well, I hope you called the sheriff to take her

146

right away!" Gwenevere got up with a rustle of silk and taffeta.

"I had to," Brock conceded.

"Well, what's going to happen to her?" Keely dropped a hand on her hip. "You can't hang someone who's sick like that."

"The sheriff wants to speak with her; I saw him this morning and told him of my suspicions."

Keely's eyes widened with surprise. "You mean he had already talked to you when I went to see him?"

Brock nodded. "I asked that he not speak to anyone until I talked to Lucy and confirmed my own beliefs."

"Well, where was Lucy that she wasn't here to talk to you after breakfast?"

"Apparently she was out prowling last night with one of her many gentleman friends and didn't come home. Once Blackie found her, all was settled but Matilda's confession. Lucy knew she'd bought the laudanum and from whom."

"So what's going to happen to Matilda now?" Gwenevere stopped in the doorway. "Burn her at the stake if you ask me."

Brock scowled. "I've made a special request that she not be charged, but be allowed to go to a niece's near Philadelphia. It's not legal, but I think I've convinced John Clark that she's harmless."

"As harmless as a shark in my mineral bath!" Gwenevere raged.

"Now Mother, do you really think that?"

Gwenevere sighed. "No, I guess not," she said quietly. "I'm just angry at the unjustice. I can't help wondering how many days, weeks, months she robbed him of."

"Maybe just hours." Brock went to his mother, leaning to brush a kiss against her cheek. "It's like you always told me, *Onna,* everything happens for a reason. Who knows, maybe she saved him from a painful, suffering death."

Gwenevere blinked back the moisture in her eyes, giving her son a pat on the cheek. "You remind me so much of your father sometimes, Brock." Then she was gone.

Keely was overcome by all that she'd just witnessed. Matilda . . . Brock . . . She'd even seen a part of Aunt Gwenevere that she'd never known before. She couldn't help wondering if her aunt still pined for Brock's father after all these years.

Suddenly Brock was before Keely, taking her hand. "I don't know about you, cousin, but I'm ready for bed. It's been a long, eventful day."

Keely's hazel eyes met his dark pools with uncertainty. A truce seemed to have been called between them, at least for tonight. "I'll get something for your arm."

"No. Water will be enough. Come on." He dropped his arm around her shoulder and led her out of the office and up the staircase to their bedchamber.

Once inside their room, Keely moved quietly about, readying herself for bed, unsure of how she was to behave. In the days after their wedding, when he was angry, it had been easy. She just ignored him, but what about now? Though she liked him no better than she had, she was overwhelmed by her desire to have him touch her . . . to make love to her, and that desire scared her.

Brock was painfully aware of Keely's movements as she washed her face and hands in the china bowl and ran a brush through her thick, shining hair. Taking a seat in a rocking chair near the window, he slipped off his stockings, watching her movement from the corner of his eye.

She was beautiful, this wife of his, and she had courage to go along with it. That was something he hadn't expected from his English cousin, something

148

he hadn't prepared for. He had thought her a mouse of a child, something to be petted and teased, but of no substance. This courage of hers was admirable, but at the same time, he knew it could be dangerous.

"Keely," Brock called.

She turned to him. She had removed her gown and was standing barefoot in a thin shift. "Yes?" Her face was still dewy from the cool water of the pitcher, the curls that framed her face damp and springy. She was a picture of innocence . . . of promised sensuality.

"Come here," he beckoned, his voice barely audible.

She came to him without hesitation, the light of the scattered bedlamps filtering through her hairs to frame her face in a fiery aura. "What is it, Brock?"

He smiled, enjoying the sound of her voice as she spoke his name. "So much has happened since you left your England. Have I been unfair?"

She came down on one knee, eye level to him. "It was stupid of me to think you would do such a terrible thing. It's true I don't know you well, but Uncle Lloyd and Aunt Gwen would never have married me off to a murderer."

He tugged at one of her damp curls. "There's no reason we can't live together in peace."

"No reason except that you say I'm English and you're not."

"Loyalties are a funny thing, Keely."

"I didn't ask to be married to a colonial; I know where I belong," she defended.

"You belong here with your husband. Where I can keep an eye on you." He reached to catch another fiery curl and she pulled away, getting up.

Keely crossed the room to retrieve the pitcher and bowl. A minute later she was removing his shirt to get a better look at the wound on his arm. "So what you're telling me is that I'm not to be trusted and that I can't go home."

He inhaled her soft, feminine scent, wishing he hadn't gotten into this conversation. Against his will he could feel the heat of desire rising within him. "I'm being honest with you. I'm telling you there's too much at stake. This is your home now. Ouch!" He looked up at her. You're taking off the skin!"

"It's only a flesh wound and it's got to be cleaned or it'll get infected and your arm will fall off. What kind of pirate could you be with one arm?"

"I'm no pirate."

"Let me go home to England when Aunt Gwen goes and I'll never be any trouble to you again," she said softly, washing the encrusted blood from his muscular arm.

"We could go round and round like this until we were too old to chew meat, Keely." He caught her arm, pulling her down on his lap. "I say I want you here where I can keep my eye on you."

His lips brushed hers and her eyes closed of their own accord. "Why are you doing this?" she whispered.

"Doing what?" He nibbled at her lower lip.

"You know, this. . . . You don't care about me, you don't love me."

"You take me to be a greater beast than I am. I do care, and I desire you, isn't that enough?" His tongue darted out to trace the outline of her lips. "I know you desire me, Keely."

"It's not right," she answered breathlessly, wanting to pull away but not having the willpower. He made her feel so alive. . . .

"That a man and a woman should desire each other?" He kissed her furrowed brow. "That's as ancient as time itself."

Before she could reply, Brock crushed Keely in his arms. His kiss was long and deep. Breathless, she pulled back, staring into his dark eyes, her hand lingering at the nape of his neck. "Your hair," she whispered, surprising them both.

He cocked his head, smiling. "What?"

"Let me see your hair." She stroked the crown of his head, feeling wickedly bold. So what if he didn't love her—she didn't love him. After all; they were married. Why shouldn't she enjoy the same pleasures he did? "I've never seen your hair. You wake before sunrise, and by the time I see you at breakfast, you've brushed and braided it again." Her hazel eyes danced inquisitively. "I just want to see what it looks like."

Brock laughed, lifting her to her feet so that he could stand. "Only if you'll let me make love to you," he said softly.

Keely's eyes narrowed. "It's my wifely duty, isn't it?"

"No." He reached back and pulled his braid of hair forward, untying the strip of leather that bound it. "I'm not talking about duties." He unwound his thick black hair as Keely watched in fascination. "I'm talking about what should be between a man and a woman," he said. "What we were made for."

Hesitantly Keely reached out to fan the long, raven locks over his bronze sculptured shoulders. "It's beautiful," she breathed.

He smiled, lifting her in his arms to carry her to their bed, his face nestled in the sweet crook of her neck. "Beautiful? Let me show you beautiful," he whispered.

Chapter Twelve

Keely looped her arms around Brock's neck, staring up into the depths of his velvet-black eyes. She brushed his broad cheek with her hand, smiling when he pressed a kiss to her palm.

Brock gently lay her down crosswise on the bed, then stripped off his breeches before sliding in beside her. "You have the most perfect mouth," he whispered, tracing her trembling lips with his finger. "How was I so lucky to find wealth *and* beautiful lips in a wife?"

Keely erupted into soft laughter. "And is it luck that you've married a woman who thinks you a murderer?" She wove her fingers through his thick hair, glorying in the feel of its silky texture.

" 'Tis all done and forgotten, cousin," he murmured, lowering his face until it was only inches from hers.

Keely's eyes drifted shut as his lips touched her lips, igniting a spark of incandescent desire deep within her. His tongue was hot and wet and probing. His kiss robbed her of all reason, pushing all thoughts aside save of him, here . . . now.

Again and again he took her breath away, his fingers teasing lightly at the bodice of her shift as

152

he rained a gentle onslaught on her mouth. "God, Keely, you taste of the heavens," he whispered huskily in her ear.

Slowly he made his way down to the neckline of her thin shift, sprinkling her pale flesh with a smattering of light, teasing kisses. With his tongue he traced the line of cotton lace, leaving a trail of damp, tingling sensation behind. Caressing a rounded breast with his hand, he lowered his mouth to the nub of her nipple, straining against the thin cloth.

Keely arched her back, moaning softly as his mouth closed over the bud of her breast, wetting the cotton material as he sent shiver after shiver of deep, resounding pleasure through her limbs.

Running a hand down the length of her thigh, Brock lifted the shift above her waist and Keely sat up, allowing him to tug it over her head and send it floating to the floor. Resting on her back again, she ran a hand over his broad chest, noting his sigh as her fingers brushed a male nipple. Smiling secretly, she touched the tiny dark nub again, surprised to find it stiffening. Fascinated by her discovery, Keely lifted her head to brush her lips against the bud, her tongue darting out to taste the salt of his flesh.

Brock groaned, running a hand through her thick, auburn hair. "And who taught you such things, witch?" he asked softly.

Keely smiled up at her husband. "Taught?" She laughed huskily. "I just thought that what was good for me must be good for you."

He nodded, his eyes drifting shut as she sucked hesitantly on his nipple. "Good rule to follow," he managed.

Smiling in the semidarkness, Keely pushed Brock over onto his back, bent on exploring this unknown entity of a man's body. Inquisitively, she moved her hands over his chest, down his long, muscular

153

arms, and over the whipcord muscles of his thighs, taking in the soft sighs of pleasure that came from her husband's lips.

A wonderful thing this male body was—so different from her own. Where she had soft curves, his skin was stretched taut over sculptured muscles. Where her pale skin was smooth and unblemished, his body was peppered with the scars of life, his suntanned flesh sprinkled with dark, crisp hair.

Brock lay still beneath Keely's innocent exploration, trying to calm his racing heartbeat. How was it that this English girl could evoke such stirrings within him? It was not the physical excitement that had him so puzzled but the emotional. Even when he'd been furiously angry with her this evening when she appeared at the tavern, a secret part of him was glad to see her. Each time he laid eyes on the little chit, against his will he felt his chest tighten, his heart skip to an unsteady beat. He prayed that he was not falling in love with her. . . .

"Enough! Enough of this," Brock said aloud, catching Keely's hand. He saw her face fall.

"You don't want me to touch you?" She knew her exploration excited him . . . that was startlingly obvious. What had she done wrong?

He chuckled, rolling her over to kiss her rosy lips. "Not unless you wish an all-too-quick finish to the whole matter, *ki-ti-hi*." His voice was soft and husky, a caress to her ears.

Keely furrowed her wispy brows in confusion, her eyes suddenly lighting up with understanding. "Oh!" She withdrew her hand from his thigh, a pale blush of color creeping across her cheeks. "Sorry . . ."

"No. Never be sorry." Brock kissed the valley between her breasts and Keely giggled. "What?" He lifted his head, a thin trace of a smile on his lips.

"Your hair, it tickles!"

"Tickles?" He smiled wickedly, dropping his head to let his long tresses brush the peaks of her breasts.

Keely laughed again, but this time softly, sensually. "Mmmm, I like that." She tilted her head back, letting her hands fall to her sides on the bed.

Moving exquisitely slowly, Brock brushed the length of her naked body with his mane of ebony hair, sending shivers of molten longing through her limbs. Nearly paralyzed with intense pleasure, Keely writhed beneath his magical assault, calling his name.

Lowering his head, Brock kissed the flat hollow of her stomach and she lifted her hips with an inherent instinct. Her mind swam with the sensations of the flesh, her body crying out to be satiated.

When Brock's lips first made contact with the web of tight curls, she cried out, shrinking back. But the soft sounds of encouragement he whispered made her relax, trusting him as he beckoned. At first, the sensations that pulsed through her were soft and flowing, but then he began to move to an ancient rhythm and she lifted her hips in response. The waves of gentle pleasure grew in strength until they became an all-consuming bittersweet pain of longing.

"Please, Brock," she cried, her voice raspy.

"Shhh," he hushed. "Lie back, it's all right."

Breathing deeply as she relaxed into the bedcovers, she felt herself being drawn up with the tide. Uncontrolled, she was being hurled higher and higher until suddenly there was a surge of ecstatic release, filling her to capacity with a joy she'd never known.

Looming over her prone body, Brock slipped into her with a single stroke, catching her as she drifted slowly to the shores of peace. Then Keely felt

155

herself moving again, lifting her hips in reception of each thrust, struggling to catch another glimpse of that indescribable peak of pleasure.

Brock's breath was hot in her ear as he moved faster, calling her name, urging her forward. In unison, they rose and fell until they both cried out in fulfillment.

When Brock rolled onto his side to relieve her of his weight, Keely lay motionless, her feathery lashes a dark smudge on her pale face. Gently, Brock brushed a lock of damp hair from her forehead. "Do you live?" he whispered.

Keely forced her eyes to open, her mouth turning up in a lazy smile. "I'm not sure . . ."

"So now you really are a woman, wife." He kissed the tip of her nose, his hand brushing over her belly.

"It was . . . it was . . ." She looked up at him, studying his bronze face in the dim light.

"I know. There are no words. Not Shakespeare, not Milton, not even Cicero could describe what love is, what it feels like."

Love, Keely thought. What did he mean? Who was he to speak of love? He'd told her there was nothing more between them than physical desire. But she said nothing, not wanting to spoil the moment.

Kissing Keely softly on the lips, Brock slid up, tossing his pillow to the floor. He never slept with a pillow. "Come here," he called, holding his arms out for her.

Crawling across the bed, Keely slipped beneath the light coverlet, snuggling down in the crook of Brock's arm. Refusing to allow herself to dwell on what she thought of her husband or her desire for him, she drifted to sleep.

* * *

The instant Keely lifted her head from the pillow, the bile rose in her throat and she moaned aloud. "Oh God, not again."

Brock pushed up out of the bed and crossed the room naked to retrieve the water bowl from the mahogany side table. Without a word he kneeled beside the bed, holding Keely as she was sick into the basin. Lifting her head she took the damp towel he offered her, pressing it to her lips. Flinging back into the pillows, she squeezed her eyes shut to force back the tears. She was so embarrassed; this made the third time this week she'd been sick.

Feeling Brock's presence bending over her, she lifted her eyelashes to see his grinning face. "What are you so happy about?" she asked irritably. "Found another British brig to pillage?"

He took the cloth from her hand and dipped it into the pitcher of cool water, wringing it out before he placed it gently over her forehead. "Are you addlepated, cousin? You're pregnant." He broke into a grin again.

Keely groaned, closing her eyes as she drew the counterpane to her chin. "Don't say that! I can't be!"

Getting to his feet, Brock moved to the mirror to brush and braid his hair. "It's November, let's see . . ." He counted comically on his fingers. "You must be quite fertile."

Keely pulled the counterpane over her head. "I don't want to be fertile. I don't want to be sick. I don't want to have a hundred screaming children and sagging breasts!"

Brock laughed, his fingers moving nimbly through his hair. "You should have thought of that before you bewitched me into your bed."

"Bewitched! Hah! They said I had to marry you. I was given no choice!"

Fastening a bit of ribbon on the end of his braid,

Brock went to the bed, easing down beside Keely to lift the covers from her face. "You never told me you didn't want children," he said quietly.

Keely looked up at Brock, sighing. "It's not that I didn't want children, just not now. Not when everything is such a mess. I wanted time to get used to being married, to running the house, and now with Aunt Gwen leaving . . ." She looked away.

"How could you have been so silly to think you wouldn't get with child eventually?" Brock couldn't help feeling angry. Why didn't she want his child? Was it because she thought she was better than he was? Did she think she lowered herself to sleep with him, a colonial? She certainly had no trouble relating to Micah. . . .

"Eventually, yes, but . . ." She looked up at Brock, "I'm sorry. You're right, I was playing with fire. I deserve what I get."

"You're my wife, damn it!" he shouted. "You make it sound as if it was something dirty and despicable. I have a right to make love to my own wife."

Keely dropped her gaze to the patterned counterpane. "And have I ever denied your right, husband?"

Brock jerked his linen shirt off the bedpost and stuffed his balled fists into the sleeves. "Don't play that game with me, cousin. You make it sound as if I forced you. I seem to recall you coming to me on more than one occasion, begging for your own rights."

Keely's cheeks colored. He was right. Though she and Brock moved cautiously through their marriage by day, more like strangers than husband and wife, by night they abandoned caution, making love and enjoying each other fully. Though Keely still did not care for her husband or his politics, she couldn't honestly deny her desire for him. Brock had awakened her sensuality and he knew it. He played her like an ancient stringed lute, teaching her the pleasures of the flesh, teaching her how to enjoy what had been bestowed upon them.

Brock sat down to roll up his hose. "I'll be late tonight, so don't expect me."

"That's fine because Micah asked me to go to the Parkers' with him; they're having a reception for their daughter and her new husband." She didn't know why she said it like that, she just did.

"I told you I don't like you seeing so much of Micah Lawrence."

"You're never here to take me anywhere, what do you care? He and Jenna are the only friends of yours who have offered any kindness. They're the only friends I have here!"

"It's not seemly. You're a married woman now."

She slid down in the bed, pulling up the covers. "Are you telling me I can't go?"

Brock forced his feet into his boots and retrieved his bayberry-colored coat from the chair. "I'm telling you it's not a good idea."

"Are you jealous, husband?"

"Have I need to be?" he asked. "It was my dear *friend* Micah who tried to marry you to save you from me."

"I'm not that stupid!" Keely didn't know why she was behaving so cruelly. She felt trapped. She was just so mad with him. What did he care if she was pregnant? It wasn't he who would suffer through childbirth.

"No, I don't think you are." He turned to her, his dark eyes piercing hers. "Because I swear to you, I would kill you both! I was cuckolded once; there will be no second time."

Tears welled in Keely's eyes at the sound of the slamming door. Brock Bartholomew had no heart, she was sure of it now. When this child is born, she vowed silently, I will leave him and go home. "Home to England," she whispered.

"What did you say, dear?" came Aunt Gwenevere's voice from behind the door.

"No . . . nothing!" Keely called, dashing at her tears with the back of her hand.

"Might I come in?"

"Please do."

Gwenevere entered the bedchamber in a flourish of flowing silks. She was wearing lavender Turkish pants, a peach-colored man's shirt, and a multi-hued silk turban around her head. "I ran into Lucy on the steps." She set down the tray she carried. "Aren't you feeling well?"

Keely forced a brief smile. "I think I'm going to have a baby . . ."

Gwenevere gave a hoot of pleasure, grabbing Keely's hands. "A baby? Have you told Brock?"

She grimaced. "He probably realized it before I did."

"I know he's pleased." She released her niece's hands and poured two cups of chamomile tea.

Keely accepted the teacup offered. "Of course he is."

Gwenevere looked up with concern. "And you're not, Keely?"

She sighed, blowing on her tea to cool it. "I don't know," she said miserably. "On one hand, the thought of holding a baby in my arms . . ." Her gaze grew distant and she smiled. "I want that." She sipped the tea. "But I can't help feeling I've fallen into some sort of trap. I've done everything everyone else wanted me to do. I came back to the Colonies because Uncle Lloyd told me to, I married Brock because you told me to, and now I'm carrying his baby. Do you know what I mean?"

"Don't worry, it will pass."

Keely took her aunt's hand impulsively. "Will you

160

take me to England with you? Back home?"

Gwenevere frowned. "Take you back? Certainly not. Where in heaven's earth did you get that idea? This is your home now. With your husband."

Keely pulled back her hand as if it had been stung. "I hate it here." She looked away. "Brock and I . . . he doesn't like me."

"He loves you," Gwenevere stated flatly.

"He does not," she challenged, her teary eyes meeting her aunt's.

"And how would you know?" Gwenevere set her teacup on the tray and went to look out the window.

"If he loved me, he'd have told me so. He barely tolerates my presence."

Gwenevere laughed. "If he'd told you, it would be more likely that he didn't. Men have a difficult time expressing their feelings, but that doesn't mean they don't feel as deeply as we do."

Keely nibbled at her biscuit. "Brock married me because he needed the money, we all know that."

"True. But that wasn't the only reason; it wouldn't have been enough for a man like my son." She turned away from the window. "I have a feeling my son was hurt very badly by a woman, Keely. Give him time to trust you."

"Why should I? He has no trust in me." She toyed with her cup. "He's afraid to speak in front of me for fear I'll go racing to the front lines to spill all of his silly secrets." She took a sip of her tea, then lifted her head to meet her aunt's gaze. "I'd never betray him. He's my husband."

"You know that and I know that, but Brock doesn't." Gwenevere sat down on the edge of Keely's bed. "It's going to take time, dear."

"Time? How much time? I can't live like this, Aunt Gwen. Can't I please go home with you?"

"And risk the life of your firstborn?"

161

Keely's face fell. Aunt Gwen was right. It would be many months before she would be fit to travel by sea again. "Then at least say you'll stay until the babe is born . . ."

"I couldn't possibly. All of the Morrow Estates need my overseeing; the arrangements have been made. I'll be traveling with Joshua Kane."

Keely bit down on her lower lip. "You're going to leave me here with Brock? This is an awful time to be making a crossing."

"Keely, I never told you I could stay," Gwenevere said gently. "I've my own interests to look after in London; I have my life and now you have yours."

Keely ran a hand through her thick hair. "Couldn't you have a life here?"

Gwenevere came to the bed and sat down, studying Keely's pale face. "Even if I wanted to, it wouldn't be fair to you and Brock."

"He wouldn't mind," she protested. "I know he wouldn't."

"Keely, if I remain here, you'll always have me to turn to, and that's not the way it should be. By my leaving you'll be forced to depend on your husband and he'll have to depend on you."

"Hah!" Keely laughed. "Brock never depends on anyone but himself."

Gwenevere took Keely's hand, brushing a stray lock of hair from her niece's cheek. "Then make him depend on you," she entreated. "Don't make the mistakes Lloyd and I made."

Keely studied her aunt's unlined face, her dark brown eyes, her bare smile. "I love you," Keely cried, hugging Gwenevere. "I love you so much."

Chapter Thirteen

May 1778

Summer came to the war-ravaged American Colonies in a rush of lush green foliage and brilliant, flowering blooms. With the winter of Valley Forge behind them, the patriot army moved with a new strength, a strength born of hardship and determination.

Joyous news had arrived from across the ocean; France had declared itself an ally of the United States. Abundant supplies were en route and the French army and navy were to cooperate wholeheartedly. Suddenly the odds were turning, and the American Colonies were becoming a true threat to the Crown.

Keely knocked lightly on the door of Jenna's parents' home, rubbing the small of her back. She was well into her eighth month of pregnancy and eager for the child to be born. When the door swung open, Keely smiled. "Good morning, Madge. Is Jenna in?" She lifted a basket of succulent red berries. "I've brought her those strawberries I promised from our garden."

The elderly dark-skinned woman grinned, baring large, square white teeth. "Good lord, chil', where's your carriage? Don't tell me you walked here?" She stepped back, letting Keely into the front hall of the brick town house on the city's green.

"It's not that far! Besides, I'm tired of sitting; I'm no invalid." Keely set the basket on a cherry side table in the hall and reached up to remove her straw bonnet.

Madge chuckled, staring openly at Keely's round stomach. "Carryin' that low it's a boy for sure. Such a big son for Master Brock."

"I know, everyone says it's a boy." She rubbed her swollen stomach, smoothing her sprigged dimity gown. "It doesn't matter to me; all I want is a healthy babe and to be able to see my feet again!"

Madge took her bonnet. "Miss Jenna's out in the garden with Max and Mistress Whitman," she said as she started down the hallway.

Keely retrieved her basket of fresh strawberries and followed her. "That's all right, Madge, I know my way by now. You go back to whatever you're doing."

"You certain, Miss Keely?"

Keely patted the old servant's arm as she passed her. "Go on with you."

Walking slowly down the center hall, Keely waved as she passed the parlor. "Morning to you, Mistress Lewes."

Jenna's mother looked up from her sewing, breaking into a smile. "Morning. Are you still carrying that child? You look big enough to bust!"

Keely laughed, continuing down the hallway. "I feel big enough to bust!" Pushing through the door that led to the garden in the rear, Keely stepped down onto the brick paved walk. "Jenna? Are you there?" She looked out over the fastidiously kept boxwood garden, smiling at the sight of the patches of Queen Anne's lace and lavender running along the walk.

"Back here!" called Jenna from within the maze of boxwood. "Near the fountain."

Following the path Keely now knew well, she found Jenna seated across from Christina Whitman on a stone bench. Christina was the wife of George Whitman, a judge in town who also belonged to Brock's patriot group. Max was playing in the grass with a kitten just beyond them.

Keely wished suddenly she hadn't come. In all the months that had passed since she and Brock had wed, there had been few people in the town who had been kind to her. Brock's friends' wives called her *the English woman,* and when she walked into the room, they immediately grew silent as if they were putting themselves at risk just being in the same room with her. Only Jenna and Micah had refused to feel any prejudice against her and she treasured their friendship greatly.

Keely forced a friendly smile. "Morning to you, Mistress Whitman."

Christina Whitman lifted her chin arrogantly. "A good morning to you," she said coldly.

Ignoring the woman's ungracious behavior, Keely took a seat beside Jenna, pushing the basket of strawberries into her friend's lap. "I brought these for you, just picked this morning."

"Thank you, Keely." Jenna leaned to brush her lips against her cheek, trying to make up for Christina's rudeness. "How are you doing?"

Keely sighed, shifting her weight in an attempt to find a more comfortable position. "Well enough, considering. Brock's been gone nearly two weeks and I'm beginning to worry. He didn't say where

165

he'd be going or how long he'd be."

Christina Whitman came up out of her seat. "Well, I should think not! Our husbands are out there risking their lives! You certainly don't think they would let you know of their movement!" She pointed angrily at Keely. "You're probably the one who informed the British soldiers about that shipment two weeks ago."

"What shipment?" Keely asked, startled.

"That's unfair, Christina," Jenna accused. "Keely would never put any of our men at risk. Brock is her husband."

The fact that Keely probably knew more of what went on in Dover's patriot circles than Christina made Keely feel no better. It was not her husband but Micah and occasionally Jenna who informed her of what occurred at those secret meetings. Though Brock regularly declared his dislike for Keely's seeing Micah, so far he had not forbidden her to do so. To keep matters civil in the house, she saw Micah only when Brock was out to sea or on one of his missions. Micah was her friend and she refused to give him up over her husband's unwarranted jealousies. Still, life was not easy for Keely. The patriots and their families in Dover shunned her and the known loyalists of the city accused her of being a traitor for marrying a patriot. "I don't know what she's talking about, but it's all right, Jenna," Keely said quietly. "It doesn't matter."

Jenna's nut-brown eyes narrowed dangerously. "It's not all right. Christina's accusations are unfounded. *I* know what's happening within the committee."

Keely turned to her friend. "And was there a leak? No one told me."

Jenna got to her feet in anger. "Brock just didn't want you to worry, being so close to your confining. The leak of information could have come from several directions. There was no evidence that it came from within us. No one was injured or caught; we just lost the shipment and it was a small one." She turned to Christina. "You shouldn't have said anything, now please apologize."

Christina laughed, her wide-brimmed straw hat tilting to and fro. "Apologize to that English bitch? I think not." She whipped a lace handkerchief from the bodice of her gown. "George says she ought to have been sent home to her precious England. Why did Brock need her here once he had her money?"

"Leave! Now!" Jenna ordered. "And you're not welcome here until you apologize."

Christina hurried down the winding brick path that led to an outside gate. "I warn you, Jenna Williams!" she called over her shoulder. "You'll rue the day you ever befriended that woman."

Christina slipped out the gate and onto the street, leaving the gate swinging open. "Max," Jenna said to her son. "Run over and hook the gate for Mama, will you?"

The towheaded little boy ran across the grass and through a flowerbed to do his mother's bidding.

"Thank you," Jenna said, smiling. "Look what Keely brought, strawberries."

Little Max broke into a grin. "Strawberries!" With a dirty fist he reached into the basket his mother offered and pulled out a handful.

"Maxwell! Don't be greedy," Jenna chided.

Keely laughed. "Oh, it's all right. That's what I brought them for." She watched as the child wandered out of earshot and then she turned to Jenna. "Why didn't anyone tell me? What shipment? What happened?"

Jenna crossed her arms over her chest, nibbling at her lower lip. She was dressed in a gown of

167

apple-green dimity, beribboned with a darker silk that made her appear a good ten years younger than her thirty years. "I'm sorry you had to find out that way from the old hen."

"Is that why Brock's been gone? Is he looking for the informant?"

"Keely, please don't ask me such questions. No one should know what goes on outside the circle. Micah's been wrong to tell you so much." Jenna motioned toward her son. "Max knows more of the goings-on in the King's Head than Christina."

"Not you too?" Keely asked, her face creased with disbelief. "You don't trust me?"

Jenna lowered her voice. "There's nothing really to tell. A shipment of our ammunition was seized by the British and not by accident."

"Is this the first time?"

Jenna glanced over at her son, then returned her gaze to Keely's hazel eyes. "The fourth time we've lost a shipment in three months. It's always been food before."

Keely pushed up off the bench. "Brock never said a word of misfortune," she said angrily. "I thought everything was going well for you. With the French into this he said the war would only go on another year!"

"Shhh," Jenna warned. "With France joining us as allies, the King and his Parliament are just beginning to realize that we're a true threat. Things may get worse before they get better. In the future we've got to be more careful where we speak and to whom."

Keely stroked her swollen belly. "Meaning me?" she asked fiercely, locking gazes with her friend.

Jenna caught Keely's hand. "Certainly not. I know you're to be trusted and Brock will learn it in time." She squeezed her friend's hand. "I even

168

know you're beginning to think what we say makes sense. You feel the need for that freedom in your heart just as we do."

Keely pulled her hand away. "I don't know what I feel. I thought you were my friend. You should have told me where Brock was going, even if he didn't."

"Where Brock went had nothing to do with the lost shipment."

Keely faced Jenna. "It didn't?"

Jenna lifted a hand in oath. "I swear it. Now sit down and let's have some of these strawberries. I'm tired of talking about this damned war!"

Keely eased down onto the bench and took the berry Jenna offered. "I wish the baby would hurry. Nothing seems to make sense these days."

Jenna plucked a cap from a berry and bit into it. "Mmm. It's not supposed to make sense when you're in love." She smiled then, waved at Max, who was floating leaves in the fountain.

Keely's eyes narrowed. "And who says I'm in love?" she asked indignantly.

Jenna kept smiling. "If only the two of you would spend less time denying your true feelings for each other and more time smoothing your relationship."

"I don't know what you're talking about." Keely looked away, watching a hummingbird hover over a long-trumpeted lily. "Our marriage was a business arrangement."

Jenna chuckled. "Yes, yes, that's what you keep telling yourselves. But I see the way you watch him when he's not looking."

"Jenna, you're being absurd."

She waved a hand, dismissing Keely's comment. "And I see the way he watches you. He's very jealous of Micah, you know. They're barely on

169

speaking terms."

"I know and it's stupid." Keely shifted her weight to find a more comfortable position. "I'm tired of his black moods and distrust of me. One minute he's kind and caring, but then he catches himself and he becomes cold and withdrawn." She put up her hands in desperation. "I can't live like this much longer."

"Things will be better once this matter is settled with the informant. It's got us all concerned. And once the baby is born, Brock will settle down. My Garrison certainly did."

Keely sighed heavily. "Well, it had better, because I'll pack my baggage and I'll return to England."

Jenna's brow furrowed. "You wouldn't leave him? Not your husband, the father of your child? Not Brock?"

"You don't live with him. You don't understand."

"Keely!" Jenna got to her feet, pacing in front of her friend. "What I see is a man who cares for you deeply. He's attentive, considerate."

Keely gave a snort. "It's all for show. He's not like that at home." She looked off into the distance. "At least not often."

"Take heed, Keely, you're lucky to have such a fine man." Jenna looked to her son, smiling sadly. "After all of this time I still miss Garrison so much. My arms still ache for him at night."

"You have your son," Keely offered quietly.

"Yes, I have my Max. He looks so much like his father that my grandmother swears she's seeing Garrison's ghost every time she lays eyes on him." Jenna smiled, calling out to Max at the fountain. "What are you doing?" she shouted, watching him dip his arm into the pool of water again and again.

"Trying to catch fish!" the little boy returned, splashing water into his lap.

170

Jenna ran down the path to kneel beside her son. Pushing up the three-quarter sleeves of her apple-green morning gown, Jenna plunged her arm into the icy water, laughing as she came up empty-handed.

Keely plucked another strawberry from the basket, laughing as Jenna tried again and again unsuccessfully to catch one of the small shimmering fish that swam in the stone pool beneath the fountain. Max hung on his mother's arm, giggling until she splashed water on him and he rolled in the grass.

Keely couldn't help wishing this was the kind of mother she would be to her son. She envied Jenna for taking motherhood so easily, so sensibly. She only hoped she would be able to do the same.

The following day Keely knelt in her garden and tugged furiously at the weeds that threatened to overrun her bed of sage. The late afternoon sun cast long shadows over the house, robbing her of the light necessary to distinguish the weeds from the herbs. "Guess I'm about done here," she told Micah, who had come for tea.

"About time." Micah stretched his long legs out in front of him, lifting his chin to soak up the last sun's rays of the day. "I'm quite certain Brock wouldn't want you out here doing this so late in your delicate condition."

Keely rubbed her nose with the back of her hand. "So don't tell him." She put out her hand. "Could you help me up? I seem to be so clumsy these last few weeks."

Micah leaped to his feet, taking Keely's gloved hand and lifting her gently.

She smiled. "Thanks," she said, taking off her garden gloves.

Micah removed a silk handkerchief from his waistcoat to dab at Keely's nose. "Stand still, Tory, you look like you've been rooting in the garden."

Keely laughed, pushing his hand aside. "Stop calling me that, it's not funny anymore. Now sit down and have your tea. You'll get your handkerchief dirty." She watched Micah return to his seat and pour them both a cup of tea from a silver pot.

"You're certainly in a sour mood today," Micah said with good humor.

Keely eased into her seat and took her teacup, sipping from it. "I'm sorry. Please accept my apologies. I don't know what's wrong with me today." She didn't want to admit to Micah that she was concerned about Brock's absence. More and more often these days she had an uneasy feeling in the pit of her stomach when he was away. I received a letter from Aunt Gwen yesterday," she said, changing the subject.

"You did?" Micah toyed with a silver-gilt button on his waistcoat. "How is she?"

"Wonderful." Keely lifted a dark eyebrow. "Although I understand one of her hounds, Rupert, came down with some sort of illness and Auntie had a surgeon sent from Rome to heal him."

"You think that's news, wait until I tell you what George Whitman's about."

Keely sighed. "Micah, are you certain you should be telling me these things? You know Brock would be furious."

Micah shrugged his broad shoulders. "I don't give a fig what Brock Bartholomew thinks, if you'll forgive me for saying so. He treats you so illy, you should have married me." He grasped her hand. "You could go away with me. We could go back to England."

Keely pulled her hand from his, laughing to make

172

light of the proposal. "You're being silly again. I don't want to hear it!"

"All right," Micah conceded, twisting a thread on his coat sleeve. "Then listen to this . . ."

After two cups of tea and half an hour's worth of gossip, Micah bid farewell to Keely and went on his way to play cards at the Golden Fleece tavern. Keely was just preparing to retire to her chamber when Jenna burst through the back gate of the garden. She had donned a simple housemaid's dress with a kerchief tied over her blond head. Had Keely not known Jenna so well, she'd never have recognized her.

"Jenna, what's wrong?" Keely cried out.

Jenna put her hand to her chest, breathing rapidly. "It's Brock, Keely, he's in danger!"

"Brock? What do you mean? Where is he?"

Jenna swallowed, trying to catch her breath. "I can't tell you the whole story, there isn't time, but I need you. Brock's going to kill me when he finds out I brought you into this, but if we don't do something, he'll be swinging from a noose by dawn."

Keely took a deep breath, fear rising in her throat. "What do you want of me? What can I do? Surely there must be—"

"No one must know I've been here, not even your servants," Jenna interrupted. "We must trust no one!"

Keely nodded, trembling. "Tell me what's wrong. How can I help?" She told herself it was for the babe, to save the child's father. Her hazel eyes were riveted to Jenna's.

"Brock is about to be set up. You must go and get him out of it."

"Me? Why can't you do it?"

She shook her head. "I think I know who's

173

betraying us . . ." Her dark eyes shone with a mixture of pain and anger.

"Who? Tell me!"

"No questions, you must promise that. The more you know, the more your life will be in danger."

"All right, no questions," Keely agreed. "But I still don't understand."

There's no time to argue." Jenna held Keely's face between her palms. "Listen to me and do exactly as I say if you want to save your husband's life."

"Yes?"

"You must go to a tavern on the docks at Leipsic, jut north of here."

"All right." Keely nodded, her eyes wide with fright.

"You must go inside and get Brock out before he passes his message."

"Spying?" Keely moaned. "He's spying? I thought he sold salt and transported soap! Micah never told me he was spying!"

"You promised no questions . . ."

Keely's face was wrought with fear for Brock. "How am I to . . . where are you going that you can't come with me?"

"Brock will be dressed as a smithy. He's been going by the name of Timothy Irons down there. Have you got that?"

"Timothy Irons, yes! I've got it."

Jenna's head snapped. "Did you hear that?"

"Hear what?" Keely looked in the direction of the house.

"I thought I heard a twig break. There's no one out here, is there?"

Keely gripped her hands until they were dead white. "No, of course not."

"Just the same, I have to go." Jenna settled her

174

dark gaze on her English friend. "Can you do it?"

"I can do it. I don't know how but I'll do it," Keely assured her.

"You know you lose your neutrality by helping us."

Keely shook her head. "I don't care about your damned causes, all I care about is my husband and this babe."

Jenna smiled. "I must go. God speed, Keely."

"God speed," Keely whispered, watching her friend disappear from the garden.

Coming around the hedge of boxwood, Keely nearly collided with Lucy. "Lucy! What are you doing here?" she demanded.

"Doin'? Takin' in the tray and teapot."

"You just came into the garden?" Keely interrogated.

The maidservant lifted the teapot onto the tray, averting her eyes. "Of course, ma'am. Ruth sent me. You know I'm not one to be looking for work."

"Where's Ruth?"

"Gone to her sister's. She's got a touch of the summer fever. You said Ruth could stay the night."

"And Blackie?"

Lucy balanced the silver tray on her hip. "I'm not supposed to say but there's a horse race down on the riverbed tonight. He's long gone."

"Good. Take the tray into the kitchen and then you may go."

"Go? Go where, Miss Keely?"

"I don't care. Wherever it is you go when you sneak out the window at night."

Lucy's eyes grew round. "Goodness me, Miss Keely, you know that wouldn't be me because I'd never—"

"You've got the night off," Keely interrupted.

175

"Now go on with you."

"You gonna be here all by yourself?" Lucy asked.

Keely hesitated for only an instant. "No . . . no, Master Brock is coming home and I want us to have the evening to ourselves."

"Ain't nothin' cooked in the kitchen."

"I'll cook something myself, now go on with you," Keely ordered tersely.

"Yes, ma'am." Lucy bobbed her head.

Keely waited until Lucy disappeared into the house and then she headed for Lloyd's office. From behind a row of dusty leather-bound books, she retrieved a pistol and then she hurried up the steps to her bedchamber. The minute Keely heard Lucy leave by the back door, Keely crossed into the servants' wing.

In the women's chamber she found one of Ruth's skirts made of blue tick, a soiled smock, and white wing cap of muslin. Stripping down to her chemise, she tugged on the woman's clothes, thankful that Ruth's abundant skirts fit over her round stomach. Adjusting the hat in a bit of cracked mirror hanging on the wall, Keely added a half handkerchief as a hood.

Scooping her clothes off the floor, she ran back to her bedchamber, dumped them onto the floor, and started for the barn. Ten minutes later Keely was headed north in an old wagon, Lloyd's ancient matchlock pistol resting beside her on the hard wooden seat.

Jenna moved silently in the darkness, her heart pounding in her ears, her fingers gripping the cold metal of a flintlock pistol. The person who waited at the end of this lonely dock on the bay was the traitor. This informant had betrayed the patriot committee and now risked Brock's life.

Jenna heard the sound of movement behind a stack of crates and she stopped, easing back the hammer of the pistol. "Come out where I can see your stinking face!" she called. The sound of footsteps echoed hollowly against the wood slats of the dock and Jenna took a deep breath, her finger poised to pull the trigger.

A dark figure appeared from behind the crates and took a step forward into the light of the three-quarter moon.

Jenna gasped in shock, the hand she held the pistol in falling uselessly to her side. "It *is* you!" she cried out.

And then there was a streak of bright light, the sound of a single shot fired, and the pungent smell of black powder in the air. Jenna crumpled to the ground under the impact of the lead bullet and for an instant she struggled for her life's breath before she surrendered and her body was still.

Chapter Fourteen

Keely wiped the perspiration from her brow with the sleeve of her borrowed clothing and looked up at the sun setting in the west. Dear God! She wasn't even sure how to find Leipsic. And what if she was too late? What if they had already taken Brock away?

Keely's hands trembled as she fingered the wide leather straps of the reins. "Come on," she urged the chestnut gelding that pulled the old wagon. "Get up!" She loosened the reins, giving them a shake, and the horse increased its steady pace down the hard-packed dirt road.

Following the road north, Keely kept her jaw set, "Stupid colonial bastard," she muttered aloud. "I told you this would come to no good end! I told you that you were a fool to put yourself up against the King and his soldiers!"

The chestnut's ears twitched at the sound of the human voice as the wagon rounded a bend and moved east toward the bay.

Impatiently, Keely lifted up a long-handled horse whip and cracked it over the gelding's head, urging him into a trot. "Stupid! Idiot! You want to be a hero? You want to leave your son with no father the way you were raised with no father?" Tears moistened her eyes and she dashed at them ruthlessly. The only reason I got into this wagon was for this child, she assured herself, running a hand over her swollen stomach. If it weren't for you, she told her unborn son, Brock Bartholomew could rot in hell for all I care!

Cursing her husband beneath her breath, Keely hung on tightly to the wagon seat, gritting her teeth as she was jarred again and again. By the time she entered the little seaport town of Leipsic, her back was aching and her stomach felt taut and achy. Spotting a sailor on the street, she called out to him. "Sir! Could you help me, please?"

Toddy MacFarlin turned to see where the pleasant feminine voice had come from but all he saw was a dirty-faced, pregnant wench passing on a wagon. He scratched his whiskered face. "You say something, sweet pie?" He stared up at Keely, wondering if the twilight was playing tricks on him.

"Yes. . . . yea," Keely returned, remembering the part she had to play. Perhaps Aunt Gwen's silly acting lessons would finally be of some use. "I'm lookin' fer the alehouse." She pulled up the reins, bringing the squeaky wagon to a holt. "My husband Timmy, I sent him to collect a fee from a cheatin' customer and we ain't seen a lick of him since. Drinkin' his pay more than likely, that or whorin'!"

Toddy laughed aloud. "Whew-wee! Glad you ain't my missus!" He smiled at the sight of her deep red hair peaking from beneath her cap. Beneath the soiled clothes and smudged face, he saw a real beauty.

"So, ye know where it is or don't ye?" she demanded, grinding her voice. "I ain't got all night. Got two babes at home to feed and the cow won't

179

come in from the pasture."

"And who might your husband be?" The sailor leaned on the wagon's wheel, taken with the girl.

Keely scowled. "The bastard's name be Timmy Irons, claims to be a smithy by trade, a louse by trade if you ask me."

Toddy chuckled. "The tavern, you think, huh?"

She nodded. "I'm in a hurry, left my oldest tendin' the fire, but he ain't really bright, Little Timmy ain't, just like his papa."

"You're in luck, 'cause I happen to be going in that very same direction! Gimme a ride?"

Keely lifted the reins, giving them a snap, and the old wagon jolted forward. "Jump in!" she called over her shoulder.

Laughing, Toddy MacFarlin ran beside the wagon and leaped aboard. "Just past that building and down that street," he told her. "Joe Galig's had that tavern on the beach for nigh on ten years now."

"This way?" Keely pulled on the right rein, urging the horse faster.

Toddy gripped the seat of the wagon as they went around the corner. "No indeed, Toddy don't envy that smithy tonight!"

Up ahead in the distance Keely spotted a large brick structure with light streaming from the windows. There was raucous laughter mixed with the sound of shrill feminine giggles coming from the tavern. "This it?"

"This be it!" The sailor pointed. "Just pull her around back."

The moment Keely pulled the wagon to a halt, she leaped to the ground. "Tie 'im up fer me, will you?" she called over her shoulder, hurrying across the grass.

Toddy laughed aloud, shaking his head as he watched the woman cross the side yard with long determined strides. "Give Timmy hell!" he hollered after her.

Racing around the building, clutching her extended stomach, Keely ran up the front steps. She swung the door open and stepped into the bright light of the smoke-filled public room. No one took notice of her in her serving woman's clothing as she stood there surveying the crowded room.

Joe Galig's tavern was a large one, built of red brick to stand the wind and salt air of the bay. Its public tap room was open, taking up half of the downstairs, while the second floor offered private rooms for dining and other pleasures. It was an honest establishment, though most of its patrons were smugglers and privateers.

The smoke from the huge fireplace along the wall mixed with the tobacco of men's pipes made Keely's stomach churn violently and her vision blurry. Pressing her hand to her stomach, she wiped at her eyes to relieve the sting. Where in the blast was Brock? It was sundown! Jenna had insisted she be there by sundown!

Then she spotted him. . . . Brock was sitting against the far wall at a small wooden table, a pewter mug in his hand. He was dressed in worn breeches and a cheaply made muslin shirt, his hair tucked beneath a three-cornered hat. He was in conversation with a dark-haired man with a mustache.

Keely took a deep breath, trying to block out the sound of her own pounding heart. Then lifting her chin, she hurried across the planked floor. "Timmy Irons, you drunken bastard!" she shouted aloud. Behind her she heard several chuckles.

Brock's head jerked up, his eyes widening for an instant before he allowed Timothy Irons's face to reappear.

"Timmy Irons, I'm calling you!" Keely shouted louder, praying no one heard the tremor in her voice. "I told you to get that money and get home!" She strode up to the table, her mouth twisted in anger.

"What are you doin' here?" Brock demanded.

"What am I doin' here? What the hell are you doin' here?" She reached out with a hand to cuff him on the ear just as she'd seen common folk do in the public square.

More masculine laughter followed as men turned to watch the incident with amusement.

"What is this, Tim?" the man across from Brock asked suspiciously.

"This is Timmy's wife, is what it is!" Keely said before Brock could open his mouth. "And Timmy's goin' home where he belongs!" She gripped Brock's arm and he came up out of his seat.

The instant he stood, Keely spotted a small brown paper packet sealed in wax resting on the center of the table. Without thought, she scooped it up. "This my money?" she demanded, giving Brock a shove toward the door. "It better be!"

Passing Brock, the packet clutched in her hand, she hurried ahead of him. The man from the table shouted after Brock, but he kept going, only a step behind Keely.

"Run!" Keely shouted as they came down the steps of the tavern. "There's a wagon around back!"

"There had better as hell be an explanation for this!" Brock insisted hotly.

Keely caught Brock's hand. "Just run!" Behind her in the distance she could hear an angry voice calling in the darkness.

"Tim? Tim, where are you? Find him!" shouted the voice. Angry voices and footsteps followed as men rushed down the tavern steps.

Coming around the side of the building, Keely climbed into the wagon as Brock untied the horse. Leaping in beside her, he cracked the horsewhip fiercely over the gelding's head and the wagon sped around the back of the tavern. "I know a way through the marsh," Brock breathed, leaning forward into the wind.

Keely clung to the side of the wagon in terror as it careened through the darkness. "Duck!" Brock shouted, and she did so without question. Hanging branches tore at her hair and arms, scratching her face, and then they were in a clearing.

Down a bumpy path they flew and then suddenly they were on softer ground. The smell of the salt air was stark and tangy as they descended into the marsh. Strange sounds filled Keely's ears and lights flickered in the distance through the tall reeds.

Brock grasped her hand, forcing it to his arm. "Hang on to me!" he ordered. "I think we've lost them, but I'm afraid to slow down. Are you all right?"

Keely nodded numbly. "Just keep moving," she insisted, raising her voice to be heard over the pounding of the horse's hooves and the creaking of the swaying wagon.

For a long time they stayed on the path through the eerie marsh and then suddenly the wagon leaped through another entryway of hanging vines and tree limbs and they were on an established road again. Brock pulled the wagon to a halt. "Keely." He took her by the shoulders. "What the hell is this all about?"

Keely's mouth fell open. Rain was beginning to fall softly, hitting her face. "You ungrateful clod! How about a thank-you?" She squirmed from his grip, taking the brown paper packet from her skirts and throwing it at him.

183

The packet of papers hit Brock in the chest and he snatched them up, stuffing them into his shirt. "You shouldn't have come. How did you know I was there?"

Her hazel eyes narrowed dangerously. "I risked my neck to get you out of there and all you can think of is how I knew where you were!"

"Don't avoid my question." He wiped the rain from his eyes. "I have to check the wagon wheel, something's loose." He swung down onto the ground and knelt by the rear left wheel. "Now tell me what you know of this. . . ."

Keely yanked the reins from off the seat and gave them a snap.

"What are you doing?" Brock shouted as the wagon rolled forward.

"I'm going home!" she returned, livid with rage. Now that Brock was safe, she could be angry with him again.

"What about me?" he called in disbelief. The rain was coming down harder now, drowning out his voice.

She turned to see Brock standing in the center of the road with his hands planted on his hips, his hat tucked beneath his arm. Rain ran down his face, plastering his raven hair to his head. "Walk!"

"Keely! What's wrong with you? What's going on?"

"You were set up," she answered over her shoulder, continuing down the road.

"I *know* that!" Brock broke into a run, going after her. "But how did you know? How did you find me? Keely, you're not going to leave me here! It's a good five miles into town!" He was running in earnest now, but the wagon was moving faster down the slick road.

"Keely!" he shouted as she disappeared into the

darkness. Realizing it was impossible to catch up with her now, he stopped running and threw his wet hat to the ground, silently cursing all women.

By the time Keely reached home, she was soaked through and shivering. The dull ache in her lower back had increased to a throbbing pain and her swollen stomach felt taut and heavy. Leaving the wagon in the barn to be unhitched by the bewildered stable boy, she hurried into the house and up to her bedchamber.

Peeling off her wet clothes, Keely slipped into a flannel sleeping gown and got into bed, shivering but too weary to get up and light a fire to drive off the chill. She fell asleep almost instantly, but woke a few hours later to a painful tightening in her abdomen.

"Oh God," Keely murmured aloud. "It can't be, not the baby!" She stroked her stomach, trying to convince herself that it was just the rough ride in the wagon and that the pain would subside. Frightened, she lay perfectly still in the bed, forcing herself to breath evenly.

What was she going to do if the pains didn't stop? Lucy and Ruth were gone, only the two stable hands were on the property, and they were long asleep. If she needed to, she decided, she would get up and call one of them to go for the midwife. How could she have been so stupid to have risked her baby's life like this, she wondered miserably.

A groan escaped her lips as the next wave of pain came and went. Catching her breath, she clutched the counterpane, trying not to panic. *I've got to get someone,* she told herself, but when she tried to rise up out of the bed, another contraction seized her, making her gasp.

Brock heard Keely cry out in pain as he opened

the front door. "Keely!" he shouted, throwing his hat to the floor. "Keely, where are you?"

There was no reply from the dark house until Keely moaned again. "Keely!" Brock raced up the front staircase and down the hall toward their bedchamber. "Keely?" he demanded.

"Here," she answered weakly as he flung open the door. "I'm here. . . ."

In the darkness Brock crossed the bedchamber in three long strides. "What is it?" he demanded, leaning over her in the bed.

Keely reached for his hand, needing his comfort. "The baby," she whispered. She felt herself rising in another wave of pain and she bit down hard on her lip to keep from crying out.

Brock swore beneath his breath as he fumbled with the lamp beside the bed. Finally succeeding in lighting it, he drew it closer to the bed. Keely's face was pale and dotted with perspiration; her hands clutched the bedsheets tightly. "You're going to be all right," he whispered, shaken. "I'll get the midwife."

Keely nodded. "Hurry," she breathed. "They're coming faster."

Brock lit two more lamps in the room then went down the back staircase, out of the house, and into the barn. "Samuel!" he bellowed. "Samuel get up and get down here before your ass is in a sling!"

A minute later, the sleepy stable hand appeared, rubbing his eyes with one hand as he hitched up his breeches with the other. "Yes, sir?"

"Take the two-seater and fetch the midwife immediately."

The boy's eyes widened. "The missus?" He gulped.

"Just go on and be quick about it!" Brock ordered sharply.

186

Samuel nodded vigorously. "Yes, sir, yes, sir!"

Brock returned to the house, stopping only to draw a bucket of cold water from the well. Rushing up the back staircase, the water sloshing down his leg, he burst into the bedroom. "I'm back," he soothed.

Keely opened her eyes long enough to see him setting the bucket on the floor. "Water. I'm so thirsty."

Picking up an empty teacup from the side table, he dipped a cup of water and brought it to her, sitting down on the edge of the bed.

Keely panted, leaning forward. "Thank you. . . ."

Lifting her gently with his hand, he guided the cup to her lips. "The midwife is on her way. It won't be long now."

"That's good because this isn't going to be long. You son is anxious. I thought this was supposed to take longer." She smiled then stiffened as another labor pain rose. Brock set the cup down, pushing his hand into hers.

"Squeeze it!" he told her. "It will help."

She did as he said, squeezing with all her might until the contraction subsided.

"Better?" he asked.

She nodded. "How did you know that would help?"

"Once I had a bullet in my leg when I was living on the Ohio. When my father's sister took it out for me, she gave me a stick wrapped with hide to squeeze." He smiled, brushing Keely's damp hair off her forehead. "It looks like you nearly did this on your own. If I'd not caught a ride halfway into town, I wouldn't have made it in time."

"It's too early for the babe," she breathed.

"A little, but he'll be fine. Remember, I was an early babe too. . . ." He grinned.

Catching the joke, Keely smiled back and then was overcome by another spasm of pain.

The minute Brock heard the front door swing open, he released Keely's hand and went into the hall. "Up here," he called. "Hurry!" Returning to Keely's side, he clasped her hand tightly. "The midwife's here now, Keely. Everything's going to be fine."

At the sound of footsteps, Brock turned to see a tall, painfully thin woman in a mobcap come through the door. "You can go now, Master Bartholomew," she ordered as she set down the basket she held in her hand. "I'll call you when it's over."

Brock looked at the slovenly dressed woman, her apron stained with blood. "Who are you?"

"Sadie Marboro. Ye called for the midwife, didn't ye?" She tucked a tangled curl behind her ear with a dirty hand.

"You're not touching my wife," Brock stated flatly.

"What?" She stared in disbelief at the savage gentleman. She'd heard that he was odd, but no one had said he was deranged.

"I said you'll not lay a hand on my wife. You're dismissed."

Sadie dropped a hand to her hip. "And why might that be?"

"You're dirty! For Christ's sake, woman, you've still got blood on your dress from the last birthing!"

The midwife shrugged. "It were a difficult one. The mother didn't make it, but Jonah White's got a fine son, his seventh, I think."

"Get out," Brock repeated, releasing Keely's hand to rise up off the bed.

"And who's going to deliver your child?" Sadie

188

indicated with her hand. "From the sound of her breathin', it's near time."

He lowered his voice, not wanting to frighten Keely any more than she already was. "I'll get someone else." He strode to the door, waiting.

She laughed. "Ain't no one else. Jesse's in Chestertown with her daughter's first layin'-in and Laura Mae's come down with an early case a' summer fever. So you're stuck with me."

"Brock," Keely called from behind him.

The sound of Keely's pained voice made him shiver. "Like hell I am!" he said through gritted teeth. "Now get your basket of filthy rags and get out!"

Sadie snatched up her basket indignantly. "And who's going to deliver this baby, *sir?* You?"

"I'll do it myself before I let you touch her with your infested ways!" he bellowed. "Now get out before I carry you out!"

Sadie hurried out of the bedchamber. "I'll be chargin' you just the same," she shouted, her voice echoing in the hallway. "Ye've wasted my precious time, ye have!"

Brock slammed the bedchamber door and went to Keely, kneeling on the floor.

"Where's the midwife?" Keely asked groggily. "Where's she going?"

Brock smoothed her brow with a bit of cloth dipped in the cool water. "She's gone."

"Gone?" Keely clutched her stomach as another labor pain invaded her thoughts. "Gone where?" she managed as the contraction subsided.

"I sent her away. She was filthy; she had the blood of a dead woman on her."

Keely forced her eyes open. "You have to get someone. Brock, it's not going to be much longer."

He patted her hand. "It's going to be all right.

You just hang on. I'll be back up in a minute."

Releasing her hand, Brock went down the back steps two at a time, mentally figuring what he needed. He'd seen only one birth out on the trail when his father's tribe had been moving. But his old aunt had instructed him well, telling him anyone over the age of eight summers, male or female, ought to know how to bring one of God's gifts into the world.

Nervously, Brock fumbled around the kitchen, and finding what he needed, he retrieved an armful of clean sheets from the linen closet. By the time he made it back to the bedchamber, Keely was half sitting up.

She looked up at him wearily. "Did you find someone?"

He shook his head. "Don't worry. I've done this before."

"You?" She pulled the sheet up. "No."

"Don't be silly." Placing the clean sheets on a chair near the bed, he sat beside her, taking her hand. "I'm your husband."

A blush crept across Keely's already flushed cheeks. "I know but —" Another labor pain rose, cutting off her words, and Brock got up to prepare for the birth of his first son.

Chapter Fifteen

Keely sighed, snuggling down in the fresh-smelling blankets, her small bundle pressed to her side. "I'm sorry the babe isn't a boy," she told Brock sleepily.

He laughed, coming to sit down beside her on the edge of the bed. "Who said I wanted a boy?" he asked, pressing a finger to the tiny starfish hands that waved in the air.

Keely smiled, tired but content. Her hazel eyes ____led with a pride for her husband she'd never ____ He had cared for her so tenderly, warding ____ears with his quiet assurance as he'd ____ir child into the world. "Every man ____," she teased softly.

____t time." He stroked the cap of dark red fuz____ covered the baby's perfectly shaped head. "But this girl-child, she was meant to be." He brushed the baby's cheek with a finger and she turned her head instinctively toward it. "I think she's hungry."

Pulling aside her clean nightgown, Keely moved the baby to her bare breast, sighing. "She's very strong."

"And only a little small," Brock assured her.

Keely's eyes met Brock's. "I'm sorry I left you on the road like that."

"In the rain . . ." he added.

She smiled. "In the rain. But you wouldn't listen to me." Her hazel eyes searched his. "Jenna said you were in danger and that I had to go."

He nodded cautiously. "So it was Jenna and not Micah?"

Keely frowned. "Did Micah know too?"

Brock brushed a lock of bright red hair off Keely's cheek. "We'll talk of it later. You get some sleep now." He motioned to the window. "It's nearly dawn."

Her eyes drifted shut. "All right, we'll talk of it later," she conceded. "But"—her eyes flew open—"we *will* talk."

"I promise." Brock lowered his head to brush his lips against Keely's. *Thank God she's all right,* was all he could think.

Keely savored the feel of Brock's lips against hers as he lingered over her. Of its own accord her hand lifted to stroke his striking jawline. "Thank you," she whispered, closing her eyes again.

Brock guided her hand beneath the co̶ leaned to kiss his daughter's tiny head. "̶ murmured. "Sleep now."

Two days later Keely sat up in bed, ̶ ̶ ̶om a dinner tray Brock had brought himself. Beside the bed, baby Laura Gwen slept contentedly in the cradle Brock had slept in as a child.

"Did you eat?" Keely asked, offering a fork full of buttered, mashed turnip.

"I did." Brock leaned forward in the chair, opening his mouth to accept the offering. "But you know me. Always hungry."

"You look like you finally got some rest." Keely sampled a slice of roasted chicken, trying to sound nonchalant. Brock had not come to her bed last night as she had expected and she was worried. Did he think that now that they had a child his husbandly duties were fulfilled? Did he intend never to sleep with her again? "Where did you sleep?" she asked.

"Lloyd's room. I didn't want to disturb you and the babe." He crossed his long legs in front of him.

"You wouldn't have disturbed us." She couldn't admit to him that she'd missed his warm body pressed against hers. She could barely admit it to herself.

Brock ran a hand through his dark hair. "Keely, I have something to tell you," he said, changing the subject.

"Oh?"

He lifted his dark gaze, settling it upon her lovely oval-shaped face. "It's Jenna. She's dead."

Keely's breath caught in her throat. "Dead?" She can't be. She was here the night I came to the tavern to get you. *She* saved your life!"

Brock leaned forward, resting his forearms on his muscular thighs. "Keely, she's been murdered. Shot. I have to know where Jenna went and who knew." His bronze face was etched with lines of vital concern.

"I . . . I don't know." Keely was in such shock that she barely heard herself speak.

"What do you mean, you don't know?" he demanded. "As far as we can figure, you were the last one to see her alive. She was killed down on the docks about the same time you were saving my hide in Leipsic."

Tears gathered in the corners of her eyes. "There

193

you go with that tone again." She pushed her tray away.

"What tone?"

Her lips trembled. "Accusing. I did nothing wrong! Jenna was my friend and I loved her!"

"You expect me to believe she didn't tell you where she was going?" Brock stood, beginning to pace the hardwood floor, his high leather boots clicking rhythmically.

"Yes, I expect you to believe me because it's the truth. All she said was that she thought she knew who was betraying you and your friends at the King's Head." Keely tried to hold back her tears. After all they'd been through, after she'd rescued him in that tavern, he still didn't trust her and the pain that that caused was almost as great as the pain she felt for the loss of her friend.

"What else did she say?"

She sighed. "That it was safer if I didn't know where she was going."

"She gave you no indication of who it might be?"

"None," Keely answered numbly.

"And no one else heard your conversation? She didn't tell Micah?"

"Micah?" Keely looked up. "He wasn't here."

"But he'd been here . . ."

"You have the servants spying on me now, do you?" She sniffed, reaching for her handkerchief. *How could Jenna be dead?*

Brock's mouth twitched. "Certainly not, but you know Lucy and her tongue."

Suddenly Keely recalled Jenna's thinking she had heard someone in the garden and then remembered the sudden appearance of Lucy. She said nothing.

"Keely, this is very serious," he continued. "Can't you remember anything Jenna said that might be of help?"

"Listen to yourself!" Keely flared, the reality of Jenna's death finally sinking in. "Jenna's been murdered and you're worried about who's telling your stupid secrets! She's dead because of you and those secrets!"

"Keely, I—"

"It's your fault. All of you!" she accused. "If it weren't for this inane *cause* of yours, Jenna would still be alive!" Tears began to roll down her cheeks. "Max would still have a mother."

"I can see that you're distraught. I'll come back later," Brock said tersely.

"Distraught! You're damned right I'm distraught! You killed Jenna just as sure as if you'd pulled the trigger," she sobbed.

Pain flickered in Brock's dark eyes. "Enough, Keely! I've had it with your sharp tongue. You don't know what you're talking about. I cared for her too!" He ran his palm over his face. "Don't you think I feel responsible enough already without you flinging accusations?"

Keely slid out of the bed, padding barefoot across the hardwood floor to stand before Brock.

"Get back in bed," he ordered, catching her wrist.

"You ought to feel guilty! Don't you see there's no sense in all of this," she shouted. "Don't you realize you can't win? He's the damned King of England!"

Brock held her in his angry dark gaze. "Don't you realize I must win?"

Keely's lower lip trembled as she lifted her hand to rest on Brock's chest. "What is it that makes me so angry with you and yet . . ." Her breath was audible in the room as she stared up at his finely sculpted bronze face.

Suddenly Brock pulled her roughly against him,

his mouth coming down hard against hers.

"Damnation, woman!" he murmured against her lips. "Sometimes you make me forget . . ."

She clung to him, still angry but needing to feel the strength of his embrace. "Forget what?"

"Nothing." He brushed a lock of hair off her cheek and then swung her into his arms, carrying her to the bed and setting her gently down. "Now rest. I'm having a meeting at the King's Head."

"Promise me you'll find her killer," she said quietly, grasping his hand.

"I'll find him . . ."

By the time Brock strode into the King's Head tavern, he had regained his composure. He forced himself to push aside his own guilt and the pain of Keely's words. If he was going to find Jenna's killer, he knew his head couldn't be clouded with emotion. He was convinced now that the betrayer, perhaps even Jenna's killer, was among them. He didn't have time to mull over his wife's accusing words, or his own mixed feelings for her.

"Afternoon, gentlemen." Brock tossed his cocked hat onto the table.

"Afternoon, Brock," came a chorus voices. They were all there — George, John, even Jenna's brother, Manessah.

Brock took a seat, studying the faces of one, of the men who sat around the trestle table. When his eyes met Manessah's, he offered his hand. "You didn't have to come today."

Manessah nodded his blond head solemnly, accepting his friend's gesture. "I know, but I wanted to."

"Your mother?"

"She's all right. She understands. It's like Jenna

196

always said." Manessah lifted his head to look at the others. "We all take the risk because we fight for what we believe in. Jenna and Garrison fought for little Max's freedom and now I fight for it. We all do."

"So what do we know?" Micah asked, pushing a small gold pick between his teeth.

"Very little," Brock responded coolly. "Keely was last to see her alive."

"Your English wife?" John's brow furrowed. "What do you mean?"

"Jenna came to our garden to tell Keely that I was in danger. She sent Keely to get me out of that tavern while she went, I presume, to meet the person she thought was betraying us."

George stroked his whiskered white chin. "So what you're saying, Brock, is that you think the person who is passing our information into the wrong hands may also be the very person who killed Jenna."

Brock waited until a barmaid had set his cup of tea in front of him and had walked away. "It's very likely, George, but it could have been an accomplice. We just don't know how deep this is."

Issac hit the table with his fist, jarring his jack of ale. "And the only connection we've got is your wife? Damn it, Brock! You should have sent her to England when we told you to."

"Issac, we've had this discussion before. I know how you all feel about Keely, but it's not her." His dark eyes met his friend's. "I'm telling you, it's not her!"

George gave a snort. "Well, it sure as hell is somebody!"

Manessah lifted his jack of ale. "It's not Keely, that's too simple. Besides, she and Jenna were friends. You know Jenna always had an instinct for this kind of thing; she'd have known if it was Keely long ago." He looked to Brock. "What of our households?"

Brock nodded slightly to Manessah, thanking him silently for his words in support of Keely's innocence. "Could be. No matter how often we warn each other that what we say is not to be repeated in any form outside this circle, I know it's done. We're all guilty. I know I am."

"Ah-hah!" Issac leaned in. "So you admit your wife may know particulars of our movement."

"No! I'm very careful. She knows less than your stable boys, for Christ's sake!"

"Now there's a thought," Manessah interrupted.

"Our servants?" Micah probed.

"Exactly. They see us come and go day and night. They move through our houses silently. We've gotten so used to them that we don't notice when they're there and when they're not."

Brock leaned back in his chair, eyeing Issac. "That's a good point, Manessah."

"So what are we going to do?" George asked.

Brock tugged at his long, dark braid. "For now, nothing. I'll continue my investigation into Jenna's murder and let you know when I find something."

Micah smiled cynically. "You'll tell us when you know something? Does that mean you don't think you can trust your friends?" he said slowly, drawling out his words.

Brock scowled. "Don't be ridiculous, Micah. Who's side are you on?"

Micah lifted his hands in surrender. "Your side, friend. Just asking."

Brock turned from Micah. "From today on we must be extra careful. Now that Sir Clinton has replaced Howe as commander of the English forces, we must take the advantage while he's regrouping.

198

With the French joining us, Mother England finally sees what a threat we are. There'll be no mercy. We're no longer just a band of outlaws in the King's mind; he finally recognizes the seriousness of the matter."

"So we just go on as before?" George asked hotly. "We just forget that Jenna was one of us and that now she's dead."

"No! We don't forget, George." Brock lifted a fist in the air. "But we go on. Jenna would have expected us to. I'll find her killer, but in the meantime business goes on as usual."

"I agree," Manessah said. "Now let's stop this bickering among us. We've been together too long to let anything like this come between us."

Brock sighed heavily, looking from one man to the next. "This first problem at hand is finding a replacement for the Timothy Irons connection."

"A pity," John spoke up. "It worked so well with the English troops in Philadelphia."

"Well, I have a feeling they may be evacuating the city soon. Anyone have any ideas?"

Everyone began to speak at once until Brock could hear no one. "Gentlemen, please." He stood to get everyone's attention. "One at a time, you'll all get a chance to have your say."

Six weeks later Keely sat in the hot June sun in the garden mending one of Brock's shirts. At her feet, in a basket, Laura slept peacefully, her tiny fist pressed to her mouth. In her slumber she sucked at her hand, making Keely laugh aloud, her breast swelling with pride.

The baby was all that she had expected, yet somehow more. Keely had never realized it would be possible for her to love anyone as much as she loved her daughter.

Laura's arrival had also raised feelings inside Keely for Brock, emotions she didn't quite understand, emotions she wasn't certain she welcomed. Brock's distrust in her infuriated Keely, and yet in the same breath she felt the need to prove herself. Too often these days she found herself thinking of Brock as she went about her daily duties. She caught herself recalling conversations with him, remembering his touch as he took Laura from her arms.

Since the baby's birth Brock had slept in Lloyd's bedchamber to keep from disturbing his wife and daughter. But sitting in the sun this morning, Keely decided it was high time her husband returned to his own bed. She missed the sound of his steady breathing in the night and she yearned for the feel of his arms wrapped around her. She had recovered from Laura's birth and it was time she claimed her wifely rights again, she thought, laughing aloud at her lewd thoughts. In the last few months she had come to terms with her desire for her husband, accepting their lovemaking as what Brock said it was, a gift from God to be treasured.

The sound of a feminine giggle broke Keely from her reverie. Lucy's shrill voice was coming from the corner of the garden near the back gate. Although Keely could not see Lucy, she could tell by the serving girl's voice that she was speaking with someone.

Curious, Keely put her mending down and moved quietly along the boxwood hedge that obscured her view of the back gate. Moving a little closer, Keely made out the rumbling sounds of a male voice, interspersed with Lucy's high-pitched tones.

"Now, Georgie, ye know ye shouldn't've come here!" came Lucy's voice, followed by a giggle.

"I know, but you didn't come last night," answered the man. "I missed you. Let me in, just for a moment."

Keely stopped, squinting to try to see through the dense green foliage of the ancient boxwood. Through a tiny hole she spotted a glimpse of Lucy's blue-tick skirt.

"A bad'en you are, Georgie. You know what would happen to me if anyone saw you here! Weren't you supposed to report back this morning?" Lucy said.

Hearing the click of the back gate, Keely pushed her hand through the hole in the boxwood, forcing back several branches. Just as the gate squeaked open, she gained full vision of Lucy, and the sight of the man that came through the gate made Keely's blood run ice cold.

The young blond-haired man was dressed in a short red coatee, faced with green. On his head was a black leather cap with a red plume.

Keely clamped her hand down hard on her mouth to keep from making a sound as Lucy flung herself into the man's arms, laughing and kissing him. *A British soldier!* Lucy's latest man was a British infantryman! Swallowing hard, Keely turned, pressing her back against the boxwood.

Was Lucy Brock's betrayer? Had her gossiping finally gotten her into trouble that she couldn't get out of? Was it Lucy who had followed Jenna and killed her or had her killed? Even with the obvious evidence against Lucy, Keely found it difficult to believe. It was too easy.

"Keely!" came Brock's voice through the hedgerow. "Keely, where are you?"

Smoothing her dimity skirts, Keely came around the boxwood hedge, smiling. "I thought you'd gone to Chestertown." She tried to look unruffled as she glanced up at him.

He lifted his daughter out of the basket and brought her to his shoulder. The infant wiggled contentedly, cooing as Brock poked her small hand with his finger. "I got a late start. I may just wait and go tomorrow. I came back for some charts I left in the study. What were you doing in the back?"

"Doing?" Keely didn't want to tell Brock anything about Lucy's British soldier until she found out more. She was determined to make no false accusations this time. "Oh, I . . . I saw a rabbit." She looked up at him, shrugging. "I wanted to see where it went."

Brock laughed, draping an arm over her shoulder. "I sometimes wish I had the time to chase after rabbits." He pressed a kiss to Keely's temple, inhaling her heavenly scent.

In the last week or so Brock often found himself coming home during the day for silly reasons, even postponing long-overdue trips. Keely's voice haunted him as he spoke with his crewmen; her scent invaded his thoughts as he tried to concentrate on columns of figures. Memories of her touch made him dreamy and unproductive. She was becoming an obsession.

Keely smoothed the fine silk of his waistcoat, adjusting his stock. "Well, get your charts and be on with you. You've wakened Laura and now she'll want to eat."

Brock laughed, leaning to press his face to the bodice of Keely's gown. "I envy her then," he teased.

Keely stroked Brock's cheeks. "Then come back to my bed, husband."

Brock lifted his head, his dark eyes sparkling. "Methinks that's an invitation," he said slowly, his

202

voice taking on an edge of eroticism.

She smiled secretly. "Is it? Give me the child and go now. I've woman's work to do." She took Laura from his arms and put her back in the basket. When she straightened up again, Brock was still standing there, dressed handsomely in a coat of burgundy with matching breeches.

"Come here," he commanded softly.

She came to him, lifting her arms to rest them on his broad shoulders. With one hand she grasped his thick ebony braid, giving it a playful tug. "I'd like to have seen what you looked like all dressed like a savage," she said thoughtfully.

"Oh, you would, hmmm?" He kissed the hollow in her shoulder.

Keely arched her neck, reveling in the feel of his hot, wet mouth pressed to her pale skin. When his lips met hers, it was a slow, sensual onslaught, a kiss of promise. Their breaths mingled and she strained against him, threading her fingers through the stray tendrils of hair at the nape of his neck. She was consumed by the force of his kiss and overwhelmed by the power he held over her.

"I don't know that I can get home tonight," Brock whispered in her ear. "I'm expected in Chestertown."

"I'll be here tomorrow," was her reply.

"I'd carry you to our bedchamber now but one of my men is waiting for me out front. I've a meeting with Caesar Rodney this morning."

Keely pushed up on her toes to kiss Brock full on the mouth. "Then go," she teased, her voice nonchalant. "And I'll see you when I see you, cousin."

"Wench!" Brock kissed her impulsively then walked away. Keely watched him until he disappeared into the house, admiring his long stride.

Once Brock's carriage had departed, Keely returned to the boxwood hedge to check on Lucy, but she was gone. Determinedly, Keely then retrieved Laura and headed for the house. She'd look into the matter of Lucy and her British soldier, and when she had sufficient evidence, she would tell Brock.

"If your papa has his culprit," she whispered to the baby, "then he'll no longer have any reason to distrust me."

Chapter Sixteen

That night Keely retired early, tucking Laura into her cradle in the small nursery connecting to her bedchamber and then climbing into her own empty bed. Though she had half hoped Brock would put off his journey to Chestertown, she had received no message, so she knew he'd gone and wouldn't return until late tomorrow.

Falling asleep almost immediately, Keely awoke a few hours later to the sound of night peepers and the caress of the soft night breeze on her face. Opening her eyes slowly, she was startled to find the large windows of her bedchamber open. As she blinked back the confusion of slumber, she came to the stark realization that the windows had been closed when she went to bed. Who had opened them? She was such a light sleeper that no one could come into their chamber without waking her.

A cold shiver of fear ran down Keely's spine as she bolted upright. Laura Gwen! Was Laura all right? Just as Keely's bare feet hit the floor, she spotted the outline of someone or something standing amid the swaying curtains. The light of the moon poured through the windows, casting a pale river of glimmering shadows across the hardwood floor and up the walls. The figure stood inhumanly still, staring into the darkness at her.

Though Keely wanted to scream, no sound came from her mouth as she stood in indecision. She could have easily gotten to the hallway door before who or whatever it was caught her, but Laura was sleeping in the nursery and she couldn't leave her daughter, not even long enough to get help.

Standing in her thin white sleeping gown, her eyes narrowed. "What do you want?" she asked shakily. Logic told her it was a person, a man, though she couldn't hear him breathe or see anything more than the glimmer of the whites of his eyes.

When the man made no response, she lifted her hand slowly to touch the porcelain knob of the nightstand next to the bed. Carefully she eased open the drawer and slipped her hand inside, all the while watching the shadowy man. When her hand touched the cold steel of Brock's long hunting knife, a smile crossed her lips. The weight of the blade in her palm gave her the confidence to take the first step forward.

"Stand back," she ordered. "You can have what you wish, but first I take my child."

The curtains moved and the man leaped from the shadows. Keely's mouth fell open as a scream rose in her throat and she lifted the knife to defend herself. The man's hand came down hard on her mouth before she could make a sound, and her knife went clattering to the floor.

"Damnation, woman," came Brock's voice. "You nearly slit my throat with that thing . . ." He slid his hand from her trembling lips.

"Br-Brock?" Keely turned to face her attacker. "You son of a—" She bit off her own words as

206

she caught the first glimpse of him.

Brock stood barefoot, his ebony hair unbound and flowing down his back, the briefest loinskin tied around his middle. His skin shimmered in the moonlight, enhancing the form of his broad shoulders and sinewy thighs. Standing here in the eerie light of midnight, he appeared more like a statue of bronze than a human of flesh.

"Wha-what are you doing?" Keely whispered, still in awe. "You scared the wits out of me!"

He laughed deep in his throat, taking her in his arms. "I'm sorry. I didn't think you'd wake up; I was just going to slip into bed beside you." He took her in his arms, kissing the hollow of her neck.

"I still don't understand." Her trembling hands grazed over the wide expanse of his back, making her shiver despite the warmth of the night's breeze.

"I'm playing *Indian*," he said, feeling rather foolish.

"You're what?" She looked up at him and he planted a kiss on the end of her nose.

"You said you wanted to see what I looked like as a Delaware brave. I had a hell of a time finding this damned loincloth."

Keely broke into a smile. "You did this for me?" She brushed her fingers over his broad cheeks, noting the splash of green color across them. "For me?"

"I didn't think you'd come after me with a knife!" He ran his hand through her mane of thick hair, relishing the feel of it. "You have a way of making me feel like an ass, cousin. I should know by now that you're not one for jokes."

"Oh, Brock." She took his face between her palms, kissing him on the mouth. "Let me see you." She was laughing, but she was touched that he would have made such a gesture. He had cared enough to grant her a whim. He had heard what she'd said and he had acted on it. The thought was startling.

Brock stepped back, releasing her begrudgingly. "It's a long time since I last shed my white man's clothing."

"And you did it for me." Keely clasped her hands together, her eyes shimmering with unshed tears. The sight of Brock's nearly naked form made her heart race and her palms grow damp and warm. Her eyes met his. "I like it, husband," she whispered, an edge of sensuality in her voice.

Brock took in the sight of his wife standing in the moonlight in her white gown, the traces of her curves outlined by the wispy-thin material. Since the birth of their daughter, her hips had widened slightly while her waist had narrowed. Her breasts had taken on a full roundness that she'd not had before.

The familiar sensation of the tightening of his groin made him reach out to her. What was this he felt inside, he wondered as he buried his face in her sweet-smelling hair. What was this ache for her? It wasn't just physical. He wanted more. He wanted to possess her thoughts, her being, and it frightened him. He had been in love with Elizabeth, he was sure of that, but these feelings for Keely were different—they ran deeper. His ache for her was constant of late.

"I've missed you here in my bed," Keely whispered as their lips met. He tasted clean and fresh with a hint of mystery, like the night air.

Her words made Brock shiver with anticipation. Who would have guessed this sassy wench of a woman-child could ever have tempted him like this? He lifted his hand to her breast, cupping it, feeling its weight as he stroked the bud of her nipple with his thumb.

Keely groaned, resting her head on Brock's bare chest, reveling in the sensations he created with his fingers. She had dreamed of him touching her like this, only the dreams were never this fulfilling, not like the heat of his caress. When Brock kissed Keely this time, she wrapped her arms around his neck, clinging to him, inviting the force of his rising desire. The feel of his strength matched to her weakness made her limbs tingle hot with bittersweet longing.

Lifting Keely into his arms, Brock carried her to their bed, laying her down gently among the tangled sheets and counterpane. "Take off the gown," he murmured quietly as he tugged on the thong of his loinskin.

Keely smiled, feeling wicked as she sat up and pulled the sleeping gown over her head, her intense gaze never breaking from his.

Stretching over her, Brock covered her soft body with his, stroking her flesh with his palm, burying his face in the valley of her breasts. The amulet she wore around her neck was cold against his lips as he lifted it over her head with his teeth and set it gently on the pillow.

Keely laughed huskily, arching her back beneath him, lifting her hips rhythmically. She was lost in a swirl of aching want. It had been too long since their bodies had met as one and she longed for that sweet union. Keely raked her nails over Brock's back, writhing, calling his name as he suckled at her breast.

Twisting Brock's thick black mane in her fingers, she forced his mouth down on hers, her tongue darting out to taste of him. "I want you," she whispered. "Now, Brock, please . . ."

Brock brushed the damp tendrils of hair from her cheek, kissing her love-bruised lips. It was difficult for him to believe that this was his wife who gazed up at him with such rapturous abandon. "God, Keely, I . . ." The word *love* was on the tip of his tongue as he slipped his engorged manhood into her, but he said no more.

Lost in the throes of full arousal, Brock's words went unheeded as Keely lifted her hips, matching his rhythm. Just a few short strokes and she was clinging to him, crying out with abandon as she surrendered to an ocean of complete and utter fulfillment. A moment later, Brock pushed home and then he, too, was silent.

It was a long time before Keely's breath finally came evenly and she lifted her dark lashes to stare up at her husband's face. It was a perfect face and suddenly she was afraid she was in love with him.

Brock lifted the lid of a barrel and peered in, then dropped it again and made a mark on his sheet of paper. He moved on to the next barrel. The dock was alive with the sights and sounds of a sunny July afternoon as he worked his way down the row of assorted kegs and crates. A scrawny half-man half-boy followed on his captain's heels, nodding vigorously.

"Yes, sir. I think I got it now," Marky Mcgraw murmured eagerly.

Brock squinted in the bright sun. "You told me that yesterday, Marky, but you still managed to lay level an entire week's worth of figures." He sighed. "Now these things have got to get to General Washington's troops. You said you could read and do sums when I hired you, son."

"Yup, yup, and that I can. My mama was a learned woman, she was, God rest her soul." Marky yanked his felt hat off his scraggly red head and crossed himself.

"Very well, I give you one more chance, but I'm

warning you"—Brock shoved the paper and quill into his hand—"if you make a muck of it again, I'll have you bailing bilge water."

"Yes, sir," Marky nodded. "I can do it, sir, and do it right this time."

Brock looked at the boy doubtfully. "Well, get to work, just don't stand there."

Leaving the lad, Brock headed down the dock toward the *Tempest*.

"Brock!" came a voice from behind. "Brock, wait."

Brock turned to see Micah Lawrence alighting from a carriage. Scowling, he waited. Since his marriage to Keely, Brock's friendship with Micah had nearly dissolved. The fact that until very recently Keely preferred the man's company over her own husband's had been more than Brock could stand, though he refused to admit it. He'd also grown aggravated with the fact that although Micah had much to say at their patriot meetings in the King's Head, he did little work, and none of it dangerous.

"How have you been, old friend?" Micah clapped Brock on the shoulder. The handsome fair-haired man was dressed today in an outrageously fashionable sapphire brocaded suit with matching shoes. "I haven't seen much of you lately."

"Do you need something?" Brock asked quietly. "I've much to do."

Micah lowered his voice, all the while grinning broadly. "Could I see you privately?" He nodded to a passerby he recognized.

"Privately?" Brock lifted a dark eyebrow.

"Your cabin, perhaps."

Curious, Brock nodded. He led Micah on board ship and across the deck. Neither man spoke again until they were in the captain's cabin with the door

211

closed.

Micah glanced down at the maps sprawled across Brock's rack. "Have you anything to drink, old friend?"

Brock leaned against the door, crossing his hands over his chest. "Water."

Micah laughed, tossing down his feathered cocked hat. "No, something of substance. A little brandy?"

"I've no brandy."

Micah sighed. "Pity."

"Get on with it, Micah. I told you I'm busy." Brock scrutinized the patriot, wondering how they could ever have once been friends.

"I want you to understand that it's only after great contemplation that I come to you. I mean to make no trouble."

"Go on."

Micah smoothed the silk of his waistcoat. "You make this so difficult. Must you stand there looming over me? I swear you look more like a savage every day!"

"Speak!" Brock barked.

"Very well." Micah took a deep breath. "I wanted you to know that Keely . . . that she's said things."

"Things?" Brock's mouth went dry.

"You mustn't ever say who told you. I don't recommend that you do anything yet except keep an eye on her. But I thought you should know." Micah turned his back to Brock, smiling to himself. "At first I just thought it was idle gossip, but last week she made mention of the Carter affair. She knows that we were the ones who captured him and gained that information on the British troop movement."

"What do you mean?" Brock clenched his fists instinctively. "I said nothing of that to her or anyone outside of the circle. She couldn't have known."

"Well, she does." Micah spun around, watching Brock carefully. "I didn't want to say anything in front of the others, for your sake."

The veins stood out on Brock's neck as he struggled to keep control. He swallowed against his rising fears. "Are you certain?"

"You think I'd say anything if I wasn't?" Micah asked quickly. "I suspected before, but then everything was quiet for a while."

"When she had Laura and was recovering . . ." Brock intoned.

Micah nodded. "Exactly. At first I thought it all coincidence . . ." He shrugged. "But now I'm not so sure."

Brock took a long time to answer. "You're not to tell the others," he finally ordered quietly.

"Of course not. We're friends, you and I. It wouldn't be your fault if your English wife turned out to be some sort of enemy spy."

"I thought you were *her* friend." Brock wiped his mouth with the back of his hand, trying to brush away the bad taste that rose in his throat.

"I'm a friend to the cause of freedom first, just as you are."

Brock studied Micah's crystal-clear blue eyes. Micah said all the right things, and yet something didn't sound as it should have. His speech was calm and collected, without remorse. All too well without emotion. Brock heard Micah's accusations; he heard his evidence and yet something deep within him made him question the validity of it all. "I'll look into it," Brock answered stiffly.

"You say that, but then we hear nothing," Micah challenged. "What do you know of Jenna's death? Nothing more than you did that night."

Brock moved away from the door to open it. "I

213

thank you for coming and I thank you for your silence in the matter."

Micah scooped up his hat from atop the pile of charts and pushed it onto his head. "Get control of your wife, friend, before it's too late for all of us."

Keely laughed, sinking her fist into the mound of dough resting on the counter. "Things never change, do they, Ruth?" she asked the old cook.

Ruth held Laura up in the air, pursing her lips to make the child smile. "That they don't, Miss Keely. That they don't."

Keely had come to the summer kitchen to check on the menu for the evening meal and had ended up kneading bread while Ruth entertained Laura. Keely enjoyed the physical labor of kneading and relished the opportunity to stand and talk idly with Ruth. It also gave her a chance to question the loyal servant on Lucy's activities.

"It certainly is taking Lucy a long time to return from the Carltons." Keely brushed the tip of her nose with her floured hand. "You must have sent her with that berry pie a good two hours ago."

Ruth kissed the baby on the cheek and pulled her against her huge bosom, cuddling her. "Got a new man, that wench has. Most likely dallying with him."

"Oh?" Keely turned and twisted the heavy bread dough. "Do you know him?"

"That's the funny thing about it. Usually she's spoutin' at the mouth about a new man, but this'in . . ." Ruth made a clicking sound between her ivory-white teeth. "She don't say much at all except that he's handsome."

Keely began to separate the dough into loaf-size pieces. "And you've never seen him?"

"None of us has. Blackie's been givi'n Lucy an awful time about it." The old black cook laughed. "He says he likes to give his approval."

"Why do you think she's being so secretive?"

Ruth's crinkled eyes narrowed as she patted Laura's diapered bottom absentmindedly. "I don't know. Maybe he's married. Why you so interested?"

Keely looked up from her bread making. "Just wondering, that's all. I worry about her. I hear her sneaking out of the house in the middle of the night. This isn't a safe time to be wandering the streets."

"Hallo!" came Brock's deep voice. "Keely?"

"Here. In the kitchen," Keely answered, her cheeks coloring. In the last two weeks she and Brock had gotten along amazingly well and it pleased her. The truth of the matter was that *he* pleased her.

Brock stuck his head in the kitchen door. "Here are my ladies." He came across the room and leaned to kiss the back of his daughter's sweet-smelling neck, then went to Keely. "You keeping her busy, Ruth?" he asked, his hand falling naturally to rest on his wife's waist.

"That I am, Masta Brock." Ruth smiled, pleased to see her master and mistress finally getting along as they should have months ago.

Keely plopped the bread dough into four pans and then wiped her floured hands on the apron of Ruth's that she wore over her sprigged cotton gown. "You're home early." She smiled, gazing up at his dark eyes, her own twinkling magically. "I didn't expect you 'til after dark."

Brock rubbed the flour off the end of her nose with a finger. "We set sail tomorrow. All's set."

Keely scowled as she turned away and removed Ruth's apron. Lately she'd found herself concerned

215

with Brock's safety and hadn't been able to resist asking him of his destinations, even though she knew she wasn't supposed to. She told herself she was concerned for him because of their daughter, but deep inside, she knew it was more. And that thought frightened her.

Brock picked up a peach from the wooden bowl on the worktable and tossed it into the air, catching it. "Can you keep her awhile?" he asked Ruth, chuckling at his daughter's antics. The child had a firm hold on the cook's hand and was trying desperately to tuck it into her own mouth.

"I was hopin' you say that, Masta Brock, cause me and the missy, we got things to do in this here kitchen, don't we?" she crooned to the babe.

"Come on, cousin." Brock gestured with a nod of his head. "Walk with me in the garden. I've been meaning to check my roses for days."

Keely smiled, catching Brock's hand as they left the kitchen. "You won't be gone long, will you?"

"A week, no more than two," he answered, biding his time until they were outside and out of earshot of any servants.

"Oh." Keely sighed.

"Why do you ask?"

She shrugged. "Just wondering. You said something of going to Annapolis and spending a night or two. I just thought it might be nice to get away from the house, you and I." She tried not to sound too disappointed.

Brock led Keely down the red brick path that wound through the verdant garden. The flowering bushes and vines were lush and sweet-smelling, their full green branches brushing at Keely's and Brock's arms and legs as they walked. Taking a deep breath, he stopped, lifting her hand to his lips. "Keely, I must ask you something."

She looked up at him innocently. "Yes." There

216

was a smile on her face as she studied his ruggedly handsome form.

"I wish I didn't have to, but"—he kissed her knuckles before lowering her hand—"but I must."

"Brock, what is it?" She blinked.

"Have you been speaking to anyone about my . . . my activities?"

"Have I what?" She pulled her hand from his. "What do you mean?"

"Just that. Have you told anyone where I've been?" He spoke faster, with more confidence. Just get this over with and be done, he told himself. She'll be angry but her anger will pass. "Have you said anything you shouldn't have?"

Anguish washed over Keely's delicate oval face. "Who in the hell would I tell?" she demanded angrily. "I have no friends, no one, only Laura." And you, she thought.

"Then you admit that you know more than you should?"

Her hazel eyes grew round with shock and indignation. "I admit to nothing. What are you accusing me of, husband?"

Brock turned away, running a hand over the crown of his head. This was more difficult than he'd anticipated. "I'm not accusing, I'm asking you."

"It's your friends, isn't it? They are accusing me, aren't they?"

"You don't understand how important our work is, Keely. You don't understand how careful we must be."

Keely's first thought was to tell Brock just how much she did know of his activities for the cause. If he knew the extent of her knowledge, he would have to believe her innocence. How many successful missions had taken place over the last nine months that she'd known about? But why should

217

she have to prove herself to her own husband? What had she done to make him distrust her except to have been brought up in England? Besides, she knew Micah wasn't supposed to be telling her the things he had. He'd only done it out of friendship, to relieve her worries, sometimes to entertain her. She couldn't betray him.

Keely turned on Brock. "You bastard," she said bitterly. "You savage bastard! You have no right!"

Brock cringed inwardly at her words, but said nothing, his fists balling at his sides.

"I've had it with your unfounded suspicions and accusations!" she shouted." I've done nothing wrong! I've tried to make this house a pleasant place to come home to. I bore you a child! I risked my life to save you in that damned tavern and what do I get for it?" She dashed at the hot tears that ran down her flushed cheeks.

"Keely, you don't understand." He wanted to tell her that he didn't believe it, but the bitter sound in her voice reminded him of other heartbreaking insults hurled long ago. Elizabeth had called him a savage bastard too.

"Oh, I understand well enough, cousin. And now you understand this," she went on. "I'm taking Laura and I'm catching the first clipper to London!"

Brock spun around in fury. "No!"

"No? And why not? It's what you want, isn't it? You got my money, my house, my uncle's good name to back you. What do you need me for? I'm just excess baggage!"

Anger rose in Brock, coloring his face. What was wrong with him to have ever thought he could love this wench? What had made him think anyone could ever love him? "You go," he said quietly.

Keely's breath caught in her throat. I didn't

218

mean it, a voice called silently from within. Don't make me leave you. Don't send me away.

"But my daughter stays."

Keely's eyes narrowed in shock. "You wouldn't!"

He rested his hands on his narrow hips, his dark eyes averted so she wouldn't see the pain she evoked. *She's leaving me.* "You're free to go — today if you like — but my daughter doesn't leave this house." He lifted a fist threateningly. "We're going to win this damned war, and when we do, my American daughter will inherit all that is mine."

"I won't go without her," Keely spit.

"Then you won't go."

Keely bit down on her lower lip to keep from crying out. "I'll hate you forever for this, Brock Bartholomew," she whispered shakily.

Brock brushed past her. "Just see that you don't take Laura from this property."

"And if I do?"

He spun around, unleashing his fury. "I'll hunt you down. To the ends of the earth."

should have told you." She shook her
. . . was . . . . "I said things I didn't
. . . . his . . . . in her . . . . Hadis but
. . . you . . . me . . .

Chapter Seventeen

"He's made all these accusations against you. Why do you stand for it?" Micah perched himself on the corner of Lloyd's desk, watching Keely thumb through a stack of household receipts. "He has no right to treat you like this."

"Micah." Keely pulled her mobcap off her head and tossed it onto a chair. "I don't think I should be talking about this with you."

"Keely! The bastard accused you of betraying him!"

She dropped a sheet of paper to the floor and leaned to pick it up. "He's still my husband." She looked up at him. "And I won't have you speak of him in that manner in front of me."

Micah got up and poured himself a healthy portion of whiskey from a decanter on the mantel. "I don't care. You never should have married him. You should have married me."

Keely scowled. "We've been through this before." She opened an ink well and dug in the desk for a goose quill. "I married Brock of my own choice and I'll live with it."

"Is it your choice that he distrust you to the

220

point of forbidding you to leave your own home?"

"I never should have told you." She shook her head. "He was just angry. I said things I didn't mean, he said things *he* didn't mean." She wondered why she was defending Brock, Hadn't she said to herself all the same things Micah was saying? Still, it didn't seem right to sit here and talk about her own husband like this with another man, no matter what he'd said or done.

"I can't believe you're taking this so calmly." Micah sipped from his glass. "It's not like you."

She added up a row of figures and marked down the number. "So *you* tell him I'm not betraying him. Who would I tell his stupid little secrets to? What do I care what warehouses his monkeys raid?"

"You know he won't listen to me. There's no reasoning with Brock Bartholomew. Never has been."

Keely sighed, setting down her quill. She just couldn't concentrate well enough right now to do the household ledgers. Besides, it was going on one o'clock and near the dinner hour. "I can't figure out where he ever got the idea that I would do such a thing. He acted like he had some sort of evidence against me."

Micah shrugged, following Keely out of Lloyd's office. "God only knows with that man." He hurried to catch up with her. "Say, Keely, is that roast duck I smell baking?"

"In orange sauce. Want to stay for dinner?"

"I was hoping you'd ask. Meals've been so boring at Fortune's Find since Mother and Father left for France."

"All right, Micah," Keely conceded as she pushed through the back door toward the summer kitchen. "You can stay for dinner, but then you have to go. I have work to do."

"One hot meal, a little dinner conversation with my favorite Tory, and I swear I'll be gone!"

Keely retied the bow of her emerald silk calash a third time. Realizing she'd go mad if she stayed in the house another day, she had decided to go visit Jenna's mother and see how Max was making out.

She didn't care that Brock had ordered she keep Laura in the house. The *Tempest* had set sail six days ago. How would he know where she had or hadn't gone? There in the garden they had met in a cold stalemate. He wanted her to return to England but said Laura must stay. What kind of monster did he think she was that she would leave her daughter behind? As much as she longed for the comfort of Aunt Gwen, she'd follow Brock Bartholomew to the gates of hell to keep her daughter.

Thought of that conversation brought tears to Keely's eyes and she dabbed them with a damp handkerchief. Even after all the cruel things he'd said, a part of her still wanted him desperately. "Stinking colonial," she muttered beneath her breath. "Fool!" Micah was right—what had she done to make Brock distrust her so? Couldn't he see that she was falling . . .

Keely leaned forward to scoop a basket of freshly baked gooseberry tarts off the floor of the entryway. It was too difficult to think about all of this. Too painful. So she wouldn't.

"I'm leaving, Ruth," Keely called aloud. "Bring her here. I'm ready."

A minute later the rotund cook came hustling

222

down the hall with Laura settled happily on her hip. "You certain you wouldn't just want to leave her here with me, Miss Keely? She'd be just fine."

Keely shook her head, reaching for her baby. "I know she would, but the summer air will do her good and I've been promising Mistress Lewes that I'd bring her by."

"All right, child. You go on and enjoy yourself. You been lookin' like you could use a friend these last few days."

Keely smoothed the light blanket Laura was wrapped in, jingling her bell and coral. "Yes, you like that, don't you, sweetie," Keely crooned to the baby.

Laura was a picture of health with her rosy cheeks and her auburn hair peeking from beneath the white lace bonnet. She had her father's eyes, dark and piercing, and her skin was slightly red in hue. To Keely, she was beautiful.

"I'm going now." Keely looked up at Ruth. "But we'll be home for supper. Something light."

Ruth threw up a huge black hand. "Go on with you. I tole that worthless stable hand of yours to get the buggy hitched. It ought to be ready to go."

Keely smiled, reaching out to take Ruth's hand. "Thank you."

"Thank me for what?" The old woman arched her heavyset eyebrows.

"For being nice to me."

"Pshaw! Get on with you, miss. I think this heat is making you dizzy."

Keely laughed, going out the front door. "Goodbye."

"Bye," came Ruth's voice as Keely stepped out onto the front stoop and took a deep breath.

The summer air was heavy with the heat of the

223

morning sun and fragrant with the scent of blooming peach blossoms. A light breeze came from the east off the bay, making the oak and maple trees that surrounded the house sway rhythmically.

Taking another deep breath, Keely shifted Laura to the opposite hip and, clutching the basket of tarts, set off down the brick-paved walk around the back of the house to the stables.

The two-seated open carriage had been hitched to the chestnut gelding and stood waiting in the middle of the brick-paved yard. The stable boy, Samuel, was nowhere to be seen.

Keely grimaced. These servants of Uncle Lloyd's were never where they were supposed to be. Samuel had probably hitched the horse and then run off to go fishing.

Lucy had left early that morning to purchase needles and some sugar and had not returned. Keely hadn't seen the servant's British lover again, but she assumed Lucy was still seeing him. If Keely could discover nothing more this week, other than that his name was Georgie, she knew she would have to tell Brock of the maid's indiscretion and possible betrayal when he returned. Then Brock would have to deal with it. Maybe he could find out what she couldn't. Maybe it was just more of Lucy's innocent games . . . but maybe it wasn't.

Setting Laura carefully in a small laundry basket on the floor of the open carriage, Keely pushed the tart basket up on the seat and swung into the vehicle. Just as she lifted the reins, she heard the sound of footsteps behind her. "Samuel, how many times —" Her voice stuck in her throat in terror. There standing only a few feet from her was an ill-clothed man aiming a cocked pistol squarely on her.

"What do you want?" Keely said with hard, clear precision. Her hand tightened around the reins as she poised to flee.

The dark-haired man laughed, tugging on the red wool cap that perched on his head. "Not much, little lady, not much a'tall."

Keely leaned forward, slapping the horse's reins, but another man came at her, catching the harness with his hand. The man's blond hair fell in long, greasy strings down his back.

"Now where you tryin' to go?" the man in the red cap questioned. He leaned over against the carriage's wheel, gesturing with his flintlock. "Don't get any ideas about screamin' or we'd have to take that there beautiful little babe of yours'en."

Keely's hand flew instinctively to Laura, but the blonde was too fast. He snatched the baby's basket from the floor of the carriage and held it high above his head, cackling with glee.

Keely stifled the fear that rose in her throat. Keeping her eyes fixed on Laura's basket, she spoke quietly. "Tell me what you want. Money? Food? Give me my baby and I'll give you what you want." She gripped the reins tightly, her knuckles turning ghostly white.

"Oh, yea. We want money." In one swift motion the leader swung up into the carriage beside her. "But we want lots of it."

His breath reeked of garlic and Keely leaned back in disgust. "So you'll have. Just give me my baby."

By now the blonde had lowered the basket and was poking Laura gently with one dirty finger.

The man in the red cap shook his head. "Sorry.

Can't be doin' that, Miss Fancy Bonnet. Our orders was to bring you in. We don't do the dealin', just the stealin'."

The blonde cackled. "That's good there, Dickie. I like the sound of that."

"Shut up, Mort, before I shut you up," Dickie barked.

Keely looked the man called Dickie in the eye. "If you're taking me, leave the child. She's of no use to you." Her hands trembled, but her voice rang clear.

Dickie shook his head. "I think not. 'Cause if I didn't take the babe, I'd have no guarantees you'd behave yourself, now would I?"

"I swear I will, I'll do what you say," she begged. "Just leave Laura behind."

Dickie snatched the reins from her hands. "I know you will, 'cause the brat's goin' with us." He nodded to his accomplice. "You best be jumpin' on the back before I leave your ass, Mort."

The blonde nodded his head, racing around to the rear of the carriage. He landed shakily just as the vehicle leaped forward.

It was all Keely could do to keep from crying out as Laura was jostled roughly in the basket. Thank God she isn't crying, Keely thought. She tried to reach behind to soothe the child with her hand but Mort jerked the basket from her reach.

Keely turned to Dickie, who had urged the horse and carriage out the back lane and through a line of trees. "Tell me where you're taking me."

"Nice of you to have the buggy hitched and ready to go. Just makes things easier fer us." He laid the pistol beside him on the leather seat. "I hate walkin'."

"I said where are you taking me?" she demanded loudly.

"Shut up, woman." He yanked the bodice of her gown, drawing her closer. "Because you cause a fuss and that little 'en is dead." His blue-green eyes were malignant. "You got it?"

Keely laid her hand on his, sinking her nails into his flesh. "You hurt either of us and you'll not get a pence. You understand?"

Dickie released the bodice of her gown. "Bitch," he murmured.

"My husband's gone. I don't know when he'll be back. I don't know when you'll get your money."

"That red bastard'll be dockin' directly if our information is right."

Keely kept her eyes open for the sight of another human being, anyone she could cry out to for help. But luck was against her. Her captors had chosen the back way out of Dover, down deserted alleys. The carriage was moving west, and they had already reached the outskirts of the town. "Information? Who gave you the information?" An image of Lucy and her convenient absence flashed through Keely's mind.

"Hee! Hee! Hee!" Mort chortled from the rear of the carriage. "Got some'en good we have, ain't we, Dickie? Some'en real close to home ye might say."

Dickie spun around angrily. "This is your last warnin', Mort. If ye don't stop flappin' your tongue, I'll cut it out."

The man holding the baby basket gulped. "Yes, sir," he mumbled compliantly.

"And you shut up, too, woman!" Dickie sunk his elbow into Keely's side. "Stop askin' your questions. The only thing you got to worry about is keepin' you and that red man's baby alive!"

Keely winced, massaging her injured waist. Peering over her shoulder, she caught a glance of Laura, her basket balanced on Mort's knees. The sight of her child made her keep quiet and think. It was obvious these men meant business. But if she kept her wits about her and did what they said, Brock would come home and pay the ransom and then they would be free. With that thought, she turned and stared straight ahead, her jaw set in determination.

Sometime later Dickie stopped the carriage, but only long enough to exchange vehicles. This time they set out in an ancient rickety wagon pulled by two mismatched mares. Dickie had forced Keely to strip down to her shift and pull on a dirty bluetick skirt and a bodice of scratchy low-grade linen. Her head was covered with an old green kerchief tied beneath her chin. Over Laura's clean blanket, Dickie threw a soiled feedsack.

"There, that's better," he told Keely. "Now you don't look so uppity. Look like you ought to." He brushed her cheek with his hand and she winced. "Look like you're mine . . ." he murmured.

So, they had set out with Keely and Dickie riding on the wagon seat and Mort on the back, his feet dangling over the side. Mort cradled a loaded flintlock rifle. Laura was still in her basket beside him, but by now she was beginning to fuss.

"Shut it up," Dickie ordered. "Shut the little bastard up, Mort!"

"Please," Keely said with all of the humility she could muster. "She's hungry."

At the sound of her mother's voice, Laura cried louder.

"So feed her! But then you give 'er back to Mort," Dickie ordered. "You got it?"

Keely nodded numbly, standing up to step into the wagon.

"Oh, no. You ain't goin' nowhere," Dickie chided. "Just sit yourself down. Mort, he's too softhearted. He's liable to let you run. He wouldn't shoot you like I would. Pass the brat up here," he called over his shoulder.

Keely sat back down, accepting Laura gratefully. Yanking the kerchief off her own head, she flung it over her shoulder, attempting to block Dickie's view. The moment she put the babe to her breast, Laura quieted and sucked hungrily.

Dickie chuckled deep in his throat, spitting a golden stream of tobacco over the side of the wagon. "Wouldn't mind havin' a little taste of that myself," he declared. "How 'bout you, Mort? Wanna try?"

Mort made no reply and Keely hugged Laura tighter against her. All too soon the child had finished nursing and fallen fast asleep.

"I think you've had that brat long enough," Dickie ordered. He yanked down the kerchief, catching a glance of one firm breast before Keely could pull down her bodice. "Stinkin' colonial," she muttered beneath her breath.

"Take it," Dickie told Mort. He turned back to Keely as his partner lifted the babe from her arms. "I ain't no colonial. Not like most of 'em round here. Loyal English subject I am. You're the stinkin' colonial," he sneered. "You and that red man of a husband."

"Why me?" Keely asked. She retied the kerchief over her head to keep the beating sun off her face. Already the bare skin of her arms was turning pink. "What made you choose me?"

"It were Elijah that did it," Mort piped up. "We

229

just work for 'im. He's a smart'en."

"Shut up, Mort." Dickie glanced at Keely. "We've had some contact with your husband now and then. Knew he was a big fish."

"Contact? How? Brock would never deal with the likes of you."

Dickie grinned. "Didn't say it was voluntary, now did I?"

She watched the passing landscape, longing to leap from the wagon and run. If only she still had Laura in her arms. But her captors both had guns. If she ran, Dickie would surely kill her and then what would become of Laura? "I don't know what you mean," she stated flatly.

"We's the ones that been interceptin' those shipments from the Chesapeake, bound for your army," Mort declared. "Sell'um for a tidy profit to the English army, we do."

"You?" Keely stared at Dickie suspiciously. " Is that where you're taking me?"

"Don't matter where we're goin'. But yea, us and others." He shot an evil glare at Mort. "Elijah said to keep your mouth shut, Mort. She knows too much . . . then we gotta kill 'er when it's done. You want her dead, Mort?"

The blonde shook his head emphatically. "Sorry, Dickie," he answered, childlike.

"But how do you know where the supplies are?" Keely asked. "Sometimes the people who are moving them don't even know where they're bound."

Dickie lifted his eyebrow, spitting tobacco over the side again. "There's some that knows, I can guarantee you that."

The sun rose directly overhead then began to fall and still the wagon moved west. Twice they stopped to drink water from a stream, but Keely

230

had time only to drink and splash water on her face and then they were moving again. Rarely did they see anyone on the road, and when they did, Dickie pressed his pistol to her side, assuring silent passage.

As the sun began to set, Keely fed Laura again and again Mort took her away. As night fell, once more Keely asked where they were headed. They were still moving due west. They had to be bound for the Chesapeake Bay.

"I told you, it ain't none of your concern," Dickie said angrily. "And I'm getting sick of your questions."

"But how will my husband know where we are?" An image of Brock flashed through her head. Despite their insurmountable differences, she longed for him. Only Brock could save her and Laura—only Brock could ever make her feel safe again, wrapped tightly in his massive arms.

"There's gonna be a note delivered," came Mort's voice from the rear.

"When?" she asked Mort.

"Soon," Dickie replied. "Now both of you shut up!"

The sun set and still they moved on. Against her will, Keely grew sleepy and dozed off. The sway of the wagon and the clip-clopping of the horses' hooves lulled her to sleep and for a short time she escaped the terror of the day's happenings. Sometime in the middle of the night she jerked herself awake. Their surroundings had changed. Trees hanging heavily over their heads had been replaced by marshland. The air was filled with the tangy scent of salt water and the sound of night birds screeching in the distance.

"Where are we?" Keely demanded. Through the

darkness she spotted Laura's sleeping form, still nestled in the laundry basket.

"Almost there," Dickie grunted.

She could hear lapping water very nearby. Had they reached their destination? Just ahead Keely could make out the outline of a makeshift dock.

"Mort!" Dickie barked. "Wake up, you worthless bastard!"

"What? What is it?" Mort murmured sleepily.

"We're here. Get your ass down and find the boat. Mister Elijah'll be waitin'." He pulled the horses to a halt and both men leaped down. Dickie held out his hand regally. "My lady."

Keely jumped out of the wagon, ignoring him. Taking Laura's basket out of the back, she clutched it tightly to her chest.

"I found it, Dickie," came Mort's voice out of the darkness. "Tied right where it was supposed to be."

Dickie laid his hand on Keely's shoulder, giving her a push. "Get in."

"What?" She blinked. "Where are you taking us?"

"Get in the bloody boat!" He pushed her again impatiently.

"Just tell me where we're going. I told you I'd do what you say." She hurried down to the water, hoping that if she did what they told her, they wouldn't take Laura away from her again.

Mort assisted her into the rocking boat. "There." He nodded toward the water. "The *Fanny.* You see her?"

Keely strained her eyes until she spotted the hull of a ship looming high in water a few hundred yards out. They seemed to be in some hidden cove. There was nothing else in sight — not a house, or another boat, or a human being.

Dickie and Mort leaped in the small boat and Mort picked up the oars and began to row toward the shadow ship farther out in the channel. Keely sat in the bow, clutching Laura's basket tightly. The salt air was cool on the bay, and her arms bristled with goose flesh. Carefully, she tucked the feed sack closer around her sleeping daughter.

Suddenly there was a shout of warning from the ship and the clatter of men's feet.

"It's Dickie," her captor shouted through cupped hands. "Permission to board."

There was a pause and then an answer. "Permission granted. Cap'n says you're late. Get your ass up here," the male voice replied.

Mort guided the boat closer to the ship, easing it gently against the hull. A rope ladder fell from above and Dickie stood up. "You first, Mort. Take the brat."

Keely jumped up. "No!"

"I said, take her," Dickie repeated gruffly.

Mort dropped the oars and stood, slipping Laura gingerly from her warm haven. The little girl struggled, crying out, her tiny arms waving in the air as the man began to make his ascent.

Keely stood up in disbelief, still clutching the empty basket. It was all she could do to remain silent and still as Mort climbed the long ladder with Laura tucked precariously under his arm.

When Dickie finally gave her the signal to proceed, she scrambled up the rope ladder without hesitation. All she could think of was Laura as she climbed higher and higher above the small boat. She gave no thought to the difficulty of the climb or the water below. All she wanted was to hold Laura in her arms again.

The instant Keely's feet hit the wooden deck of the ship, she snatched Laura from Mort's arms. "Thank you." she whispered.

Mort grinned sheepishly, then turned away.

As soon as Dickie was on deck, Keely was ushered across the dark ship and down into its bowels. Faintly, she could hear the sound of men's voices and the lap of water at the hull, but mostly she heard the beating of her own heart.

Dickie kept his hand possessively on her right shoulder as he guided her down a long, stinking passageway. Then he pushed open a door and shoved her forward into a blinding light.

Keely blinked in confusion, trying to adjust to the white light of the cabin's lanterns.

There was a tall man with dark hair tied in a club, sitting at a rough pine table. Chicken bones were strewn across the table and onto the floor. The man reached for a bottle of wine and took a swig, baring a full set of shiny gold teeth. "Good even to you, missus," he said through a mouthful of wine and chicken. "Have ye dined?"

Keely swallowed hard. The cabin reeked of unwashed bodies and rotting food with a distinct overlay of cheap ladies' perfume. "I . . . I'm not hungry," she managed, clutching Laura.

The man turned to Dickie, the smile falling from his face. "Yer late, Dickie-boy. Expected you hours ago." He plucked a wing from the chicken carcass on the table and gnawed at it. "Run into problems?"

Dickie yanked off his red knit cap. "No, sir. Not exactly, Mister Elijah. Just took longer than we thought . . ." He glanced up at Keely. "Ah . . . carryin' the brat and all."

Elijah looked up at Keely and smiled. "Pretty

234

lady. She knows why she's here?"

Keely lifted her chin, meeting the man's stare head on. "I do."

Elijah looked to Dickie. "Ye weren't supposed to bring the child. My orders were just her."

Dickie bobbed his head. "I know, sir, but we just thought she'd behave better on the way. We didn't have no problems with 'er tryin' to get away or nuthin'."

"I should think not." Elijah took another swig of wine. "Well, now that the little thing's done her purpose, she can be on her way."

Keely tightened her grip on Laura. "No! You can't have her!"

Elijah got up from the chair. Wiping his hands on his breeches, he came slowly toward Keely. "Now, little lady, we're just sendin' her home to her papa. A good faith offering to go with the ransom request." He put out his hands. "Now just give the sweet little thing to Elijah and no one will get hurt."

Keely's hands trembled. "You're going to take her back to Dover?"

He nodded, the light of the lamps glimmering off his gold teeth. "I'm a man of my word. Now give her up."

Keely's breath quickened. *He promises she'll be returned to Brock,* she reasoned. She kissed the tiny forehead, cradling her against her breast. *If I don't give her up, he'll take her and then she might get hurt.* Showering the baby's face with kisses, Keely slowly, agonizingly, offered the bundle. She looked up at Elijah. "If you harm a hair on her head, you won't have to worry about my husband, because I'll kill you myself," she whispered.

"I don't like threats." A flicker of red-hot anger streaked across Elijah's face and then was gone. He smiled down on Laura, holding her as if she were spun glass. "There ye go, little thing," he crooned, heading for the door. "Dickie, outside."

"Where are you taking her?" Keely demanded, coming across the room.

"You stay!" Elijah barked. "And then she remains safe."

Keely didn't dare take another step closer.

"I'm just sending her on her way like I promised."

Keely nodded, swallowing to hold back the tears as she watched Laura disappear from view.

Elijah stepped out the door behind Dickie and closed it. "Here, take the little bastard," he ordered, dropping Laura into Dickie's arms.

"Me? What'll I do with her?"

The baby began to wail, flailing its arms.

Elijah chuckled. "Dump 'er overboard, of course."

Chapter Eighteen

Brock leaned into the wind, lowering his head against the driving rain. He sank his heels into the gelding's sides, urging him faster. He was anxious to get home.

In the last few days he had turned the past month's events over and over in his mind. Keely professed to be innocent of any wrongdoing, yet everyone in his circle of friends was quick to believe her guilty. Even Micah, who had been her friend, made accusations. But when Brock thought it out, he'd realized that the evidence against his wife amounted to little more than suspicions and prejudices. She was English and they were not, and it frightened them. Brock of all men could understand prejudices. They put a fear in people that sometimes obscured the truth. Besides, to blame her was just too obvious. Keely couldn't be the person betraying him and the patriot cause here in Dover; she just couldn't be. He feared the truth ran deeper.

Wiping the rain from his mouth, Brock guided

his steed west, peering through the darkness ahead. The dirt road into Dover had turned soft with the summer downpour, making the track dangerous. Water splashed high against the gelding's sides, covering Brock with a fine layer of gritty mud. More than once the animal slipped in the mire but Brock held on tightly, guiding his mount to safer ground.

Brock wondered if he should have taken the carriage; it would have been a damn sight drier. But it would have been slower, too.

All he could think of was Keely. Had her anger passed? Would she listen to him when he told her he didn't think she was guilty? He thought of her perfectly shaped mouth and the way it had quivered when they'd argued in the garden. He hadn't meant to hurt her like that. He hadn't meant what he'd said, but she'd made him so damned mad!

And she had hurt him. . . . Brock had sworn he would never get himself into a position again where a woman could have so much power over him, but he'd done it.

And now Keely wanted to leave him. She said she wanted to take Laura across the sea to England and never return again. Well, he wouldn't allow it. He'd find a way to make Keely happy here in Dover. He'd tell her he loved her.

Love . . . Brock smiled in the darkness. It felt good to love again.

Not an hour later, Brock flung open the front door of the house. "Keely?" He yanked the wet hat off his head, his fingers moving to the buttons of his rain-soaked cloak. "Keely, are you here?"

Lamps were lit in the front hallway, casting eerie shadows across the handpainted wallpaper. The house was silent.

"Keely?"

Brock turned at the sound of footsteps and smiled with relief. "Keely, I—" But it wasn't Keely, only Ruth.

"Evenin', Masta Brock." The old cook's face hung.

"Ruth, what is it?" He pushed his wet hair off his forehead. "Where's my daughter? Where's Keely?"

Ruth shook her head ominously. "Don't know, Masta Brock."

"What do you mean, you don't know?" he bellowed. "I left strict instructions for them to remain in this house until I returned."

Ruth hung her head; her plump black hands twisted in her apron. "Yes, sir."

"Then where the hell are they? Where did she take Laura?" He paced, ignoring the water that ran off him and pooled on the hardwood floor.

Ruth lifted her head, her dark eyes meeting Brock's. "This mornin' she said she was goin' over to see Mistress Lewes. She took tarts."

He scowled. "And she never came back?"

"Never went. I sent Blackie lookin' for her just afore dark. The missus never saw her."

Brock swore beneath his breath. "She's gone," he whispered. "She's left me."

Ruth stood stock-still, her eyes fixed on Brock. "Don't know what happened here a few days ago with you two, but I can tell ya she was mighty upset."

Brock turned his back to the servant. "I told her not to leave. I told her Laura Gwen was not to leave this house!" He slammed his fist on a small table, sending a Chinese vase smashing to the floor.

Ruth just shook her head, mumbling as she went back down the hall toward the kitchen. "I got some supper for ya, sir, when you want it."

Brock stared into the tiny gilt mirror in the entryway. "God damn her!" he muttered. "She couldn't wait. She couldn't give me a chance. She never gave me a goddamned chance!" Lines of pain, of betrayal, were etched deeply in his bronzed face. In the reflection he saw dark, menacing eyes . . . eyes a person could fear.

All night Brock sat at the old desk in Lloyd's office, listening to the sound of the rain pelting the windows. He was deathly tired, but he couldn't bring himself to go up to his bedchamber . . . to their bedchamber. He had ridden to see Mistress Lewes himself, but the woman had only verified Ruth's statement. Keely had never reached her home. No one had seen Keely all day. It was if she had just disappeared. Samuel had left the carriage for her, though he admitted sheepishly that he'd gone fishing directly after that, not waiting to see her off. But Ruth was positive she'd heard the carriage depart.

Brock decided that when morning came he would go down to the docks and see if Keely had been there inquiring about passage to England. She couldn't have gotten out of town this fast. He'd find her and there'd be hell to pay. . . .

Mort pushed off the side of the ship in the smallboat and began to row. At his feet lay the baby Dickie had passed on to him.

Mort could just make out the outline of the

wee little thing kicking and squirming as he rowed farther from the ship and downriver toward the bay. The baby didn't fuss or wail as it had in Dickie's arms. The little lass seemed to trust him.

Navigating by the light of the moon, Mort took his time, putting more distance between the smallboat and the sailing ship. When he'd gotten into the rowboat, he'd told himself he was doing it to get the baby farther away from the ship. "Don't want it bobbin' up on the morning tide," he'd told the night watch as he'd shimmied down the rope ladder. But the truth was that he kind of liked the little thing.

Her mother had said her name was Laura.

"Laura," Mort called softly. He lifted the oars out of the water and dropped them into their cradle. Carefully he picked up the baby, tucking the old feed sack tighter against her chin. "Purty little thing, you are," he murmured. "A pity to feed ya to the fish." He lifted her gently onto his shoulder the way he'd seen his mother do with his own little brothers and sisters at home in Virginia.

"But what am I gonna do with ya?" he asked quietly. "Dickie's expectin' me back any minute. I take ya back and he'll throw you over before you can say. 'Mama's tit.' "

He patted the little bonneted head and the babe gurgled, lifting a tiny hand to grasp a strand of long bond hair.

Mort laughed, prying his dirty lock from the child's clean hand. "Sweet little'n."

From the direction of the ship came a voice and Mort looked up.

"Mort!" he could hear. "Mort, where the hell are you?" It was Dickie's voice.

Mort looked to the shadow of the ship and

241

back to the baby in his arms. "Only got one idear," he whispered, brushing a dirty finger against the baby's cheek. "Your mama ever tell you the Bible tale of a man called Moses?"

Laura opened her mouth, trying to close it around his finger.

"Well, this Moses, his mama put 'im in a basket and someone picked him up and made him one of the Pha-row's sons." He chuckled. "Maybe the Pha-row'll find you."

Kissing her forehead he laid her gently on the floor of the rocking boat. Then standing up, he slipped into the cold water of the Chesapeake Bay. For a moment he hung on to the side, staring at the little girl in the bottom of the boat, then he turned and swam away.

Halfway to the ship Mort turned onto his back and twisted to see the little rowboat floating gently down river. "God bless ya, little mite," he whispered. Then he turned back toward the ship and started across the water in smooth, even strokes.

When Mort came up the rope ladder to the deck of the ship, Dickie was standing in wait, a lantern swinging from his hand.

"Where the hell you been, Mort?" He swung a fist, striking the blond in the arm. "I told you to throw the brat overboard and the watch says you went rowin' off with her! Mister Elijah gonna be cussin' mad, now where is she?"

Mort swallowed hard. "I . . . well, Dickie, see I didn't want the carcass floatin' right here next to the ship where the woman could see it so . . . so I rowed off a little ways and then . . ."

"Then you dumped her over?" Dickie demanded.

242

"Uh-huh."

"Then where in the bloody hell is the smallboat, Mort? Why are you soakin' wet?" He held the lantern up in Mort's face.

Mort blinked. "I, well . . . I . . . I fell in throwin' 'er over!" he declared.

"You what?"

Mort nodded, more sure of himself. "When I threw 'er over, I slipped and went in myself and the dingy got caught in the current and done floated away." He gestured dramatically with a hand.

Dickie exhaled in exasperation. "You damned crotch-infested Virginians! I never known one that had any sense!" He whacked the man on the shoulder again. "All right, get below and get some sleep. It'll be dawn soon."

"Yes, sir." Mort nodded compliantly. "Right away."

The morning sun came pouring through the windows, filling Lloyd's office with the brilliant light of another day. Quietly, Ruth moved from window to window, pushing them open to let in the fresh garden air.

Brock slept leaning back in Lloyd's chair, his feet propped on the desk. He'd shed his coat and waistcoat along with his stock and wet stockings. The breeches and linen shirt he still wore from the night before were wrinkled and damp. His usually handsome face was dark with the shadow of a beard and with worry lines etched around his eyes.

Ruth sighed, staring at the sleeping man. "Ah, Masta Brock, what ya done?" she whispered. "Ya

243

never told her you loved her, did ya? Never told her ya needed her . . ."

Brock opened his eyes slowly. "No," he answered, "I never did."

Unruffled by the fact that Brock had heard her, Ruth smiled sadly. "She's grown up so much since ya married her. Don't you see it? All she wanted was to make ya happy."

Brock shook his head, dropping his booted feet to the floor. He wiped his mouth with a palm. "So why'd she leave me?"

Ruth picked up a glass still half full of whiskey. She replaced the decanter on a shelf. "How would I know? I'm just an old woman." She turned back to him. "But maybe she'd had enough. You know as well as I do that she ain't no more a traitor to you than that there apple tree in the garden." She pointed to the windows. "Somethin's funny here, all right, but it ain't Miss Keely."

"She's my wife. She belongs here." Brock stood, stretching his cramped legs.

"Maybe she wasn't feelin' much like a wife . . ."

"Is there a servant in this house who hasn't got mouth?" he demanded irritably. "I thought you were supposed to be seen and not heard."

Ruth started for the door. "You asked, Masta Brock, I was just answerin'."

A knock sounded at the front door and Brock brushed past her. "I'll see who it is."

Flinging open the front door, Brock stood face to face with Micah.

"Christ! Why didn't you come by last night?" Micah asked, coming in. He swept off his cocked hat and dropped it on the table. "I just heard."

Brock closed his eyes for a moment. Micah was the last person in the world he wanted to see at

244

this moment. "I saw no need to contact you," he responded stiffly. "I take it you know nothing about the incident."

Micah's blue eyes widened. "God sakes, man. Of course I don't. I was in New Castle until dinnertime last night." He started down the hallway. "I need a drink."

Brock followed him. "This is really none of your concern, Micah."

"The hell it isn't!" He went into the office and snatched the decanter of whiskey off the shelf. "Don't you see? Something's happened to her, Brock."

"Happened?" He sat on the arm of a wingback chair. Micah seemed to be genuinely concerned. "What do you mean? She threatened to return to England. I take it that was her purpose in going."

Micah poured himself an ample glass of the amber liquid and took a long swallow. "I don't think so. She wouldn't have gone without telling *me*."

The hair on the back of Brock's neck bristled, but his voice remained constant. "Meaning what? She was my wife, damn it! She didn't tell me."

Micah slipped out of his fustian frock coat and perched himself on the corner of Lloyd's desk. "I saw her two days ago. She was fightin' mad at you, but she had no intentions of going anywhere. Not without Laura."

Brock rolled his dark eyes heavenward. "Is there nothing confidential in my life?"

"With Jenna gone, who else does she have to talk to?"

Brock cracked his knuckles, studying Micah closely. "You don't think she fled out of anger?"

245

"The girl's too sensible."

"So what are you saying happened? She took the baby, she took the carriage, and she left."

Micah sipped his whiskey. "With a basket of fresh tarts?"

Brock leaped up. "You think she's been kidnapped?"

"It's a distinct possibility. Too many people know you."

"Well, if she had been taken, why haven't I heard from the kidnappers?"

"It's early yet. Go bathe and get yourself a clean set of clothes. Then go down to the ship and be sure nothing's been heard there. I'll wait here just in case."

Micah's revelation started the wheels of Brock's mind churning. It hadn't occurred to him before that she could have been kidnapped. It had certainly happened before. Not more than six weeks ago a Chestertown merchant's only son had been kidnapped and ransomed for a substantial sum of gold.

Why had he been so quick to judge her? The thought that Keely might not have left him, that she might have been forced, fired an uncontrollable anger within him. At the same time he felt a sense of relief, of hope. Maybe they still had a chance. If he could just bring her home and tell her how he felt . . . He knotted his fists. But first he had to find her.

Brock lifted his head to look at Micah. "Tell me one thing. Why are you doing this? Why are you helping me? You never hid the fact that you thought us ill matched or that you'd wished she was your own."

Micah tugged at the blond queue at the nape

246

of his neck. "It's for her that I'm concerned, not you, friend."

"You accused her of betraying us." Brock began to unbutton his water-stained shirt.

"It doesn't matter." He smiled. "She's a woman. What do women know of loyalties? I still care for her and her welfare. Deeply."

Brock nodded. "Fair enough." He lifted a finger. "But I'm warning you. I get her back, and she's mine. She was never meant for you." His dark eyes met Micah's with a challenge, and then he was gone.

Micah sipped his whiskey. "Don't be so certain, friend," he whispered to the empty room. "Don't be so certain."

The sound of voices echoed in the front hallway as Brock came down the grand staircase. He had shaved, taken a bath, and dressed in a fresh pair of doeskin breeches and a soft cotton shirt. Today was no day for a gentleman's coat and stock.

"Brock, I think you'd better hear this," called Micah from below.

At the bottom of the steps, Lucy, Blackie, and Ruth parted to let their master through. Micah stood at the door with a poorly clothed boy of twelve or thirteen.

"He says he has a message for Captain Brock Bartholomew."

" 'Tis only for 'is ears," the boy piped up.

Brock pushed past Micah. "I'm Captain Bartholomew. What is it, lad?"

The boy blinked. "The message, sir, is that the price is what ye carry in the *Tempest*'s hold plus two pieces of gold. If the demands ain't met, your property feeds the fishes."

"What?" Brock caught the boy by the front of his worn tunic. "What do ye speak of? Tell me!"

The boy cringed. "Don't 'it me, sir. 'E said ye'd know what I spoke of. I don' know no more."

"Who?" Brock crouched until he was eye level with the frightened boy. "You must tell me who."

"I . . . I don't know. Just a man in buckskins. 'E said 'e was a messenger too."

Brock released the boy's shirt. "You swear you know nothing more?"

He put up a dirty hand. "I swear it, sir."

"Did the man say where or when?"

The ruffian nodded. " E said fer you just to go to yer ship and wait. Another messenger'll come."

"Did he say when?"

"No, sir."

Brock stroked his chin. "I'm just to wait? You're certain that was the message?"

"Yes, sir." The boy bit down on his lip. " 'E also said ye'd pay me, sir . . ." His eyes pleaded poverty.

"Of course," Brock turned around. "Ruth. Take the lad into the kitchen, feed him, and take a few pence out of the jar."

"Yes, sir," Ruth replied. "Come here, boy." She signaled with a black hand.

The lad slipped past Brock and hurried down the back hall after Ruth.

"I'll be damned." Brock muttered.

Micah shook his head. "I knew she didn't run! I knew it!"

Brock glanced up. "I've got to go. Blackie, saddle a horse."

The servant nodded vigorously and ran down

248

the hall. Brock started back up the grand staircase with Micah directly behind him.

"I'm going with you, Brock," Micah could barely keep up.

"The hell you are. I don't know how long I'll be gone. You must go to the King's Head tonight. We're expected. You've got to tell them what's happened."

"What are you going to do? You're going to give them what they want, aren't you?"

Brock gave a snort. "Certainly not!"

"What do you mean?" Micah caught Brock's arm and both stopped on the landing. "You have to hand it over. She's your wife, for God's sake!"

"Those supplies are not mine to give. They belong to our army now. They're being unloaded at this very minute." He snatched his arm away and went down the front hallway toward his bedchamber.

"So what are you going to do?" Micah demanded.

"Fight. What else can I do? Brock Bartholomew is not a man who pays ransom."

"And what if Keely is killed? Think of the child, for Christ's sake!"

Brock pushed open his bedchamber door and spun around. "Don't you tell me what's at stake. You think I don't know?" He snatched a leather pack off a chair and began to stuff it with a clean shirt and his shaving equipment.

Micah stood in the middle of the room, baffled. "The *cause* is more important than your wife's life?" His voice quivered with each word.

Brock turned slowly. "I won't lose. No man can face me on the open sea and win." He stuffed his hat on his head and strode toward the door. "I'll

249

see you when I get back with my wife and daughter."

Brock took his leave and Micah just stood in the bedchamber, staring at the massive poster bed. On a chair lay a silky sleeping gown. He picked it up and brought it to his nose, inhaling the feminine scent that clung to it. Squeezing his eyes tightly closed, he prayed beneath his breath. "Please, God," he murmured. "Let her live."

Chapter Nineteen

Keely woke to find herself alone in her jailor's cabin. Running her fingers through her tangled hair, she sat up, taking in her surroundings by the light of the day. After Elijah had taken Laura from her, he'd told her to get into his rack and go to sleep. He'd promised not to hurt her as long as she did what he said, and he swore that Laura was on her way back to Dover with the ransom note.

Keely's heart ached for her daughter, but she knew she'd done the right thing. So far, her captors had kept their word. What else was she to do? They'd given her no choice. Sitting up, she pressed her hands to her breasts, wincing. She knew Laura must be crying to be fed.

Pushing out of the rack built into the wall, she stepped over a pile of chicken bones and an empty ale bottle. Her hand went to the doorknob. It was locked.

Not surprised, she turned away with a sigh. How long would it be before Brock received the note? How long would it take him to fulfill their demands? Would he comply? Or would he take this as good luck and be done with his traitorous wife?

She laughed aloud at the irony of it all. If the kidnappers were going to steal someone's wife, they could have at least taken one in good favor with her husband. They'd have done better to keep Laura—at least she was certain Brock would have paid for *her* release.

A key scraped at the door and Keely turned apprehensively.

Mort entered the captain's cabin, carrying a bowl and a tankard. He pushed the door shut with his foot and set the food carefully on the table. With the back of his hand he pushed a pile of chicken bones and orange peels to the floor to clear a place for her. "Thought ya might want to break the fast." He looked up at her and then to the floor, stuffing his hands in the pockets of his filthy breeches.

Keely studied the man with the stringy blond hair. "My daughter, can you tell me if she's all right?"

Mort kicked at a bone on the floor with the toe of his boot. "Just fine when I last seed her. Purty little thing."

"And how long will it be before my husband receives the demands?"

Mort shrugged, his eyes still fixed on the floor. "Can't tell you that, ma'am, 'cause I don't know. Dickie and Mister Elijah don't tell me 'bout that stuff. I jest do as I'm told."

Keely took a step toward him and laid her hand hesitantly on his shoulder. "You think you could

252

do something for me, Mort?"

He grinned sheepishly. "What ya need?"

"When you go, could you just forget to lock the door?" She held her breath.

For an instant Mort contemplated her words, but then his eyes got round with fright and he shook his head emphatically. "Oh, no. I'm sorry, but I couldn't do that! If ya got away 'cause of me, Mister Elijah'd hang me from my thumbs till I was dead."

She dropped her hand from his shoulder. "I'm not even sure my husband will pay the ransom," she confessed dejectedly.

Mort's head bobbed up. "For criminy sakes, don't tell Mister Elijah that!"

"Why?"

" 'Cause he'll kill ya if he thinks he can't make no coin off ya."

Keely paled. "He said he wouldn't hurt me if I did as he said. It would be no fault of mine if my husband didn't pay. Why would Elijah kill me?"

"I'm tellin' ya, he's a bad'en." Mort looked up at her with concern in his dull brown eyes. "He smiles a lot with them fancy gold teeth, but they say he smiles when he's cuttin' your throat, too."

"I thank you for the warning, then." She pushed a lock of auburn hair off her shoulder.

"Well, eat a'fore it gets cold and I'll be back later. I got paintin' on the fo'c'sle to do." He paused at the door, thinking of the baby floating down the river in the rowboat, and then he turned and went. Better for her not to know, he thought to himself. Because if she don't live through this, it won't make much difference what

253

happened to the little mite.

Jenny Lynn Lassiter raced down the hill beyond her house, laughing as she slipped in the dewy grass and slid the rest of the way to the bottom of the hill on her backside.

"Jenny Lynn, wait for us," cried one of her sisters.

"It's my turn to empty the first crab pot. Mama said!" chided another breathlessly.

Coming to her feet, Jenny brushed the grass from the back of her patched homespun skirt. "Wait? I spend my whole life waitin' on somebody!" The yellow-headed teenage girl snatched a stick off the ground and hurled it into the air, watching it hit the water with a satisfying splash.

The Chester River flowed into the Chesapeake Bay, providing the inhabitants of its shore with abundant food and a mode of transportation. Like many families, the Lassiters depended on the river not only to feed them but also to provide income in a time when coin was sparse.

"Beat ya!" Maggie, the second eldest of the six Lassiter sisters, stuck out her tongue as she passed Jenny Lynn. Reaching the dock that their father had built years ago, she dropped to her knees and began to tug at a rope that descended into the water.

"It's not fair!" Sally cried from the grassy bank. "Make her stop, Jenny Lynn! Mama said it was my turn!"

Jenny ignored her sisters' quibbling, walking slowly down the wooden dock. Suddenly, she broke into a grin. "Look at that," she breathed.

"What?" Maggie continued to draw the crab pot up while Sally sulked at the water's edge.

"A boat!" Jenny exclaimed.

"A boat?" Sally looked up.

Jenny Lynn tugged at her skirt, dropping it onto the dock. "A boat, and looks to be in right good shape." She pulled her bodice over her head and dove into the water in her thin chemise. "Mama says we could sure use a boat."

"Mama didn't say we could go swimming," Sally complained.

Jenny Lynn swam in even strokes toward the peacefully drifting boat. When she reached it, no more than a hundred yards off the shore, she caught it with one hand and hoisted herself up to look for holes in its hull.

"God a'mighty," she breathed, blinking in the bright sunlight.

"Is it in good shape?" Maggie called from the dock. "We got a dozen blue claws."

Jenny Lynn stared at the baby in the bottom of the boat. Was it an angel? She'd never seen anything so beautiful in her life. The rosy-cheeked infant was dressed in a long silken white gown and matching lace bonnet with golden-red curls peeking from beneath it. A fluffy white blanket cushioned its head and attached to the blanket was a silver bell and coral.

Jenny Lynn swallowed in awe, sticking out a finger to touch the baby's cheek. The exquisite angel-baby turned its head, catching her finger with its tiny rosebud mouth. "You're real," Jenny Lynn breathed. "And you're hungry."

Never taking her eyes off the fascinating creature, Jenny began to swim toward the bank, drag-

255

ging the wooden rowboat behind her. When she reached the shore, she beached it and lifted the baby to her shoulder.

"A baby," Sally cried. "Look, Maggie, Jenny Lynn's found a boat and a baby!"

Turning toward the house, Jenny Lynn began to run, the infant cradled in her arms. "Mama! Mama!" she cried. "You'll never guess what I found!"

Brock added the column of figures for a fourth time before he threw down his quill, swearing beneath his breath. Three days had passed since the young boy had come with the message that Keely and Laura had been kidnapped, and still he waited for the second messenger. Pushing away from the chart table, Brock got to his feet. He needed to go topside; he needed the fresh air.

For three days he had done nothing but pace the deck of the *Tempest* waiting for word of where he was to meet the kidnappers so that the goods could be transferred. Of course, by the end of the first day all the precious casks of flour, salt pork, and cornmeal had been unloaded and sent on to Washington's troops by land transport. Brock had no intentions of bartering for the lives of his wife and child.

Instead, he had filled the armory with as many cast iron shots and barrels of powder as she could hold, and added six more gunners to his crew. He'd also sent for his cousin, Tigiana, who lived on the shores of the Delaware Bay at Lewes. His father's nephew was a brave young man with a powerful devotion to his people, though he now lived among the white men as a fisherman.

Brock's plan to rescue Keely and Laura was simple. He would trick the kidnappers into handing over his wife and child and then he would blast the bastards out of the water.

Leaving his cabin, Brock went down the passageway. Just as he started up the ladder, Blackie started down.

"God a'mercy, Master Brock. You got to come with me. Ruth says you're to come to the house right away!" The servant ran back up the steps and waited on deck for his master.

"Come to the house? That's impossible. What is it that Ruth can't handle? I have to wait here for word of Mistress Keely and the babe. You know that."

Blackie shook his head vigorously. "No sir, you got to come straight away. I brought your horse."

"What is it? A messenger? Has word come?"

Blackie's head bobbed this way and that. "No, sir," he said breathlessly. "It's the little one! Laura. Someone's done brought her home!"

"And the misses?"

Blackie grew still, refusing to meet his master's gaze.

"Mr. Jameson!" Brock shouted, striding toward the gangway. "Elmer!"

"Sir?" the two men replied, almost in unison.

"Quartermaster, Mr. Jameson has the deck."

"Aye, sir," Elmer acknowledged, turning to the ship's log.

"Aye, sir," Jameson responded with a salute.

Hurrying down the gangplank just ahead of his master, Blackie untied the horse he'd brought for Brock. "Here you go, sir. Brought you Tally. Took

257

him right behind old Mable here." He indicated a mare tied to a post.

Brock snatched the reins from Blackie's hand and an instant later was mounted and pounding down the planked dock.

Leaving the servant behind on the slower horse, Brock pressed his knees to the gelding, spurring him forward at breakneck speed. "Come on, Tally," he murmured urgently. "Home, boy."

The dirt road leading through Dover was a blur to Brock as he hung low, clinging to the massive steed. Images of Keely passed again and again through his mind, the outline of her soft mouth, the texture of her thick auburn hair between his fingers, the scent of her heady flesh, damp from lovemaking. Why had the babe been returned and not his wife? Brock's chest was so tight that he found it difficult to breathe. Would he never see Keely again? Would he never again hear the sound of his name on her lips?

When he reached home, Brock jumped off his horse, letting the reins fall haphazardly to the ground. Alongside the house on the brick-paved drive stood an unfamiliar wagon hitched to a pair of mules. Taking the front steps two at a time, Brock flung open the front door and rushed in. "Ruth! Ruth!" he shouted. "Where the hell are you?"

"Here, sir," Ruth answered, sticking her head out of the parlor. In her arms she held a small bundle.

In a breath's time Brock was beside her, taking his baby from her arms. "Laura?" he murmured softly. "Laura, sweet?"

His daughter peered back with ebony eyes that

258

mirrored his own. She whimpered and he lifted her to his shoulder, squeezing his eyes shut in pain. "Where's your mama," he whispered, his voice thick. "Where's your mama gone, Laura Gwen?"

"Masta Brock." Ruth laid her hand gently on his shoulder, bringing him back to reality. "Masta Brock, there's someone here you should meet."

He nodded, smoothing the downy red hair on the crown of Laura's tiny head. Stepping into the parlor behind Ruth he saw a woman and five little girls ranging in age from only a few months old to about fourteen years.

"Mathter Bartholomew," the woman lisped, getting to her feet.

"This is the woman who brought little Laura back to us, sir. Her name is Bessie Lassiter. She comes from down off the Chester River."

Shifting Laura to the opposite shoulder, Brock came to the woman, offering his hand. "Mistress Lassiter, I can't thank you enough. You'll be well paid."

Bessie blushed, accepting his hand hesitantly and then withdrawing. She fingered her well-patched skirt, staring at the planked floor of the parlor. "Thertainly not, thir. It was my oldetht, Jenny Lynn, who found her." She grasped the arm of the eldest girl. The yellow-blonde bobbed a curtsy with a giggle.

"Found her? What do you mean?" Brock gestured with his free hand. "Please sit, Mistress Lassiter."

Bessie sat down nervously on the edge of a brocaded chair. "Juth that, thir. I thent my girlth down to the river to wath clotheth and they come

259

up totin' the little darlin'."

Brock turned to Jenny Lynn in disbelief. "You found my daughter down by the river?"

Jenny bobbed her head. "That I did, sir. The boat just come bobbin' by and so I waded out to catch it. Didn't know there was baby a'ridin' in it. I was just thinkin' it'd be nice to have another rowboat for crabbin', seein' as how them stinkin' rebels stole the last one we had."

"Jenny Lynn!" Bessie admonished sharply.

Brock patted Laura on his shoulder rhythmically. Tories, he reasoned. "She was just lying in the bottom of the boat?"

Jenny Lynn nodded enthusiastically, taking a step forward in honor of her sudden importance. "She wasn't cryin' or nothin', just suckin' on the corner of that old feed blanket she come wrapped in." She pointed to a dirty feed sack sitting folded neatly on a small round table next to the settee.

Brock looked to Bessie, his face reddening with anger. "And you don't know where she came from or who put her in the boat and sent her adrift?" He fingered the harsh material of the feedsack.

"Not an idea, thir." Bessie took a fussing baby from one of her children's arms. "But I can tell you the's been well fed. Thuckled her at my own brethst, I did. And the wath a hungry little mite."

"How long ago did you find her and how did you know she was ours?" He kissed the little head and handed Laura gently to Ruth.

Bessie smiled but blushed and turned away, unable to stand under the scrutiny of the handsome half-breed. "That were three dayths ago thith morning. We found you becauth of the bell and

260

coral, thir."

"The bell and coral?" Brock frowned. "I don't understand."

Ruth jingled the tiny silver bell attached to the coral teething ring Keely had pinned on Laura's blanket four days ago. "The bell and coral, Masta Brock."

He shook his head, smoothing his braid absent-mindedly. "I'm not following."

Jenny Lynn spoke up. "It was my grandmama." The girl poked her finger in and out of a small hole in her smock. "She looked at the mark of the silversmithy on the little bell. She knowd it from a candlestick she'd seen where she works sewin', so . . ."

"So?" Brock urged.

"So, Grandmama, she went right to Mistress Creekins's house and asked who the smithy was. Mistress Creekins said the candlestick had come from Dover so Mama loaded us into the wagon and we come here. Mama found the smithy right on the main street and he could tell us a Captain Bartholomew had the bell and coral made a fortnight back."

"I'll be damned," Brock muttered in astonishment, turning away. "A chance in a million." He glanced at Laura cooing at Ruth. It was true what his father's sister had told him. The great Manito protects those who cannot protect themselves. Please God, please Manito, he prayed silently. Protect my wife. Protect Keely.

"I cannot thank enough, Mistress Lassiter, Jenny Lynn." He nodded to the young girl and she giggled. "What can I do to repay you?"

Bessie shook her head. "Nu-nuthin', thir. We

261

exthpected no payment. We only wanted the child to be returned." She bowed her head. "I only with that I could tell you of her mama. Thith warring ith a dirty buthineth. Men do what they'd never dared before."

Brock held out his hands. "You live on a farm?"

Bessie shifted the baby on her lap. "We do, thir."

"Could I speak to you, Masta Brock?" Ruth asked quietly.

Brock followed the old servant out of the parlor and into the hallway. "Yes, Ruth."

She lowered her voice. "Her husband is with a Tory regiment with Clinton's army. I'm sure they need food and like, sir, whether they say so or not."

He nodded. "True enough. Have Blackie load the wagon with two sacks of flour, a hogshead of salt pork, a packet of sugar and salt, and whatever else you see fit from the larder."

Ruth smiled, baring perfect white teeth. "Yes, sir."

"And Ruth . . ."

"Sir?"

Brock slipped two silver coins from a small bag beneath his coat. "Put these in with the sugar."

Ruth gave him a wink. "I always said you were a goodin' Masta Brock. Ain't no matter what others say."

At that moment Blackie came bursting through the back door from the kitchen. "Master Brock! Got a message from your first officer!"

"A message?" Brock put out his hand to accept the crumpled note.

"Just as I was leavin', sir, a man with a peg leg come hobblin' down the dock. He said he had to speak personal to you but that Mister Jameson, he said you wasn't there and if the man didn't give *him* the message he was gonna cut off the man's other leg!"

Brock grinned, unfolding the piece of foolscap. His first officer had always had a way of convincing unwilling parties. The note was in Jameson's own spiraled handwriting.

Brock,
   The meet is tomorrow, sunset. Fools Cove on the Chester River. The *Tempest* is ready to get under way at your command.

Looking up, Brock crushed the bit of paper in his massive hand. "Keely," he whispered. "The game is on."

Chapter Twenty

Brock stood on the quarterdeck of the *Tempest,* staring straight ahead as the sharp-hulled topsail schooner cut through the water at a remarkable speed. The salt spray of the Chesapeake Bay covered his bronzed face in a light mist, filling his nostrils with the scent of the sea. His midnight-black hair fell down his back, unbound and free to ripple in the leeward wind. Across his left cheekbone he wore two diagonally painted lines, one blue, one red. The blue represented the courage of his men, and the red, the blood of the enemy that would surely follow.

The deck of the ship was alive with movement as men hastened to set full sail.

"Leave no scallops in your staysails!" called the sailmaster's voice, which was carried on the wind. "We'll need every bit she can give us."

Brock turned to his cousin, Tigiana, standing beside him on the quarterdeck. "I'm honored that you came, brother."

Tigiana nodded solemnly, matching Brock's

dark gaze with his own. "It is an honor that I am asked. We of the wolf clan of the Lenni Lenape are one always." He clasped his hands. "Just as our father's were one on earth and now are one in spirit."

The bronze-skinned brave was a good head shorter than Brock, but his shoulders were broad and his biceps exceptionally well formed. He had his half-breed cousin's piercing dark eyes and high cheekbones, but Tigiana's face was distinguished by a long sloping nose and heavy eyebrows.

Brock rested his hand on Tigiana's muscular forearm. The Lenni Lenape was a man of honor and a man to depend upon. "I know this is a bad time for you in the midst of fishing season and with your wife about to give birth, but I ask because I had no one else to ask."

"Say no more, Brock-Forrester. You ask and I come just as you would come if I asked. No explanations are needed, not among the wolf clan."

Brock smiled, nodded in understanding. "You will like my Keely. Her hair is the color of the autumn leaves, alive and glowing with a flame that can't be extinguished. Her eyes are as blue-green as the depths of the ocean before a great storm."

"She is good to you, brother?"

Brock chuckled. "We've had our misunderstandings, but she is as good to me as I am to her."

"As long as you love her and she loves you," Tigiana said quietly. "That is all that is important in this earthly life."

"Yes." Brock sighed, reaching for a chart his navigator held out for him. "I love her, and when I find her, we will make amends or die trying."

Keely stood on the deck of the smuggler's vessel beside Elijah, plucking at the folds of her soiled gown. Her captor rested his filthy hand possessively on her shoulder.

"Ye see that sailin' ship comin' this way? The *Tempest,* she's one of the fastest you bloody rebels have got."

Keely shook her head, an ironic smile playing on her lips. *Bloody Rebel,* that was a change. Someone was actually calling *her* a bloody rebel. "She is beautiful," she responded.

"Beautiful, hell!" Elijah's golden teeth flashed in the sunlight. "Her belly's full of salt pork, flour, and sugar stolen from King Georgie Porgie himself. It'll bring a pretty price when I sell it back to him for his troops."

Keely's eyes widened. "And you call yourself a loyal English subject?" She gave a laugh. "You have no loyalties. You're nothing more than a pirate!"

Elijah applied even pressure to her shoulder until her knees buckled beneath the pain. "Shut your mouth, woman, or I'll toss you to my crew." His beady eyes glimmered like those of the rats she'd seen below deck. "I warrant ye won't be so uppity when they finished with you!"

"You promised to return me unharmed if my husband complied with your wishes." She lifted a hand, pointing up the Chester River. "He comes now with his end of the bargain."

Elijah chuckled, pulling a silver flask from beneath his short red sea jacket with the buttons missing. "If this little deal works out well, the captain and I might work out a nice arrangement.

Something permanentlike; I've been looking for a trustworthy supplier."

Keely pushed a strand of hair from her mouth. "You can't do that. The agreement was the contents of the *Tempest*'s hold in exchange for my life. Brock would have no dealing with a man like you!"

Elijah jerked her arm viciously. "I know where ye live now, pretty lady. I know every time your half-breed bastard husband leaves the dock." He smiled, lowering his leering face a hair's breath from hers. "Next time I took ye, I'd not be such a kind and friendly host, if you know what I mean?"

Their eyes locked and Keely struggled to free herself from his grasp.

"The *Tempest*, she's closin' in on us, Cap'n," shouted one of the seamen.

Releasing Keely, Elijah gave her a shove, forcing her to her knees. "Ye'll stay put if ye know what's good for ye."

Holding her breath, she nodded.

"All right, mates," Elijah shouted, walking away. "Man your stations. Find my horn, Dickie, and let's talk to these bastards."

Carefully Brock eased the *Tempest* toward the dilapidated smuggling vessel just ahead. The ancient two-masted sloop was half the *Tempest*'s size and flying Dutch colors; across its bow its name was barely readable and missing one letter.

Moving to the bow of the ship, Brock lifted his speaking trumpet to his lips. On board the other vessel he could make out a man in a red coat, the man he assumed to be the captain of the ragtag outfit.

"There on board the *Fanny!* I want to see my wife," Brock ordered, his booming voice carrying easily between the two ships.

A minute later the captain was holding Keely by a thick chunk of her auburn hair. "Belong to you, you red bastard?" he shouted with his own battered trumpet. "A pretty thing." He released Keely, swatting her backside with his hand. "Very nice," he shouted.

Brock cringed as he watched Keely swing at the captain and the man cuff her back, clipping her in the chin.

"You hurt her," Brock warned, his anger barely in check, "and I'll slit your greedy throats one and all!"

The captain nodded, smiling, his gold teeth reflecting the sun's failing light. "Let's just get this exchange over with and get the hell out of here, Injun."

Brock glanced at Tigiana standing beside him.

"Don't let your anger rule you," his cousin warned quietly in the Lenni Lenape tongue. "They are without intelligence. You will best them with clear thought."

Brock nodded, taking a deep breath before he lifted the brass speaking trumpet to his lips. "Send my wife over in a smallboat and then we will begin transporting the goods!"

The pirate captain lifted his own horn to his mouth and laughed long and hard. "Start loading the barrels on your smallboats. When she's all here in my hold, I'll gladly surrender the lady."

It was Brock's turn to chuckle. "I think not," he called.

"Then what do you suggest?"

268

"A plan I think we can both see safety in." Brock lifted his head to let the breeze caress his cheek. The wind was westerly off the *Tempest*'s port bow, just as he had calculated; the tide was going out. "I will pass you on your starboard side," he continued on the horn. "You anchor here, I'll anchor a few thousand yards directly off your bow."

The captain in the red coat nodded. "So my cannon can't reach ye and yours can't reach me. Smart Injun, you are. Must be quite a woman, this wench."

"You will set my wife in a smallboat to the southern bank where one of my men will wait with her. To the northern shore, I will send my first mate; you will send yours." Brock paused, wetting his lips. "If there is treachery on either side, recourse will be simple enough."

The gold-toothed captain paused in thought, spoke to a mate beside him, then nodded slowly. "Sounds fair enough to me," he shouted.

Brock lowered his horn, turning away. He chuckled. " 'Twas simple enough, Mr. Lassiter."

It was nearly dusk when the *Tempest* set anchor and Brock lowered a smallboat to transport Tigiana to the southern bank of the river. All was moving as planned. The pirate ship *Fanny* had anchored where she sat, downwind of the *Tempest*. Just as Brock had instructed, Keely was rowed ashore and the first mate began rowing back across the Chester River to the northern shore.

As Brock's men prepared silently for battle, moving nonchalantly about the deck, he ordered that one smallboat be filled with barrels and cloth

269

sacks from below deck and be sent across for appearance' sake.

When the first barrel was hauled up on the deck of the *Fanny*, Brock watched the red-coated captain shove a long blade into the top of the cask. He withdrew the knife, studied it, then smiled, holding it over his head to his crew's delight. Taking the speaking trumpet, he shouted, "Yer an honest man, Brock Bartholomew. Too bad yer a bloody Injun!"

Brock lifted a hand to wave and turned his head ever so slightly. "Mr. Jameson."

"Captain?" the first officer responded.

"Is my wife safely ashore?"

"She is, sir. Tigiana gave the signal a good ten minutes ago."

Brock swept his leather three-cornered hat off his head, banging it on his knee. "Cut anchor!" he shouted. "Quarters, gentlemen!"

Suddenly, the *Tempest*'s deck was alive with movement. Men overflowed from below deck, racing to reach their stations. Topmen under the boatswain's command scurried aloft to ready extra rigging while gunners cast off the lashings of their prized carronade cannon and the assorted four-pounders that lurked behind the gunports.

"Anchor's cut, Cap'n," shouted one of Brock's officers.

Brock lowered his hand to the gilt-handled pistol that rested in his belt. "Good job, Larry." With long sure strides he walked the length of the *Tempest*'s deck toward the stern. Already, the tide and the wind off the bow were pushing the *Tempest* straight into range to fire on the *Fanny*.

"God damn it!" shouted Elijah from the bow

270

of the *Fanny*. "The bloody red bastard's tricked us. Pull anchor! Pull anchor!" he shouted, kicking at Dickie as the man ran by. "She's blowing straight for us!"

The deck of the pirate ship *Fanny* erupted into sheer pandemonium. Men ran and shouted, tripping and running into each other as they hastened to set sail and retrieve their anchor.

From the southern shore of the Chester River, Keely paced the grassy bank. "What is he doing?" she demanded of Tigiana. "They're moving! Why are they moving?"

Tigiana crossed his arms over his bare chest. "It was the plan. There are no supplies for exchange aboard." The red man smiled at his cousin's cleverness. "Only large cannon."

"Well, you've got to get me on board!" she shouted as the first boom of a cannon echoed over the water. "I must be with my husband!"

Tigiana shook his head. "You will stay here with me. Here where you are safe. It is what Brock-Forrester wanted."

Keely glanced up at Tigiana's solemn red-hued face. "Is *he* where it's safe?" she demanded, running to the smallboat beached on the shore. "No! He isn't and I have to go to him."

Just as Keely lifted her foot over the smallboat's bow, Tigiana's iron hand closed over her arm. "I cannot let you go," he said in the same even-toned voice. "I gave my word."

Realizing that she obviously couldn't outwrestle the stocky Lenni Lenape brave, Keely lowered her head in mock surrender. "Very well, if you say it's what my husband wished."

Tigiana nodded, turning to watch the *Tempest*

as it neared the *Fanny*, which was still pulling up anchor. "It is. You are a wise woman to know your husband is wiser."

Silently, Keely lifted one of the smallboat's oars and swung it as hard as she could at Tigiana's dark head. "Sorry," she muttered, cringing as the oar connected with the brave's head, making a dull thud.

Tigiana fell to the grass without a sound and Keely dropped the oar, running to kneel beside him. Guiltily, she held her palm over his mouth. "Still breathing," she said aloud. "And no blood, just a bump." Scrambling to her feet, she pushed the smallboat into the water and waded out beside it, jumping in. A minute later, she was rowing in the direction of the *Tempest* and the *Fanny*.

The sun hung low in the west beyond the battling ships, ablaze with the reds and oranges of near nightfall. The sky was streaked with the last rays of sunlight and filled with the sound of booming cannon and rapid gunfire.

Praying feverishly, Keely rowed with all her might, amazed that she was actually making progress toward the ships . . . toward Brock.

"Captain! Captain Bartholomew!" shouted First Officer Jameson above the din of gunfire. "You're not going to like this, sir." He saluted the American colors the *Tempest* flew and stepped onto the quarterdeck.

"What is it?" Brock lowered his spyglass.

"There's a smallboat coming for starboard side, sir. I think it's your wife."

Brock's face paled, his hand nearly crushing the delicate spyglass. "Damnation," he groaned. "Get her aboard before they spot her and blow her out

272

of the water!"

"Yes, sir." Jameson sped off, ducking at the sound of cannon fire as a ball whizzed through the air.

Out of the darkness, through the smoke of the cannon, Keely made out a rope ladder being dropped from the *Tempest*. The vessel was still moving, being blown by the wind downriver, but her stern was scraping the *Fanny*'s bow.

"Mistress Bartholomew," came a voice from the *Tempest*. "Mistress Bartholomew, can you hear me?"

Keely lifted the oars from the water. "Yes! I can hear you!" she shouted above the gunfire and creaking wood.

"You'll have to bring her up against the hull. It's the only way we can get you on board. Can you do it?" cried the voice.

With determination, Keely lowered the oars and began to row again. All she could think of was Brock . . . his broad shoulders, his smirking grin, his long, thick, black hair. "I'm coming," she whispered. "I'm coming, Brock."

The instant the side of the smallboat scraped the hull of the *Tempest,* a man came shimmying down a rope ladder and dropped into the boat. Keely recognized him as Brock's first officer.

"You all right, ma'am?"

Keely nodded, although her palms were bloody from gripping the oars. "I will be," she replied, wiping her hands on her skirt. "Where's my husband, Mr. Jameson?"

"On the quarterdeck, ma'am. Do you think you can get up the ladder, or do I need to carry you?"

Keely looked up doubtfully at the rope ladder looming above. "I can manage, sir."

Jameson smiled in the semidarkness. "Be right behind you, Mistress Bartholomew."

When Keely reached the deck of the ship, she swung over its rail and began picking her way through the men toward the quarterdeck. Cannon sounded, filling the air with the thick, burning odor of gunpowder as men reloaded to fire again. A bit of sail came crashing down from above and Keely ducked as the huge piece of canvas rigging fell haphazardly to the deck.

"Prepare to board!" Keely heard Brock shout just ahead of her.

"Brock!" Keely cried out, running. "Brock?"

"Keely?"

Through a mist of salt spray and the cloud of blackpowder Brock made out the outline of Keely running toward him. His chest constricted unnaturally as his arms opened of their own accord.

Hitting his broad chest, Keely clutched Brock desperately, glorying in the feel of his arms wrapped tightly around her.

"You should have stayed on the shore where you were safe," he murmured into her hair. "What the hell was wrong with Tigiana, letting you go."

Keely lifted her cheek from Brock's chest, staring up into his remarkable ebony eyes. "It wasn't Tigiana's fault, it was mine." Brock smelled of gunpowder and the salt air, a heavenly masculine scent that made her quiver within.

He ran his hand through her thick hair. "You look like hell, Keely Bartholomew. Where's Tigiana?" He brushed his mouth against her honey lips again and again and for an instant no one

274

existed but the two of them . . . locked in an eternal, bittersweet embrace.

Keely's lower lip trembled and her tongue darted out to savor the taste of him. "On the shore . . . I . . . I hit him."

"Hit him?" Brock covered her head with his hands as the ricochet of a gun sounded and wood splintered a few feet above their heads. "How hard?"

"He wouldn't let me come to you. I had to come and he didn't understand."

"Prepare to board!" Brock shouted to his men. Turning back to Keely, he kissed her hard on the mouth. "You have to go below." He pulled his pistol from his belt and pressed it into her hand. "Bar yourself up in my cabin. Open the door for no one but me. If anyone breaks through, shoot the bloody fool."

Keely nodded numbly.

"Go on! Hurry!" he ordered.

Already the first wave of gunners from the *Tempest* were leaping onto the pirate vessel, weapons drawn. The battle rattle clacked wildly as men rushed forward wielding boarding pikes, swords, and boat hooks for hand-to-hand combat. Screams filled the air as the experienced seamen clashed with the unorganized pirate crew.

Trembling, Keely clutched Brock's pistol to her breast, inhaling deeply. She knew Brock had ordered her below, but the idea of moving was too frightening. Besides, how could she retreat to the safety of his cabin while he stayed above, battling her captors? What if he should be wounded? Rationalizing her decision, Keely pressed her back to a wooden crate, holding the pistol with both

275

hands as she watched the brutal fight.

Within half an hour the gunfire had nearly ceased and the crew aboard the *Tempest* were taking prisoners and lashing them on board the deck. A stubby little man with a patch over one eye escaped from the group of prisoners and came straight for Keely. Without hesitation she raised the pistol and pulled back the hammer.

The explosion of a pistol startled her and she watched the man fall lifeless at her feet.

"I thought I told you to get below," Brock chastised tersely. Taking the pistol from her trembling hands, he tucked it into his belt and lifted her off her feet with one motion.

"I'd have shot him if he'd taken another step closer," Keely told Brock shakily.

"Is this the same woman I married?" Brock kicked open the door to his cabin.

"Laura? Is she all right?" Keely asked as he lowered her to his rack.

"She's fine. Ruth found her a wet nurse the day she came home." He kissed her brow.

Keely stroked his bronze cheek with her palm, smearing the blue and red streaks of paint. With her hand, she guided his head down until his lips met hers. "I knew she was all right. I knew it in my heart."

"Stay here," he whispered, pulling away while he still had the resistance. "Wait for me."

Keely smiled, letting go of his hand. "I'll wait," she whispered.

The next thing Keely knew, Brock was shaking her gently. "Keely, wake up."

She lifted her heavy lids. "Brock." She could hear the swoosh of water as the *Tempest* moved upriver. "Is it over?" She wiped at her face with her blood-encrusted hand.

Brock caught her hand, opening her fingers to study her palm. "It's over, the *Fanny* is sinking where she rests. She wasn't worth salvaging. What happened here?" He pressed his lips to her injured palm.

"The oars, I guess. It didn't hurt at the time."

He smiled wryly. "I just sent a smallboat for Tigiana. This is quite embarrassing for him, you know."

She shrugged. "I didn't know what else to do."

Their gazes locked. "I thought," Brock said quietly, "that we'd row ashore and spend the night on the beach. We could both use a swim."

"I'd like that," she breathed. "Will it be all right . . . the ship I mean."

"Jameson can keep her as well as I can. It's only for the night. We'll set sail for Dover on the morning tide."

"Good. I want to hold Laura."

Brock brushed his lips against hers. "And hold her you will."

Chapter Twenty-one

Keely laughed, running down the bank of the river as she peeled off her clothes. "Come on," she shouted over her shoulder.

Brock followed, stepping over the bits of feminine clothing she'd left in a trail behind her. "Who is this mad woman?" he called, joining in her laughter. By the pale, golden light of the half moon, he watched her stop at the water's edge and remove the last remnant of her soiled clothing. The silky white shift caressed her shapely breasts and long lithe legs as it floated to the ground.

"Are you coming?" Keely beckoned. Already she was wading out into the cool river's water, the gentle waves lapping at her hips.

Brock stood on the shore, stripping off his linen shirt and tight buckskin breeches. He couldn't take his eyes from her lovely form as she cupped the water with her hands, letting it flow in rivulets over her shoulders and down into the valley between her breasts.

She smiled seductively, putting her arms out to him. Entranced, he entered the river and took her in his arms.

"Keely?" He pressed his lips to her brow, to her cheek, to her lips. "Are you mad, wench?" he teased. "What have these men done to you?"

"No harm came to me." She traced his lower lip with the tip of her tongue. "But I missed you. God, I missed you." She lifted her dark lashes, gazing up at him as she stroked his cheek.

Brock's brows furrowed. "This is the same woman I married last fall? This woman who hits Lenni Lenape warriors over the head with oars and seduces her husband on the beach. It can't be," he whispered.

She smiled. "It is. You just didn't know me." She ran her fingers through his thick black hair. "And maybe I didn't know me either," she added thoughtfully.

"Ahhh, Keely." He exhaled, pulling her against his chest so that she might rest her head on his shoulder. "I thought you'd left me. I thought you'd taken Laura and fled."

She shook her head, caressing his muscular shoulders with her hands. "I spoke out of anger; I could never leave you. But I thought you didn't want me. You told me to go. I thought you had what you wanted, Uncle Lloyd's money, an heir. You accused me of telling your silly secrets. I thought you wanted to get rid of me."

Brock sighed, lifting a wet hand to caress her cheek. "My words came of anger too, anger and fear. But want you to go? Hell no, I didn't want you to leave." He kissed her mouth, his hand sliding down her back to cup her bare backside.

"You've become an obsession with me, cousin."

Keely's heartbeat quickened as their breaths mingled. Already there was a burning inside her, a burning that rose from deep within her to radiate through every limb of her trembling body.

"I think of you night and day," he went on. "I can't sleep, I can't reason." His lips were warm against hers, warm and feverishly demanding. She couldn't breathe as they twisted their tongues in a dance of desire, yet she couldn't pull away.

"Let me wash you," he murmured in her ear. "Let me rinse away their filth."

Keely's eyes drifted shut as he dribbled the cool river water over her breasts and down her arms. Letting her feet lift from the bottom, she drifted in Brock's arms, seeming to float as his hand caressed her flesh, erasing all memory of the fear and humiliation of the past few days.

"I was afraid you wouldn't come," she whispered. Brock's hand brushed over her stomach and instinctively she lifted her hips. "I was afraid I'd never see you or Laura again."

"That's nonsense," he whispered as he lowered his body in the water. "You are my wife. Of course I came."

Keely half sat up in surprise as his lips closed over her nipple. "Mmmm," she sighed. "I've missed this too." With one hand looped around his neck, she brushed at his hair with the other.

Tugging at her nipple with his teeth, Brock cradled Keely in his arms, glorying in the scent of her, in the sound of her labored breathing. Reaching down with a hand, he scooped a bit of sand from the river bottom and dropped it onto her belly, rubbing it gently in a circular motion.

Keely's eyes flew open. "What are you doing?"

"It's the way my father's people wash," he told her. "The clean sand brushes away the dirt from your skin."

Keely's stomach tingled where he had rubbed the slightly abrasive sand. "It feels nice," she answered. She turned her head, trying to make out the dim outline of the *Tempest* downriver from them. "They can't see us from the ship, can they?"

"A little late to be worried," he teased, scooping up another handful of sand. "But no, they can't see us from this far off. I made certain of it."

Arching her spine, Keely let her head fall back into the water, still floating in Brock's arms. "This is wonderful. It's been days since I felt so clean."

He laughed, kissing her mouth then nibbling at her damp neck. "You're easy to please . . ."

Keely lowered her feet until they touched bottom and she stood up, encircling his neck with her arms. "Not as easy as you think," she whispered huskily. Her entire body was hot and tingling from the sand he had brushed over her flesh. She pushed her leg between his, rubbing against the distinctive male hardness of his loins.

Brock groaned, easing onto his back and pulling Keely down on top of him.

"You're going to drown us," she laughed, kissing his bare chest.

"What a glorious way to go." He ran his fingers through his hair, rinsing it thoroughly. "And now," he told her, "it's time we go ashore."

Hand in hand, Brock and Keely waded from the river and walked up the grassy bank. Just

281

beyond the bank, in a bluff of trees, a small fire blazed. Near the fire a quilted comforter was spread out invitingly.

Without a word the two walked to the blanket and stretched out beside each other.

Brock ran his hand over Keely's silky, damp flesh, dropping brief, fleeting kisses over her torso. The flames from the fire glowed red, illuminating them in soft shadows of light and dark.

Moaning softly as Keely stroked his inner thighs, Brock nibbled at the peak of her breast and moved lower. Leaving a burning trail of desire behind, he forged a path to the core of her womanhood. Keely's fingers grew tangled in Brock's hair as she lifted her hips, in awe of the intensity of her own pleasure. A sweet aching coursed through her veins, filling her to overflowing with a throbbing, incandescent heat.

"Brock," she murmured huskily. "Brock . . ."

Stretching out beside Keely, Brock caught her by the waist and lifted her over him. Heavy-lidded with passion, she lowered herself onto his manhood, crying out in ecstasy as flesh met flesh.

Taking his hands in hers, Keely opened her eyes to stare down at him as she moved slowly, stroking him with her velvety softness. Brock groaned, murmuring her name again and again, lifting his hips to match her rhythm. Lowering her mouth to his, she kissed him gently, her lips lingering over his as she began to move faster.

High and higher the two spiraled as one, locked in an impassioned embrace that seemed eternal. Then suddenly Keely cried out in abandon, and against his will, Brock rose in fulfillment, sighing as he drifted to earth.

Keely flattened herself over him, still holding the throbbing evidence of his masculinity within her. Smiling dreamily, she lifted her heavy eyelids and kissed his dark brow. "No one has ever made me feel like you do. No one ever could."

Brock stroked her damp hair. "I was once warned of witches disguised as English ladies," he murmured. "You've caught me in your spell and I've no wish to escape."

Keely smiled, resting her head on his broad shoulder. She liked the feeling of him still within her, warm and comforting. "A spell." She laughed, snuggling against him. "You sound like Aunt Gwen."

Brock sighed, stroking her head. "Christ, I love you, Keely."

She lifted her head in surprise. "What?" she breathed.

"I said I love you."

"You love me?" she asked in disbelief.

He nodded, twirling a bit of her auburn hair around his finger. "I think I've loved you since the first day I laid eyes on you, there on board the *Tempest*. I just couldn't admit it, not to you, not even to myself."

She laughed, nearly hysterical with emotion. "I don't believe you! I thought you hated me. I was afraid to love you. I was afraid to tell you that I had fallen in love with you."

He kissed the corner of her mouth. "We've been fools, haven't we — with it all."

She smiled down at him, still in shock at his revelation. "I was so certain our marriage would never work. . . . Maybe I was afraid it would."

Brock laughed, his eyes drifting shut, and Keely

laid her head down on him again. The fire was warm on her backside and her thighs tingled as she felt his manhood growing within her.

"I can't believe it," she repeated. "You love me." She moved slightly, rubbing against him, and he groaned. "Say it again," she whispered. "Tell me you love me, Brock."

"I love you," he answered.' With one swift motion he flipped her over onto her back, still lodged deep within her. "I'll love you 'til the end of time and then beyond."

"Show me," she breathed, looping her arms around his neck. "Please show me again . . ."

Later, Keely rested on her side in Brock's arms, tired but content from their lovemaking. She watched the small campfire spit and sputter as it grew smaller, casting eerie fingers of light over their prone bodies. Brock lay with his eyes closed, his arms encircled around Keely's waist. His breath rose and fell so easily that she wasn't certain if he was asleep or awake.

"Brock," she whispered hesitantly.

"Mmmm?" He toyed with her father's amulet that hung between her breasts.

"I have to tell you something."

"You're a Tory spy and you're about to murder me . . ."

She elbowed him sharply. "Brock, that's not funny!"

"Ouch!" He grabbed his side, rolling onto his back. "You've got sharp elbows, woman!"

She rolled over to face him. "I can't believe you'd say that after what people have accused me of doing."

Brock's face sobered. "I'm sorry. You're right, it isn't funny. Now what is it you have to tell me?" He ran a finger down the slope of her breast to tease her nipple.

She pushed his hand away. "It's a serious matter, Brock!"

Sighing, he rolled onto his back, tucking his hands beneath his head. "Tell me then, cousin."

She took a deep breath. "It's Lucy."

"Lucy?"

"I saw her with an English soldier. They seem pretty familiar with each other."

Brock frowned. "You think perhaps she's the one . . ."

"I think we'd be foolish not to consider the possibility." Keely rested her head on her hand, bringing her face only inches from his. "You say that someone is betraying you, and I swear to you it's not me, Brock."

He took her hand, pressing his lips to it. "I know."

"You know? But you said . . ."

"I wasn't thinking clearly. I listened to others instead of listening to my heart. I know you'd never betray me." He smoothed her gloriously disheveled hair, entranced by its red hue in the firelight.

"So what do we do now? I could find out nothing except that his name is Georgie and she's seeing him secretly. You know she hears everything that's said in the house, meant for her ears or not. What if she's been leaking information to your enemies?"

Brock shook his head. "I can't believe I could

ever have said enough in the house that Lucy could have known what the informer knows."

"But the meetings in your study, the things Micah's said to me . . ."

Brock's eyes narrowed. "Micah?" Involuntarily, he stiffened. "What's Micah said?"

Keely wet her lips. She didn't want to get Micah in trouble, and she knew he wasn't supposed to be telling her the things he had. "Noth—nothing important," she said, looking away. "Don't you think the men who kidnapped me have something to do with the informant? They knew what you were carrying in your hold and where you'd been. They told me someone close to you was passing information to them."

Brock didn't miss Keely's hasty change of subject but he pretended not to notice. "Perhaps, but I tend to think not. This bunch was too unorganized to be the major force behind our troubles. I may be able to get something out of one of the crew members, but that Elijah, he'd let me kill him before he talked."

Keely sighed, laying her head down on Brock's chest. Chilled by the night air, she pulled over them a corner of the blanket they rested on. "I'll do anything I can to help you, if you'll just trust me," she said quietly.

Brock stroked her head, running his fingers through her hair. "Go to sleep now and in the morning we'll start for home."

"Home to Laura," Keely whispered.

Brock's eyes drifted shut. "I still can't believe she's safe. How did the little thing survive in the bottom of the boat? How long was she there?" he wondered aloud.

286

Keely lifted her head in confusion. "Alone? Alone where? What boat are you talking about?"

Brock opened his eyes. "The one she was set adrift in."

"What are you talking about?" Her throat constricted with fear. "The man Elijah told me she'd been sent home with the ransom note. You said she was safe at home."

"Shh," Brock soothed. "She is safe, home in her cradle right now. But they lied, sweet. They had no intentions of returning her. I'd guess she wasn't supposed to have been brought along with you. Someone put her in a small rowboat and left it to drift down the river. Three little girls found her the day after you were kidnapped. It was a ways upstream of here."

Tears formed at the corners of Keely's eyes, threatening to spill over. "I didn't know," she breathed, stricken. "They said they wouldn't hurt her if I handed her over. They swore they were returning her to you."

Brock wrapped his arms around Keely, holding her tightly against him. "It's all right. No need to cry now, she's fine," he whispered. "You did what you had to. Don't you know the spirits watch over little children like Laura?"

"Spirits?" Keely sniffed. "What spirits?"

"When I was with the Delawares across the Ohio River, my aunt told me of good spirits that protected and guided us. She said there were spirits who protected children too."

Keely snuggled closer to Brock. She was suddenly so sleepy that she could no longer keep her eyes open. "Elijah, the captain, is he still alive?" she asked groggily.

"He is." Brock kissed the top of her head.

"Are you going to turn him over to the authorities?"

"For treason. They'll hang him."

"Good." She sighed. "He deserves it if anyone does. He's the worst kind of traitor, a man with no loyalty."

"Keely!" Brock opened his eyes. "I can't believe you'd say that." He chuckled.

"And why not? A person has to take a side and stand with their decision."

"And what side do you stand on, cousin?" he asked gently.

She rested her head on Brock's chest. "I don't know," she whispered. "I was born English, it's all I've ever known. But so many of the things you've said, things Jenna told me that I never knew that I . . . I just don't know anymore," she finished quietly. "The life you seek for Laura is so idealistic. Could it ever truly exist?"

Brock pulled the comforter tighter around them, tucking it over her shoulders. "It can, love." He brushed his lips against hers. "And it will . . .

Keely lay stretched across her bed on her stomach with Laura lying beside her. Keely shook a silver rattle over the baby's head and watched the little hand reach for it. "She's so smart, Brock! I think she knows what I'm saying."

Brock looked up from the small desk he'd had brought to their bedchamber. The desk was piled high with documents and loose papers; charts littered the floor around him. "Of course she's

288

smart, she's her papa's girl."

Keely grinned, pushing the rattle into Laura's hand. "Are you Mama's girl too?" she crooned.

It had been such a relief to arrive home two days ago and find Laura in perfect health, safe in Ruth's arms. Keely suddenly found herself so happy that she thought she would burst with joy. Everything was perfect, war or no. Her husband loved her, and she had a beautiful daughter. She was shocked and in awe of the change in her world with the simple revelation of love. Only a few months ago, she thought nothing would ever be right again and now she had more than she'd ever dreamed of. Somehow Brock's love for her had changed her life forever.

"I tracked down Lucy's soldier," Brock told her, dipping his goose quill into a pot of ink.

His words immediately tapped Keely's attention. "Did you?" She got up from the bed and came to him.

"I don't think he's our answer."

"Why not?" She rested her hands on Brock's bare shoulders and he laid down his quill.

"It seems that the young man in question, Georgie Henricks, is a habitual English deserter. He apparently just walks off, leaving his company behind, and then appears a few days later. Manessah had no trouble finding him at all . . . in an English brig in Jersey."

"Damn!" Keely muttered.

Brock chuckled, catching her around the waist. "Damn, the lady says? Damn?"

She covered her mouth with her palm. "I don't know where I've picked that up"—her eyes sparkled with laughter—"you maybe?"

Brock pulled her down onto his lap, nuzzling her neck. "I thought we should talk to Lucy, though Manessah says the boy is too stupid to be a go-between. Manessah also found out that he was in the brig for two weeks last month when we lost that shipment being carried overland from Chestertown. He couldn't have had anything to do with that."

"Doesn't sound like it, does it?"

He kissed her mouth softly. "No, but we'll ask just the same."

Keely pushed off Brock's lap. "Let go!" She tugged at the skirt of her shift. "I've got to get dressed . . ."

Brock smiled, getting up from the chair, the corner of her lacy shift still held tightly in his hand. "A kiss for your shift . . ." he teased.

"And if I'm not up to kissing?"

He tugged the shift. "Then I take it with me . . ."

Smiling, Keely pushed up on her toes to give him a chaste kiss on the cheek.

"Oh, no." He shook his dark head. "Insufficient payment. I want a *real* kiss, madam."

Lowering her dark lashes, Keely rested her hands on his muscular bare chest and pressed her lips to his. Brock released her undergarment, encircling her waist with his arms. She deepened the kiss, thrusting her tongue into his mouth, and he accepted it greedily. It seemed that these days he could never get enough of his English wife.

Laughing, Keely pulled away. "Sufficient?" Her cheeks were flushed, her heart palpitating.

He nodded. "Almost too sufficient." He reached for his clean shirt on the bedpost.

290

Keely scooped Laura off the bed and pushed her into Brock's arms. "Take her to Ruth and I'll meet you in the kitchen. Lucy's supposed to be peeling apples for preserves."

Ten minutes later, Keely met Brock in the kitchen. He was perched on a stool, eating the apple peels Lucy dropped on the wooden worktable. "Where's Laura?"

Brock glanced up. "I told Ruth to take her out for a walk in the garden."

Keely nodded, fingering the nape of her neck where she had pulled her hair back to get it off her face. "How's the new man Mort working out?" she asked Lucy, who stood at the table peeling apples furiously.

"F-fine, mistress." Lucy looked up and then down at the apple she held in her hand. "He's chopped enough wood today to last us into September. I keep tellin' him he ain't got to work so hard 'round here, but he just keeps choppin'." She wiped her forehead with the back of her hand. "He says he's grateful ya didn't have him carried off with the rest of the baddies."

Keely looked at Brock. "I told you he was harmless without Dickie. I knew he'd be a good worker."

Brock bit into another juicy apple peel. "It seems to me I remember a certain lady complaining of her uncle's habit of collecting stray servants."

Keely wrinkled her nose at him and turned to Lucy. "Lucy, we need to talk to you about something."

The servant shifted from one bare foot to the other. "I figured as much."

291

"We're not accusing you, Lucy, but we need to know about Georgie Henricks."

The paring knife slipped from Lucy's hand and fell to the floor with a clatter. "G-Georgie?"

"Whatever you've done for him, Lucy, you've got to tell us."

The blonde scooped the knife off the floor and dropped it on the table. "D-done for him?" she asked, seemingly confused. "Didn't do anything for him, 'cept what any woman does for a man."

Brock broke into a grin and turned away.

Color rose on Keely's face. "That . . . that's your own matter, Lucy, but what I mean is, did you repeat anything you'd heard here in the house to Georgie?"

Lucy's brow creased. "Certainly not!" she cried out indignantly. "He's an English soldier . . . some days at least. This here's a patriot household. I'd not give him a drink of water from this well, never'less tell him anything you or Mister Brock said!"

Keely sighed, coming around the table to the young servant. "You're quite sure you never said anything about where Master Brock was going, not even accidentally?"

Lucy brushed her finger across her lips. "Never a word. I wouldn't do that to Master Brock. He's been good to me. The only reason I went with Georgie was because he was such a good—" She clamped her mouth shut, realizing whose presence she was in. "Well, you know, Mistress Keely."

Brock got off the stool and came to Lucy, resting his hand possessively on Keely's hip. "Thank you for being honest, Lucy. And watch yourself. Georgie was not a good choice for these times."

Lucy dropped a curtsy. "I give up on him two weeks back." She smiled. "Got a new man now. An apprentice to a smithy right here in Dover."

She grinned and Brock burst into laughter, steering Keely out of the kitchen.

Chapter Twenty-two

One evening early in August, Keely and Brock sat in the parlor, intent on a game of chess. They had each won a match in the last week and she was determined to take the upper hand tonight.

Sir Clinton's retreat with the English forces from Philadelphia north into New Jersey and Pennsylvania made Brock's duties much easier, and he found more time to remain at home with his wife and daughter. With the British army north again, and the French sending supplies on a regular basis, the patriots on the Eastern shore had heaved a sigh of relief. Shipments of food, ammunition, and medical supplies were being transported daily and their rebel army for once was reasonably well off.

"Queen to king two." Brock looked up, a smirk on his face. "And you've got one dead knight, my sweet."

Keely studied the ivory inlaid chessboard then raised her dark lashes, smiling coyly. She lifted the white queen and moved it across the board. "And then my queen's bishop takes your queen."

"Damn!" Brock murmured. "How'd you manage that?"

She laughed. "You've been too good a teacher. I think I've gotten much better, don't you?"

He pressed his elbows to the small teak table, leaning forward to stroke his chin. "I hate to lose, you know."

"I know." She sipped from her glass of claret. "Would you like to concede now?"

"Haven't you got anything better to do than harass me? Tend to children, bake bread, run my bath? You can see I'm trying to think."

Keely bit back a chuckle. "No. I've nothing to do. Patience is feeding Laura and I don't bake bread." She lowered her voice until it was husky with insinuation. "Your bath, I'll take care of later."

Patience was the wet nurse Brock had hired to care for Laura after she was returned. Although Keely tried to nurse the baby again when she got home, her milk had dried up. Keely was disappointed that she could no longer feed her baby herself, but she was pleased with Patience. Not only did the woman suckle Laura regularly, but she was at Keely's call to care for the babe whenever Keely desired.

Brock lifted his castle and then set it down in the same place. "Micah said he came by today."

"He did, but I told him I was busy." Keely toyed with the stem of her glass. "I lied."

"Oh?" Brock looked up.

"He's been acting so strangely since I was kidnapped."

"Strange how?" Brock leaned back in his chair, crossing his arms over his chest.

"I don't know. He's here a lot. He's just not his old self anymore. He always seems nervous. He follows me around like one of your hound

295

pups."

"I can tell him he's no longer welcome when I'm gone," Brock suggested hesitantly.

"No." She shook her head. "Don't do that. I can handle him." Her eyes met her husband's. "He's still my friend."

He nodded, unsmiling. "Very well."

She squeezed his hand. This new trust between her and Brock had made all the difference in the world in their relationship. A huge burden seemed to have been lifted from both of them.

After several minutes of silence, Keely leaned forward. "So? Are you going to make your move or not," she teased.

"I—" An abrupt knock at the front door interrupted his reply.

"Who could that be?" Keely got up from her chair. "It's after nine."

"Probably another problem on the *Tempest*. Marty's got watch tonight. Things always go wrong when Marty's got the watch." He started to get up. "I'll answer it."

"Oh, no." Keely came around to his side of the table and laid her hand on his chest, pushing him back into the chair.

The pounding at the door came again, louder.

"I'll get it," Keely insisted, kissing him lightly. "It's still your move."

She smiled at Brock's laughter as she left the parlor and went down the hall to the front entranceway. "Yes . . ." She swung open the front door. "May I—"

English soldiers.

A shiver of ominous fear trickled down Keely's spine. Several seconds passed before she regained enough composure to speak. "May I help you?"

296

"Good evening, mistress." A tall soldier dressed in the red coat of the British regulars swept off his plumed hat. "Is Captain Bartholomew in?"

The man's native English accent seemed strangely foreign to Keely's ears. "May I ask what you want?" She stepped forward, pulling the door behind her a bit.

"With all due respect, ma'am, my orders are to speak to Captain Bartholomew of the *Tempest*."

She dropped her hands to hips, defiantly. "Well, he's not here and I don't know when he'll be back."

The uniformed officer stiffened. "Then we shall wait."

"I'm Brock Bartholomew." Brock swung open the door, coming up behind Keely. She instinctively took a step back as if somehow her presence could shield him from the soldiers.

"Brock Bartholomew . . ." The redcoat officer pushed his way into the front hall, followed by the other soldiers. "We have a warrant here for your arrest." He held up a rolled sheet of paper. "You'll have to come with us."

"On what grounds?" Keely demanded. "You have no right to break into my home like this!"

"Keely," Brock said sharply. He took her arm. "It's best I go with them. They have no viable proof I've committed any wrongdoing."

Keely sunk her fingernails into the flesh of his arm. "You can't just let them take you away!"

"I'll talk to them. I'll be home by morning," he assured her.

"Come along, sir." The officer tucked the warrant into the sleeve of his sharp red uniform.

"Get my coat," Brock told Keely, "and bring down Laura." His dark eyes were grave. "Hurry!"

Keely turned and ran up the grand staircase. Running down the hall to the second wing, she grabbed Brock's azure coat off the bed and lifted a pile of coins from the table near the door. Dropping them into the inside pocket she'd sewn in the lining, she burst into the nursery. "Patience! Give me Laura!"

"She hasn't had her fill yet, mistress." The girl switched Laura from one breast to the other. "I can bring her down when she's done."

"Patience!" Keely's voice trembled. "Please give her to me. I'll bring her back up in a minute."

The wet nurse stood up. "What is it?" She wiped Laura's little rosebud mouth, handing the whimpering child to her mother.

"English soldiers," Keely muttered. "They've arrested Master Brock." Her voice rose in pitch. "They're taking him away."

Patience followed Keely down the hall. "God damn King George! Damn 'im straight to hell!"

"Go down to the kitchen and find Blackie. Tell him to saddle a horse for me. I'll be out as soon as they leave."

"Yes, mistress." Patience hurried for the back staircase and Keely went down to her husband.

"Here's your coat," Keely murmured shakily, handing it to him. "There's coin in the inside pocket," she whispered.

Brock nodded ever so slightly. "Good girl." He put out his arms. "Give Papa a kiss and I'll see you tomorrow, Laura." He took the babe from Keely's arms, holding her tightly to his chest. He brushed his lips over her small head and she puckered her mouth, swinging her tiny hands excitedly.

The British officer cleared his throat. "I have to

298

insist we go, sir."

Gently, Keely took Laura from Brock. "I can't believe they're going to take you this way," she said, trying not to become hysterical.

Brock grasped her shoulders. "I'll be all right." He pressed his lips to hers and she clung to him. He pulled back. "I love you," he whispered.

Before Keely could answer, Brock stepped forward, lifting his wrists. "Intend to chain me?" he asked the redcoat officer, his voice thick with sarcasm.

"Only if need be," the man answered. He took Brock by the arm. "Now come along."

"Where are you taking him?" Keely demanded. She pushed Laura into Patience's hands as the servant passed them in the hall and then Keely followed the soldiers outside. "Where are you going?"

"You'll be notified," one of the redcoats answered.

"Notified, hell!" Keely yanked the soldier's arm and he stopped short, snapping his arm from her grasp.

"Unless you wish to be arrested as an accomplice, ma'am, I suggest you take your leave."

"Keely!" Brock called. "Go inside!"

She stood on the brick walk watching the soldiers load Brock into a wagon. The minute the vehicle started down the street, she ran back up the steps and into the house.

"Lucy! Patience! Somebody get me my cloak!"

Patience came running from the kitchen. "Yes, mistress." She started straight up the steps. Hurrying into the kitchen, Keely found Ruth holding Laura.

"Has Blackie saddled a horse for me?"

Ruth gave a nod. "He has, but it ain't safe fer ya to be goin' out alone, Miss Keely. Not after what just happened here."

"I've got to go notify someone in the committee. Who knows who else they'll be picking up."

"Here it is, mistress." Patience came running into the kitchen and dropped the light wool cloak over Keely's shoulders. "You sure you gonna be all right? Blackie says the streets are crawlin' with redcoats."

Keely kissed Laura's cheek. "Keep the doors locked and open them for no one but me."

Out in the back courtyard, Keely made out the silhouette of Blackie standing beside a saddled horse. "Thanks, Blackie."

Blackie put out his hands to help her mount, and just as she was seated, another rider came out of the barn.

"I'm comin' with ya," Mort called out of the darkness. "It ain't safe fer a lady like you to be travelin' on a night like this."

Keely would have protested, but she knew Mort was right. "Have you got a weapon?" she asked, taking her horse's reins from Blackie.

Mort patted a lump beneath his patched coat. "Ya been too good to me, Mistress Keely, fer me to let ye down."

She nodded, sinking her heels into her mount. "Then let's go . . ."

Keely pounded her fists on the front door of the white brick plantation house at Fortune's Find. She hesitated only an instant and began to bang again. "Micah! Micah!"

"Got to be somebody there," Mort called from

his horse. "Plenty of light comin' from the windas. Give 'em a chance to answer, Mistress Keely."

"I haven't got time to wait!" She rapped again viciously and was rewarded by the sound of scraping metal as the lock was turned.

The minute the door opened, Keely pushed her way in. "Just wait there, Mort," she ordered over her shoulder. Bursting into the candlelit hall, she came face to face with a tall black servant. "Where's Micah? I have to speak with him. It's urgent."

The manservant closed the door behind her. "Master Lawrence has retired for the evening, ma'am. If you wish to make an appointment . . ."

She shook her head. Her waist-length auburn hair had escaped its silver hairpins to cascade heavily down her back. "I've got to see him now!" Turning, she ran across the entrance hallway and started up the grand, curving staircase.

"You can't go up there, ma'am," the servant protested, hurrying after her.

"Micah!" Keely shouted. "Micah!"

A door opened at the top of the steps and Micah appeared in a long, floral-patterned banyan. "Keely! What is it?" He put out his arms to her and she flung herself into them.

"Micah, you've got to help me . . ." The frantic words tumbled from her mouth. "I didn't know who else to come to! You're the only one who can help." The tears she had held back too long began to run down her pale cheeks.

Micah's eyes drifted shut as he gathered her in his arms, inhaling her mysterious intoxicating fragrance. He had dreamed of holding her like this. He could barely breathe for thoughts of her soft ample breasts pressed against his chest. His slow, diligent patience had finally paid off. She had finally come to him. "Solomon."

"Yes, sir?" The manservant who'd come up the steps behind Keely took a step back, lowering his head.

"Send for tea. But have Cain bring it up. And brandy. I'm not to be disturbed!"

"Yes, sir!"

"Come on, love," Micah soothed, pushing a lace handkerchief gently into her hand. "Come into my room, where you can sit down."

Wiping her mouth with the bit of lace, Keely nodded, leaning against Micah as they entered his bedchamber. "I knew you would help me," she told him. "I knew you'd be here. You always said that if I needed something, I could come to you."

Unwilling to release her hand, Micah led her to a two-seated velvet settee and sat down, pulling her down next to him. "Tell me . . ." he whispered, taking the handkerchief from her hands to wipe her eyes himself. "Tell me how I can help you."

"It's Brock," she confessed, appealing to his brilliant blue eyes. "He's been arrested."

"So soon?" Micah stood up. The damp handkerchief floated to the floor.

"What do you mean?" Her brows furrowed in confusion.

"I . . . I just meant I didn't think he'd get caught yet. He takes so many unnecessary chances. Surely you knew this would happen eventually."

"You have to help me . . ." A knock came at the door and she let her sentence go unfinished. She knew she couldn't risk speaking in front of anyone.

302

"Come in, Cain," Micah called, seemingly agitated.

A huge, burly man with dark hair came into the room, carrying a silver tea service. When the man turned toward Keely, she saw that the entire left side of his face was severely scarred . . . a burn, she supposed.

"Put it down and be gone," Micah ordered.

The man set the silver tray on a table in front of the settee, glaring at Keely. The upper lip on the left side was turned up perpetually, his face frozen in a sinister sneer. "Anything else?" Cain boomed, his deep bass voice echoing in the paneled room.

"Wait outside, Cain."

"Yes, sir."

The man left the room and Keely came to Micah's side. "They didn't even tell me where they've taken him. How do I get him released?"

"I don't think you can; I don't think anyone can." Micah smoothed the front of his exquisitely made brocade, silk-lined dressing gown.

"You don't?" She laid her hand on his arm beseechingly. "There's got to be some way."

Micah gazed into the depths of her hazel eyes. "There's no helping him now. Once an arrest like this is made, the man can't be helped."

Keely shook her head. "Don't say that."

"I'm so sorry all of this has happened." He laid his hand on hers, his voice taking on a strange air. "But don't worry, I'll take care of you."

"What?" Confused, Keely shrank back. What was Micah saying? Didn't he care about Brock? He wasn't making any sense.

"I can care for you better than he ever could have." Micah grasped her arms, speaking more

303

rapidly. "I'm leaving here. You can come with me. You know I've loved you since the day I first saw you there on the road to Dover."

"Micah," Keely protested, "what's wrong with you?" She struggled, trying to twist from his grasp. There was a strange light in his eyes that frightened her to the depths of her soul. "Why are you saying these things? You talk as if he's already dead!"

"You'll never want for anything, I swear it," he insisted, pushing her backward.

"Micah! Let go of me, now!" she shouted. She was powerless to escape his iron-clad grip as he propelled her backward, flinging her onto his bed.

"I'll give you anything. Tell me what you want, land, jewels, artwork!" He pinned her arms to the bed, pressing his mouth hard against hers.

Disgusted and frightened, Keely twisted away. "Micah, please!"

"Just tell me you love me and that you'll be my wife," he begged, trying to turn her face toward his.

Recovering from her initial shock over Micah's attack, Keely gained control of her emotions. She ceased struggling and lay limp beneath him. "Get off me, Micah," she ordered forcefully. "Get off me now. You're hurting me."

He rolled off her, but still held her wrists. "What's the matter, darling? Why are you angry with me?"

Their gazes locked. "This isn't like you. I thought you were my friend."

He loosened his grip, his handsome face lighting up. "You'll come with me then?"

Fear of what Micah might do made her choose her words carefully. "I can't come with you be-

304

cause they're not going to hang Brock. I won't let them."

"But . . . but if they did? If he was dead . . . you'd come with me? You'd be my wife then, wouldn't you?"

The instant Micah released Keely's wrists, she scrambled from the bed and ran for the door.

"Keely, where are you going?"

She opened the door and rushed passed Cain. Down the hallway she went and toward the stairs with Micah at her heels.

"Keely, you can't go now. We have to make plans." He lifted the skirts of his brocade banyan and followed her down the steps.

Swinging open the front door, she stepped onto the front stoop, illuminated by two brass lamps. "Mort! My horse."

Mort leaped off his own horse and came running with Keely's. He led the bay gelding up the three steps and onto the stoop. Without hesitation, he put out his hand and helped Keely into the saddle.

Micah came bursting through the door. "Where are you going?" he demanded angrily. "I want you to stay here and talk to me!"

Keely lifted the reins, staring down at Micah bitterly. "You son of a bitch!" she snapped. "I trusted you! Brock was your friend. When I tell him what you said, what you suggested, he's going to kill you!"

Micah tipped back his blond head in laughter "*When* you tell him? You're not going to tell him. They're going to hang him, you stupid girl. He'll swing from a rope till there's no breath left in him." He shook his finger. "Then what will you do? You'll come to me, just wait, you'll see."

"Never!" Wheeling around, Keely sank her heels into the gelding's flanks, and horse and rider flew off the stoop and into the darkness.

Brock paced the stone floor of the interrogation room, his hands tucked behind him. "I've told you, gentlemen," he continued calmly. "I know nothing of any such raid on the King's army a fortnight past. I know nothing of the supplies missing from your storehouse, and I am unfamiliar with the British brigs *Charlotte* and *Lady Anne*." He glanced up at them, his voice calm and placating. "A pity they were lost to those pirates . . ."

"Captain Bartholomew!" Major Victor Hughs slammed his fist on the table. "We have had enough of your antics! I must have your cooperation!"

Brock slipped off his azure sleeveless waistcoat and laid it carefully over his frock coat on an empty chair. "I told you, gentlemen"—he nodded respectfully—"I'm willing to cooperate to my fullest ability, but you must ask something that I can answer."

Lieutenant Colonel Klaus Von Bueren, detached from the Brunswick Infantry, stood up and came around the table. "You red rebel bastard! Tell me vhat this is!" He pushed a piece of rolled-up parchment into Brock's hand.

Brock unrolled the paper, glanced over the list of names, and handed it back. "It says it's a list of captains commissioned as privateers for these United States."

A red-faced Von Bueren threw the rolled paper across the room. He inhaled and exhaled rapidly, the buttons of his blue and red coat nearly bursting from their threads. "I know vhat it says! Vhy is your name here?"

"My family has been in the shipping business in Dover for over fifty years."

The German lieutenant colonel tossed his powdered head from side to side. "That has nothing to do vith anything! There is a new ship being built in Chestertown at this moment. Vhy is your name on the deed?"

"I told you." Brock sighed, stifling a well-placed yawn. "My family is in the shipping business. To transport goods, we must have sailing vessels."

Red veins pulsed at the officer's temples. "There is no shipping now!"

Brock pulled a gold-cased watch from inside his waistcoat on the chair. It had been Lloyd's watch, one given to him by his brother, and now it was his. "It's near three in the morning, gentlemen. Couldn't this be continued after we've all gone home and had some sleep?"

Major Hues stood up, his hands resting on the lapels of his red coat. He was dressed in the uniform of the Queen's Regiment of the Light Dragoons. The white epaulettes at his shoulders fluttered as he walked. "It is obvious, sir, that you arc not taking these accusations seriously." He glanced over at Von Bueren and back at Brock. "That gives us no choice but to have you transported."

Brock stiffened. "Transported? Transported where?" They wouldn't take him away from his Keely, not now! He had known it was a possibility when he'd married her, but it hadn't mattered. So much had passed between them since then. She loved him now . . . they had Laura . . . they

307

had an entire lifetime ahead of them!

Major Hues returned to the table, took a seat, and picked up a goose quill. He scrawled a few large, flowery words across the sheet of paper and slid it across the table to Von Bueren. The German officer signed the sheet and Major Hues sprinkled a bit of sand across the page.

Brock clenched his fists at his sides. *I love you, Keely,* his brain pounded. *I love you, ki-ti-hi!*

Major Hues cleared his throat, lifting the sheet of paper. "Brock Forrester Bartholomew is to be transported to the prison ship *Jersey* in the New York Harbor." He looked up at the patriot, a silly smile on his face. "There he will be interrogated as to his treasonous actions, then hanged from his neck until dead."

Chapter Twenty-three

"Mistress Bartholomew," George Whitman reasoned calmly. "We can't possibly allow you to go."

"Allow me?" She laughed, her feminine voice stark in the lantern-lit tavern. "I'm a free woman. I can come and go as I please. My husband has been transported to a prison ship in New York. I intend to go to him with or without the committee's approval."

George ran a hand through his powdered hair. "Don't you think this would be better left to us? I'm certain Brock would never approve."

Keely rested her hands on the plank table, her eyes passing from committee member to committee member. The same men she had met nearly a year ago were all here — Jenna's brother Manessah, George, John, Issac, and a few new faces. Only Micah was missing. "Gentlemen, I know what all of you have been saying about me. Brock's English wife, the traitor . . " She locked gazes with George, and ashamed, he turned away. "But I don't care."

"Then why are you here?" John questioned.

"I came to tell you that I was going. I also

came to warn you. I'm afraid Brock will not be the last to be carried off in the night."

George chuckled, lifting his jack of ale to his lips. "You think business is going to cease because you say it's for our own good?"

"Let her speak, George," Manessah urged.

"No, George!" Keely answered sharply. "I came to tell you to be careful. All of you. You've come too far to let them best you now."

Issac studied the young red-haired woman who sat across the table from him. "Why would an English woman come here to the King's Head to warn a band of rebels?"

"I was born in this town. My husband fights for the rights of our child, of yours."

Manessah smiled, pushing back from the table to prop up his boots. "I think the lady is trying to tell us that she believes in the battle we fight for."

She looked at Manessah. "I believe in my husband."

There was a moment of silence and then one of the new members of the committee spoke up. "Charles Lutton, Mistress Bartholomew."

Keely acknowledged him with a nod. "Mr. Lutton?"

"I'd just like to ask what you hope to accomplish by going to New York." His tone was not condemning, but rather curious.

She folded her hands on her lap. "I don't know."

"You don't know?" George was unable to contain his laughter.

"All I know is that I have to go."

"But it's absurd, a woman traveling that far, right into the hands of the British!"

Keely sighed impatiently. "Tell me something, George. If your wife was taken prisoner in the middle of the night, wouldn't you go looking for her? Wouldn't you try to have her set free?"

George shook his head so violently that puffs of white powder rose in a cloud above him. "It's not the same thing, Mistress Bartholomew. Not at all."

Manessah stood up. "It is *exactly* the same thing. Wouldn't Jenna have said so?"

Keely smiled up at Manessah in silent thanks. "Well, gentlemen, if you have no messages for my husband, I'll be on my way. I leave at dawn."

Manessah came around the table, offering his arm to her. "Let me walk you out."

She pushed away from the table. "Thank you, but it's not necessary. My manservant is outside. He'll see to my safety."

Manessah took her hand, linking it through his arm. "It would be an honor, ma'am."

Smiling, Keely accepted his hand and together they walked to the door. "Thank you for supporting me."

He squeezed her hand. "You were terrific."

"I was scared, but I felt like I should come and tell you myself before I went. I wouldn't want to endanger any of you. But I have to go to him. You understand." She looked up at him with her hazel eyes, seeing Jenna's face in his.

"Completely. Give Brock my best and tell him we're doing all we can here. Micah is supposed to be looking into a prisoner exchange."

Keely smoothed her hair. She wore it pulled back and tied with a ribbon in a long mane of curls cascading down her back. "Is that why he isn't here?" She forced her voice to remain steady.

What had happened at Fortune's Find with Micah had disturbed her greatly.

"I assume so. John brought the message that he wouldn't be attending tonight's meeting."

"Well, Manessah, I've got to be going. I still have things to take care of at home."

"Do you want me to go to New York with you? I can."

"No. I think it's safer if I go alone. None of you should be involved. I'm taking a man with me. I'll be safe enough."

Manessah offered his hand in friendship. "I want you to know I never believed any of what they said about you."

"I know." She smiled, taking his hand. "It doesn't matter. All I want is to get Brock back safely."

"Mistress Bartholomew," George Whitman came up behind her.

"Yes, George."

"If you manage to see Brock, tell him we're behind him. Tell him we'll get him out."

"I will, George."

He bowed gracefully. "Godspeed to you."

Keely and Manessah watched George return to the table of men. "The older ones, they're all so suspicious," Manessah told her gently.

Keely opened the door and lifted up on her toes to kiss her newfound friend on the cheek. "Good night, Manessah, give your mother and Max my love."

"I will."

Keely closed the door quietly and crossed the dark street to where Mort waited on horseback.

"You all right, Miss Keely?"

"Fine, Mort." She swung into her saddle. "Now

312

let's go home."

The carriage lurched forward, came to an abrupt stop, and rolled forward again. Keely groaned aloud, clutching her stomach. It had taken her over a week to make it to New York City, and she was sick to death of the tedious, jolting ride. While she would have preferred to have come by horseback, she had realized that she must give the proper appearance. No woman of her position would be riding horseback across country with one male servant, she would undoubtedly have been stopped and questioned.

Instead, Keely had chosen the slower mode of transportation and it had worked. Her ruse had been that she was traveling north to the English-held city to visit her Tory cousin. The cousin, widow Valerie Goldson, was actually a patriot informant and a friend of Manessah's. Jenna's brother had been kind enough to send a message ahead, making arrangements for Keely to stay with the widow while she was in New York trying to gain her husband's freedom.

Wiping her perspiration-soaked brow with a linen handkerchief, Keely peered out the window at the brick and wood-frame warehouses lining the waterfront of the harbor. The streets were a flurry of activity with wagons of goods being transported and armies of soldiers marching to and fro. Everywhere she looked there were men in the uniforms of the King—redcoats, bluecoats, greencoats—swarming the streets.

There had been no word from Brock since the night he had been taken away. She had not been notified as the soldiers had promised. The only way she knew where he had been taken was through Manessah's diligence and the aid of several silver coins.

"Mort!" Keely rapped on the roof of the carriage. "Mort!"

Mort swung down from beside the driver and stood on a sideboard, sticking his head in the carriage window. "Yes, ma'am?"

"Mort, how much farther?"

"The driver says a little ways, but we got to pass through guards. They don' jest let anyone down on them docks."

Keely nodded, tugging at the low-cut bodice of her gown. Vigorously, she waved a silvered paper leaf fan. "Good, because I'm about to roast in here."

Mort grinned, nodding his head. His appearance had improved greatly since he'd come to work for Keely. His clothes were clean, his hair was washed and pulled back neatly in a club, and he no longer reeked of sour sweat. It was Ruth he had to thank for the change in his personal upkeep. The cook had insisted he come to her table clean, or he'd not eat, so after two days of no meals, Mort had bowed his head to the old tyrant and done her bidding. Since that episode he had been diligent in his tidiness.

"Just hang in there, Miss Keely. With Mistress Goldston's coach, her driver says we won't have no problem gettin' through. Seems she got her a friend down here. Some fat German called Von Bueren."

Keely sighed, leaning back on the coach seat. "Precisely who I intend to see. Thank you, Mort, you've been good to me and it won't be forgotten."

He flushed with pleasure and climbed back up on the carriage seat beside the driver.

A few minutes later, the carriage came to a halt and a soldier in a red uniform, carrying a rifle, stepped forward. "No civilians past here," he told Mort and the driver. "I don't know where you think you're headed, but you'll have to turn around."

Keely watched through the window as Mort tugged off his hat and reached into his shirt for a slip of paper the widow Goldston had given them. The soldier glanced at the sheet of paper. "I'll have to check with my officer," he said, then he disappeared into a small wooden building.

A minute later the soldier returned with an officer at his side. Taking a deep breath, Keely forced her sweaty hands into a pair of lady's gloves. Then, she lifted the latch and alighted from the carriage in a great flurry of silk skirts.

"Sir." She lifted her eyebrows, offering him her gloved hand.

She'd dressed carefully this morning under the widow Goldston's direction. She wore an elaborate silk taffeta gown patterned in spirals of green and red vining with a silver gilt stomacher laced so tightly that she could barely breathe. When she had protested to the widow that the gown was far too elegant to wear to the docks, the young woman had winked, giving her a smile. "It's what will get you in to see who you need to see," she assured Keely. "Trust me."

The officer, wearing a British regular's uniform, accepted Keely's hand, bringing it to his lips. "Ma'am." His dark eyes wandered to the low-cut bodice of her gown and his cheeks colored. "How might I help you?"

315

Keely smiled coyly, trying to remember everything the widow Goldston had told her about winning these men over. "I ... I have an appointment, sir." She tugged her hand from his grasp and he straightened up with disappointment.

"You do? And with whom might that be?"

She lifted her fan, concealing her mouth with it. "I'd rather not say," she whispered.

"Oh." Then the officer's eyes brightened. "Oh, oh, oh, yes, I understand. Any friend of Mistress Goldston's is certainly welcome."

Keely lowered the fan. "Thank you, Major."

"It's been a pleasure." He opened the carriage door and offered his hand in assistance. "If there's anything I can ever do for you again, ma'am ..."

"I shall surely call on you!" She took a seat and reached to close the door, but the officer held on to it, sticking his head inside the carriage.

"Ah, how long do you think you'll be in New York?"

"Well, that depends." She grasped the door handle and pulled the carriage door shut, giving the major just enough time to pull his head free. "That depends on how well I like it here." She rapped on the roof of the carriage with her fan. "Mort! Drive on!"

The carriage rolled forward and Keely waved out the rear window. The moment they had passed through the wall of soldiers blocking the entrance to the dock, she slid back in the seat, heaving a sigh of relief.

Mort jumped down onto the sideboard. "You all right, Miss Keely?"

"I'll be all right when I find Mr. Bartholomew."

316

"We're gonna find him if he's to be found, I swear it."

Ten minutes later the carriage arrived at the designated warehouse and Keely adjusted her silk bonnet. Murmuring a prayer beneath her breath, she left the safety of the carriage and marched up the plank dock with Mort following in her footsteps.

"Yeah, what you want?" A bearded man in a loyalist unit's uniform stepped in front of Keely, barring her passage into the warehouse where she was to meet with Von Bueren.

"I'm Lucy MacDaniels and I've an appointment with Lieutenant Colonel Klaus Von Bueren." She fluttered her fan.

"An appointment? Hah!" The loyalist hocked and spat at the ground, just missing her gown. "That what you ladies are callin' it these days? Stinkin' whores!"

"Sir, let me pass or you will regret your mistake," she threatened, tight-lipped.

The man shrugged, stepping aside. "Don't make no difference to me if you get the runnin' clap." He allowed Keely to pass but then dropped his rifle in the doorway, cutting off Mort. "But *he* ain't goin' nowhere."

Mort slid his hand beneath his coat to rest it on the hilt of his knife, but Keely shook her head. "Stay here and wait for me."

Her manservant nodded in obedience. "You need me and all ya have to do is hollar," he told her. "I can slit this crud's throat as easy as I can slit the next man's."

"I don't think that will be necessary, Mort." She forced a smile then opened the door and disappeared from his sight.

Following a long passageway, Keely encountered a German officer; however, this man was expecting her. "Right this vay," he told her politely.

The middle-age soldier escorted her to a small sitting room somewhere in the warehouse and then disappeared, promising that the lieutenant colonel would be with her shortly.

Nervous, Keely sat down on the edge of a velvet settee, toying with her gloves. She was amazed that such a room could exist in an old brick warehouse among barrels of salt pork and casks of wine. The room had been wallpapered, the floor covered with thick carpets, and a small rectangular stove added to one corner. There was a mahogany desk with stacks of papers piled on it, the settee, two chairs, and several hand-carved oriental tables. A silver tea service sat on the table in front of the settee. Steam rose from the teapot.

When the door latch lifted, Keely jumped. A rotund man with a red face and hanging jowls came bouncing into the room. "Mistress MacDaniel, how good to meet you." He extended his hand and Keely rose to take it. "No, no, you must sit. It is too varm in these Colonies, don't you think?"

Keely smiled. Here I go, she thought. This is my chance. If I'm to see Brock, this is the man who can get me there. "It's so good to meet you, sir. Val has told me so much about you."

The lieutenant colonel lifted his coattails and seated himself in a chair across from Keely. "That Val, she is a good voman. Wunderbar!" He lifted the teapot. "Tea?"

"Please."

The German officer poured a cup of tea and

318

handed it to her, then poured himself a cup. Lifting a napkin from a tray, he clapped his hand on his knee. "Bonbons! Vould you like one?"

She glanced at the dark mounds of chocolate with pink icing tips. If she hadn't known better, she'd have thought the small sweets had been molded to resemble breasts. "No." She swallowed a gulp of boiling tea. "None for me, thank you."

Von Bueren popped one of the delicacies into his mouth and reached for another. "So how might I help a voman as beautiful as you, Miss Lucy?"

The plan ticked through Keely's mind. She was Brock's mistress, come to say farewell before he was hanged. Mistress Goldston said it was the only way. She said they would never allow her to board the prison ship if they knew she was nothing but a wife. "Well, sir, as you know, my . . ." She cleared her throat. "A Captain Bartholomew has been taken prisoner by your men."

"Yes, yes!" the German officer took a big gulp of tea, splashing some down the front of his light blue coat, staining the yellow facing.

"Here, let me." Forcing herself up off the settee, Keely pulled her handkerchief from her sleeve and blotted the man's coat. He likes to be fussed over, the Widow Goldston had advised.

Von Bueren grinned, leaning back in the plush chair. "Yes, yes. I saw to that arrest myself. Ve have been on the man for quite some time."

Keely returned to her seat. "So, Klaus." She smiled prettily. "Do you think I could see him, just this one last time?" She let her lower lip droop in a coy pout.

He reached for another bonbon, smacking his lips in delight. "I think, yes, I think this could be

319

done, maybe. Of course certain gentlemen will expect payment." He shrugged, noncommittal.

"I understand. Just tell me what it will take." She picked up her drawstring purse from the settee.

"Not now. After tea." Von Bueren waved a chubby hand and lifted the plate of bonbons. "Are you certain you wouldn't like a sweet? They are quite exquisite!"

Seated at the bow, Keely held tightly to the sides of the rowboat, squinting to see into the darkness. Water lapped at the smallboat's sides as it skimmed the surface of the bay. The British prison ship *Jersey*'s rotting hulk had been anchored in the harbor just off Brooklyn. There, she was told, Captain Brock Bartholomew was being held until his sentencing. His charge was treason to the Crown. His sentence, if found guilty, was to hang.

"There she is, miss," called the sailor rowing the boat. "See her. Right ugly thing, ain't she?"

Keely pulled her cotton wrap closer around her shoulders. Mort had not been permitted to come with her. He was waiting on the dock, while this sailor brought her to the prison ship. The sailor would wait but ten minutes once she was aboard and then he would leave, with or without her. If she wished to return to land, ten minutes was all she had.

"Yes, I think I see it," she answered. Ahead she could make out the outline of a ship's hull, resting in the water at an odd angle.

"Ya only got ten minutes, so make it quick-like. Ya'd not live a night on board. Them soldiers can get purty rough. They's the only ones they put on board for guards, ye know."

Keely nodded. "Ten minutes and I promise I'll be back in this boat."

The sailor guided the tiny rowboat up against the ship's hull and cupped his hands around his mouth. "Yo! On board!"

"Yeah?" came a mocking voice from far above. "What ye need, laddy?"

"Got a friend of Von Bueren's here. 'E says if ye split a hair on 'er, any of ya, 'e'll skin yer hides!"

"Who's she wanna see? This is the third one this week. The man's making a profit, ain't he?"

"I don't know nothin'," called the sailor. "I just do the rowin'."

Keely stood up, leaning against the ship's slimy hull to keep from tumbling into the water. "Captain Bartholomew. I'm here to see Brock Bartholomew."

A rope ladder fell from above and Keely started the treacherous climb.

Once on board, a bare-chested sailor in short pants led her across the deck. "Got no parlor, ma'am." He chuckled. He toted a lantern and a long wooden staff. Tucked in the top of his breeches was a pistol and a long-bladed knife.

The oil lantern the sailor carried cast an aura of golden light across the deck, sending squealing rats in every direction. Keely stifled a scream as a rodent came straight for her, bumping into her boot.

The sailor chuckled, smacking the rat over the head with his staff. The animal screamed in pain and scurried off into the darkness. "Make nice bed partners, don't ye think?"

Keely shivered, hugging her wrap to her sides.

"Right down this way." The sailor led her below into the bowels of the ship, where the stench was nearly unbearable.

She held her cotton wrap over her mouth and nose to keep from being ill. The odor of human excrement and sweat combined with that of rotting wood and food made her light-headed.

"Ye can wait here." The sailor kicked open a door. "Want the lantern?"

She put out her hand, trembling. "Please." Too frightened to move, Keely just stood there, clutching the lantern as her escort disappeared into the darkness. She could hear footsteps below and above her, mingling with the sound of the ocean lapping at the ship's dilapidated hull. Men groaned while others laughed. She could even detect the sound of someone crying pitifully.

The sailor, Charlie Loden, pushed open an iron grate. "There a Capt'n Bartholomew in here?"

"Yes. Here," Brock answered quietly.

"Yer wanted."

"Christ," Brock breathed. "Now? In the middle of the night?" he shouted from the pitch-black hold.

"Get yer ass out here, unless you want me to come in!" Charlie ran his staff against the iron bars impatiently. "And hurry about it. I got a card game waitin' on me."

Brock pushed up off the filthy floor, running a hand through his hair. He stepped over two men, tripping over a third. He shared the dark eight-foot by eight-foot cabin with fourteen other men. Stepping gingerly over the slop bucket, he crouched and crawled through the doorway. Behind him the sailor slammed the iron grate, sliding the bolt home.

"You can't take me away like this," Brock told him. "I haven't been sentenced yet. I've had no trial."

"Shut up and get on!" Charlie poked him with the staff. "Tonight ain't your hangin'. Someone here to see ya." Leading Brock down a pitch-black passageway, he kicked open a door.

Brock turned.

In a halo of golden light, Keely stood stock-still. Over her head she wore a cotton shawl like a veil falling to cover her magical hair. "Brock . . ." she whispered.

"Keely?" Brock groaned, his eyes filling with tears. For a moment he wondered if she was real. Was this just another dream? "How the hell did you get here?" he managed huskily.

She ran and flung herself into his arms, tears rolling down her cheeks. "It doesn't matter," she whispered. "Just hold me, Brock. Hold me . . ."

Chapter Twenty-four

Keely trembled in Brock's arms. "Thank God you're safe. I didn't know what to do. I don't know how to help you."

Brock took the lantern from her hand and set it on the floor. "I can't believe you came. You shouldn't have endangered your life like this."

She laughed as he brushed the tears from her cheeks with his dirty palm. "What is my life without you?"

Brock crushed her to him, kissing the top of her sweet-smelling head. How could he tell her that there was little chance of escaping the sentence? How could he tell her just to go home and start her life anew? "Keely," he whispered.

She lifted her chin to stare into his dark eyes. His face was covered in a ragged beard, his cheeks sinking in an unnatural hollow. He was missing his coat and waistcoat and his shirt was torn nearly to shreds. Even in the dim light of the lantern she could make out the outline of purple bruises across his cheeks and forehead and down his arms. "What, love, tell me. I'll do anything."

"There's nothing to be done, *ki-ti-hi*. They have

no evidence except for a man's word in Dover, but I don't think it matters. They want me badly. They think that if they kill me, other privateers will take heed. They don't understand our commitment; the Crown still sees us as a band of rebels."

"What man?" she pleaded. "Didn't they say who?" She ran her fingers through his long black hair, trying to push it back into some kind of order.

"No. But I think it's someone within the circle," he answered.

She gasped. "A committee member?"

He nodded gravely. "It seems to be the most logical deduction."

"Micah is working on a prisoner exchange. Maybe he can get you out of here. Wouldn't that work?"

"It would." He kissed the tip of her nose. "But I don't know that they'll agree to it. I seem to be quite a catch."

"I've got to go," Keely whispered in Brock's ear. "There's a man waiting in a rowboat for me."

"How the hell did you get here in the first place?"

"It's a long story. One I can save until you're set free." Her lips met his and they kissed feverishly.

"Go then and see what you can find, love."

She nodded bravely. "I brought you coin. Manessah said you would need it."

"Manessah is right. You must pay for food here, have it brought in, or starve. There are two men with nothing, so I share what I can with them. My money's dwindled to nothing."

"Here then." She pushed a tiny sack into his

palm. "I have to hurry or I'll be left here."

"Go then," Brock murmured, catching her around the waist. "Another kiss and then go."

"I promise I'll be back," Keely murmured, accepting his lips. She clung to him desperately, terrified that this would be the last time she'd ever see him. The last time she'd ever feel his embrace. "I love you," she whispered.

"I love you." Pulling away, Brock took her hand and retrieved the lantern. "Now go, sweet, while there's still time. Go."

Taking one last look at the bronzed face of her husband, Keely picked up the lantern and ran from the room, leaving Brock in darkness.

Three nights later, the sailor, Charlie, again came to Brock in his dark cell. "Capt'n Bartholomew!" he shouted.

"Here," Brock answered. "It's about time someone came. The poor man's been dead more than a day. The stench is unbearable!" He got up from the corner of the dark cell and moved toward the lantern light. He had no idea if it was day or night. It was always dark below deck in the windowless cell and the soldiers had confiscated Lloyd's watch. He wasn't even certain how long ago Keely had come, but her image in his mind was what kept him alive, what made him believe there was hope for his release.

"I ain't come for the poor bastard, that ain't my job. I come for you."

"Me?" Brock stepped over a sleeping man. Asleep or dead. "Why me? Has my trial come?"

"The Lieutenant Colonel Von Bueren wants you."

Brock cringed. Not more interrogation, he prayed. His bruises hadn't yet healed from the last session. "What's he want?"

"How the 'ell should I know!" Charlie opened the iron grate and let Brock crawl through.

The echo of the falling bars rang in Brock's ears as he started down the passageway. "You taking me ashore?"

"Not me. Got someone waitin' to row you."

Charlie led him down the passageway and up on deck.

The fresh night air hit Brock so hard that his head went dizzy. He had never felt anything so glorious as the salty breeze that caressed his worn body. The moon hung full in the sky casting bright light over the water to illuminate the way.

"Get along, Capt'n."

Brock nodded, following his jailor, intoxicated by the cool night air. How long had he been below deck? How long had it been since he'd seen the water or tasted its salt on the tip of his tongue?

"Down the jacob's." Charlie threw the rope ladder overboard, giving his captor a prod with his staff.

"Will I be returning?" Brock asked.

Charlie shrugged. "Like it here that well, do ye?" He dissolved into laughter then, spotting a rat, went running across the deck in pursuit of the rodent.

Climbing down the ship's ladder, Brock descended into the smallboat below. A sailor nodded his head, lifted his oars, and began to row steadily toward shore.

That ride in the rowboat was the most glorious Brock thought he had ever experienced. He just couldn't get enough of the night air. He gulped its freshness, expanding his chest again and again until he thought he would grow drunk on it. All too soon, though, the smallboat hit the side of the dock and two uniformed soldiers dragged him roughly to his feet, leading him down the dock.

The streets were quiet except for the occasional bark of a stray dog, or the laughter of a soldier on watch. Just as Brock's jailor had promised, the soldiers led him directly to the brick warehouse where Von Bueren had seen him on two other occasions. But this time, instead of leading him in a door off the alley to the side, the soldiers took him to the front and down a long passageway. Before Brock knew what was happening, a door was unlocked and he was shoved inside.

Brock lifted his hand to shield his eyes from the bright light of the lanterns. Confused, he blinked his dark eyes, trying to clear the cobwebs from his head. He was in someone's parlor!

The sound of a doorknob turning made him gaze across the room. The door on the far side opened and Keely appeared.

"This way," she ordered with a sweep of her hand.

Two soldiers carried in a copper bathing tub and disappeared out the door.

"Keely?" Brock's voice was weak and strained. He was so thirsty. There was never enough water to drink in his cell for one man, much less fifteen.

Keely smiled, lifting her finger to her lips to tell him to be silent. She stood with her back against the open door as the soldiers appeared with buckets of steaming water and poured them into the tub. Again and again they came as Brock watched in disbelief. What was going on here? Had he been released? No—if so, she would surely have taken him far from here.

When the tub was filled nearly to the rim, the two red-coated soldiers returned one last time with a tray of heavenly-smelling foods and two bottles of wine. Finally they took their leave and Keely closed the door behind them.

She turned, smiling. "Well?" She lifted her hands, palms up. "Hungry? I thought you might like a bath first."

"What is this? I don't understand. Are they letting me go?"

Unable to stand the sight of Brock's haggard face, Keely came to him, putting her arms around his waist. "No," she said softly. "Not yet." She laid her head on his chest, oblivious to his filthy clothing.

"Then why am I here? Why are you here?" He caught her by the shoulders. "What's going on, Keely? Who let you in here?"

"Von Bueren, and the price was steep, so I hope you approve."

Brock's eyes narrowed dangerously. He knew what a lecher the German was. "How steep?"

She couldn't help laughing. "Not *that* steep! I paid him in cold hard coin, though other arrangements were offered."

"I'm afraid to ask how much."

"Then don't. I'd be ashamed to admit it to you." She stood on her toes to kiss him gently. His scruffy beard tickled her face. "There's a razor there by the tub. The mirror's on the wall. Why don't you shave and take a bath and then we'll eat."

"First a drink of water." Brock pushed his hair back off his face. "Then could you explain to me exactly what's going on here?"

"I can." She poured him a tankard of water from a glass pitcher and handed it to him.

Brock drank the cold water greedily. "God, but that's good!"

Keely smiled, working on the buttons at his neck to remove his torn shirt. "It seems the lieutenant colonel runs quite a business here. Not only does he allow people to see the prisoners on the *Jersey,* but for a King's ransom, he rents out his little parlor here for *entertaining,* as he calls it." She took the empty tankard from his hand.

Brock located the razor and bar of soap Keely had brought and began to lather his face. "Von Bueren *knew* you would be meeting me here tonight?"

"He arranged it. He thinks I'm your mistress, come to bid you a fond farewell." Keely couldn't help smiling as she sat on the edge of a large desk in the corner of the room to watch Brock shave.

He shook his head. "Well, I'll be damned. I wouldn't believe it if I didn't see it myself."

"I only wish I'd been as successful with your release."

"What'd you find out?" Brock scraped his chin with the razor, removing weeks worth of black beard.

"Manessah's friend, the widow Val Goldston, is trying to help all she can. I'm staying with her here in the city. She says they want to hang you to set an example to other privateers. She's already tried bribery but neither Von Bueren nor anyone else will agree to it. It seems you're too

330

important." Keely got up and began pacing the floor. "Val says I should go home and see about that prisoner exchange. She also says we need to find out who the informant was. It may be helpful in your release."

Brock laid down the razor, running his hand over his clean-shaven face. "She's probably right, you know."

"I know," she answered softly. "But I'm afraid to leave you. No one can tell us when your sentencing will be. What if . . ."

Brock took her in his arms. "God, Keely, can't we not talk about this for a while?" He stroked her head, kissing her temple. "I've missed you so much. I do nothing all day but lie there and think of you . . . of you and Laura, of the mistakes I've made . . ."

She touched his lips with her fingers." The mistakes *we've* made."

He smiled. "I didn't realize how dark my life was until you came and filled it with your light."

"I think your confinement's made you addlepated, husband." Keely brushed her fingers across his high cheekbones. The weeks below deck on the prison ship had taken their toll. Brock's skin was pale, his eyes sunken. "Now take those dirty things off and have your bath. I'm starved."

Not needing any more encouragement, Brock slipped off his shoes and stockings then added his breeches to the pile. Sinking gingerly into the steaming bath water, he sighed. "I can't believe you thought of a bath." He scrubbed his chest with a bar of soap and a soft square of cotton.

"I had no desire to dine with the likes of Mort." She opened one of the bottles of wine the soldiers had brought in and poured them both a

331

glass.

"How's Laura? Tell me what she's doing. What's she like."

Keely laughed. "How much can I tell you? You'd only been gone a few days when I left for New York." She handed him a glass of wine, bringing her own to her lips.

"I guess you're right."

"But she's fine. With Ruth and Patience fighting over her, no baby could be better treated."

He nodded, sipping the wine. "What time is it? How long have we got tonight?"

"Only until one, and it's already after nine. At one someone will come to take you back to the ship."

"What about you? How will you get back to where you're staying?" He set down his glass and began to scrub his entire body vigorously.

"Mort is waiting outside with Val's carriage. He's been very good to me, Brock. We couldn't have found a more loyal man."

"When the time comes, I'll see he's repaid handsomely."

Brock stood and Keely handed him a large towel. Heat rose in her cheeks as she watched him dry his wet limbs. Unable to take her eyes from his magnificent form, she handed him a pair of clean breeches.

"Why are you looking at me like that?" He smiled, the breeches dangling from his fingers.

"Because I love you," Keely answered.

Brock let the clothing slip to the floor as he leaned to kiss her perfect lips. She moaned softly, pressing her body to his. He tasted of wine and desperation. He threaded his fingers through her hair, deepening the kiss, trying to chase away the

332

demons of the past weeks.

"Brock," Keely whispered. "Let's eat before it gets cold."

"No," he answered huskily, taking the wineglass from her hand and setting it on a table. "I need you, Keely. I need you now." He traced the outline of her bodice with his fingers as he pressed hot, damp kisses to her collarbone.

Keely arched her back, slowly succumbing to his smoldering passions. Night after night she had dreamed of this, of Brock holding her in his arms, of Brock crushing her fears with the heat of his desire.

Her breath came faster as he released her breasts from the confines of her bodice. His wet mouth teased the peaks of her breasts until her nipples stood erect and throbbing against the thin material of her shift.

Lifting her into his arms, Brock knelt, lowering her gently to the carpeted floor. She ran her hands through his wet hair, writhing against his damp, naked flesh as he took her nipple in his mouth. Pulling her bodice off her shoulders to aid him, she pushed the material down around her waist, ignoring the tiny stitches she split asunder. She didn't care about the gown; she didn't care where they were or under what circumstances. All that mattered was their love — nothing, no one, could take that from them.

"Brock," Keely whispered. "Brock . . ." All conscious thought slipped from her mind as she caressed the hard, sinewy muscles of his back and shoulders. She dug into his flesh with her nails as he stroked her inner thighs, murmuring endearments beneath his breath. Pressing his knee between her legs, she lifted her skirts, too consumed with desire to try and remove them.

Brock lowered his head over hers to take in her brilliant hazel eyes. "Now?" he asked.

"Now," she answered, her voice strained and throaty.

He entered her with one thrust and Keely lifted her hips, smiling up at Brock as he moved over her. Her entire body pulsed with sensation as they moved faster toward some right, throbbing light of fulfillment. Closer and closer they moved, their breaths mingling, their hearts beating as one until together they called out in ecstasy and he spilled his life's blood into her.

Keely dropped her head to the floor, laughing in relief. Chuckling, Brock kissed her perspiration-beaded forehead, pushing tendrils of hair off her cheeks. "Not much of a gentleman, am I?" he teased. "Ravishing you here on the floor." He rolled off her and onto his side, pushing her abundant skirts down. "The least I could have done was taken off your dress."

Keely laughed, looping her hands around his neck. "Later, after dinner. Then you can take it off."

He kissed her rosy mouth impulsively. "I love you, Keely. No matter what happens, I want you to know I love you."

"Nothing is going to happen except that I'm going to have you released." She pushed his chest with her hands, forcing him onto his back. "Now let's eat."

He got up, offering her his hand. "With or without my breeches?" he asked, standing in naked glory.

Keely came to her feet, trying to smooth her rumpled skirts. Deftly, she slipped her arms back into the bodice of her gown and raised the material to cover her breasts. "With the breeches," she told him, laughing. "Or we'll never get to eat!"

All too quickly, the hours slipped by. Keely and Brock shared a sumptuous meal of roast duck and fresh garden vegetables, completing the meal with cherry tarts and a second bottle of sweet wine. Cross-legged, they sat on Von Bueren's costly carpet, laughing and talking as if they were picnicing in their own garden as they had done the night of the wedding. Neither mentioned that this might be their last dinner together.

After dinner they made love again, this time with delicious slowness. Keely savored every touch, every whisper, every gentle kiss, terrified that it would be their last. Their passion spent, she lay cradled in Brock's arms on the floor, twirling a lock of his long black hair around her finger.

"You have to go soon," Brock whispered. With a finger he traced the bridge of her nose.

"I can't."

"You have to. You made a bargain with the lieutenant colonel. He kept his end, you have to keep yours." His voice was rich and filled with emotion.

"But how can I go back to Val's and sleep in that bed when I know you'll be there on that horrid boat?" She lifted her dark lashes to meet his gaze.

"You will, because you have to, *ki-ti-hi*."

"*Ki-ti-hi*, what does that mean?"

"It means—" He took her hand, pressing it to his bare chest so that she could feel the beat of his heart. "My heart, my love," he whispered, "only in my father's language it means more."

She kissed his bare chest. "I like that."

335

"Now, you must get up and get dressed before the guards come and carry us off stark naked."

She laughed. "It would be a sight, wouldn't it?"

"It would."

"So they take you away. What do I do then?"

He stroked her cheek with the back of his hand. "Then, in the morning you have Val find you a ship bound for Dover."

"A ship? Why a ship? I can't just leave you here!"

"Now listen to me." He caught her wrists. "You go home to Dover and you find Manessah. Tell him that we suspect the informer is among us. Tell him we must know who it is. Also have him check into Micah's prisoner exchange. Micah is sometimes slow to follow through. You know how —"

At the sound of Micah's name, she stiffened involuntarily. After this was all over, she would tell Brock what he had said, what he had tried to do, but for now, all that was important was to have Brock set free.

"Keely, are you listening to me?"

She blinked. "Y-yes. Micah. I'll have Manessah check up on Micah."

"All right, now you'd better get dressed. It's nearly one o'clock." Gently he pushed Keely off his lap and stood up, helping her to her feet. They embraced, pressing bare flesh to bare flesh, just holding each other for a moment, and then he broke away.

"Here's your shift," Brock said gently.

Slowly they dressed. Suddenly there seemed nothing left to say. When Keely had her gown in some sort of order, she brushed out her hair and tied it in a bit of ribbon from her purse.

She handed the brush to Brock. "This is for you. There are also fresh clothes, a toothbrush, and some other things for you in the bag." She indicated a canvas satchel on the floor. "Val's made arrangements for someone to bring you food and water every day."

He smiled. "Thank you."

Keely watched as he brushed out his hair and began to braid it. When he reached the end of the thick plait and began to secure it with a strand of hair, Keely pulled the black ribbon from her head. "Here, let me." Gently she tied the ribbon in his hair. "All done."

Brock took her by the waist, forcing her to meet his gaze. "Thank you," he whispered.

"For what?"

"For everything, Keely. For coming into my life, for giving me a beautiful daughter, for giving me your love."

"You're going to get off that prison ship," she told him shakily.

"I know," he insisted, not wanting to scare her. He couldn't bring himself to tell her that the odds were against it. "But if I don't, I want you to go home to England. Take Laura and go live with Mother."

"Dover is Laura's home. It's where she belongs." Keely smoothed his linen shirt, trying to hold back the tears that threatened to flow.

"Do what you wish, but I want you to know I'd understand."

"Oh, Brock," Keely cried. "It's so hard to leave you . . ."

"I know. But you must. Just leave the room and go on to the carriage. I'll wait here for the soldiers. It's the best way."

337

Silent sobs racked her body as Keely clung to Brock.

"Go," he whispered as he forced his mouth down hard on hers. There was no tenderness in their kiss, only raw, unyielding passion. It was a kiss of final desperation.

Tearing herself from Brock's arms, Keely turned and went, closing the door quietly behind her.

Chapter Twenty-five

Keely hurried down a brick-paved street in Dover, her blue cotton chintz skirts swaying as she walked. After leaving Brock that night in the warehouse in New York, she had found a small sloop departing for Lewes, Delaware. The widow Goldston had made all the arrangements and in a week Keely found herself home. It was a great comfort to hold Laura again, but having the babe in her arms made the ache for Brock even greater.

"Afternoon to you," a woman in a straw bonnet called as she passed Keely on the street. "Any word of your husband?" She stopped on the walk.

Taken unawares, Keely hesitated. This was the first time anyone had spoken to her civilly in public since she'd arrived in Dover. "Thank you for asking." She dared a cautious smile. "No word of his release, but I saw him only a week ago in New York. His spirits are high. I'm certain he'll be home soon."

The woman in the bonnet lowered her voice. "I'm Sally Thorner. My husband fights with our Delaware Regiment."

Keely accepted the hand the patriot woman offered. "Thank you for your kind words."

"Sometimes people make mistakes, Mistress Bartholomew. I hope you're not one to hold anything against them."

Keely nodded in understanding. "I have to be going, but it was nice speaking with you."

"We ladies of the Patriot Society meet occasionally for tea and talk. Would you like to come sometime?"

"Yes, I would, when this is all over and my husband's home safe again. Thank you."

Sally nodded. "I'll send a message next time we gather. Have a good day, Mistress Bartholomew."

Keely watched the patriot woman walk away and then turned to head back up the street. I guess I'm one of them now, she thought with amusement. I'm a patriot, a traitor to our King. It was funny that the transformation had come so slowly that she hadn't realized it was happening. When had she stopped being an English woman and become an American?

With a sigh, Keely hurried along, refusing to dwell on the matter. Right now she had to meet with Manessah and discuss the possibility of the informer being a member of the committee. Manessah had been on the eastern shore of Maryland when she'd returned from New York three days ago, but he'd returned last night. Keely had sent Mort with a message that it was urgent they speak in private. Manessah suggested they meet at the Golden Fleece tavern on the Green just after noon.

"Keely! Keely!" a voice called, startling her.

She looked up to see a covered carriage pulling up beside her on the street.

"Keely! Thank God you're safe, sweetheart! I've been mad with worry!" Micah alighted from the carriage dressed in a gold silk voided suit with

340

matching gold shoes.

"Micah!" Keely dropped her hands to her hips. "I don't want to talk to you!"

"Nonsense, love. We have so many plans to make. Come home to Fortune's Find and sup with me." He clasped her arm, and she tried to twist it free.

"Micah, release me. This isn't funny anymore!"

"Why are you so angry, sweetheart? I know that jaunt to New York was tiring. That's all it is, isn't it? You're just tired?"

She took a deep breath. "Micah, I went to see my husband."

"I know. And you told him about us? You told him you were going with me?"

Keely tried to take a step back, but he held fast to her arm. The carriage blocked her view of the street, in the same turn blocking anyone else's view of the two of them. "Micah, you must stop this. I'm not going anywhere with you! I don't love you! I love Brock!"

Micah snapped her arm viciously, pulling her against him. "Don't say that! Don't ever say that again. You should have married me. I wanted you." He lowered his voice. "I'll have you . . ."

Keely swung with her free arm, clipping Micah in the chin, but he twisted her arm behind her, making her cry out in pain. "Shut up," he ordered, "or someone will hear you!"

She opened her mouth to scream, but he clamped his hand hard down against it. She bit down on the soft flesh of his palm and he cursed her beneath his breath.

"Cain! Get down here and help me!" he ordered, stifling her voice with his injured hand.

Keely struggled, kicking as the manservant with the scarred face lifted her and shoved her into the carriage. She fell forward under the force of his

341

hands and struck her forehead on the corner of the seat. Dazed, she struggled to sit up, all too aware that Micah had jumped into the carriage and it was pulling away.

"Micah," she begged. "What are you doing to me?"

"Oh, love, you're bleeding. What has that beast Cain done to you?" Micah pulled a silk handkerchief from his sleeve and leaned to dab gently at her head.

She snatched the handkerchief from his hand, still on her knees on the carriage floor. "Don't touch me," she threatened. "Don't you ever touch me again!"

"Keely!" Micah sat back in the seat. "How can you talk to me like that?" He sounded like a schoolboy whose tender feelings had been injured. "I love you, sweetheart. I'd never hurt you." He studied her intently, his clear blue eyes wide with honesty. "I love you. I'm going to make you my wife."

"I'm Brock's wife," she insisted, making no attempt to cover the utter contempt in her voice. She held the handkerchief to her forehead and slowly the white silk turned crimson with her blood.

"I know. But I took care of all of that, sweet."

Keely lifted her head to stare at the handsome blond-haired man. Her throat constricted in fear until she thought she would suffocate. Suddenly everything was swirling; blackness threatened to overcome her. "Y-you did what?"

Micah folded his hands neatly on his lap. "I took care of it. Once Brock is out of the way, you'll be free to marry me, right?"

Feeling dizzy, Keely got up off her knees and sat down on the seat across from Micah. The carriage careened down the dirt road, heading east out of Dover at an alarming speed. It was very quickly becoming obvious to Keely that this was no silly infatuation Micah had for her. The man was disturbed!

Seeing her head sway, Micah caught her hand and set her upright. "I've no smelling salts with me," he cried in panic. "Keely, are you all right?"

She forced the stifling black void from her mind, clearing her thoughts. This was no time for silly fainting spells. If she was going to get herself out of this mess, she would need all her wits about her. "I—I'm all right, Micah." She wiped her mouth with the soiled handkerchief. "Could you . . . could you just open the window so I can get some air?"

He sighed. "Sorry, sweet, but then you might holler out and someone might hear you. We'll be at Fortune's Find in just a few minutes."

She lifted her head to stare at him. "Micah, how could you do this to me . . . to Brock? They may hang him, for God's sake!"

"I told you you never should have married the red bastard." He shook his head. "I told you he'd come to ill ends."

"Because of you!"

"Me—the next man? What difference would it make? He can thank me for keeping him safe as long as I did."

She took a deep breath, trying to clear her head. Micah wasn't making any sense. She was so confused. What did he mean, he'd kept Brock safe? "Where are you taking me?"

"I told you," he said exasperated. "To Fortune's Find."

"And what? You're going to hold me there against my will forever?"

He laughed. "Certainly not, love. I wouldn't do that to you. I'm going to take you with me."

343

"With you where?" she demanded.

Micah smoothed the golden silk coat he wore. "To my new assignment." He smiled. "We're going north and to the west!"

"Micah, I don't understand. What new assignment? What are you talking about? Your duties are here in Dover giving aid to the committee."

"We're going to a fort, in Detroit."

"Detroit?" Her eyebrows furrowed in confusion. "But those forts are Brit—" Keely stopped in mid-sentence, the nausea rising in her throat. All of a sudden, it all made sense, everything that had happened in the last year. Micah was the British informant. . . .

"Micah, how could you?" Keely paced the floor of his bedchamber. Cain stood outside the closed door, barring her escape. "He was your friend. You wouldn't really see him hang," she declared, still in shock.

Micah leaned back in an upholstered chair, tugging on his neat blond queue. "It's true enough that I didn't think they'd be quite so serious about the whole matter, but"—he shrugged—"it's a simple solution. My superiors wanted Brock, I wanted you."

Keely stared at Micah. How could he speak so calmly of Brock's impending death? It all seemed so unreal, Micah kidnapping her like this, his obsession with her. She had known for some time now that he was infatuated with her, but it had never entered her mind that his kind words and friendship would result in such a bizarre turn of events. "You started all of this, you could end it. You could save him, couldn't you?" she said, her voice barely audible in the opulent bedchamber.

He lifted his chin with interest. "I suppose I

could if I wanted to." His chest swelled with self-importance.

Keely forced herself to walk toward him, her gaze steady. "Would you do it for *me?*" Treat him like a child, she told herself. Treat him like Von Bueren, only remember, he's more dangerous.

Micah licked his lips, his breath quickening. She was so breathtakingly lovely, an angel with a halo of red-gold hair. "But if I saved him from the noose, you'd go running back to him. I'd have nothing."

Without thought, she spoke again. "No. If you give me your word that he'd be set free, Micah, I . . ." Her breath caught in her throat and she lowered her lashes. "I'd go with you," she finished. Her own words echoed in her ears.

"I don't know." Micah shook his head. "There could be no tricks. I could just have him arrested again."

"No, no tricks. I swear it." She touched her hand to her forehead. She had finally stanched the bleeding with Micah's handkerchief and now the wide gash was growing crusty. "I've never lied to you, Micah. You and I, we've been friends since I came to Dover."

His brows furrowed in puzzlement. "But you said you loved him . . ."

"I . . . could learn to love you, Micah."

He beamed. "You could?"

"Tell me you'll have him released."

"I'll think about it."

Keely went down on one knee, clasping Micah's hand. It seemed so tiny and pale compared to Brock's. "Please—for me?"

He turned her hand in his, lifting it to his lips. "Of your own free will, you would come?"

"Yes," she breathed. "But he has to be safe. You have to guarantee he'll never be arrested again," she pleaded desperately.

"I don't know . . ."

"You could do it, you know you could!" She stared up at him, her hazel eyes fixed on his face. "You must be a very important man to the British."

He bobbed his head. "I am. You know I am."

Keely withdrew her hand and walked away. "You'll have to free him if you really want me, Micah."

He jumped up out of his chair. "You're all that matters to me in this world, my love."

Keely shuddered. The same words that Brock had once uttered sounded so twisted coming from Micah. "If you love me as you say you do, you'll have to prove it to me."

Micah rested his hand on her shoulder, turning her around. "Of course I love you; I could never live without you. Don't you see that? That's why I must have you!" He released her, running to his bed. Getting down on his knees, he pulled a small chest from beneath the bed. "Look at the things I've saved," he told her eagerly. "Things of yours. At night, in my bed, I surrounded myself with your belongings because I don't have you."

As the minutes ticked by, the hideous strength of Micah's obsession was becoming more apparent to Keely. She watched him withdraw one of her handkerchiefs, a glove, a pressed rose from the box.

"Where did you get those things?" she demanded. "They're mine!"

"I hope you're not angry with me, love. I would have asked, but you'd have said no, so I just took them."

Keely snatched the glove from his hand. She'd lost it at a party he'd escorted her to in February. The lace handkerchief had been missing more than a month. She watched incredulously as he removed one item after another from the box . . . a button, a bit of green ribbon, even a long strand of red hair. In disgust, Keely turned away.

"Tell me you'll have him set free, Micah," she ordered firmly. "If you want me, I must have your solemn promise that he'll be all right."

Carefully, Micah returned each item to the box. "What of his child?"

Keely lifted her dark lashes, suddenly very tired. "She will stay with her father. If you're to drag me into the wilderness, she's better left here with him."

"Yes, yes, I think you're right, darling." Micah put out his hand. "The glove, might I have it back?"

Keely threw it at him in surrender. Nothing seemed real anymore. How could life be so cruel? Brock's life would be spared, but in order for that to happen, she would have to go with this madman! But once Brock was free and he returned home, he would find her gone and come searching for her. Keely knew in her heart that Brock would go to the ends of the earth to find her. It was her only hope.

Micah returned Keely's glove to his treasure chest and slipped it under his bed. "I think we should leave tomorrow. I have business at a fort in Penn's Colony. We'll stay there a few days and then on to Detroit."

"When will Brock be set free?" Keely asked without emotion.

"I could have a message sent tonight," he answered hesitantly. "The captain could be released by the end of the week." Micah moved to the tea table beside the settee and poured two porcelain cups full. "Would that suit, love?"

Keely lowered herself into the chair across from

347

Micah. Her head was spinning and her throat was dry. She took the teacup he offered. "You want me to go with you. What's expected of me?"

He peered over the rim of his teacup. "I just want you to love me . . ." he told her innocently.

The hot tea soothed her throat. "You don't expect me to bed you tonight, do you?" she asked starkly. She could go with him, she could even pretend to care for him, but she knew she could never ever let him touch her.

"What kind of beast do you think I am, Keely?" He dumped a second spoon of sugar into his teacup, then added another. "I know that will take time, love. And I'm willing to wait. What kind of gentleman would force a woman into intimacies against her will?"

"What kind of gentleman would kidnap a woman and take her from her husband and child?" The moment the words were out of her mouth, she regretted them.

Sadistic anger flashed across Micah's face. "I'm not kidnapping you," he snapped. "You agreed to go! Do you or don't you want the red bastard set free?"

"Yes!" She leaned forward in the chair. "I'm sorry, Micah. I didn't mean it!"

His anger faded. "I didn't think you did. Now finish your tea. I'll be taking you back to your house to get whatever you want to take with you."

"All right. But first you have to write the message that will have Brock released. I want to see it."

He shrugged. "Very well." Getting up from the settee, he walked to a small desk and sat down. In a matter of moments he was bringing a sheet of paper for her approval.

Keely took the document, taking care not to

348

smudge the wet ink. She read the letter quickly. "You didn't say why he was to be released. Don't you have to make up a reason?" She looked up at Micah.

"No. They've gotten enough information out of me in the last two years to humor me on this one. Besides, Von Bueren owes me a favor."

She handed him back the letter. "You promise it will actually be sent?"

"Cain," Micah called.

The manservant stepped inside the bedchamber. "Sir?"

"Get Charles Lutton to deliver this to Major Perkins. I want it sent to Lieutenant Colonel Von Bueren in New York immediately."

"Right away, sir." The man with the scarred face took the note from his master and exited the bedchamber.

"Charles Lutton?" Keely asked. "Isn't he one of the new members of the committee?"

Micah returned to the settee and lifted the silver teapot to pour himself another cup. "Very observant. He's to replace me here in Dover. Such a nice young man; I recruited him myself. More tea, darling?"

"Now remember . . ." Micah caught Keely by the arm as she started up the steps of the house. "You do anything to give me or our plan away and I swear Brock Bartholomew will be dead by sunset tomorrow."

Keely pulled her hand from his grasp, staring at him in the darkness. "I understand."

"Let's go then. Pack as little as possible. I'll buy you new gowns. When I finish this assignment, I thought maybe we'd do the tour, Paris, Venice, perhaps the Orient. Would you like that, dearest?" He followed her up the front steps.

"It would be lovely . . ." she lied.

It was near midnight when the two entered the front hall of her and Brock's home. A lamp stood burning on the table in anticipation of her return.

Carrying the lamp, Keely went straight to the bedchamber she and Brock had shared, just as Micah had instructed. Hurrying, she gathered a few necessary items, trying to ignore evidence of Brock lying everywhere. She pushed aside his shirts to gather two clean shifts. A cocked hat he wore with his Sunday best fell haphazardly to the floor as she gathered a hairbrush, a small box of hairpins, and a handful of ribbons to tie back her hair. Micah followed behind her, filling a kidskin bag he'd brought from Fortune's Find.

"Miss Keely?" The sound of the nursery door startled Keely, making her drop the silver-handled toothbrush Brock had given her only weeks ago.

"Miss Keely, thank God yer home! We was worried sick about ye!"

"Patience, go back to bed," Keely said in a tired voice.

"Miss Keely, is that Master Micah?" She shifted from one bare foot to the other.

"Patience, I said you may go back to bed. I'll be in to see Laura in a minute."

"Where you been all day? Everyone's been lookin' fer ye. Master Manessah, he's been here—"

"Patience!" Keely interrupted sharply. "I said you're dismissed."

Patience gave a gulp, staring from her mistress to the man who stood in the shadows behind her. "Yes, ma'am." Nodding her head, she backed into the nursery and closed the door behind her.

Micah kneeled to retrieve the toothbrush. "Excellent, darling. I can see we're going to get along just fine."

"That's it," Keely answered quietly. "I want to say good-bye to Laura and then we can go."

"This is all you're taking? Don't you think you need at least one clean gown?"

"The one I have on is fine. Just let me kiss Laura." Her face remained inanimate.

He followed behind her and Keely stopped. "Might I go alone?" she asked. If only she could be alone with Patience for just a minute . . .

"I'm sorry, dear, but I can't risk it. What if you were to reveal something to your maid? You just can't be trusted yet, my love. I must be careful until we're a safe distance from here."

With a sigh of defeat, Keely entered the small nursery. Micah stood in the doorway.

Staring down at the sleeping infant, tears welled in Keely's eyes. Slowly she leaned to kiss the baby's downy red head. "Good-bye, sweetheart," she whispered. "Mama loves you."

"Where ye goin' Miss Keely? Goin' all the way to New York again?"

Keely wiped her eyes with the back of her hand. She couldn't let herself cry, because if she started, she knew she wouldn't be able to stop. "Patience, I want you to stay here in the nursery with Laura. You're not to follow me downstairs."

The maid pressed herself to the nursery wall, frightened by the strange tone of her mistress's voice. "Yes, ma'am."

"Let's go." Keely turned, brushing past Micah.

He closed the door to the nursery. "There's just one more thing, Keely, before we go."

"What's that?"

"A note." He went to Brock's writing desk. "Sit down here and tell Brock that you've left him for me."

351

Horrified, she took a step back. "No, Micah." Suddenly everything was slipping. How would Brock know to come rescue her? He would think she'd truly betrayed him! "I couldn't!" she choked.

"You must. I know the man; if he loses fairly, he'll accept his lot in life. He won't come looking for you."

She shook her head. "I couldn't possibly," she cried desperately. "You do it, if you must."

"Oh, no. It must be in your own handwriting. It's the only way he'll believe it."

"Please. Don't make me do it, Micah . . ."

He took her arm. "It's the only way. If you don't do it, the deal is off and Captain Bartholomew dies. Now sit. We have to hurry. Cain's waiting with the carriage." He pushed her roughly into the chair and retrieved the lamp, setting it on the edge of the desk. "Pick up the quill and write exactly what I tell you," he instructed.

Numb, Keely did as she was told. Just as she was signing her name at the bottom of the letter, Lucy came bursting into the bedchamber.

"God sakes! Miss Keely, have you lost your head? What are you and Mr. Micah doin' in your chamber in the middle of the night?" The maid was dressed in nothing but a thin shift, her long blond hair falling unplaited down her back.

"Lucy. Go back to bed, this is none of your concern," Micah told her, helping Keely up from the chair.

Keely moved in a dazed state. She couldn't believe what she had just written. In releasing Brock from his death sentence, she had signed her own. Now he would never come looking for her. He would never attempt to rescue her from this twisted fate. He would think she had betrayed their love. She was doomed. If she couldn't escape from Micah on her own, she would never see Laura again. She would never get a chance to explain to Brock what had happened.

"Oh, shut your mouth, Mr. Micah, I was talkin' to Miss Keely!" Lucy spat angrily.

Micah struck out with his hand, catching Lucy sharply on the cheek. The maidservant gasped, her hand flying to her face.

Micah picked up the leather bag that held Keely's possessions and started out of the bedchamber. "Come on, Keely."

Keely fell in behind, too ashamed even to speak to Lucy. Her hand went to her neckline as she struggled to breathe and then she stopped in midstep. Shoving her hand below the neckline of her gown, she pulled out the amulet her father had given her so many years ago and yanked the copper tuppence from the chain.

"Keely," Micah insisted from the hallway. "Come along, dear."

With one swift motion Keely tossed the amulet to a surprised Lucy and then hurried out of the room.

Chapter Twenty-six

Just after dawn the following morning Keely dressed at Micah's insistence and prepared to leave Fortune's Find. She had slept soundly through the night, a dreamless sleep of hopelessness. When Micah had come to her bedchamber to wake her, he'd brought tea and muffins. She sent him away with the meal, telling him she would be down in a few minutes. Without thought, she packed her small bag and met him in the front hallway.

"I'm sorry you didn't get much sleep, love." Micah kissed her cheek affectionately. "But once we're a safe distance from here, we'll take the time to rest and enjoy ourselves." He turned to a maid scurrying down the hall. "Connie, have the bags been loaded into the carriage?"

"Aye, sir." The dark-haired girl dropped her head in submission. "Mr. Cain is waitin' out front for you and the missus."

"Perfect." Micah dropped his hand on Keely's shoulder. "If you're ready, sweet, we can go. I've taken care of everything here. The staff will stay on to care for the house until Mother and Father return."

"They don't know you're leaving?" Keely asked.

"They'll find out soon enough. I was the one that encouraged them to go to Europe in the first place. Things were just getting too hot here."

"They never knew who you were, what you did?"

He applied even pressure to her shoulder, propelling her forward. "Shall we go, darling?"

Clutching the cotton wrap that hung on her shoulders, Keely went out the front door and down the steps to the waiting carriage. The sound of pounding hooves caught her attention as Micah offered his hand to help her in.

Down the long lane that led to the plantation house came a lone rider on a dark steed. The horse moved at breakneck speed headed directly for them.

"Who in the blast is that?" Micah demanded.

"Don't know, sir." Cain leaped down from the driver's seat of the coach, a French rifle cradled in his arm.

"Keely, get into the carriage at once; Cain will take care of it," Micah insisted sharply.

She balked, squinting to see who the rider was. She recognized the horse, and her heart skipped a beat. It had come from her husband's stables.

Tearing her arm from Micah's grasp, Keely dashed around the side of the coach.

"Miss Keely!" the rider called frantically.

"Keely, come back here, damn you," Micah shouted.

"Mort!" Lifting her skirts, she ran toward him, her heart pumping wildly.

"Cain, you shoot her and I'll have you castrated," Micah shouted. He yanked the rifle from his henchman's hand.

A single shot sounded and Keely screamed, covering her ears as the rider's hat flew off and he was unseated. Mort fell beneath his horse, his

355

blond hair turning crimson. Keely sank to her knees in utter revulsion as the man who had tried to save her was crushed beneath the hooves of the frantic animal.

Keely lay there in the damp grass sobbing until Micah tugged gently on her arm. "Come," he insisted. "We have to go."

"What about Mort?" she demanded angrily. "He was my friend."

"Cain will take care of the body and then catch up." He shifted the rifle to the opposite hand and pulled her to her feet. "Now come along. We have to hurry, dear."

Dazed, Keely followed him. A minute later, the carriage pulled out of the drive of Fortune's Find, bound for Detroit.

Keely winced, rubbing the small of her back as she eased the strained muscles of her buttocks. Three days ago she and Micah had left the carriage behind and begun to move northwest on horseback. They traveled from sunup to sundown, stopping only for water and to eat a quick meal. Micah was nervous, frequently sending men back to be certain no one was following them. Tonight it had been well after dark before Micah finally declared it time to put up camp for the night.

Continuing to massage her sore limbs, Keely peered out of her tent. Twenty feet away was a campfire, and over it was a spit holding three plump rabbits. The smell tantalized Keely's nose and made her stomach growl in protest. She had refused the noonday meal Micah offered her and now she was nearly faint with hunger.

Shifting her weight, Keely slipped off her boot and studied her blistered heel. She knew Micah carried medicinal salves on one of the pack horses, but she couldn't bring herself to ask him for anything. Instead, she washed her feet with cool water she'd brought from a nearby stream and then replaced her cotton stockings.

Keely swatted at a mosquito and watched one of Cain's ruffians cut off a piece of roasting rabbit and pop it into his mouth. She licked her lips, sorely tempted to abandon her pride and venture out to share in the meal.

She put her hand on the tent flap and froze when she spotted Micah deep in conversation with Cain just beyond the light of the fire. Micah's shadow, distorted by the crackling flames, seemed the outline of some grotesque demon.

Keely shivered despite the hot summer night's breeze. She was more frightened of Micah now than when they had left Dover a week ago. There was no pattern to his bizarre behavior. One minute Micah would be coddling her, speaking gently, laughing, being his old charming self and then the next minute he became irrational. Without reason he would strike out at the servants or beat his horse mercilessly. Once he had threatened to strike her. Over and over again Micah swore that he loved her, yet Keely could see a sadistic violence bubbling beneath the surface of his conscious mind.

The thought of escape taunted her day and night. All she wanted was Brock and her baby, yet if she did manage to escape and make it back across the wilderness, how could she explain to Brock what had happened? The letter left behind had been in her own handwriting. Brock would never believe she had been taken by force. Micah was an important man in the community, a patriot hero . . . a man Brock had been jealous of from the beginning. Brock would see only betrayal in her disappearance.

Sensing that Micah was watching her, Keely lifted her gaze to meet his. He puffed on a small cigar, rolling it between his fingers, studying her, a silly smile on his face.

Keely's hand fell from the tent flap and she drew a ragged breath. Tonight? she wondered. Will you come to my tent tonight? The thought of Micah's hands on her made her flesh crawl. I'd sooner die than let you touch me. After Brock, she could belong to no other man, not ever. Keely lifted her chin in defiance. "You'll have to kill me first," she whispered beneath her breath.

Fueled by that thought, Keely crawled out of the tent. Ignoring Micah's stares, she took a plate one of the men offered and accepted a thick slice of roasted rabbit.

"I'm so glad you've found your appetite, love," Micah said, moving closer.

Keely went to the edge of the firelight and sat on a fallen log.

"You have to keep up your strength." He followed her. "I know the trip is difficult on you, but once we're safe within a fort, there'll be time to rest."

Keely ignored him, sampling the succulent dark meat.

He knelt in front of her. "Keely?" He caught her chin with his hand and forced her to look at him. "Are you all right? Are you ill?"

"I'm fine," she answered without emotion. Their eyes locked and he dropped his hand.

"God's teeth, woman, then what ails you?" he asked irritably. He crushed out his cigar in the dirt at her feet. "You've been sulking since we left Dover."

She continued to chew at the rabbit. "You killed

Mort."

He laughed harshly. "Is that all it is?"

"Mort was good to me."

Micah toyed with the hem of Keely's blue dress. ". . . Not the only friend of yours I've killed."

She choked on the meat. "What did you say?"

He smiled. "I just said he's not the first." He chuckled.

She didn't want to ask, yet she couldn't help herself. "Who . . . who else?"

An unholy light flickered in Micah's bright blue eyes. "The woman. She had to go. I was the logical choice." He shrugged. "She knew it was me. Couldn't have her telling tales, could we?"

"What woman?" Keely demanded.

"Jenna, of course. You didn't know?" His mouth twitched into a smile. "I guess I thought you were brighter than you are."

"You son of a bitch," she murmured.

Without warning, Micah struck her sharply on the cheek and her plate fell from her lap.

Keely's mouth trembled, but she refused to look away. Her face stung from his blow, but she didn't lift her hand to ease the pain.

Micah stood up. "I don't like that. No lady speaks to her husband in that manner."

"You're not my husband," she managed through tight lips. Oh God, not Jenna, she thought. It can't be true. But in her heart she knew he told the truth. Was there no end to this nightmare?

Micah smoothed the front of his sleeveless leather waistcoat. "I am if I say I am!" he shouted.

She swatted at a mosquito buzzing around her head. If she thought about Jenna now, if she thought about any of it, she'd surely go mad. "I think I'll go to sleep."

Micah grabbed her arm, pulling her to her feet.

"You said you'd come with me." His tone softened. "I kept my part of the bargain, you have to keep yours." He tried to smooth the long red tresses that tumbled from her chignon, but she pulled back.

"I came with you, didn't I?"

"You said you could love me." He spoke faster. "We're going to have a good life together. I'm going to make you happier than that red bastard could have made you."

She knew there was no arguing with him. Crossing him would only make him more agitated. "Micah, I'm tired." She stared at him, her face without emotion. So much had happened that she was almost devoid of any feeling. "I want to go to sleep now."

He lifted her hand to his lips, kissing it gently. "Sleep well, my love. Another week and we should reach the first fort. We'll stay there until you're rested. I promise."

She pulled her hand from his grasp and went to her tent, dropping the flap behind her.

The last mile seemed longer to Brock than it had ever been. Everything looked the same, the brickhouses, the giant oak trees, the fields of corn and rye that spread in every direction, yet it all somehow seemed different. Urging his horse faster, Brock turned the corner past the Golden Fleece tavern. There hadn't been time to send Keely a note after he'd been released. He'd found a smuggling vessel headed south only hours after he'd been let off the *Jersey* and the trip had been brief. With the wind and tides in their favor, it had taken only three days to make the port at Dover.

Brock took a deep breath, inhaling the soft breeze of late summer. It had been only a year since Keely had come into his life, and now it seemed as if she had always been his. Thoughts of her, of her long, thick auburn hair, her laughing mouth, her stormy hazel eyes, made his chest tighten and his heart beat more rapidly. All he wanted was to hold her again. She would take away the pain; she would chase away the fears. In her arms lay salvation.

Sitting there beneath the decks of that blasted prison ship, Brock had come to realize that although the fight for independence was important, it was not as vital to his life as Keely was. Priorities, that was what Lloyd had said was necessary. He had said that Brock had to know the importance of each thing in his life and then he must live accordingly. The war was of great consequence, but without Keely, nothing mattered.

Dismounting at the front stoop of the house, Brock ran up the front steps and flung open the door. He tossed his battered cocked hat on the side table, running a hand through his dark hair. "Keely! Keely," he shouted. "Keely, where are you?"

"Masta Brock?" came Ruth's voice from the kitchen. "God's sake, man, is that you?" She came running from the back of the house.

"I think so, Ruthie." He laughed. "Where's Keely? Where's Laura?"

The old servant threw her arms around Brock's middle. "Never thought I'd be so happy to see any man, Masta Brock!"

Brock laughed, hugging the old woman.

"Loose me, Masta Brock, 'fore you squeeze the life right out of me!" The cook took a step back, wiping the corners of her eyes with her floured apron.

"Master Brock!" Lucy shouted, coming down the grand staircase. "You a ghost?" Laura rode contentedly on the maid's hip.

Brock patted his chest. "I don't think so, Lucy. Give me that sweetheart." He held out his hands, taking his daughter from her.

Little Laura cooed and chewed at the strings of her bonnet.

"I can't believe how much you've grown," he marveled. "Aren't you beautiful?" He tugged off the infant's white cap to kiss her head of tight red curls. "Where's your mama," he crooned, looking into her dark eyes. "Where's your mama, princess?"

Lucy scuffed at the floor with her bare foot, and Ruth turned away to straighten a portrait hanging on the wall.

Brock's face fell. "What? What is it?" His palms grew damp as he looked from Lucy's face to Ruth's. "Tell me . . ."

Ruth reached to take Laura gently from his arms. "Take Masta Brock upstairs and show 'im the note, Lucy."

Lucy turned and went up the front staircase, the bounce gone from her walk. "It just don't make any sense, Master Brock, after all she went through."

"Lucy, what are you talking about? Where's my wife?"

"Gone."

"Gone? Gone where?" he demanded.

"Don't know. She didn't say." Lucy pushed open the bedchamber door and went to open the heavy drapes to let in the sunlight. "The note she left is there on the desk, sir. We didn't touch it. We didn't touch anythin'."

Confused, Brock picked up the note, recognizing Keely's handwriting. "How long's she been gone?" he asked quietly.

"A good fortnight, sir." Lucy tucked her hands behind her, at a loss as to what to do.

"You can go now, Lucy."

"Aren't you gonna read the letter?"

Brock sat down on a chair, suddenly weary. "Go on, Lucy."

She bobbed a curtsy. "Yes, sir. If . . . if there's anything you want . . ."

"I'll call you, Lucy."

Lucy studied her master's striking face for a moment, feeling the pain that seeped through him, and then she left, closing the door quietly behind her.

Brock took a deep breath, rising to go to the window. He stared down at the garden below, taking notice of the bright wildflowers that bloomed in every nook and cranny of the small boxwood garden. Wearily, he lifted the sheet of paper and read it.

Brock,

By the time you receive this letter, I will be gone. Please don't try to follow me; I've made my choice. I tried to live with you and be a good wife, but my love for Micah was too great. Please forgive me for the pain I've caused you, but believe me when I tell you this is better for all concerned.

Keely

Brock crushed the delicate paper in his hand, the tears welling in his dark eyes. "No, Keely, please, no." For a moment the pain was so great that Brock thought he would die of it. Then it eased, slowly replacing itself with a red-hot anger, an anger more intense than any he'd ever felt before.

"God damn you, Keely!" he shouted. He threw the paper to the floor, crushing it with the heel of his boot. Without thinking, he lifted a French vase from a table and sent it spiraling across the room. It shattered over the bed, splinters of bone china falling onto the pillows.

"God damn you! How could you?" he shouted. He kicked over a small teak table and his chess set fell to the floor, pieces rolling in every direction. "For him . . . how could you?"

Outside the bedchamber door, Lucy and Ruth stood, their backs pressed against the wall. "I never heard Master Brock carry on like that," Lucy murmured shakily. "He's gonna hurt himself, or hurt one of us."

Ruth shook her head, wiping her brow with the hem of her apron. In the past two weeks she felt as if she'd aged a century. It just didn't make any sense, Miss Keely running off with that dandy, Micah Lawrence. She thought she was too good a judge of character to have been so gravely mistaken about the girl. Ruth glanced up at Lucy. "He won't hurt nobody. No need to be afraid. Masta Brock just isn't that kind of man."

"What'll we do?" Lucy asked, twisting her hands.

"What can we do, child?"

"Lucy!" Brock boomed from inside the bedchamber. The door flew open. "Lucy!"

"Y-yes, sir?" The maidservant took a step back in fright.

"You saw your mistress the night she left?"

"Yes, sir. Me and Patience. Ruth and Blacki was sleepin'."

Brock waved a broad hand. "Come in here. I want to talk to Patience, too."

Lucy gulped. "She's gone to fetch flax for spinnin'. Ruth told her it was all right. She won't be back 'fore dusk."

"Don't just stand there, come in here!" Brock glanced at Ruth. "I'm all right, Ruthie. You go back to Laura." He turned his back on the women and Lucy followed on his heels.

Brock walked to the windows to stare out at the garden. He pushed one of them open and the heavy drapes fluttered in the warm breeze. "Tell me what you saw, Lucy," he said starkly. "What you heard that night."

"W-well, sir." She got down on her knees and began to retrieve the chess pieces that littered the floor. "Miss Keely, she went out earlier in the day. Said she had business. Then she just didn't come home. Mr. Manessah, he come lookin' for her."

Brock stroked his chin. "What time?"

The girl set several chess pieces on the bed and got down on her hands and knees again. "I don't know, but it was dark outside. Mister Manessah, he was a sight worried . . . said she was supposed to meet him hours ago at the Golden Fleece."

"Why?"

"Didn't say. Just told us to let 'im know when she come in." Lucy uprighted the teak table and returned the chessboard to its proper place.

"So when did she come home?" he asked bitterly.

"Midnight."

"Did she come alone?"

Lucy made an event of arranging the chess pieces. "N-no sir. She come with Master Lawrence."

Brock caught Lucy by the wrist. "Leave it. You're doing it all wrong. I'll set it right later. Just clean up the rest of the mess."

Lucy backed away.

"Go on." Brock returned to the window, fingering the drapes. "She came with Micah."

"I come into the chamber here and asked wha
she was doin'. Guess my mouth was a little smar
because . . . because Mr. Micah, he slapped me.

Brock turned, frowning. "He slapped you?"

She bobbed her head. "Hard."

"What was your mistress doing?"

"Just sittin' there at the desk" — Lucy pointed — "
queer look on her face. Then he told her it wa
time to go and they went."

Brock rubbed his forehead, trying to make sens
of it all. "And she never said anything to you
Lucy?"

"Nothin'."

He began to pace the floor. The evidence wa
obvious, she'd left him for Micah. But somethin
just didn't sound right. A spark of hope ignite
deep within him. "Sit down, Lucy."

The girl plopped herself in a chair.

"Now I want you to think and think hard." H
spoke quietly, putting emphasis on each word
"You said she looked queer, what do you mean?

Lucy shrugged. "Just didn't look like herself
kinda nervous-like."

"Lucy," he said, gazing intently at the girl. "Ca
you remember anything she did that seeme
strange? Was she trying to tell you anything eve
though she didn't speak?"

She looked at him blankly. "No. She just lef
with him." The servant paused. "Wait a second
Master Brock." Her eyes lit up. "She *did* do some
thing kind of odd."

"What?"

She put up a finger. "Wait a minute." Lucy ra
out of the bedchamber, returning a minute late
with something in her hand. "I don't know if it
means anything, but she yanked this off her neck

366

and threw it to me as she was goin' out the door."

Brock opened his hand to receive the tiny object. It was her copper pence, the one she always wore around her neck on a chain. The copper pence her father had given to her. "Lucy, she gave you this and she didn't say anything?" he asked excitedly.

"Didn't say a word, just tossed it when she was going out the door."

He rubbed the sentimental object between his fingers thoughtfully. "Did Micah see her give it to you?"

"No, sir. He'd gone into the hall. He was in an awful hurry," she added disdainfully.

Brock closed his hand over the object, his eyes drifting shut for a brief moment. "I'm so sorry, love," he whispered. "I never should have doubted you."

"Brock!" A masculine voice from down the hall startled Brock. "Brock, where the hell are you?"

"Manessah, that you?" Brock met Jenna's brother in the hallway.

"Sorry to come into your home like this, but I just got word from the shipyard that you'd returned."

"Manessah, you're not going to believe what's happened."

The tall patriot's eyes met Brock's. "It's Micah."

"God damn him!" Brock clenched the amulet tightly in his fist. "Come in so we can talk."

The men entered the bedchamber and Lucy fled. Brock closed the door behind her. "How long have you known?"

Manessah lifted an eyebrow, surveying the broken china and scattered chess pieces. "Just since this morning."

"He's taken her, you know."

"I know."

Brock's eyes were riveted to his friend's face. "Do you know where he's headed?"

"It's bad, Brock. Detroit. And if he gets that far, I don't know if we can get her out."

Brock looked away.

"The good thing is," Manessah continued, "he's scheduled for a stop at an English-held fort in Penn's state. "

"That's where we'll catch up with him then," Brock said quietly. He looked up again. "Anyone owe you any favors? We're going to need a regiment or two."

Chapter Twenty-seven

Keely sat quietly on a rough wooden bench, her back pressed to one of the inner walls of the fort. She hugged her knees to her chest, her eyes drifting shut. The sound of crude male laughter filled her ears as she leaned forward to rest her forehead on her knees.

She and Micah and his men had been here in this fort for two weeks and hour by hour she felt as though she was drifting farther from reality. For days Micah had been promising they would move on, but each morning he admitted they might stay one more day.

The fort was a log structure built behind walls of cut timber somewhere in the wilderness of Pennsylvania. It was defended by a ragtag assortment of misfit English officers and enlisted men, and was overrun with Indians dressed in breechcloths and English uniform coats. Though the Englishmen claimed to be here at the command of their superiors in New York, Keely wondered if they hadn't just been long forgotten and left to their own devices. A few women lived within the protective walls of the fort, but they were dirty ignorant females who peddled their bodies in desperation to feed themselves and their children.

The degradation that ruled the encampment disgusted Keely and she'd told Micah so. He'd only laughed and said it was good to see how the "other side" lived. His reply had infuriated Keely, but she didn't dare demonstrate her anger too forcefully. Although he had not hurt her other than an occasional slap, she knew she had to tread softly. Not far beneath the surface of his charming veneer lurked an uncontrollable violence.

"Keely!"

Micah's voice startled her and she looked up. The crude, windowless room was well lit with hanging lanterns. In the center stood a wooden table with six men seated around it engrossed in a game of cards. Several Iroquois Indian guards sat on the dirt floor talking among themselves in a strange mixture of French and their native tongue.

"Keely," Micah repeated. "Did you hear me? Come here . . ." He pushed his chair back from the table, signaling her with his finger.

Wearily, she stood up. She knew there was no sense in resisting his demands. If she didn't get up and come to him, he'd drag her across the room, to the delight of the other men.

"What is it?" she asked, her voice barely above a whisper.

"Fill my cup again. I told you to keep it full."

As she lifted the bottle of whiskey from the table and poured, Micah caressed her backside with his hand. "Micah, stop it," she warned.

An officer with a pipe in his mouth chuckled, tossing down a card. "Your turn, Lawrence. Can't you keep your hands off your pretty wife in our presence?" He lifted his eyes to meet Keely's meaningfully. "Makes a man awful jealous." He tapped

370

his empty tankard. "Have her give me a douse too."

Keely cringed at the word *wife*. When they had arrived at the fort, Micah had explained to her that the only way she would be safe from the other men was to say she was his wife. Even then, she was not to leave his sight. If she did, he had warned, he couldn't be responsible for her virtue. So, she remained a prisoner of the worst kind. There were no chains to hold her here. She remained with Micah of her own choosing . . . because she knew she must.

Keely moved out of the way of Micah's hand and filled the officer's tankard. Then she moved around the table, filling the others' cups. An Iroquois with a shaved head brushed against her as she leaned to fill his tankard. The man grinned, reaching out to catch a lock of her hair. Keely glanced across the table at Micah, but he was engrossed in his cards.

Keely's eyes met pitch black. "Let go," she insisted through clenched teeth.

The Iroquois laughed deep in his throat. "Very beautiful." He grinned, grasping a large hunk of hair. "More beautiful a scalp I never see. It would hang well on my belt."

She grimaced at the pain he caused her as he twisted her hair around his hand, forcing her to draw closer. Tears stung Keely's eyes. "Micah . . ." She looked across the table to see Micah staring intently, a strange glimmer of interest in his eyes. He seemed to enjoy seeing this man hurt her!

"Micah!" she said loudly. "Make him stop."

The odd expression was gone from Micah's face as fast as it had appeared. "John, let her go. I've warned you before." He returned his attention to his game.

The Iroquois brave laughed aloud, releasing Keely. She took a step back, rubbing her head. Filling two more cups, she went to return the bottle

371

to Micah. As she backed up, he caught her arm. "Not so fast, *wife,*" he chided. "A kiss for your master."

"Micah, no," she hissed. "Let go."

"Is it too much for a husband to ask his wife for such a small favor?"

"Micah, you're hurting me, let go."

Several of the other men glanced up with interest.

Micah pushed up out of his chair. "I said a kiss, wife," he threatened.

She rested her hands on his chest. "Micah, you're drunk!"

He pulled her away from the table by her arm, out of earshot of the other men. "Don't you do this to me," he warned. "You came of your own free will. I won't be embarrassed by you in front of the other men."

"I said I would come with you," she challenged. "I didn't agree to be mauled in public."

He pulled her against him. "I've had enough of this bitchy behavior, Keely. This is not the woman I fell in love with."

She laughed bitterly, turning her face from his so that she didn't have to feel his breath on her lips. "She's dead, Micah. She's gone."

"Nonsense!" He grasped her by the shoulders, giving her a shake. "Now you wise up and start behaving yourself." He turned her face to his with his hand and forced his lips against hers.

Keely closed her eyes, her face stony, her flesh unyielding. When he received no response, he pushed her aside and she fell back, catching herself before she hit the wall.

"Go sit down," Micah ordered. Then he returned to the card table. One of the officers patted him on the back as he sat down and Micah laughed, lifting his tankard.

Keely went back to her bench and sat down,

drawing up her knees again. Weary, she closed her eyes, blocking out the sounds of the men's voices and the harsh laughter directed toward her.

Brock . . . Her lips turned ever so slightly into a smile. She thought of his dark eyes filled with laughter, his broad bronze hands that caressed her so gently, his voice that filled her heart with joy. *Ki-ti-hi* . . . that was what he called her.

She wondered what he was doing now. Was he holding Laura? Was he on the *Tempest* somewhere on the Chesapeake? Keely's heart twisted beneath her breast until it became a physical hurt. Brock would never know that she truly loved him. To him, she was a betrayer, and when Laura grew into a woman, he would tell her what her mother had done.

A tear slipped down Keely's cheek and she brushed it away hastily. It was thoughts of Laura and Brock that kept her from going mad. She spent hours dreaming of them, reliving past moments, laughing to herself at her own foolishness. Now that Brock was gone from her life forever, she desperately regretted those first months of her marriage. How could she have been so obstinate? It wasn't until after Laura's birth that she had realized she was in love with her husband. Their time as man and wife had been so brief. If only she could have had those first few months back . . . she'd live them differently now.

Keely dozed on and off until the sound of movement in the room made her open her eyes. The men who had been playing cards with Micah were getting up and hurrying out of the room. A buzz of excitement flowed through the knot of Iroquois at the far end of the room as they gathered rifles from a heap in the corner.

Spotting Micah speaking to one of the Englishmen, she went to him. "What is it? What's going on?"

Micah turned to her, his mouth twitching nervously. "A silly little uprising, apparently. Nothing to worry your pretty head over." He looked unconvinced.

"What kind of uprising? I don't understand."

The officer pulled on his coat and began to button it up. "No need to worry Mistress Lawrence. It happens on occasion, but I can promise you we're perfectly safe within these walls. These Injuns love to get into an uproar. We let them do the fighting; we watch from the rampart. Care to come?"

A mixture of fear and hope colored her face. "Someone is attacking the fort? Who?"

The officer shrugged, strapping a pistol around his waist. "Never know. Could be a bunch of Injuns; every once in a while a band of patriot rebels breaks through." He smiled. "But they never get out alive."

Rebels? Keely thought. Maybe they could get her out. Maybe they could help.

"You stay here, Keely." Micah picked up his tankard and the bottle of whiskey from the table.

"No. I want to go with you to . . . to watch." She touched his arm lightly.

"I said stay here. Mark says he'll leave one of his red bastards to watch after you; you'll be safe enough."

"But Micah, I'm scared," she said, feigning weakness. "I want to be with you."

Micah glanced at Mark, smiling with self-importance. "I'm sorry, love, but you'll be safest here. They're not even certain who it is yet."

At that moment a sound of gunshot echoed, followed by several more. Somewhere within the walls of the fort an Iroquois emitted a high-pitched hoot of victory. Through the doorway that led into a corridor Keely could see men and Indians filing by with rifles flung over their shoulders. Somewhere a bell clanged.

374

"Damnation," the officer muttered. "Fire. Every time we let these damned Indians fight, they set the place on fire! You coming, Lawrence?"

Micah smiled at Keely. "You stay, love and I'll send for you if I think it's safe. All right?" He brushed his lips across her cheek.

A moment later there was no one left in the room but Keely and a tall, gangly Indian dressed in blue breeches and a hide tunic. He sat on the bench on the far wall from Keely, whittling on a stick. For a long time Keely just sat on the bench listening to the gunfire and the bloodcurdling shouts of glee coming from the Indians. Then she got up and began to pace. The Iroquois guard paid no attention to her.

Keely kept glancing at the door each time she passed it. Then, with each turn, as she started across the room again, her path grew closer to the door. Finally the Indian brave stood up, walked to the door, and sat down on the log bench beside it.

Keely sighed and began to pace again. Then, suddenly she stopped in midstride. "Is that smoke I smell?"

The Iroquois lifted his head, twitched his nose, then returned his attention to his whittling. "Yes."

She crossed her arms over her chest. "Don't you think you should go find out if they're burning the place down?" she demanded.

He looked up. "No." He dropped his head.

Exasperated, Keely walked faster, past the bench, around the table to the wall and back again. The smell of smoke grew stronger with each passing minute until finally it began to seep into the room.

For a moment she stood in indecision, then she walked up to the door. "Well, if you're not going to do anything about it, I am! Damned if I'll burn to death in this hole!"

Without bothering to look up at her, the brave in the blue breeches lowered his rifle, barring her exit.

"We stay here."

Keely turned away angrily, lifting the hem of her dress to wipe her brow. Though it was September it was still warm . . . and it seemed to be getting warmer by the minute.

"Don't you understand?" She turned on her captor suddenly. "They're burning down the fort. We've got to get out of here!"

He wrinkled his nose again. "Just bark, no big fires yet."

A woman's scream sounded somewhere within the walls of the fort and Keely shivered. Panic rose within her as she paced the floor faster. Gunfire sounded regularly now and occasionally a man cried out in pain. Slowly, smoke filled the room and it began to sting her eyes.

The Iroquois brave looked up, wrinkled his nose, then tucked his whittling beneath his jerkin. Unhurried, he stood and gathered his rifle and a small pouch on the bench beside him.

"Finally . . ." Keely muttered.

The brave walked out the door into the passageway, which was filling rapidly with smoke.

"Where are you going?" Keely shouted, running after him.

"The fort's burning. I go home now," he answered simply.

Keely stepped out into the hall and began to cough violently. She could see nothing in the billows of black smoke. The Indian had disappeared and she didn't know which way he'd gone. "I can't see you! Wait for me! You're supposed to be protecting me!"

There was no answer but the steady sound of ricocheting bullets and exploding black powder.

Choking, Keely stepped back into the windowless room and slammed the door shut. Is this my fate? she wondered bitterly as she lowered herself onto her hands and knees. Is this to be my tomb? Am I to die here alone with no one to know when I'm gone?

No . . . she told herself. *No!* Down on the floor the air was much cleaner and her head was functioning again. I've got to get out of here. This is my chance . . .

But she didn't know how to get out. She didn't even know where she was. And who was out there? If she did manage to find her way out of the fort, what if it was a band of wild Indians burning them out? Would she escape only to be captured and carried off by some devils? Brock had told her about the Iroquois . . . the enemy of the Lenni Lenape. The Iroquois were a fierce warring bunch with none of the laws of the Eastern tribes. They hated the white man and took great pride in torturing their captives.

Pushing the self-defeating thoughts aside, Keely crawled on the floor toward the far corner of the room. Feeling with her hands, she located the bucket of water she recalled seeing earlier. With her teeth, she tore at the skirt of the blue cotton chintz gown she'd been wearing for weeks. The worn material tore easily and she soon had a large rectangle to submerge in the bucket. When the material was sufficiently soaked, she wrung it out and threw it over her head. Filled with a new determination, Keely crawled to the door, flung it open, and started down the smoke-filled corridor on her hands and knees. If she was going to die, she'd be damned if she'd die hiding in a corner somewhere.

Although the smoke still stung her eyes and made her cough, the wet material protected Keely from the noxious fumes. Slowly she made her way down one hallway and into the next. Twice she met with burning timbers. The first time, she made her way through them; the second time, she had to turn back. She didn't know where she was going, but she followed her instincts. Brock had always told her to follow her instincts when she was lost or confused.

She moved slowly, circling through the maze of log walls in search of fresher air. Soon, she could hear the loud sound of gunfire and the shouts of men. She bumped into a set of hand-hewn stairs and scurried up them.

Fresh air filled Keely's lungs and she threw off the wet material. Rubbing her eyes, she realized she was on the rampart of the fort walls. Men raced in every direction, shouting and firing their weapons. Occasionally the roar of cannon sounded. The scent of black powder and warm blood filled Keely's nostrils as it had that night on the *Tempest.*

She grabbed the arm of the next red-coated soldier that passed her. "What's happening?" she demanded.

The bearded man laughed, reloading his flintlock. "The damned rebels are attacking us with a vengeance! Seems they're lookin' for Mr. Lawrence."

Keely's heart skipped a beat. "Where is he?"

"Who, your husband? Don't know, but you'd best find him. A bunch of Iroquois are supposed to be taking him out through the back. He's looking for you."

Keely nodded in disbelief as the man hurried off. *Rebels?* The rebels were here! They could help her! They would get her out!

She stepped over the prone body of a dead man and ran to the side of the fort to look down through the trees. Hanging over the crudely cut wall, she squinted, trying to make out something. But through the smoke, she could see nothing but a glimpse of men running, and the streaks of fire as guns sounded.

Convinced there was no way down from here, Keely ran for the steps. All she could think of was freedom. She didn't know what had happened to

Micah, and she didn't care. All she wanted was to go home. These men would take her . . . they were obviously winning. She would make Brock understand what had happened when she reached home.

"Where the hell do you think you're going?"

A rough hand clasped Keely's shoulder and she gasped. Through the billows of smoke she made out the scarred face of Micah's henchman, Cain. "Let go of me," she insisted wildly.

He leaped to catch her but Keely ducked and ran down along the rampart. Flames shot up through the floor, the heat so intense that she could smell her hair singeing. Behind her she could hear the pounding of Cain's feet. He caught her around the waist and she screamed, turning to pummel his hideous face. Cain stumbled backward and the floor groaned, splintering then giving way. Tangled in Cain's arms, Keely grew light-headed as she felt herself falling. . .

On horseback within the compound of the wilderness fort, Brock raced to and fro, shouting through the smoke. "Find them! Damn you! The place is coming down around us!"

He wheeled his horse around just in time to see an Iroquois take aim at his back. Without a moment's thought, Brock flung himself from the horse and hit the ground running. His rifle fell to the ground, but in his hand he carried a steel-honed knife.

The Iroquois's lead shot bounced recklessly off a burning wall as Brock caught him in the neck with his knife. It was a clean cut and the brave fell to the dirt in an honorable death.

Tucking the knife into the waistband of his breeches, Brock sprinted to catch the reins of his fleeing horse. In confusion the crazed animal ran beneath a burning timber and into a gap in the structured walls of the fort.

Cursing beneath his breath, Brock went after the spooked horse, following him into the burning inner walls of the fort. Coughing and choking, he squinted to see. There, another ten feet beyond stood the horse, blocked by a pile of charred lumber.

"Come on, boy, good boy . . ." Brock soothed, walking forward slowly. "Come on now. That's it." He caught the reins and the horse reared in terror. Pulling off his linen shirt, Brock threw it over the horse's head and immediately the animal calmed down. Murmuring soothing words, he began to lead his mount toward safety. Just as he started to duck beneath the last wall of burning timber, he thought he spied a splash of blue in a pile of splintered wood.

Holding tightly to the reins, Brock pushed a length of timber with the toe of his boot. It fell to the dirt floor. But then, of its own accord, another piece fell.

"Help me!" a muffled voice begged.

Brock dropped the horse's reins, uncovered its head, and gave it a pat on the backside. The horse ran out of the inner wall and into the compound. A minute later Brock was pulling up one piece of charred wood after another. "I'm coming, it's all right." The first body he uncovered was lifeless. He rolled it over and through the smoke he recognized Micah's personal manservant. In a frenzy, Brock began to toss wood in every direction. He could see the blue now. It was a woman's skirt! A woman!

A hand came up from the rubble and Brock grasped it. A brilliant white light filled his head. He knew that hand! It was Keely!

"Keely!" he shouted. "Keely!" Dropping on his hands and knees, Brock pushed aside two more boards and she rose, her face blackened, her auburn hair tangled and singed.

"Brock!" Her sooty face lit up. "Oh God, Brock. I'm so sorry. I didn't mean what I said in that letter." The words tumbled from her mouth in a flurry. "I had to do it. They were going to hang you . . . Micah, he said . . ."

Brock crushed her to his bare chest, brushing his lips over the dirty crown of her head. He was laughing, he was crying. "Keely, it's all right . . ."

"I'm so sorry . . ." she told him, holding on to him with all her might. "I didn't know what to do! I love you so much!"

He lifted her from the rubble. "Come on!" Running through a wall of burning timber, Brock carried her into the compound. Setting her on her feet, he brushed the hair from her face. "Are you all right?"

She smiled, nodding. "I just look bad. I'm not hurt. Cain must have cushioned my fall."

Brock shook his head in amazement. "Stand here while I get a horse. I want you out of here."

Keely watched him disappear into the smoke and a moment later he was back, leading a horse. "Can you ride?"

She laughed, her heart bursting with joy. "With you, anywhere . . ."

Brock swung onto the mount and put out his hand to help her up behind him. "Hold on," he urged, "and let's see if we can find our way out of here."

Keely clasped her hands around Brock's waist, her fingers resting on the flat muscles of his stomach. She leaned forward, her head against his back. He smelled of black powder and smoke, but beneath those harsh odors was that familiar masculine scent of his that always made her warm in the pit of her stomach.

Brock urged the horse through the smoke toward the entrance to the walls of the fort. They skirted an Iroquois brave and a Pennsylvania rifleman in hand-to-hand combat and pushed forward into the forest. Brock brought the horse to a stop just outside the walls. "Do you see Manessah?" he shouted above the sound of rifle fire.

"No."

Brock led the horse around the side of the fort and toward the back. Tree limbs brushed at Keely's back and she pressed herself against Brock.

"So there you are . . ."

Brock pulled on the reins, halting the horse. Leaning against the crude fort wall stood Micah. His clothes were blackened, his blond hair was pulled from his neat queue, and he was bleeding at his chin, but other than that, he had fared the battle well. In his hands he held a rifle, aimed at Brock's middle.

Brock's voice was frightfully low. "Haven't you done enough, Micah?"

Keely leaned forward, staring at Micah venomously. "He killed Jenna! He shot her on that dock!"

"I know," Brock responded.

"Keely, get down from that horse and come with me," Micah ordered. "We made a deal. You're mine."

She laughed, tightening her arms around her husband's bare midsection. "I was never yours, Micah. Never!"

His lower lip quivered. "Don't say that. You told me you could love me. You said we would go to Europe. I was going to take you to Paris."

"I lied."

Micah dashed at the corners of his eyes as moisture formed in them. "All I wanted was for you to love me, Keely. Like you loved him."

She stared at the pitiful man. "Let us go, Micah."

"No!" He shook his head adamantly and raised the rifle. He pulled back the hammer. "One ball and you're both dead. Clean through the both of you. If I can't have you, he can't . . . no one can."

Brock moved his hands slightly, and Micah waved the rifle. "Don't move! You move and I shoot!"

"You said you were going to shoot anyway," Brock retorted.

Keely watched his tears trickle, making winding paths down Micah's sooty face. Her hand brushed against the pistol in Brock's waistband and he stiffened slightly. She couldn't let this madman ruin her life. He had tried once; he'd not succeed this time. She wasn't certain she could fire the gun. She'd never killed another living thing, but for Brock, for her baby, for their love . . . If someone has to die, she thought, it must be Micah.

Beneath Brock's arm, Keely moved her hand ever so slightly, slipping the pistol from Brock's waistband. "Don't do this, Micah," she begged.

"I have to, Keely. I can't let him take you." Micah's hands shook and the tears flowed down his face, so twisted with pain. "I loved you so much . . ."

Time lost all meaning as Keely saw Micah close his eyes. She pulled back the hammer of Brock's pistol and squeezed the trigger just as Micah pulled the trigger on his rifle. Two shots fired almost simultaneously and she watched in horror as Micah fell back under the impact of the bullet that pierced his chest. In a second it was over and Micah was dead, his lifeless body slumping to the ground.

Brock twisted in the saddle, his bronze face reflecting a mixture of sorrow and relief. "I'm sorry you had to do that." He took the pistol gently from Keely's shaking hand.

"I'm sorry too," she answered, still stunned.

Brock kissed her mouth, brushing her rich red hair from her cheek. "I have a little girl at home looking for her mama."

Keely smiled, her eyes filled with tears. "I love you," she whispered, staring into the depths of his ebony eyes.

"I love you, *ki-ti-hi*."

Turning, Brock lifted the reins and sank his heels into the steed's sides, and together the two rode off through the forest.